CONTENTS

INTRODUCTION

Last year's Introduction suggested *New Writing Scotland* 30 was our strongest issue yet. This current issue has forced us to revise that opinion. For the first time, we had to reject submissions on the grounds of space. Had we editors been permitted to follow our initial urges, this volume would be less a tantalising taster and more a surfeit of riches. Many eminently publishable submissions had to be turned down because there simply wasn't room, even though this collection, like the last, runs to more than three hundred pages.

We had a difficult and time-consuming cull, where we tried to be fair and representative while maintaining our original remit, to publish the best of new Scottish writing. Sometimes it was a question of taking fewer poems by one individual, sometimes a more brutal decision based on duplicated or, dare we say, overly familiar subject matter. All of our decisions were made in the spirit of camaraderie; we're writers too, and we know how hard it is to produce something good, and how dispiriting when that SAE flops back through the letterbox. Our approach is broad and open though, and we believe this anthology provides a stimulating illustration of what is happening in contemporary Scottish writing. We're pleased to follow one of *New Writing Scotland*'s proudest traditions, and present stories and poems by debut writers alongside new work by familiar, established names. Brand new in both respects, then.

Since we changed our submission guidelines, the number and quality of submissions have been astonishing, not to say time-consuming. It is gratifying that we have more to read, and more from which to choose. As a result, we are confident that what we are publishing is more representative of Scottish writing across the board. We have not only widened the submissions base, but we have invited work from writers who may not otherwise have submitted (never, we may add, with any guarantee that it will be accepted and published; instead of *Black Middens*, we might have pinched Toby Young's title, *How to Lose Friends and Alienate People*). We have offered suggestions for the kind of future submissions we'd like to read, and are happy to report that these have, in the main, been ignored.

For example, we thought the myriad of issues raised in the next year's referendum would be more appealing. We thought it likely writers would want to engage with the result or imagine a post-referendum Scotland of whatever persuasion. Apparently not, though it is something we may see in a future collection.

Submissions come to us from all over the diaspora, and we welcome work in translation. But the ethnic diversity of the country we live in remains unrepresented. If you have a talented friend, colleague or neighbour who may not know of us, please point them in our direction.

In the last issue we suggested there was space to 'raise our game: there's everything to play for'. We published our first graphic short story and, again, suggested writers could look to other media or find new ways of addressing the familiar. We stand by that: raise your game, surprise and challenge us.

So, the advice for new or potential submissions has changed slightly – given what we've said, read what we are publishing and send us what you believe is your strongest work.

New Writing Scotland 32 will have one new editor (and one veteran), which will obviously mean new choices and maybe even a further change of direction. But we are confident *New Writing Scotland* will continue to do what the title dictates – offer exciting, thought-provoking, enjoyable new writing from Scots by nationality, habitation or persuasion, as well as continuing to showcase work by new writers. There is, we believe, nothing more rewarding for a new writer than to have their work appear in the same pages as someone whose name is familiar and whose work one might even have long admired.

The editors have dedicated this issue to Gavin Wallace, a man whose service and commitment to Scottish literature, firstly with the Scottish Arts Council and latterly with Creative Scotland, were second to none. Again and again he showed he was much more than the acceptable face of arts administration. There is barely a Scottish writer or literary organisation that has not benefited from Gavin's dedication and his loss is especially acute at this time of transition and reconstruction. As well as that, of course, he was a reader, and one of the best. When next you raise a Scottish book, raise it to Gavin.

Finally, it's customary for editors, especially departing editors, to congratulate themselves on their achievements. A new editor joins *New Writing Scotland*. Another leaves in the belief that this publication is in a healthier state than it has been for many years.

On we go.

Carl MacDougall
Zoë Strachan

NEW WRITING SCOTLAND 32
SUBMISSION INSTRUCTIONS

The thirty-second volume of *New Writing Scotland* will be published in summer 2014. Submissions are invited from writers resident in Scotland or Scots by birth, upbringing or inclination. All forms of writing are welcome: autobiography and memoirs; creative responses to events and experiences; drama; graphic artwork (monochrome only); poetry; political and cultural commentary and satire; short fiction; travel writing or any other creative prose may be submitted, but not full-length plays or novels, though self-contained extracts are acceptable. The work must be neither previously published nor accepted for publication and may be in any of the languages of Scotland.

Submissions should be typed on one side of the paper only and the sheets secured at the top left corner. Prose pieces should be double-spaced and carry an approximate word-count. **You should provide a covering letter, clearly marked with your name and address.** *Please also put your name on the individual works.* If you would like to receive an acknowledgement of receipt of your manuscript, please enclose a stamped addressed postcard. If you would like to be informed if your submission is unsuccessful, or would like your submissions returned, you should enclose a stamped addressed envelope with sufficient postage. Submissions should be sent by **30 September 2013**, in an A4 envelope, to the address below. We are sorry but we cannot accept submissions by fax or email.

Please be aware that we have limited space in each edition, and therefore shorter pieces are more suitable – although longer items of exceptional quality may still be included. **Please send no more than four poems, or no more than two prose work(s) to a maximum of 3,500 words in total**. Successful contributors will be paid at the rate of £20 per published page. Authors retain all rights to their work(s), and are free to submit and/or publish the same work(s) elsewhere after they appear in *New Writing Scotland*.

ASLS
Scottish Literature
7 University Gardens
University of Glasgow
Glasgow G12 8QH, Scotland

Tel +44 (0)141 330 5309
www.asls.org.uk

Gregor Addison

'TERMEN NE MRET: THEREMIN DOES NOT DIE'
(Lev Sergeyevich, 1896–1993)

Clara Rockmore raises hands in supplication,
conducts the ether; *Valse Sentimentale*,
waspish, thin, coaxed from the wireless air, buzzing

like bees on daffodils. But still
no-one knows the whereabouts of Lev Sergeyevich.
In his two room flat on Leninsky Prospekt

the great man weeps for his beloved Elena,
fifty years his junior, who gave herself, trembling
and tremulous, to desperation. Life

flickers on the static, whistles in the drum.
All notes lose the air they breathe.
Lev, who outlived Eisenstein in Hollywood, even

his party card, succumbed to Faustian sleep.
In Kuncevskoye Cemetery, Moscow:
the slow glissando,
                                        the solo sighing of the wind.

Jean Atkin

HARE'S GRACE

For all of August a leveret
loped past the cottage.
At every dawn and dusk it
tracked our steps. Sometimes
it crossed them, as if
the wind changed or
the shape of the hills.
The weeks turned hesitant,
green and full of paths.

The last time, I saw it crouching
in the flowers. The afternoon
whined like a hawser.
The hare laid down its ears
on its silk-sprung back. Then,
meek as a tailor, it
cut out from a rose leaf
the perfect
shape of its mouth.

I put on my coat and went out
to touch the leaf's
shirred edge.
And my hand remembered
the blind faith
of the fingers pressed so
gently, by so
many, into the roots
of the Tree of Jesse.

*Pilgrims touch the Tree of Jesse as they enter the Cathedral of
Santiago de Compostela.*

Dorothy Baird

WITHOUT WITNESS

On my own in a caravan
overlooking the Sound of Mull
rain thrumming on its old roof,

I think of you at home dozing as you do
on the couch (daughter on lap-top
or out tip-tapping on too high heels)

but after five days amongst the hills
my thoughts float over the Sound
like the tuwhit of a seeking owl

but there's no tuwho because there's no you
to reply and now I'm not even sure
you exist or if you're memory's

quirky trick because you're fading
and, knowing nobody here, I can walk
into the shop and be anybody,

so which of my possible selves
will I pull on today: one with husband and daughter
or the one untrammelled as the tides?

The hills are strewn with juniper and bog-cotton
and, frankly, do not care. After twenty-five years,
you are my long-haul witness, carrying the truth of me.

But you are far away if you're anywhere at all,
and I'm in a rain-drummed box,
eyes full of wind and sea.

Helen Boden

IN SUBURBIA

One of the first things to become familiar was the pair
of mop-haired brothers who unhurried delivered
the *Evening News* to the old man opposite
in their school clothes and sneakers around five o'clock
sack straps across their left shoulders and fluorescent
under their right arms they would walk calmly up his path
and down again then turn right off the Drive
out of sight along the lane around the back before
appearing again on the bridge down the cutting
and onto the Loan.
                  It cheered me to see them through
that first sad summer then the turning back of the
clocks and the heavy snows and my first spring here
and sometime before the second winter the smaller
boy was gone and his brother already a close-cropped
young man did the paper round on his own at the same pace.
Next season the old man stopped cutting his own lawn
one of his neighbours went into residential care
the other side had a second child by which time I had homed in
on the best places to find blossom
                      bluebells
                          autumn leaves.

Jane Bonnyman

AUGUST PICNIC
'and the frogs came up, and covered the land'
—Exodus 8:6

So they journey at my toes,
blades of grass shiver to their beat.
I think of those that were,
the sudden darkness passing over;
their chill as I lowered each sole.
When we raced towards
this place, you said the sunlight
had picked it out for us.
I held a tub of raspberries,
you waved the blanket like a flag.
I came to you as you stood,
a matador against the apple glow –
how could I know about the tiny selves
set by some unearthly sense
to march across this forest floor,
dry shadows so far from the river.
They are everywhere now,
on oily peat, moss, pine needles.
Not even a whisper between us,
you reach out your hand,
we leap quick from the clearing
and run, feet heavy to the road.
The blanket crumples in your arms,
the raspberries spill,
and fall like meteors.

John Burnside

TRAVELLING SOUTH, SCOTLAND, AUGUST 2012
'Necessity is not the mother of invention; play is.'
—*Ian D. Suttie*

It gets late early out here
in the lacklustre places,
wind in the trees and the foodstalls'
ricepaper lamplight, fading and blurred with rain,
the wire fence studded with fleece
and indelible traces
of polythene wrapping; marrowfat clogging the drains
on the road that runs out to the coast
then disappears.
A last bleed of gold in the west, like a Shan Shui painting,
then darkness.

The animals are gone
that hunted here:
wolves coming down from the hills, that
immaculate hunger,
rumours of bear and cat, quick
martens and raptors.
The rain is darker now,
though not so black,
oil-iridescent, streaked with the smell of lard
– *it gets late early out here*; though *late*, out here,
has a different meaning:

stars in the road
and the absence of something more
than birchwoods or song,
pallet fires, tyre-tracks,
grubbed fields clouded with grease
and palm oil, hints
of molasses and lanolin, tarpaper,
iron filings.
A narrow band of weather on the road,
then houses; though we scarcely think of them
as that.

I remember a meadow at dusk
in another rain
(and this is nostalgia now); I remember
I stood in a wind like gossamer and watched
three roe fawns and a doe
come quietly, one by one, through the silvering grasses,
wary, but curious, giving me just enough space
to feel safe,
their watchfulness reminding me of something
lost, a creaturely
awareness I could only glimpse

in passing.
That meadow is gone, and dusk
isn't dusk any more
– or not out here –
just miles of tract and lay-by on the way
to junkyards and dead allotments,
guard dogs on tether,
biomass, factory outlets,
the half-light of ersatz dairies petering out
on rotting fields
of rape and mustardseed.

We've been going at this for years:
a steady delete
of anything that tells us what we are,
a long
distaste for the blood warmth and bloom
of the creaturely: local
fauna and words for colour, all the shapes
of ritual and lust
surrendered where they fell, beneath a fog
of smut and grime and counting-house
as church, the old gods

buried undead beneath the rural sprawl
that bears their names, or wandering the hills
of Lammermuir and Whitelee, waiting out
the rule of Mammon, till the land returns
– with or without us –
chainlink going down
to bindweed, drunken
thistles in a sway
of wind and goldfinch on the dead estates, fat
clusters of moss
and gentian, broken

tarmac with new shoots
of coltsfoot breaking through
like velvet, till the darkness of the leaf
unfurls into a light we could have known
but failed to see
by choosing not to find
the kingdom-at-hand:
this order;
this dialectic;
this mother of invention,
ceaseless play.

Margaret Callaghan

MÖBIUS STRIP

Emily is eight. Her mum is pressing an eyeliner pencil hard against the white-blue skin beneath her eyes, drawing in slanting Japanese eyes for a Halloween costume. Every so often her mum stops to correct mistakes with the spit-moistened end of a handkerchief. Emily wears the silk pyjamas her dad brought back from Japan when he was in the merchant navy. For her gran he'd brought a china tea set, bought from a wee boat that had sidled up to the ship. Her gran showed Emily how to hold a cup up to the light so that she could see the face of a geisha girl in the base. On the walk home from the Brownie party the pyjamas will be trailed in mud and puddles and the wet silk will cling to her legs. Emily's red hair is plaited so tightly that it pulls her eyes up at the sides. She is wearing a straw hat stolen from her brother's Spanish donkey. The next day it will become part of a Mexican costume for the Cubs' party, coffee grounds rubbed into his face, moustache drawn on with more eyeliner, guns in a holster, and a colourful shawl around his shoulders. Do all Mexicans have guns? Emily thinks that they must. She imagines dusty plains stretching out to touch the end of the sky, a broken-down bar, a yellow three-legged dog tied up outside, a man on a donkey, a cactus. Years later she will spend her thirtieth birthday dancing with a Mexican cowboy on a farm in La Gloria and he will leave sweaty palm prints on her silk shirt.

When he was nineteen and in the merchant navy, her dad missed his boat in New Orleans, 'Drunk,' he says, 'at a party,' he adds. Woke up across town from the harbour, doesn't know how he got there. The navy diverted another boat to fetch him and charged him six months' wages for timewasting. He didn't have a passport and had to stay in prison with America's illegal immigrants. That's his American memory. His memories of South Africa are of good dentistry and segregation, of Saudi Arabia of muezzin calls and long waits while grain was unloaded by hand, scooped up into bags and sewn shut. In Hawaii harbour they played cards to see who got shore leave. At the church hall dance, in between Irish jig displays and songs about spinning wheels, he tells people he's been round the world four and a quarter times and waits for them to ask about the quarter. He'd been followed in Japan by a crowd of girls, he claimed. 'They thought I was one of the Beatles but of course I was better looking than any of them.' When he knows that her mum is listening he says that he was going to jump ship and go off with a Norwegian girl and her mum mutters that she wishes he had. At school Emily says *Arigato* and *Sayonara* and is upset when the teachers laugh.

Emily is nine and given the part of Mary Magdalene in the school play, because she has the longest hair. Her hair is unravelled into orange crinkles, so that she can dry the feet of the priest that plays Jesus. 'My daughter's the one playing the prostitute,' her dad tells everyone. 'Shut up, Patrick,' her mum says. Emily doesn't know what he is talking about but she's glad that she has got the only female part: twelve boys in the class, twelve apostles, and her. A few weeks later it is unexpectedly summer and her mum collects her from school wearing shorts and a halter neck. The headmistress-nun pulls her into the office and tells her she is disgraceful. 'It's clear you're not a Catholic,' she says. 'It's clear she's a frustrated old bitch,' her thirty-year-old mother tells her friends in the baker's afterwards. The other mothers sip sweet milky tea and giggle over éclairs. Emily's mum has a black coffee and waves a cigarette; her bright pink shoes match her nail polish. Emily glances up from her book and watches the column of ash from the cigarette. Waiting for it to fall.

The following day Sally-Anne comes skipping up the road, bunches flying, to tell Emily's mum that the teacher banged her brother's head off a wall 'cause he got his sums wrong. Matthew refuses to comment, stoical ten-year-old in his green school uniform, tie askew, grubby cuffs and ink on sleeves. The mothers flock around, squawking with glee to see what her mum will do. She changes into her shorts and goes to the school. 'I won't go to court right now,' she informs the startled headmistress-nun coolly. 'I'll think it over.' Emily wins school prizes again.

A few weeks later Emily's mum returns home to find her Irish granny has let herself in through the kitchen window and is mixing soda scone bread. The worktops are covered in flour and the breakfast plates hidden under mixing spoons in the washing-up bowl. 'Nine o'clock in the morning and neither the dishes done nor the beds made?' Her granny purses her lips. 'Oh and you're out of milk.' She has never forgiven Emily's mother for not being a Catholic and for marrying her only boy. When Emily is fifty and cross, her friends will tell her she has the face of a disapproving Irish granny.

Later in the afternoon Emily's granny and her mum drink advocaat and lemonade and smoke their way through the cigarettes in the onyx cigarette box, given with a matching lighter as a wedding present. The soda scone is put aside for Emily's dad. Emily's granny shows her the silver scars on her hands and arms for making mistakes in her sums forty years before. 'The teacher would send someone to cut down a branch to hit you with,' she tells Emily. 'It was the waiting that was the worst. Some of the men teachers didn't like hitting girls so they'd hit your brother instead.' Emily asks her granny if that upset her more but her granny says she was just glad it wasn't her. Emily licks the ends of the midget gems her granny has brought and sticks them on her earlobes to see if she would suit earrings.

Emily's Irish granny asks her mum who Emily was called after. 'You,' her mum replies looking puzzled. 'No, my name is Emily McGinity Moran, she's just Emily Moran.' She'd come to Glasgow on the immigrant ship and met Emily's grandpa at an Irish dance in the Gorbals. Every summer she takes the bus straight from the car park in the Gorbals to the bus stop outside her sister's farm in Monaghan. On second Sundays she takes a turn of cleaning the chapel with the other women, where they whisper about the priest's wee drink problem. Her husband grows potatoes, turnips and lettuce in the garden of his council house and gives a percentage of his wages to the church and a percentage back to the farm. He couldn't get a job in Ireland or in the shipyards of Glasgow where they turned him away because they had met their Catholic quota. He works on a building site until he is seventy-five and at the weekend digs in one of his nine daughters' gardens. His meals are served at seven o'clock, noon and five every day and he watches the ten o'clock news each night with soda scone and tea. Emily can't remember hearing him speak. When Emily's granny is in hospital he teaches himself to fry a steak and make cheese on toast. Her other grandpa hadn't liked the Catholics because he said they didn't strike but took the pay rises when the unions negotiated them.

Emily's mum meets her dad at the door, fuming, when he returns from work. 'I don't even like the name Emily,' she tells him. 'I just had to even it up 'cause of calling Matthew after my dad. I wanted to call her Caroline.' Emily listens with one ear, the other on *Little House on the Prairie*. She wants to be called Caroline too, or Laura, not Mary though. She closes her eyes, sticks out her arms and imagines being blind. 'Anyway, the last time she arrived unannounced the beds were made and she says, "Oh I see you don't air your sheets",' her mum goes on. Emily's dad is tired and clutching bread with holes that they're experimenting with at work. 'Bagels, I think they're called,' he says. 'American.' At lunchtime the next day Emily will eat them in the school playground with cooked chicken breasts and a pill jar filled with mayonnaise. Her friends will have egg sandwiches and hot orange juice in a flask and will make faces at her food.

Matty, Emily's maternal grandpa, died aged fifty. Five and half stone. Joined the navy at fifteen. Her granny still has the report card of his behaviour that was sent home to his dad every six months. 'January, *Poor*, February, *Fair*, March, *Good*,' it says in tea-stain scrawls. Emily remembers visiting him in hospital where crumpled white and grey men disappeared into the white sheets. He sneaked her peppermints and told stories of being six days on an open boat. Years after the war ended, medals came through the post and he threw them all in the bin. One New Year after singing songs about 'Nobody's Child' and 'Blanket on the Ground' Emily's dad and granny argue while drinking a bottle of whisky. 'I wish it had been you that had died instead of Matty,' Emily's dad tells her granny. 'So do I,' her granny shouts back spitting through loose false teeth. Matthew tops up the whisky bottle with water and sits with Emily on the back doorstep. They wrap themselves up in coats borrowed from the pile on the bed and play card games in the light of the torch Matthew got for Christmas as part of his Secret Agent set.

Each Tuesday Emily's gran collects her from school, her half-day from work. She fries her a steak, makes milky tea and buys a cake with hard icing and a cherry from the corner shop. After lunch her gran gives her twenty pence and takes her back to school, gripping her hand tightly. Emily saves the money in her secret drawer. Her gran's fingers are gnarled ginger roots and her knees the size of melons from cleaning the floors of Marks and Spencer's for thirty years. When she cuddles her, her gran smells of Bromley hand cream and Charlie perfume and Emily feels trapped. Emily's gran spends her wages on getting dresses for Emily that she doesn't like and once, a red raincoat that she did. She lost her mum when she was eight and her brother died of tuberculosis when he was sixteen. They couldn't afford to call the doctor so he walked three miles to the Royal Infirmary, blood spots scattered behind. Emily's gran lost her sense of smell in the war. 'There was nothing nice to smell in those days so her nose gave up,' Emily's mum had once explained. Her gran's house stinks of bleach and she bathes all the time.

During the night Emily's mum has started to make gypsy skirts for Emily and then her friends. Soon strangers start to turn up at the door clutching fabric. She runs an eye over them and guesses their sizes. Over breakfast she will ask Emily to convert inches into centimetres while she yawns over Rice Krispies. Emily has a hazy memory of being pulled out of bed half asleep to try something on and feeling resentful when she realises it's not for her. Sometimes her mum will wake up Matthew to measure a skirt against him. All his life he walks in his sleep and has a phobia of buttons. 'Not on clothes,' he'll explain to puzzled girlfriends, 'just in a jar.'

Emily's dad is made redundant when she is thirteen, 'one of Maggie's millions,' he says, and goes off to Ireland to help on his uncle's farm. On the news a taxi driver is killed when miners drop a concrete slab on his car filled with scabs. Emily remembers the scabs on her knees when she fell from the swing and imagines men's faces leaking pus. Her dad tells everyone he is returning to the land to be a Paddy tatty howker. He puts on her grandpa's Northern Irish accent and sings songs about Ballyjamesduff, accompanying himself on an imaginary fiddle. He tells her to stop calling him 'dad'. My name is Aloysius Joseph O'Flannery O'Brien. Emily doesn't see him for two years. Sometimes when she is lying in bed she tries to remember his face. Her brother returns from a visit and tells her that Ireland is damp peat and cows and rain and pots of tea and pubs.

Whilst he is gone, her mum learns Italian from tapes and starts to drink espresso and red wine. She returns home from her job in the west end clutching courgettes and aubergines, fries them with tins of tomatoes and makes up a name for each new dish. Emily's friends come round to watch but refuse to eat. Their mums have swapped their tea and éclairs for fizzy

Lambrusco. By now her mum is thirty-five and complains to her gran that she never got the chance to go to art school. Her gran tells her it wasn't worth it for a lassie and points out that she decided to marry a Catholic so she's lucky not to have hundreds of weans. Her mum takes up life drawing classes and gets an evening job in the cinema. On a long bus journey she acts out the whole of *One Flew Over the Cuckoo's Nest* for Emily and Matthew. Sometimes at the weekend Emily's granny looks after them and her mum goes out with her friends. Emily lies in bed listening for the tapping high heels up the close to signal her mum's return.

When she is fifteen, Emily meets a Hindu boy at the chess club. They huddle in bus shelters when it rains, dazed on kisses. He teaches her to ride a bike by holding on to the back and running behind her while she shouts 'don't let go'. He reads her Indian poetry in a mournful tone and she tries not to yawn. They do their homework together at his kitchen table and his mum brings them samosas and sometimes tinned creamed rice and pears as an exotic British treat. His parents talk of partitioning and Emily imagines a big sliding door across the map of India. When she was younger, her brother told her that you could land a small helicopter on the Iron Curtain and she had believed him, but pretended not to. Her boyfriend's mum asks her if her parents are Christian and Emily doesn't know how to reply. His dad asks Emily to help him with the crossword and shakes his head at his son's bad attempts. 'All that expensive education,' he says. 'Wasted.' Emily's dad returns from Ireland and refers to her boyfriend as her exotic friend. 'Shut up, Patrick,' her mum says.

Emily is sixteen and on a fortnight's school exchange in Rome. She flies round on the back of the host's son's moped and tries to smoke coolly like the slim serious Italian girls. She also tries to like espresso and rolls the word *prosciutto* on her tongue, practising until the gets the soft *c* and long *o*. At night she reads Primo Levi in bed and imagines walking across Italy. The host's son teaches her to swear in Italian, calls her *cara*, and tries to undo the dress her mum had made for the trip. Emily sighs and avoids him. When she returns home her parents tell her that they are getting divorced.

In the long summer after university she meets Mark at a kibbutz where they both work in the chicken coop. At night they sit around campfires at the end of the desert, yellow stars scratched out in a crayon-black sky. They talk of Zionism and the IRA and sing Bob Dylan and Billy Bragg. He teaches her the guitar and teases her because she makes up the words of the songs. Mark's girlfriend, Miriam, is at Oxford where she is writing a thesis on anti-Semitism in Shakespeare's plays and learning Hebrew in her spare time. Emily imagines her dark shadowed eyes, curly hair and thin clever olive face. At the end of the summer Mark tells her that he has called Miriam to tell her that it is over and asks if she wants to come back with him to London to meet his parents.

Mark's parents live in Golders Green and early in the morning Mark and Emily breakfast in a café on bagels and turkey rashers and she tries not to stare at the monochrome people, women with wigs and men with ringlets and tall black hats. His parents live in a dusty Victorian house, decorated in the Seventies and unchanged since. On the wall outside the bathroom, there are pencil marks to show Mark and his brother growing and Emily imagines a childhood where the walls don't change colour through the night. That evening his parents are celebrating a family birthday and have invited their friends from the university. Apple juice and sweet sherry are poured into wedding-present crystal and pickled gherkins and gefilte fish set out in small silver bowls. Emily is sitting next to a Nobel prize-winner. He sounds English but he tells Emily that his father was a miner in Lanarkshire. He asks her what percentage of her school went to Oxbridge and tells her a joke, the punch line of which is Möbius Strip. She laughs and looks it up later.

That night she and Mark sleep squashed into his single bed, surrounded by textbooks and bits of computers. She wears his brother's pyjamas, loose at the waist, and they giggle beneath the thin duvet. The next day Mark takes her to visit Marx's grave in Highgate cemetery as part of his alternative London tour, and says they have to drink a toast in vodka to his memory. They sing Ra Ra Rasputin on the bus back to his parents' house where his mum looks at the vodka bottle and asks Emily if she often drinks in the day. The following week they go to Glasgow to see Matthew's band. Later in a club, Mark and Matthew drunkenly bond over Jerry Sadowitz; Glasgow and Jewishness combined in a person.

A few years later Emily and Mark are living in a long thin house in Oxford. On the pine kitchen table Emily leaves 'to do' lists scrawled on the back of envelopes. 'Send birthday card, pay credit card, buy train tickets', and more ambitiously 'learn Italian'. Mark adds things to these lists. 'Kiss Mark, make him sandwiches for work, learn Hebrew'. Every second Friday they leave work early, meet in the High Street, chain their bikes to a railing outside the exam halls and take the slow coach to London for Friday night dinner with Mark's family. Mark's mum talks to her of cooking and Judaism in the kitchen while the men discuss science prizes in the lounge. Sometimes in the morning Emily accompanies them to the synagogue and carries the keys and money to save the family breaking the Sabbath. His mum calls her the carrier goy in Hebrew and Mark bites the inside of his gums.

Mark's grandfather moved to Palestine from Latvia in the Thirties. He was trained as a dentist, 'Jews choose professions that they can take with them,' he tells people, but there was no shortage of dentists in Thirties Palestine. He opened up a shop that failed because he kept giving things away to new immigrants. He couldn't afford to send his daughter to university and so she worked in the labs in the evening to pay her way through her biology degree. His other grandpa came from Poland to the east end of London in the Thirties, where he had a shop selling buttons and zips. Mosley's lot regularly smashed its windows but he remained calm. 'It could have been much worse,' he says but doesn't say how. On Friday nights the family talk of friends who are survivors in hushed voices. They eat salt with unleavened bread to remind them of the tears of the Israelites and drink sweet wine from yellowed silver.

Emily is twenty-four and preparing the kiddush at the back of the synagogue. Mark's mum tells him she has bought him pyjamas in case he ever wants to stay at home. Emily's knife slips and blood mixes in with the radishes. His mum takes Mark away to introduce him to a friend's daughter and they share science jokes and reminisce about his ex-girlfriend. Emily gazes at the woman's one thick eyebrow and refuses to be included. She feels her phone vibrating in her pocket. It's her dad. He's just flown for the first time and is dying to tell someone. 'Over-rated,' he says, 'and I'm not doing it again until they reintroduce smoking.' He asks her what perfume he should bring back for Emily's mum. By this time they've been divorced for ten years but meet weekly for lunch and an argument. A few moments later she receives a text from a friend in Tokyo where she is teaching little Japanese children 'American English'. You should come, she texts. 'Sayonara,' Emily texts back, forgetting what it means.

Six months later Emily is working in Japan. She has a bedside rug which heats up when she stands on it and a toilet that automatically flushes. She is listening to 'The Times They Are a-Changin'' in a karaoke bar and is waiting until it's her turn to sing 'Nobody's Child'. She sits with her friend on a high metal stool in the modern bar. 'I never understood what went wrong with you and Mark,' her friend says. Emily looks at the cigarette smouldering in the ashtray, stained with the pink lipstick she'd chosen to match her shoes. She shrugs in the Jewish way Mark had laughed at; shoulders raised, hands splayed, lip pursed. 'Nothing in common,' she says. Her friend raises her *sake* glass. 'Slàinte,' she says. 'L'chaim,' Emily replies.

Kate Campbell

MAGENTA

I saw magenta on the moor
I lost a mountain hare in snow
I heard the curlew circling low
I watched the moon out in the storm

I lost a mountain hare in snow
I traced the marking on the stone
I watched the moon out in the storm
I held the white grass in my hand

I traced the marking on the stone
I found an old ring to take home
I held the white grass in my hand
I picked an opal washed in cloud

I found an old ring to take home
I tracked the peregrine in flight
I picked an opal washed in cloud
I knew the crow unseen at night

I tracked the peregrine in flight
I touched the reed bent under hail
I knew the crow unseen at night
I marked the headlight on the hill

I touched the reed bent under hail
I felt the wind that lifts your hair
I marked the headlight on the hill
I read a map you do not know

I felt the wind that lifts your hair
I heard the curlew circling low
I read a map you do not know
I saw magenta on the moor.

Jim Carruth

VISIONARY

He could see
the promise in a heifer
poison in an udder's hard quarter
pneumonia in a calf shiver
early abortion in a ewe tremor
new birth in a pacing and tail raise.

He could see
hare stew in paw prints in the snow
slow death in the oak's soft bark
fledglings in a sparrow's speckled nest
late harvest in the first shoots
foot rot in the cob's hobble.

He could see
danger in a bull's stare and stamp
the first prize rosette in a judge's nod
the expense of a new tractor
in the belching smoke of the old
a small grave in his collie's walk.

He could see
debt in the depth of milk in the tank
departure in his son's scowl
selling up in a neighbour's eyes
the clutch of seasons left for him
hunched in the mirror's reply.

18

Defne Çizakça

THE BIGGEST LIBRARY OF ISTANBUL, Κωνσταντινούπολη, ‎دىن‌ىطن‌طسق

The Messenger of Allah said: 'The jinn are of three types: a type that has wings, and they fly through the air; a type that looks like snakes and dogs; and a type that stops for a rest then resumes its journey.'
[Shaykh al-Albaani said in al-Mishkaat (2/1206, no. 4148): al-Tahhaawi and Abu'l-Shaykh reported it with a saheeh isnaad]

My destiny was decided by a footnote in the Christian year of 1688, in the Muslim month of Recep, and just as the crescent moon was rising above the Bosphorus.

What was being sealed was not only my fate. Recaizade son of Cemaleddin dipped his quill into the inkpot and my grandparents', my parents', my siblings' lives changed. For always.

I don't know if the ones I shall father will be affected by this minuscule piece of writing too. A lot of time has passed. Many books have been burnt. Recaizade son of Cemaleddin is long dead and so are the poor calligraphers that continued his project. Nevertheless, I have never been one to under-estimate words. We have been cursed time and again by things that appear unassuming: sighs, secretions, gasps. Endnotes, side notes, footnotes.

It was Recaizade's plan to write the first Ottoman novel. The Turks did not write novels till Recaizade came along. They had poems and miniatures and they told stories in coffeehouses. They had the Qur'an, the hadith, gossip and hearsay, but they did not have fictitious prose. So when the first novels known to men arrived to the rainy winter of Istanbul, Recaizade son of Cemaleddin became as excited as a child drinking *sahlep* for the first time.

That rainy day had been ordinary on all accounts but this: Recaizade was to encounter, by kismet, pages that would begin to haunt him. They were piled in a perfectly ordinary-looking trousseau casket. How the novels had ended up in there, and how the casket had ended up in the bazaar of Eyüp from the plethora of bazaars it could have ended up in, no one knew. Recaizade had glimpsed the pages and bought the old box. To entertain the seller boy who thought the chest was for a new wife, he put a sly smile on his face. Then, leaning on his rosewood cane he shuffled back home.

Recaizade had told his wife he had found a treasure, so she had made a fresh pot of tea. He had closed the wooden shutters of their home. They had put incense into silver cups. One after another the times of prayer had passed as they got lost in a cloud of words, and husband and wife had not been drawn to bed even by the longing for one another, and they had read for a straight day and a straight night, and only then had they fallen asleep, resting their heads each on a book, with narrow-bellied glasses of stale tea in their left hands, the right ones tightly holding on to each other.

The idea to write the first Ottoman novel had occurred to them at the same time but they had had different beginnings for it. Recaizade had begun all things only when he had left his little village in Thrace and moved to Istanbul. So he thought the story should start with a dirt road leading to this city and then progress in it.

She had thought of faces first, because the faces in Istanbul were the most melancholic she had ever seen. They appeared to her every night in a sad procession before she went to sleep. She also wrote about places loved and lost; burnt houses, burning houses, houses readying themselves for fire. The places, faces and fires formed out of nothing, became solid, turned into words. But a story never came to stay.

At the beginning, they waited. They were certain the story would arrive sooner or later. They treaded patiently. They hoped it would come along as the characters got acquainted with one another, or as the city gained edges and curves. But the story never arrived. And they discovered with a knot in their stomachs, that they were, in fact, not writing the first Ottoman novel. Their ink-stained hands had produced something they would rather abort: an encyclopaedia of Istanbul.

They could not stop, though they thought they should. It became more and more difficult to contain the chapters because, just like the neighbourhoods of the city, they multiplied inexplicably. The pages were copious, the letters cast shadows.

The footnote that was to change everything arrived with the entry 'Alif'. A first letter. An intake of breath on a misty morning. A gulp like the one that changed Jonah. The end and beginning of things.

*

My grandfather was the third one to read the footnote. After Recaizade son of Cemaleddin and his beloved wife.

My grandfather did not talk much but people talked to him all the time. It was like he had a cardboard attached to his chest that read: 'tell me things'. Everyone took notice. All the *mecnun* of Istanbul, and those that couldn't find a priest to confess to, told him stories.

My grandfather was a creature of habits. He took the same walk every day by the shore of Eminönü, he bought fish and bread from the same vender around three-fifteen, then he sat at his favourite bench and looked over at the sea, at the caiques, and at the bigger boats, and the rich people that came from Europe, and the poor people that went to Europe and their small suitcases but most of all, he liked to stare at the Italian ships because they passed by Greece.

He always told of the event this way: 'It was a rainy day. I had a yellow umbrella. I cleared the raindrops with the back of my hand and noticed there was a heavy book on the edge of the bench. I picked it up.'

There were gold geometric lines on its cover, he noticed, alike the calligraphy in mosques, or in the palaces of Alhambra. Lines like the contours of cheekbones and smiles. Pretty, sudden, elegant.

He opened the book. He opened it mostly so that he could see its dedication. He was more interested in people than he was in books, and more interested in dedications than he was in stories.

But instead of a dedication, he found an introduction.

This is the foreword of those that have prepared the pages for publication

We found these notes written in handwriting, compiled in over fourteen books, signed by a Recaizade son of Cemaleddin. We found these handwritten notes, in fourteen books, signed and then packed in straw-coloured paper, on our doorstep, us being the brothers Uziyeddin the famous travelling calligraphers of the land of Osman.

On the first book of the fourteen books we have found – signed by Recaizade son of Cemaleddin – a preliminary title, a title in progress: The Habits of Deep-sea Istanbulites. Needless to say, we were intrigued by the title as there is no deep-sea diving in Istanbul whether it be on the Bosphorus; or on the shores that open up to the Black Sea on one side, and to the Marmara on the other. Being intrigued as we were, us being the brothers Uziyeddin, there was little we could do other than proceed with deep humility with the reading of these fourteen books wrapped in straw-coloured paper. We are of the ones that believe if something is left at your doorstep it has been put there by Allah. It matters not whether the thing is a cat, a book, or a babe; God requires that you adopt it.

These fourteen books took us a long time to read. When one of us fell asleep the other took the lead and in this manner, amongst the two of us, we finished the notes in about twenty-five days and a quarter – and three days more if you add breakfast, lunch and dinner and the various lokums in between and the unexpected guests who are always on the coming. Despite these forced breaks, we quickly fathomed there was going to be nothing in these books regarding deep-sea Istanbulites. Rather the writer was referring to the depths of the mind when he used the word sea; the depths of the mind and the depths of the heart, the depths of fear and even the depths of hope and the methods of remembering. The word 'deep sea' was used in the style of a metaphor. Seeing as it is that we are interested in metaphors, and in all sorts of seas and divers, and methods of remembering we proceeded with our reading.

The introduction continued. There was no mention of us: of grandfather or of me. But who could blame the brothers Uziyeddin, how could they have known? We know Recaizade never saw us directly. Recaizade son of Cemaleddin, only a few times in the passing, saw us as the following: a sorrowful-looking cat, a shiny engagement ring, Avram the jeweller's dog, the ink into which he dipped his quill. There is, usually, no reason to suspect such things.

*

My grandfather went on reading, reached the footnote, fell in love with it, was convinced, and that was that. He needed no second reading. But, as fate would have it, one minute he held the book in his hands, and the next minute, he had lost it. I think grandfather began stitching pockets for himself on that day. Pockets that could carry books, notes, envelopes. And finally, but much later, keys.

Like any man that loses his beloved my grandfather became short tempered, and dopey eyed upon the loss of the encyclopaedia. It took us years to find the book again. Tracing it back became a family pastime. I grew up thinking it was a natural thing like eating smoked aubergines, or sleeping on satin. And before we located it, we had to live in sad times because all we had to show in way of justification for our lives was a rumour. And a thin one at that. The rumour of an encyclopaedia no one had ever read, the rumour of a footnote inside of it. We lived purely on faith like the downtrodden do.

I remember my childhood came and passed away in the backstreets of the city in those bookshops that swarm with cats. We would spend long afternoons there crammed amidst the smell of books, sickening sweet, like crumbled leaves or home-made jam. I thought this was what everyone my age did: the going down winding streets, the hopping on boats, the searching for lost things. I was perplexed as to why I didn't see more of my kind. I kept on checking mirrors, and shadows, and back lanes. I pricked my ears. But there were no others amidst memorabilia and broken book spines and the thick glasses of the men who fix them. These men tended to disorder the pages as they stitched the books back. Sometimes out of blindness, and sometimes because they had the devil in them. It took years and years for us to hear the encyclopaedia mentioned, but my grandfather never gave up. Once he saw a thing of beauty, he never forgot about it.

Much later, when I had reached my early adulthood, we understood why those expeditions to the bookshops never bore any fruit. We could not find the footnote, we could not find the encyclopaedia because they weren't in Istanbul. They had been taken to Kudüs, the holy city. And there, by sheer luck, the encyclopaedia was gifted again to an Istanbulite man who, together with his wife, took the book with the fragile spine back to its home. And together they built a dwelling place for it. A house in the neighbourhood of Kuzguncuk. The house that was to become the biggest library of Istanbul.

A. C. Clarke

FINGERS CROSSED

Spilt salt reddens in a pool of wine.
You heap it with the flat of your knife.

Yesterday a mirror cracked: its jagged faultline
split my face. I read how someone found

a Celtic head in a junkshop, cradled it home,
set it on her bedside table for luck.

The creature that it harboured woke,
loped down stairs in its wolf-pelt. The house shivered.

I think of a skinned rabbit, pink as a baby,
laid at the foot of a standing stone; remember

the mess of bone and feather in the cellar.
Something cries in the dark outside.

All the lights are on. The fridge is humming.
I tell myself everything will be fine.

Stewart Conn

THE ROOMS OF THE SWEET ORANGES
Palazzo Ducale, Urbino

Scented citrus in their loggias formerly
intended for guests, we were instantly
at ease in their bright airiness, survivors
of the decline and plunder of centuries.

Back home reading the guide I could swear
to an aroma of oranges, and struck by such
powers of suggestion head for the kitchen
to top up my coffee only to laugh out loud

on finding you adroitly doing the peeling
and slicing for a fruit compote, its fragrance
so intensely evoking those ornate rooms
it must surely be more than happenstance;

a reminder, say, that those blissful
days of late summer giving way
to autumnal chill, on our first and doubtless
last visit, must not become simply

part of an undifferentiated past
unspooling with ever greater
rapidity but, added to memory's trove,
flavour the remainder of the life we share.

Ian Crockatt

FOUR POEMS
Four poems translated from the Old Norse poetry of Rögnvaldr Kali Kolsson – viking, crusader, lover, skald – Earl of Orkney from 1135 to 1158

The lady and the castle

Chaste Ermengarde hastens
     to serve – the snow-curve of
her broidered brow silvered,
     poured-wine beauty shining.
So swung swords gleamed – tempered
     In fire's sheath, warm-flame wreathed –
when war-hardened heroes
     assaulted that castle.

He makes a poem about a man in a wall-hung tapestry

There in the frieze – frozen,
     fighting Time's tight-wefted
weave – stands Old Age; rigid,
     arm raised. His blade's needling
icicle-gleams shimmer
     in an arrow-shower-
braving berserk's eyes. *Move!*
     Old Bandy's still standing.

His friend Erlingr – brother-in-law of the king – falls off the pier into mud, perhaps an open sewer, while returning to the ship after a night out in Imbólum

Guttered were you Erlingr?
　　　　Too gallus to rally
your wits, mouth *miðhæfi** –
　　　　muck-lover! Unlucky
almost – our king's in-law
　　　　bums-up in Imbólum's
mire! Our crown-prince clowning –
　　　　clarted in shite's motley!

* It was the custom in Imbólum when meeting in a narrow place to call out 'miðhæfi' – midway, or perhaps 'don't cross' – to indicate right of way.

He laments his wife's illness, seeks comfort in shaping words

I brood at her bedside
　　　　– I've brought lace, necklaces,
bone combs – who lies, limbs and
　　　　lips feverish – wishing
back our glad hours hawking
　　　　low-isled water-meadows;
I shape grave words – heart-deep,
　　　　honed, brief – to imprison grief.

Caitlynn Cummings

TASTE BUDS

Borscht

A red soup, a beet soup. My dad skins the beets and shows me how to shred them through the cheese grater. 'No problem,' I say, 'I'll do that job.' After one beet my palm is stained, I look as though I've just committed a murder, and my bicep aches. My dad takes over, he finishes where I've left off, he helps me. He shreds the beets, the onions, the carrots, and the cabbage, his strong arm accustomed to the rhythmic motion. A vibration of my dad's lips issues in a hum.

I pick up two intact carrots and make them dance across the oak kitchen table. They get stuck in the pockmarks and the gouges of the wood, but jump out into the next dance step. They dance around the ashtray and my dad grabs one partner with a grin on his face. 'Time for the shredder!' he says.

'No! What about the dancing?' I exclaim as my carrot friend becomes a lump of mush.

'They'll dance in your stomach in about an hour,' he explains, stopping for a second and widening his eyes while looking at me. 'With all the stomach juices!' He lunges at me and tickles my stomach insufferably.

'Stop! Stop!' I plead. 'Let's make the bore-ashhh already!'

'Borscht,' my dad corrects slowly, moving his mouth exaggeratedly to show me how all the sounds are made. I mimic his mouth's movements, never being more aware of how my lips moved. 'Perfect!' he says with a clap. I beam. My dad puts a can to his lips.

'Borscht, borscht, borscht.' My new favourite word.

My dad dumps the vegetable carcasses into a pot with some broth and vinegar. Nothing else exciting happens. Hmmph. 'This takes for ever,' I complain, rising on my tiptoes to see into the big steel pot of bubbling borscht. 'What kind of food is this?' I ask to quell my boredom.

'It's Russian,' my dad teaches, 'they use a lot of cabbage. You better watch out tonight after dinner.'

'What do you mean?' I ask.

'Cabbage makes you toot.'

'Gross!'

'It's good for you, don't worry; we need these vegetables to be strong.'

Finally we dish out the soup into white ceramic bowls. It is a deep, deep red. The onions, carrots, and cabbage seemed to have disguised themselves as beets, wearing the same dresses and hats as the beets, dyeing their skin the same colour. I can't tell which vegetable is which. My dad must be a beet, I think, not those cheating orange sticks who lie. Good for the eyes, but full of lies. Stupid carrots. Beets are honest; they are who they say they are. And they look so cool!

'Now,' my dad informs me, 'the biggest decision you will ever make: are you going to put sour cream in or not?' We are very serious. My dad watches me intently. I think intently, looking to the sour cream container and back to my bowl of borscht.

'Yes,' I decide, a huge grin enveloping my face. My dad slides the sour cream towards me. I take a big spoonful and plop it in my soup. I stir it in and it makes a Pepto-Bismol pink colour. 'Cool!' I exclaim. I put my nose over the steaming bowl and whiffs of vinegar and dairy accost my nostrils. It is strange. My spoon is small, my dad's is big, but they both have the same four-quadrant flower design on the end of the handle. In the cutlery drawer are heaps of spoons from different sets. I work up my nerve and jam a spoonful of Pepto-Bismol borscht into my mouth. My face contorts in disgust. The spoon retrogrades and I spit onto the table. 'Ewwwww!' I exclaim. 'This is disgusting!' My dad smiles understandingly, with a hint of disappointment in his hazel eyes.

Spaghetti

Salted water is boiling. A pan is heating up spattering butter. I throw celery and onions into the pan. My dad, erudite as he is, lectures on making pasta: 'Always begin with a rolling boil, a rolling boil.'

'A rooooolllllllliiinngggg boil, eh?' I ask, one eyebrow arched. 'And where did you hear that?'

'Well … Umberto,' he explains after a pause.

'In a very intimate conversation, those being very rare, with the famous Italian chef and restaurant owner, I assume?' I ask.

'No, okay, it's in his pasta book,' my dad admits, pointing to the book lying open on the kitchen table, full of glossy pictures and spaghetti sauce stains. He sits down on one of the old, stained kitchen chairs. 'Then we are to chop the tomatoes and the peppers, sauté the venison, and put it all together with another can of tomato sauce.'

Oh, that imperial we, I think. I begin to chop the vegetables and my dad takes out the ground venison from the package and puts it into the pan. Those Bambi movies really made having a hunting father difficult. When I was younger I used to cry 'But Bambi!' every time venison was talked about, made, or (the worst) seen in the yard. Now, after countless circle-of-life conversations with my dad, I realise it's just another animal, another type of meat … one I may come across living one day in the forest and dead the next day in my spaghetti, but meat nonetheless. The venison gives a little punch to the sauce, and the sauce drowns out any excesses of gamey flavour found in the meat.

The sauce boils, though I don't know if it constitutes rolling. 'Remember what you used to say about our spaghetti when you were a little girl?' my dad asks with a nostalgic paternal smile.

'The Stevens' Strawberries thing?' I ask.

'Yes. Daddy,' my dad assumes a little girl falsetto, 'this spaghetti is so good we should sell it to people like the Stevens sell their strawberries in their patch.'

'Well it is pretty good,' I say. 'Maybe you should diversify your farm income with a little spaghetti on the side business.'

He chuckles. 'Do you want to check the spaghetti?' he asks. He takes a swig of his beer.

'Yeah I do,' I say. I fish a noodle from the boiling water with a fork. It falls off; it always falls off. I try again and succeed. I pick the piping hot noodle up with my right hand, unwind it off the fork, and throw it against the cupboard. It sticks. 'It's ready,' I chime. My mom hates that; she thinks it's extremely inane to have to make something dirty to see if something's done. It's fun, we tell her, it's cooking. She doesn't get it.

We dish up and eat at the table. We twirl, we shovel, we *mangiamo*. What's with those families who cut up their pasta anyway? My dad gets a big bite on his fork and plunges it into his mouth. He closes his mouth, squints one eye, arches one eyebrow, and tries to let a little air in to dispel the scorching fire in his mouth. Overeager.

Chilled Almond Soup and Kiwi Spinach Salad

'Okay, Dad, we need to go to town and get some bulk blanched whole almonds, lots of garlic, kiwis, fresh spinach – not that frozen stuff – onions, balsamic vinegar, and virgin olive oil,' I say as I read off my list. We go to town, getting most ingredients at the grocery store, but also stop at a speciality store, Nutters, for the nuts.

At home I read out the recipes a number of times, asking my dad to help with certain tasks. 'We – I mean, you – have to get out the food processor and grind up the almonds very finely,' I joke. My dad stands on a chair to get the processor off the top of the cupboards, wobbling slightly. He grabs it, lurches onto the ground, and steadies himself. A shrill, destructive noise issues from the food processor as the nuts are blown to bits. I press innumerable cloves of garlic. My dad processes onions into similarly discombobulated bits, sitting down immediately after his work is done. I mix all the ingredients, add a little bit of milk, heat it up briefly, and chill until serving.

We begin to make the salad. My dad eyes the kiwis suspiciously. I wash the spinach. 'Did you know that spinach is full of antioxidants?' I ask.

'Yes,' my dad responds. 'We do need to annihilate those free radicals.'

'Indeed,' I concur. I pick up a kiwi. My dad's eyes follow my hand. I peel off the skin and begin to cut it into cubes.

He has had enough and can't contain himself any longer: 'What exactly are you doing?'

'Ummm, cutting kiwis,' I respond obviously.

'Yes, but why?' he asks. 'Are you making dessert or something?'

'No, I'm making kiwi spinach salad.'

My dad grimaces. 'Fruit in salad salad?' he asks.

'Welcome to the twenty-first century, Father, we aren't bound to pair red meat with red wines and – gasp – we can put fruit not only in fruit salads but in salad salads! And to think you were a progressive hippie in the sixties,' I say.

My dad smiles and motions me to go on blaspheming with my kiwis. He sits down and sips his shot of vodka.

We eat my new dishes. The chilled almond soup goes over well, nice on a hot summer day. My dad doesn't like the salad, but I do, eating his leftovers.

Empty Fridge

I come down and visit my father at the farm. The yard is desolate, swept with snow, vehicles rusting everywhere. My two golden retrievers greet me like they haven't seen a person in a long time. I knock on the front door to no answer. I turn the handle and hip check the door to make it open. It always did stick.

'Dad,' I call.

No answer.

I take off my shoes and coat and walk up to the kitchen. Orange peels litter the table as do twenty-six-ounce empty vodka bottles. Fruit flies are rampant; I try hard not to breathe them in. The counter has an old, dirty pot sitting on it, caked with the remnants of spaghetti I made for my dad two or three weeks ago. A half-empty package of peanuts sits on the table, some shells in an ashtray. There is a strange burgundy stain on the table; I don't think it's from borscht. I open the fridge. It is empty except for more orange peels in the crisper and years-old condiments. I put my hand to my mouth. 'Dad!' I shout. Nothing.

I race around the foyer, the living room, the bathroom, and come to my father's shut bedroom door. My heart pounds the beat to an experimental jazz tune, loud and irregular. I decide and burst into the room. My dad lies on the bed, still, face up. Clothes are strewn around. A potted plant has been overturned, its soil and white fertiliser particles cascading onto the grey, stained carpet.

I yell, 'Dad!'

He doesn't move.

I move to his bedside and grab his arm, shaking violently while screaming, 'Dad! Dad!'

His eyelids flutter and he looks at me. 'Candace,' he says, 'you're here.'
My heart slows down.

He looks to an empty vodka bottle on his bedside table and looks back
at me. He closes his eyes.

'Of course I'm here,' I say, 'it's five o'clock. Right on time. Let's go make
you something to eat.' I then think of the absent ingredients in the kitchen,
the empty places in the cupboards where they used to reside.

'I'm not hungry,' he says. He's never hungry any more. Even when he
does eat he says he can't taste anything. He used to tell me that taste buds
can change. When I didn't like borscht, he said wait a while, I might later.
His taste buds no longer work; I'm surprised his liver does. That is one
thing we never ate: liver.

Jenni Daiches

OMISSION

If with more care I had woken into that morning
perhaps I'd have found a sign that when you left

the house with holiday postcards in your hand
I would never see you again. If I'd tuned my ear

to the garden of birdsong, or breathed less bluntly, I might
have remembered some small thing to mention, and you

might have paused just long enough. If I'd attended
to the spaces between words, the empty margins,

the unspoken, or let something slip from inept fingers
so the sound of breaking glass turned you aside,

if I'd directed your eyes to an idle drift
of cloud in an arc of diffused affirmative light,

you might have strolled back smiling, pleased the day
was fine, ready to start the journey home.

SCIENCE

You'd think nothing could be simpler,
here in the woods, especially in winter,
stripped and lean, minimal,
no supernumerary leaf or lustre.

Sky open as a peal of bells,
and no impediment to hinder
the clean fabric of a naked, frugal picture,
as earth and increase hang fire.

But a goldfinch flare
betrays the forest's tension, flaunts
defiance to the message from the sun
and under my feet there is rebellion.

Decay teems with unseen creatures
impatient for the signal to begin,
dismays all efforts to impose order. Even
the giving of names seems crudely human.

Katy Ewing

PERSEID

The August night was clear, dark mooned.
We carried flutes of cava mixed with sloe gin, pink and sparkling,
out of artificial bright
in coats and hats, with giggles,
hoping judging neighbours wouldn't see.
The real dark pulled us on
out of the orange glow garden,
across the now dead street-lit main road,
towards the quiet.

Once there, we lay down on our backs to see the sky
without neck-ache,
the night road hard under our heads,
cool and gritty.

Now the sky became the universe,
a turning vast machine, the deepest sea of giant stars,
of worlds unknown,
and we were small, our lives just moments,
flickers in the planet's mind.

But then, you said,
it was also all so far away, so tiny,
and me and you so big, so warm, alive,
the centre of it all.

We held hands, watched, as shooting stars
glanced wishing trails above us, happy
when we saw the same one.

Each time the lonely distant sound of
middle-of-the-night car came close,
we jumped up, pretended to be normal,
just innocent everyday types walking in the night,
feeling like naughty kids, sneaking out after bedtime.
Then when the coast was clear we'd lie back down,
for just a little longer.

Elizaveta Feklistova

PHENOMENOLOGY

There's a linden tree outside her window, and its leaves lead rustle-restless lives. 'Take me with you!' they hiss. 'Take me away. Out, out and away.' The breeze teases; first bates its breath (they hang their heads) then breathes, breathes. Evie watches them, remembers that

'Take me with you.' That murmur against her neck, those hands restless and rustling through the fabric of her shirt. 'Take me away. Out, out and away.'

Then there had been footsteps and voices and she'd panicked for no good reason. The moment passed in a blur of 'so close' and 'not now' and she'd stepped back from her before their friends could turn the corner.

That had been a fluke, a one-time thing at seventeen and stupid. What did she expect?

'In the end,' says Rita, 'I traded guilt for a pack of playing cards.'

'That's a weird way of putting it.'

'Yeah, but it sounds awesome, admit it. And anyway, you know what I mean, I'd rather hide out here gambling—'

'We're not gambling. We're betting on whose turn it is to buy everyone a coffee, Rita. As if that counts.'

' 'Course it does. So. I'd rather hide out here with you gambling than go back and look Dan in the face and watch' (she's dead serious now, and tries to hide it; exaggerates each word, turns her tone mockingbird sweet) 'the last, few remaining vestiges of our relationship go ...'

The tip of Rita's cigarette glares red in the feeble evening light. Slender fingers swoop and close around a card, slide it out from the middle of her deck. She tilts her head, considers, then simply lets go and it falls unceremoniously

'... all the way down ...'

onto the table top and her voice wafts over through a haze of smoke. Evie can't counter. She picks up another card from the pile. She still can't counter, she shakes her head the leaves shake she had been shaking like a leaf that night,

'... knowing that there's nothing I can do to prevent ...'

feeling vulnerable and vain and oh, so triumphant; and the flow of her
thoughts had stilled to a hush, but her blood had been raucous and roaring
and rushing and for far too long she had been stupid enough not to realise
that none of that – not even

'… the two of us …'

soaring high on the absurdity of it all, not even the hand (tightening, tight-
ening) on the back of her neck, or the way her own mouth had stuttered
over skin – none of that had mattered. She had been

'… falling apart.'

drunk as in sort-of-tipsy, but she hadn't been drunk enough to run. Footsteps,
voices. Seconds later the rest of the group had turned the corner and

'There you two are. We've been looking for you!' they had said and

none of it had mattered.

'You and Dan are still together though, right?' she asks, laying down a seven.
Rita covers it with a ten.
  'Well … um … yes. But …' Rita grins, looks rueful, gnaws at her lip.
It's what she always does when she's about to embark on a long explan-
ation about something she knows Evic couldn't care less about. Rita turns
her face towards the window. Rustle-restless shadows waltz across her
cheek.
  'I just wanted to tell you abou— no, it doesn't matter. You won't be
interested.'
  A fleck of dust drifts down and nestles between her lashes. Rita shuts
her eyes, brushes it away, opens them, takes another drag. Her lips bleed.
A cloud outside shifts, and suddenly all Evie sees is sunset red. Then the
sky darkens again and Rita swerves around. Something about her grin looks
a little bit faded and her eyeliner on one side looks a little bit smudged, and
Evie wants, so badly, more than anything, to listen to whatever it is she
won't be interested in.
  'Well whatever it is you're gonna inflict on me,' she says, 'don't worry. I'll
listen.'
  'You sure? Okay. Well a few days ago, in class, we talked about this philo-
sophical theory called phen … phenology? No, not phenology. But something
like that. There's a "phen" and an "ology" in there somewhere at any rate.'
She taps her cigarette against the ashtray.
  'Yes?'

'And I think it's really interesting. Basically, like, um, how do I explain it? Well, from what I understood, it's this theory that, um, the way an individual perceives an object is, like, part of that object's essence.'

'Okay, go on.'

'It's sort of … take that tree outside for example. A scientist or a realist would say that it is made of wood and has bark and leaves, right. And that it was planted a certain amount of years ago, and that it's an oak—'

'It's a linden.'

'Doesn't matter. It's a specific type of tree anyway. And a pheno-something-ologist would say that …'

Leaves lean left, yearn yellow. Take me with you! they whisper. Take me away. Out, out and away. Branches strain towards the sky, taut and tense and

'… the essence of the tree is the way you, you Evie, perceive it to be …'

perfectly hopeless.

Rita pauses.

'You all right, Eves? You're rather quiet today.'

'I'm fine, Rita.'

'The reason I thought of phen-blah-ology in the first place is because you asked, remember? 'Bout me and Dan, whether we were still together.'

'Yes.'

'Well, I've been thinking, we are still together, technically, but I don't want us to be, and we won't be for long any more, so I already started thinking of him as my ex. And, you know, in phenology, he really would already be my ex, simply because I perceive him that way. I like that. I like the thought of that. Like my mind controls the world around me.'

'I wish,' Evie says, and wishes that:

'Come on! Let's go!'

'What?'

'They're all coming round the corner! Let's run for it.'

'Not enough time!'

'Who the hell cares?'

Minutes and metres away, lips met. Laughter in the dark cut short.

The sidewalk stretched around them like an asphalt river. It had—

'Your turn, Evie.'

It hadn't happened that way of course. They had stayed put. They had returned to that stupid party. They had fallen asleep friends, they had woken up friends. But Evie had thought, for a second, clinging to her in an empty suburban street, she had thought—

'Evie. It's your turn.'

'I don't want to play any more.'

'Damn it,' says Rita, 'I was winning.' She drops her cards. She drums her fingers on the table top. She finishes her cigarette. She lights a new one.

'Also, I forgot to tell you!' she says suddenly. 'The guy from the bookstore asked me out.'

'Yeah?'

'Yeah. Turned him down 'cause of Dan, but told him I'd call him once we break up.'

'Ah.'

'So now I just have to figure out a way to ditch him and not make it too brutal. Hate dumping people. Never have the guts to do it.'

'You,' Evie interjects, 'have more guts than anybody I have ever met in my life.'

'Can't have met many brave people then. And yeah, of course I have the guts to do it. But just ... it's just such a goddamn pity, isn't it? Dan and me not being able to make it through.'

'I know.'

'Hanging out with him used to feel like the best thing in the world, Evie. But now it's mostly just dull. And other times he pisses me off so much it's like I could kill him.'

'If you do,' Evie mutters, 'just remember, friends help you move, best friends help you move bodies.'

'I'll bear that in mind.'

Rita gathers up the cards into a neat pile. 'Can I ask you something, Evie?'

'Sure.'

'Why do you hate Dan so much?'

The door slams shut with a bang. Rita jumps. 'Close the window,' she says and Evie gets up, takes three steps, turns the latch. Outside, the linden leaves rain down in a muted storm of bright. It's all so devastating, really. She watches. She speaks:

'Hey, Rita?'

'Hm?'

Evie Hayes comes close to telling her one nervous weekday afternoon, when the air isn't yet quite cold enough to cut. 'Can I have a cigarette?' she says instead.

And the reason for it being so devastating, she thinks, as she watches them fall, is that blatant beauty is simply too rude. It barges in and knocks you

down and there's a radiant flash of awe or pain, but then you're free to go.
The subtle makes you think it's safe to look so

'You don't smoke!'
'No, not usually. But I get these moments, and …'

you stare, stare, stare and the more you stare the more you see: her mouth,
rough and red and a little too thin, her imperfect skin, and her sparrow-
brown hair and her feather-slight smiles and her fluttering hands and the
weight of her eyes and then it happens, that one disastrous night

'… I'm having one right now, when …'

you think you'd rather die than look away. And it's a year later and she sits
opposite you, in all that damned, dishevelled glory of bleeding lips and
bitten nails, and

'… I want to. I want—'

                              you

sink down into your vacant chair and close your eyes as slender fingers
slowly slide a cigarette into your mouth. Rita, too lazy to fish out her lighter,
leans forward and (it would be, you think, so easy to simply reach out and)
the flame is an ache that spreads and spreads and the tip of her cigarette
glares red in the feeble evening light and the tip of yours ignites and then
it's over. Life goes on. Leaves crash to the ground. Car wheels tear them to
shreds. Meaningless music (so quiet it's barely audible) won't stop playing
in one of the neighbouring flats.

'What's that noise?' Rita remarks. 'D'you hear it?'

Rita's referring to the far-away tune. She registers it only dimly, the way
adults do when they strain their ears and try to hear one of those high-
pitched beeps that drive children wild with annoyance.

'Yes,' you mutter.
'Yes what?'
'Yes,' you say. 'I hear it. It's the soundtrack to our lives.'

She doesn't get it. She laughs anyway. You take another drag. Smoke sighs
its way in a long, pointless coil towards the ceiling.

Gerrie Fellows

PILOT

In another season
he could pinpoint the summits
the passes between them   skipped
gullies   the cliffs' vertiginous riffs
            a mapped scribble of rock
            over which he plies his art

        He knows the chart
but now he flies a terrain
obliterated by snowfall
the mountains God's mistake
lochans null grey   ridges erased
corries turned to violet shadow
rims fanning out from icefall
over which windslab plates   fractures
to a blank   in which he's alone

                and all he knows
is the air rush he moves in
even the wind gives no quarter
the sky a perfect blue
clueless as the white beneath him
not even a comb of cirrus
tarnishes its thinning mirror
            Astray in finned aluminium
            he has forgotten   who he is

                or what he knows
kept alive by numbers, readings
the lights of the instrument panel

the forest   lifting its living needles
            to rescue him

Olivia Ferguson

MY MAD GIRL

She turned things on and couldn't turn them off,
panicked in doorways and narrow places,
fought off chairs with all her hands,
devised falls and fires. Each time
she woke up from a transatlantic night
you were there, to swab her armpits
with her shirt and lay her head down.

The hair you should cut –
thickened to a flap – but it's old
and it's full of old smells found nowhere else.
She wears it like a blanket round her neck
while she sleeps. She moves
before you, too proud to run and too late
to walk. She hatches trees you can see through.

Back home there was no forest:
trees were travellers stomaching the road.
She said it was so beautiful
it made her sick. She said there's one kind of beauty
does that to you, twists your insides gently with
forks, like spaghetti.

UNDER THE TREE

On the last judgement day, they say, his wife came home from the shops and found him under the tree at the back, between home and work. She dropped all her bags on the ground to come for him, they say, and he just sat and he just watched the stuff inside slide apart.

He could've said, I didn't know what I was doing. Maybe, if I was more cautious by nature, I'd have gone and seen someone. It was braver to do nothing now. The neighbours knew, and no longer cared, but like always they hid their ears between the leaves above him.

He thought about being sick in the queue for vaccinations when he was fifteen. The six pinpricks like a magic ring on his shoulder, and the wonderful scab that grew there big as a coin.

It was hot, they say. Since Kyle's girl was born the ground had sweat dry. Days at North Berwick were better than ever, though not the ones they remember when the beaches were wetter, and the dog had the worm casts all to itself.

He could've said, I've got it on my hands and can't get it off. It was smarter to do nothing now. The work had been shameful for months. The tree, they say, wasn't listening to him. It had its own complaints: the dry bit just there, the dog, the problem root.

Seonaid Francis

DON'T BURY ME HERE
If I should die, think only this of me ...

Don't bury me here,
where grey sky meets grey sea,
cut only by the pale grasses
of the shifting dunes,

where the wind laments across the moor,
the endless siren song of wilderness,
and black plastic flaps
like prayer flags caught on wire.

Don't bury me here,
on this waning codicil of land,
weather bleached,
where the sodden earth lies beaten under rain

and the relentlessness of water
washes away the stars
and leaves nothing but a pious
lithography of days.

Don't bury me here.
My body would lie heavy
in this cold, sandy earth,
and the foreignness of my thoughts

would nourish nothing.

Graham Fulton

FOR A MOMENT

Past a man and a wee boy
who's inspecting the wrappers
stuffed into a hedge

And the man says
Am goani huv ti ask yi
        ti walk a wee bit faster Andrew
yur dad huz ti go ti iz work
                    and his wee boy says
        Faster?
and his dad says
Aye Andrew
        walk a wee bit faster
and his wee boy says *Walk faster?*
and his dad says *Aye Andrew*
        walk a wee bit faster
yur dad huz ti
go ti iz work

And the wee boy takes off
with a determined clumping run
and says *Like this Dad?*
as he passes me with my shopping bag and moves
to the left to avoid a Jack Russell and steps
onto the grass outside my flat
as his dad laughs and says
Someone will come an chase yi
        fur standin oan thur grass Andrew

an come here
fur a moment
        yur nose iz aw snot

And once I've shelved
the things in my bag
I stand at the window right now

and can still see them far away
walking slowly
hand in hand
towards the bridge   talking to each other
gone

Harry Giles

BRAVE

Acause incomer will aywis be a clarty wird,
acause this tongue I gabber wi will nivver be the real Mackay, I
    sing.
Acause fer aw that wur aw Jock Tamson's etcetera, are we tho? Eh?
Acause o muntains, castles, tenements n backlans,
acause o whisky exports, acause o airports,
acause o islans, I sing.
acause o pubs whit arena daein sae weel oot o the smokin ban, I
    sing.
acause hit's grand tae sit wi a lexicon n a deeskit mynd, I sing.
acause o the pish in the stair, I sing.
acause o ye,

I sing o a Scotland whit wadna ken workin class authenticity gin
    hit cam reelin aff an ile rig douned six pints o Tennent's n
    glasst hit in the cunt,
        whit it wadna
            by the way.

I sing o google Scotland,
        o laptop Scotland,
                o a Scotland sae dowf on bit-torrentit HBO
    drama series n DLC packs fer paistapocalyptic RPGs that hit
    disna ken hits gowk fae hits gadjie,
                tae whas lips n fingers amazebawz cams mair
    freely as bangin.

I sing o a Scotland whit hinks the preservation o an evendoun
    Scots leeteratur is o parteecular vailyie n importance bit cadna
    write hit wi a reproduction claymore shairp on
    hits craig,
        whit hinks Walter Scott scrievit in an either tide,
        whit hinks Irvine Welsh scrievit in an either tide.

I sing o a Scotland whit wants independence fae Tories
        n patronisin keeks
                n chips on shouders
                        bit sprattles tae assert ony kin o
    cultural awtonomy whit isna grundit in honeytraps.

I sing o a Scotland whit hinks thare's likely some sort o God, rite?
          whit wad like tae gang for sushi wan nite but cadna
haundle chopsticks,
          whit sines up fur internet datin profiles n nivver replies tae
the messages,
          whit dreams o bidin in London.

I sing o a Scotland whit fires tourists weirin See You Jimmy hats
          the puir deathstare,
              n made a pynt o learnin aw the varses tae Auld Lang Syne,
                    n awns a hail sined collection o Belle n
Sebastian EPs.

I sing o a Scotland bidin in real dreid o wan day findin oot chuist
          hou parochial aw hits cultural references mey be,
              n cin only cope wi the intertextuality o the Scots
Renaissance wi whappin annotatit editions,
                    n weens hits the same wi awbdy else.

I sing o a Scotland that hasna geid tae Skye,
          or Scrabster,
                or Scone,
                          bit cin do ye an absolute dymont o
a rant on the plurality o Scots identity fae Alexandair mac
Alexandair tae Wee Eck.

I sing o a Scotland whit cadna hink o a grander wey tae end a nite
          as wi a poke o chips n curry sauce,
          whit chacks the date o Bannockburn on Wikipedia,
          whit's no sae shuir aboot proportional representation,
          whit draws chairts on the backs o beermats tae lear ye
aboot rifts n glaciation
                    n when hit dis hit feels this oorie dunk,
                          this undesairvt wairmth
                                o inexplicable luve,

whit is heavt up,
      in the blenks afore anxiety is heavt up
         by the lithe curve o a firth.
Whit wants ye tae catch the drift.
Whit's stairtin tae loss the pynt.

I sing o a Scotland whit'll chant hits hairt oot dounstairs o the
Royal Oak, whit'll pouk hits timmer clarsach hairtstrangs,
whit like glamour will sing hits hairt intae existence, whit
haps sang aroon hits bluidy nieve hairt,
    whit sings.

Rody Gorman

FIR NAM BEANN

Chunnaic mi air bhàrr sìthein dà chràc
Is dh'fhairich mi 'n uair sin dùrd nan adharc
Is am beuc 's an geum 's an ràn 's an raoic
Aig luchd-fiadhaich nan cròic is nam bràc
Ann an glac a' falbh às an fhradharc
Agus thuirt mi rium fhìn: *Teich, a ghlaoic!*

THE CORNERSTEPREGARDROCKPEAKHORN MANONES

i saw on the harvestbranchtopcreamcroptop of a flowerfairyhill
two poundingantlers and i smeltfeltheard that hourtimethen the
humsyllablemutter of the sounding horns and the yellclamour
and the roarlow and the cry and the belchbellow of the
boisterouswild hideragevenisonantler and branchbellowdeer
foresthunters in a catch-hollow going out of pupilsight and i said
to myself: *desertretreatflee, you gowk!*

Alison Grant

ADDING AIR

You need to get up from that desk,
book a sailing course, learn about
reef knots and gunwales, how to cast off.

Try bungee jumping or go-ape in trees
with three children under ten. Teach yourself
to bake, feel the dough, watch it rise.

Me? I breathe in mountains, grow broad beans,
chop eight tons of wood each winter.

But you should build a dry stone wall
with volunteers in Kendal,
each flat slab interlocked
to underpin a well-shaped cope,
each gap home to toads
and the green creep of moss.

Katharine Grant

WEARING SILK

The old man is waking the old woman with the resolute tap he perfected during the war. She's been expecting the tap for a week or more. At once, she gathers herself. She must prepare to move, these days. When all her strength is mustered, she pushes back the eiderdown, lowers her legs and carefully places each foot into slippers she knits for them both every year. She sniffs the air. Without touching the shutters she gauges that it's dawn. It's not cold, though. Summer has reached the farm.

'Coffee, Joska?' She's standing by the range, still warm from the night before.

He's going to refuse, as usual, but the diminutive of his name, not usual, catches at him. He'll take the coffee today. Perhaps its bitterness will help. What nonsense, he thinks. Of course it won't help. Nevertheless, he drinks the coffee, the scour adding to the sickness in his throat. He wipes his mouth. She's never been a good coffee maker.

His wife doesn't light the lamp, not out of economy or in deference to today's business but because she's spent so long in this kitchen she no longer needs her eyes. She moves around with blind confidence, familiar with every mote of dust in the cupboards and every tear in the cloth over the chest under the window. She usually smoothes it, that cloth. Today she must steel herself to touch it. There's nothing wrong with the cloth, or with the chest on which, for years, they've sat of an evening. What's in the chest is a different matter. The old woman knows she must help the old man, so steeling herself with a small jerk, she pulls the cloth off and lets it drop onto the floor. The old man blenches. He wants to say 'stop, stop, I've made a mistake – not today'. He says nothing, though, as the chest's hinges grind, closely followed by the rustle of tissue and the soft slip of leather. 'Joska?' The diminutive again. There can be no stopping. He knows it and is grateful that she knows it too. She's a good wife.

The old woman is holding out two items retrieved from the chest. He takes the first, a bridle, then hefts the proffered saddle clumsily into the crook of his arm. The saddle's not heavy; he's just not used to it. His wife shuts the chest and pads over the flags to the back door. She opens it, forgetting her own coat in her care to hand the old man his cap.

In the makeshift stable attached to the house, Dronski swishes his tail. He knows the pattern of things. The old man will try to pull back the bolt on the stable door. The bolt will stick. The old man will curse and give the door a sharp nudge with his knee. The bolt will slide and the door will open. The old man, murmuring greetings, will grapple with the feedbin, lean in, then ease himself upright, shuffle over to the stall and offer Dronski oats from his hand before tipping a plump scoop into the manger. Dronski will drop a few oats for the pleasure of searching for them in the straw with his tongue.

Except that's not how it is today because the old woman is with the old man. No matter. This, then, will be the pattern. Whilst the old man gets the oats, the old woman will scratch the horse's skinny neck and, if allowed, kiss the dents that time has worn above his eyes. Dronski will allow those kisses this morning. Why not? Summer is come.

But nothing quite conforms. The old woman tries the bolt and the old man has to put something down to help her. When the door opens, it's the old woman who goes to the feedbin. She doesn't know the stable as she knows the kitchen, so must feel for the scoop. She forgets to offer oats in her hand. Disappointed, Dronski nudges her, then goes to his manger and begins to grind corn between yellow teeth. The old woman gives a small exclamation and emerges from the stall. Her husband looks up. No silks, she says, we've no silks.

She leaves the stable and returns to the chest. From the bottom, she draws up tissue, lays it on the table, and from the tissue unfolds her wedding dress. It's plain, stitched by her mother and aunts in a noisier lifetime. She touches the silk with her little finger. She has no thought this morning for the daughter who might have worn the dress. She thinks only *yes, yes, this is perfect*. She fetches scissors, hooks on a pair of spectacles and still without lighting the lamp, spreads the cloth. She should unpick the stitches – that's what her mother would have done – but she only puzzles how best to go about the delicate business of cutting. She pulls the dress this way and that. Ah, there it is: the small brown stain where a drop of wine from the wedding breakfast spilled. She brushes the silk against her nose. No smell. Still, she pauses to remember not so much the wedding meal with its coarse gaiety, her father's silly speech and her mother's tears at 'my little Mushkin' pre-ferring the thin comforts of a farm boy's home to the fat comforts of her own. She remembers earlier in the day, when she had to pull this dress over her head because one of her aunts had stitched up the bottom buttonholes by mistake. Shielded momentarily from her mother's scolding and her aunt's wailing, she had felt the silk rub against her nose and in that shiny cocoon had realised with a sense of surprise that she really did love the skinny farm boy who had singled her out. When her head re-emerged, she'd felt like a proper bride.

She sniffs some more, then shakes her old woman's hair, finds chalk in a jug and begins to draw. At first, she's cautious and the strokes waver and break, but as she works, her strokes become bolder. Wavery strokes are not good strokes and these strokes must be worthy. Finally, she's ready to cut, and always aware of her husband in the stable, of Dronski in his stall and of what must be done, she pushes the scissors hard over her knuckles and begins. Her spectacles fog. She pulls them off and brings the silk closer.

Her face smoothes in concentration; her fingers gain confidence; her cutting is deft and uncompromising. As the last of the unwanted silk flows onto the floor, she does not pin or tack, she just threads the sewing machine, her foot already poised on the treadle. Her fingers hold the silk firmly; her foot drives up and down. She hums the song she brought from her child-hood, the one she used to sing when they had calving cows. József teased her, yet always called her to the byre. He's a good husband.

Back in the stable, Dronski is already saddled and when the old woman sees him, she stops short. The horse's back is so dipped that the saddle barely needs a girth, and the pale, un-oiled leather of the bridle strikes a gaudy note against his coarsened coat. The old man's attempt to remove straw from his tail and draw a comb through his mane has only increased the horse's dishevelment. The old woman's heart contracts. The old man, sickness rising again, begins to shake his head. The horse can barely move. This is madness.

The old woman recovers herself. She holds up the silk blouse she has created and Dronski cocks his ears. The old man reaches out. 'Your wedding dress, Mariska?' His wife nods. Her husband hesitates, then drops Dronski's rein, takes the blouse, pulls it on and tucks the fraying edges into his trousers.

'Wait!' The old woman goes into the stable, dips her skirt in Dronski's water bucket, then kneels in front of her husband and polishes his boots. 'There.'

They move out of the yard, the old woman leading the way, the old man leading the horse. A hundred yards up the track, the old man stops at the upended plough. Dronski prepares himself for the shafts. The old man shakes his head. 'Not today,' he says and hauls himself onto the wheel. Dronski watches. 'Come, then,' the old woman says, and the horse obediently positions himself so that the old man can clamber into the saddle. Dronski braces. This is unusual indeed. The old woman murmurs. The old man checks the girth.

The horse hobbles off, as he supposes he should. The old man crouches stiffly, pitching back and forth. Out on the plain, the grass is short and damp. A breeze caresses Dronski's ears and lifts the old man's cap. The old man adjusts the stirrups with awkward and uncertain fingers. The horse, still puzzled but always willing, feels the old man's fumbling and sees, from the corner of his eye, the old woman standing on the plough, holding up her handkerchief. The curl of white stirs something.

The old woman knows what she's about. She's everything: starter, steward, crowd. She drops the handkerchief.

The old horse sees the handkerchief falling and vaguely remembers not the detail but the thrust of a silken day when, cosseted and compelled, a similar fall of white had him leaping forward and galloping past painted stands and blue furlong markers, round the corner and onto the straight, cutting through the tunnelled roar of the crowd. Had this really happened? Yes, he can feel it through the crackle in his veins. Once or many times? He's not sure. He walks more quickly and when the old woman shouts his old name, the name they changed as unfitting for a plough horse but which is still his name, he breaks into a trot, then a canter. Immediately pain tears him. His tendons howl. But he keeps going – he's galloping now – because far stronger than the pain is the pleasure, the agonising pleasure, of spring and speed and the stretch of the leg. He flies, creakily.

The old man is still unsure, yet as the horse's neck flattens, he leans forward, cheeks flushing, sap rising. He has no sense of Dronksi's racetrack. How could he? He's never been further than the town from which he extracted his wife. The old man is back at the docks, once again paying the paltry price for a Derby winner reduced in the space of two years from a jewel over which rich men slavered, to a printed name on an august list of heroes, to a number on a bill of lading. Underneath him, the horse snorts and in answer the old man grins briefly. Racing people might have lost interest in Dronski but Dronski has always known his worth. The trouble they had, breaking a racehorse to the plough! The silk blouse billows and flattens against his chest. How smooth and cool it is, though not as smooth and cool as his wife's skin when he'd drawn the dress over her head the night he brought her here. He could have choked at the loveliness. He could choke now. How glad he is they made that promise to the horse, he and Mariska, but oh, the pain of fulfilment.

The horse is racing, eager in the dawn; his jockey is tight and light and driving him on; his supporting crowd is a wrinkled dancer, her arms in the sky.

One circuit is all they manage, then the horse is slowing, gasping for breath. He stumbles; the man rattles; the woman's arms slump. Eventually, the horse staggers to a halt. He trembles, ribs heaving. His jockey climbs down, legs buckling. His supporter shrivels, crumpled and exhausted. It's some time before they manage the walk back to the stable: an old man, an old woman, an old horse.

'I'll see to him, then I'll be in,' says the old man. The old woman touches her husband's arm, then kisses the horse's sunken eyes, and kisses them again, just for love. She returns to the house, pulls herself up the stairs and into the bed, eyes fixed, hands locked together. She braces herself. When the retort comes, she shudders.

Eventually, the old man climbs in beside her, still wearing the silk blouse. It's now fully light and there are chores waiting. They fold themselves together, unspeaking, only when they find their loss too hard to bear, she touches the blouse with her nose and he touches the back of her neck with his thumb.

Jen Hadfield

CRYPTOGRAPHY

Those interminable lunches at my grandmother's. Plunged sauna-style from the dining room, which was the chilliest room in the house, to the sitting room, the hottest. Dazed, bored, resentful after unsatisfying, pale-green English food – a gooseberry fool, celery growing *post-mortem*, like the fingernails, in a glass of a water – I'd pass the time by writing. I was afraid my relatives might read what I wrote, watch my pen moving across the paper like a lie-detector. To establish a secret space for myself, I devised a cryptogrammic alphabet. I wrote fluently in code into my early adolescence.

When I finally abandoned hieroglyphics, I allowed, instead, my handwriting to become so degraded – like the contorted script of the folded, volcanic coastline of Grunasound – that no-one would be able to decipher it. The strata have been tilted, crumpled, and eroded into a consolidation of welded blades, or the corrupted leaves of a great, blackened census, jolting down to the waves. Rabbits shelter in the rotten rock, bask and skitter over igneous runnels. Here and there the strata sandwich a thick chapter of concrete-coloured rock, a paste of greyish quartz.

I remember when the urge to publish was the urge to raise a cairn, a private cache in a public place. If I could only publish a book of poems I could move on. Usually, a letter for the unattainable beloved, left where they might find it. Would they recognise it was addressed to them? How tantalising that impulse was, and how unhealthy.

I honestly do want to *communicate* now – preferably face to face and in real time if I can manage it. But my handwriting's a relic from that other era. Even I can't read it, nor can I often remember what I wrote. Sometimes when I can't make out a word, I substitute whatever word it looks like, often one whose sound is more apt than its literal meaning. Often I wish the substitution had occurred to me spontaneously. I'm fed up with being so much in control – this is what I'll tell people who are irritated by my illegible handwriting, whose regular, well-formed letters sit on demand, with tails neatly tucked beside them – I've a hunger for the dynamic, impulsive and unintentional.

Sylvia Hays

CHANGING, OR, THE MAN WHO KNEW THOMAS MANN

It is the end of the summer in which my mother died. I need to go very deep into the south to administer her estate. I will, but for the time being I am sitting on the end of a pier netting crabs, with pieces of leftover chicken on a line for bait. They are greedy things, the crabs, and it isn't long before I have a bucketful in time for lunch. The sun's heat forces smells up out of the silvered timber – salt, creosote and the very essence of the wood. I have this part of the inlet almost to myself. The holiday-makers will be keeping cool on screened verandas, or jumping the breakers on the Atlantic side.

I drive back to the hotel my friend Winifred owns. 'Hotel' is an odd name for this building, which is actually a wood-shingled structure built on stilts with their feet in the sand. It has three parts, with breezeways between each one, verandas on the outer four sides and a steep roof sheltering the whole thing. Winifred keeps half the top floor for herself. She has had a dormer window replaced by a door, and a deck built that projects to command a view of the beach.

I've been staying here for a week and helping out as necessary around the hotel: I take an occasional turn at the reception desk, or practise my skill at lettering signs, or advise on refurbishing some of the rooms. The bucket of crabs goes up to her kitchen and into a cauldron of boiling water. Winifred and I lunch on the deck. I notice that hunger renews itself at approximately the same rate that the crabs can be unpicked, so the process could in theory go on for ever.

The next day I dye a crinkle-cotton shirt in the crab pot (now thoroughly scrubbed). The turmeric I spotted on the kitchen shelf turns the Indian cloth a beautiful, vibrant shade of deep yellow. There is something satisfying about doing non-holiday things in this beachy place. The shirt dries quickly in the sea breeze. I'll wear it tomorrow with a pair of shorts when I start driving south again.

South. Until my mother's funeral earlier this summer I haven't been so far south as I am about to go since I was eighteen, half the age I am now. I hardly know it, am tempted to deny any knowledge of it; yet my gene pool is there. The south, though I am already in it, is a big country; too far to drive in a single day. I have arranged to stay overnight with an old friend I haven't seen in many years. I have heard that he was devastated by the death of his wife a few years ago.

First I have to turn the car north again to recross the bridge that holds this long spit of land at arm's length from the mainland. The road snakes around the shallow waters of the sound and cuts a dry route through the Dismal Swamp. I expected cypress knees and Spanish moss hanging from the trees, but there is only this two-lane strip of grey, shimmering in the mounting heat. Even in shorts and the thin Indian yellow shirt (yes! that is exactly the colour it has become: Indian yellow) I am too hot. My thighs stick to the seat of my mother's car.

After the funeral I had driven her nearly new car north, filled with odds and ends I didn't want to risk leaving in the house. The car has air conditioning, unlike my own, but even that isn't coping with the humid heat of the Dismal Swamp. It is the climate that may have exterminated the first English settlement not far from here, and the climate that played a part in decimating the colonists at Jamestown nearly a generation later. Pine trees growing as tall and straight as the telephone poles they may become line the road for miles. Occasionally a track disappears between them into the woods, the swamp. I certainly do not expect to see a low brick building divided into a few small shops, which is off to my right with a parking lot in front. I am thirsty now as well as hot, so I pull in, get out and slam the door shut.

What have I done! The act and the sound of the door slamming already belong to the past. In silence the sun beats down on this empty place. I have locked myself out of my mother's unfamiliar car. The keys are visible in the ignition. If there is a spare set I do not have them. I try all the doors, just in case; every button is firmly pushed down. Because of the heat I have left the front windows open just a crack, too narrow for an arm to reach through. None of the small businesses lined up in front of me has anything to do with motor vehicles. *There must be a way out of this.* Over there is a dry cleaner's. An idea. The woman behind the counter is perfectly calm and cool. If she has observed my difficulty through the plate glass window, or thought I was trying to steal the car, she gives no sign of it. I explain, and ask for a wire coat-hanger. She seems to hesitate, then hands one over.

Standing beside the car, I untwist the wire from the hook end of the hanger and straighten it as much as I can. The wire is not as heavy as I would wish; it waves around and keeps trying to fold itself back into its own shape. I feed the wire through the opening at the top of the window and aim the hook at the key ring. It touches, but veers off this way and that. I am sweating almost too much to grasp the wire firmly. A dozen, maybe twenty tries to catch the keys and all fail. Then – oh, how beautiful! – the hook is secure in the key ring. From the opposite end of the wobbling wire, I *pull*. The keys spring out of the ignition, recoil off the wire and fall to the floor.

I can barely see them now. They are almost hidden by the seat. What now? Thoughts of breaking in flash through my mind followed by *it is not even my car. My mother may be dead but it is not my car.* No-one enters or leaves the parking lot. The sun bleaches everything like an overexposed photograph. I say to myself *there will be an end to this story.* When I think of it as a story desperation starts changing into curiosity: *On a global scale this is only a minor difficulty. My life will not end with me forever standing in an empty parking lot locked out of a car in the middle of the Dismal Swamp. I wonder how this story will end?* Feeling slightly cheered at the thought, I reshape the coat-hanger and feed it through the gap above the window. It just touches the keys. I try to prod the keys without knocking them under the seat or out of sight. Many attempts later they jump forward on the floor mat and I can see them clearly. Now the critical business begins. Is it possible to hook the coat-hanger into the key ring when it is lying flat on the floor? Time passes without sound except for the impotent dinging of wire against a metal ring. Eventually the impossible happens: I have caught the keys! Now to drag them across and lift them slowly, steadily to the window. I concentrate on keeping my hands from shaking while I coax the keys through the gap and into my grasp.

So glad am I to be gone that I take no notice of my thirst. I don't return the coat-hanger; I don't suppose she would have wanted it back. It is strange that life has shifted back into almost-normal again, as if nothing had happened. Before I cross another state line I stop at a textile mill, one of a good many in this region. Cotton is still king, though its days must be numbered; I have met polyester. I stroll into the cooled air of the mill shop as if on an ordinary errand. No-one looks at me strangely. The dirty seaweed that I have felt clinging to my shoulders and dripping down my body ever since my experience is invisible.

I have a history of acquiring cloth. I am fascinated by mill shops with their goods piled high next to the place where they are made, and the penetrating noise and chemical smells of the manufacturing process. This is one of the major mills. Walking up and down the aisles between tables of cloth has a soothing effect. My hands skim over the smooth texture of fabric that might be made into sheets or shirts. I linger over making a choice: a modest purchase of two lengths of blue cotton, one plain, one checked.

Gustav is expecting me by drinks time, and I have one more state to cross. My route is as much west as south, and the Spanish moss I thought I would see must be somewhere to the east of this highway. To while away the time I play with the cruise control and decide I don't like it, then switch on the radio to find gospel music on all the stations, so I drive in silence.

As I get more deeply into the south, small memories like snapshots come to mind from the times I travelled as a young child with my parents to the destination I'll reach tomorrow. Crossing hill and mountain country I remember tobacco patches beside wooden houses, shacks really, built of unpainted board-and-batten. There was always a porch across the front and there always seemed to be an old man sitting in a hickory straight chair tipped back against the wall. Always the man would be dressed in bib overalls and wearing a straw hat. If ever he were to take it off it would leave a line of dirt and sweat indented across his forehead and above that, pinkish skin that seldom met the powerful sun. The memory of this man, which is probably a composite memory, stays with me as an image of pure stillness, as if it were possible to seize time and hold it captive. On the gable ends of barns would be painted advertisers' slogans, and all along the road intermittent signs promoting Burma-Shave and the fact that Jesus Saves. There's none of that to be seen now, apart from a scatter of signs about Jesus, or maybe I'm in the wrong place to see it. The standard sort of house is one-storey brick, and the inhabitants are indoors keeping cool. The road is good, and I whizz across the state.

Gustav changed jobs some years ago and no longer lives in the university town where I first knew him. He was in the archaeology department then, and I was a returning student, there to study art at last. How we all met – my husband and I, Gustav and his wife – I can't remember; I just have a small collection of memories I take out and turn over from time to time.

We had been invited for Christmas Eve at their house, built of white clapboard; like so many old southern houses it had a veranda across the front. Double doors gave onto a central entrance hall in which stood a tall fragrant Christmas tree covered with real candles, all lit. I was captivated by its magic even though safety warnings flashed somewhere in the back of my head. We were in the sitting room having drinks before dinner while I regarded the Tintorettos on the walls and the ancient artifacts on shelves. Tintoretto was never one of my favourite painters, but these were real, and in a private house they had a different kind of presence. In the midst of our conversation there was a whoosh, gentle enough at the sound's edges that I might have ignored it but Gustav didn't. With one continuous graceful motion he left his chair, entered the hall, opened the front doors and pitched the flaming tree out onto the dark lawn.

Another time – cold for a southern winter's day – they came to us. Greetings were exchanged and, having unbuttoned his coat, Gustav spread his arms wide and embraced me. I was completely encircled and held fast within the soft fur lining of the coat. He released me with a gentle laugh, but the erotic possibilities of that moment had been stated. Was it on that occasion that we playfully began to waltz? I don't remember; we only would have done a few turns, but his movements were natural and sure. It was in his blood.

He belonged to a family of ancient pedigree – when and why he left Europe I never thought to ask. Even if I had thought of it I would probably not have done so; it would have felt to me then like a vulgar intrusion. When my husband asked him how he came to be attached to a university in the Bible Belt (it had been a minor culture shock to us too), Gustav replied simply, 'I have to earn a living.' It was said of Gustav that he was a terrible snob. This seemed plausible enough, but I had no direct evidence of it. Nor was I able to hold it against him that he was excruciatingly handsome. His impeccable manners, his aristocratic bearing and yes, perhaps the rumoured snobbishness, made him the object of various practical jokes which he would relate with some relish. And out of the mouths of others, Gustav stories abounded.

What I remember with the most pleasure and gratitude – gratitude for a sudden though temporary escape from the student routine, from inter-mittent but growing domestic misery – were occasional ventures on some archaeological errand into the country. If we met by chance on the campus he'd scoop me up and into his department's little green van. He'd drive it like a Ferrari on country roads where I'd never been, creating a tornado of gravel and dust after the tarmac ended. Someone had turned up some Indian artifacts on a farm – might it be worth starting a dig there? Gustav, with me in tow, would rush off to investigate. He took me to see, from an awed distance, sacred green hills which were Indian burial mounds. In deepest country we came upon a horse, like in size to the Trojan horse, standing in splendour in a large field. Real horses grazed at its feet under-standing that they were cousins. Gustav explained that it had been constructed of welded steel some years before by the daughter of the farm, who had been a sculpture student in the same department in which I was studying painting.

I have crossed the state line, so I haven't much farther to go. Gustav has sent some perfectly clear directions, which are laid out beside me on the passenger seat. I will be on time despite my earlier experience. I think I will say nothing about it. The white clapboard house with its veranda is not unlike his old one, perhaps less charming in proportion but somewhat bigger. As I come up the drive Gustav steps out to meet me. At least fifteen years have passed; he is remarkably little changed.

I never knew his age; I can't guess it now. He is considerably older than I am – who can I compare him with? My father, older or younger? He seems ageless, as handsome and prepossessing as ever. The day's end still holds the heat, but in the cooler interior of the high-ceilinged entrance hall I am awkwardly conscious of my state of dress: the crumpled shorts, the Indian yellow shirt. I have been sweating in it all day from heat or from stress, and now I stink powerfully, unmistakably, of curry. I can feel Gustav surveying me from head to toe. He explains that we are to dine out tonight. His piercing blue eyes look down to mine while, in his slightly nasal Viennese accent, he intones, 'My clu-u-b is only *sli-i-ghtly* elegant but you mi-i-ght want to change.'

Gustav insists that we have drinks before he shows me upstairs to my room. He mixes dry gin martinis, with ice. While we sit on the sofa under one of the Tintorettos the condensation from the cold glass drips onto my bare thighs like a modest reprimand. I notice things about the room that give me delight: some of the antique oriental rugs are placed cater-cornered across the polished wooden floor. I used to think that anything placed in that manner was tacky; in this moment my taste has changed. The rugs are beautiful; the arrangement is beautiful.

I unpack, shower and change for the evening. I know Gustav well enough to have brought a long dress. It is not the sleek sophisticated garment I would like to have possessed, but one I have made myself, with tiers of contrasting floral linen below an Empire bodice. It will do, I hope, as a take on the peasant look, still au courant. The air of the southern nightfall is heavy, rich and fragrant. At the club, the dining room is upstairs. A low hum of conversations from other tables blends with our own talk. Gustav speaks of friends and acquaintances from the past. When he mentions Thomas Mann among them I am reminded that those who accused him of snobbery also said he was a dreadful name-dropper, but I don't care. The food, the wine, the conversation are a heady mix. I am still just naïve enough, even after marriage and divorce, to believe that attraction isn't necessarily symmetrical, yet I sense warmth growing between us. After dinner we take the elevator. Gustav presses the 'door close' button immediately. Without hesitation or restraint we are upon each other for those brief moments of our descent, stopping only when the doors open on our private space. I am sure Gustav is no more fit to drive than I am, but somehow he gets us home. This night my sleep is dreamless and deep.

In the morning I find that the table has been laid and breakfast prepared by the servant I never see. There is still much driving to do before I reach my destination, the place of my mother's birth and death. Gustav has to leave early, too. He is director of a museum that he says is 'mostly full of stuffed squirrels'. So we part with a kiss that is almost chaste.

I must cross this entire state from east to west, and cross one more before I enter into the one that usually comes last in tables of things like per capita income; miles of roads paved; average years of schooling – the lists can and do go on. A native of the state once remarked, 'They tell us we can't read, but we sure can write,' and then reeled off a list of names to which prizes were attached: Pulitzer, Nobel. The road to the large house my mother shared with my grandmother is still not paved. The land has grown up in timber that ought to be cut. That is where the main value of the estate lies.

Choosing a gravestone will be my first duty after I arrive. The lawyer has advised me to find someone to cruise the timber. I know roughly what this means. When I was eleven and there for a year, I was half in love with the state forester who came out to demonstrate how this is done. That year I became president of the Young Forestry Club. I've packed my shorts and turmeric shirt in isolation in a plastic bag. My long dress is in the suitcase. I will accompany whoever it is who comes to cruise the timber. For that reason, beside the plastic bag and the suitcase in the back of the car is my pair of snake-proof boots.

Audrey Henderson

NATIONAL LIBRARY OF SCOTLAND

The National Library of Scotland was like an iceberg,
only one-sixteenth of it showed above the surface;
or it was like one of those fungi with a relatively small
fruiting body and mycelia that go on for miles, knitting
whole fields together. We should have guessed, because
it took so long to get a book, especially the *Iconography
of Cosmic Kingship* by H. P. L'Orange, which came back
crypt-cool and old-smelling, so you could tell someone
had been down to the deep-delved earth, but when the fire
alarm went off, we finally had proof. There they were, mile
upon mile of troglodytic book people standing in a straggly
line past the People's Dispensary for Sick Animals where
you might see a German Shepherd with a bucket
round its neck, past the shop that sold prosthetic devices
in tan plastic – as if anyone in Edinburgh needed a tan
prosthesis – and all the way to the other bank. Indeed,
we could have guessed the size of it before because
George IV Bridge is actually a bridge, and you can peek
over the edge beside Bauermeister's, where Escher-like
eighteenth-century facades recede down to the Canongate
and you can gauge the fathoms of the NLS. Sometimes
we would catch sight of a book person, the chief of the book
people behind the Cerberus-headed librarian, but often not.
The noises of the others, their breaths, their footsteps
the squeaking of their little carts were all subsumed
into the purr of an air-handling machine which extracted
dampness out of every word ever written about Scotland.

Once on a cloudy day, shortly before tea-time an incident
occurred. I say on a cloudy day, because it was usually
a cloudy day and if not, then the acid-etched roof glass
let in only hazy light, dulled further by chicken-wire
embedded in the panels to ward off adventurous book thieves.
The muffling carpet was an orchid-lichen green, the colour
of things that have a vicarious relationship to life and it did
nothing to remediate the gloom. The silence in the reading
room was so intense that you could hear ear-hair growing,
when suddenly a rock crashed through the ceiling, leaving
a neat little hole and landing with a thud on the dense

woollen carpet. Nobody looked up, but more remarkable
still, without any apparent stirring or sign of communication,
after an interval of three minutes, maybe less, a homunculus
appeared with a dust-pan and brush and whisked the thing
away, as if he had been standing for years behind a panel
of fake books, waiting, on the off-chance that he should
have to retrieve an asteroid from the reading room floor.
After that there were no more irregularities, just our parting
on the mezzanine, your offering me help in perpetuity,
and my leaving you there, with the etched thistles
and jade terrazzo and the people who sweep away stardust.

Angela Hughes

THE DANCE

In a sunlit plaza, just off one of the narrow cobbled streets of the Parte Vieja, a woman sits cross-legged with her back against a drinking fountain. She is partially obscured by the afternoon shadow of a balcony. Her eyes are half-closed and she strums a battered guitar. A breeze trails 'El Corazón' over the heads of the passers-by walking off their siestas. Opposite the woman, a young man crouches to watch, wide-eyed. He keeps his gaze on her hands. His name is Phil. He is thirty-three years old and he has come to San Sebastian to begin to say goodbye.

The woman, Ellie, recently turned thirty. She returned to San Sebastian to teach English. Nights are spent improving her Spanish in the many bars and cafes of the old part of the city. She lingers longest in The Iguana, a bar with sawdust on the floor, and barmen with an intuitive feel for the best music and a generous approach to sharing wine and joints. Ellie's face empathises with that of the locals – prominent jaw, heavy-browed eyes and wide forehead. She enjoys the anonymity this allows her.

It is her hands that continue to fascinate Phil. Small, slim and long-fingered. The nails are uneven, broken and bitten, but not to the quick. The little finger on her left hand is slightly crooked and swells at the knuckle. She wears a plain silver band on her right thumb. The tune changes tempo and the movement blurs her fingers. It gives the impression of a smeared charcoal drawing. Phil's legs begin to shake: his balance fails him and he falls backwards. Ellie looks up and smiles. She loses the rhythm, throws her head back and laughs. Phil straightens himself out and sits on the ground. The scent of garlic fried in olive oil curls around him from an open apartment window. At the end of the song Phil watches Ellie raise her hand and run it through her hair. This is where their story begins. In less than a year it will end and Phil will be dead.

'Etxe Kalte, you know it? On the harbour front, Calle de Mari.' Her accent, similar to his own, wrong-foots him for a second.

'Aye,' he says and swallows.

'Meet me there tonight at three, after the bars close.' She stands up, laughing. He looks up at her, nods. His stomach tightens and he nods again. She turns to walk away and he realises he is shaking.

*

It wasn't when she made the tea that Phil noticed the twitch in his mother's hand. It wasn't when she filled the kettle with water or when she poured first the water into the teapot and then the tea into the mug. It was when she added the sugar. Phil noticed then. He watched the granules fall from the spoon. He saw the trickle of tea working its way down the side of the

cracked white mug with the red and green Basque flag. He watched a
sugar-slick form on the uneven wooden table, covered in ring-marked
hieroglyphs. His flesh felt clammy and the sweetness of the hot liquid
turned bitter in his mouth.

Phil willed his mother to catch his eye but her bowed head was resolute.
Botticelli blonde curls covered her face. Hair that he had inherited, along
with her blue eyes, yet on him the overall effect had never quite lived up to
the expectations of its individual features.

And so he knew it had begun. *Chorea,* from the Greek, χορεία, 'to dance'
– uncontrollable limb movements, the first visible signs of Huntington's,
an incurable disease that robbed him of his father, then his mother, and
then his future. He was twenty-two when she died. His own diagnosis was
confirmed three years later. His father had left home nine years before.

*

Just after three o'clock, Phil watches the crowd thin and Ellie move unsteadily
towards him. She seems lost in her thoughts and is almost in front of him
before she realises he is there. Her short hair is flattened on one side and
her eyes have a dreamlike expression. He can't decide if she is tired or
stoned. She smiles a slightly crooked smile before she takes him by the hand
and leads him into the club. He follows her past the bar and down the
narrow, wooden stairs. The final step trips him and he stumbles; his eyes
struggle to adjust to the half-dark.

A room no more than twenty feet square. The floor moves with dancers,
heads skimmed by an aurora of light. Porous walls stream with rivulets of
perspiration. For a moment he is disorientated. The sound vibrates through
his body. Ellie drops his hand, throws her arms in the air, and pours herself
into the middle of the horde. Phil takes a deep breath and dives in. He flails
wildly against the current before he gives in and allows it to carry him. Eyes
closed he absorbs the music. A couple of hours later, drenched in sweat and
barely able to stand, he opens his eyes and once again follows Ellie's lead.

*

The next day Phil stands beside Ellie on the balcony, a whisper of air between
them. The hair at the nape of his neck is sticky with the late afternoon sun.
His eyes follow the line of white shuttered windows, each surrounded by
ochre coving with a number painted in black above. In the Plaza de la
Constitution below, families are sprinkled around tables. Ash escapes their
cigarettes and dances in the shafts of sunlight. Children's laughter and adult
voices merge, and the day drifts into the arms of the early evening.

Phil turns to look at Ellie in profile. The curve of her cheek. A mole in
line with the corner of her eye, just below where her eyebrow ends. A slight
bump on the bridge of her nose. They stand close but he senses the distance.
When do you tell someone that you are going to die?

'I should go,' he says.

They face each other, a foot apart; both have their hands in their pockets. The space between them begins to collapse and Phil wills his feet to take root, to steady himself.

'I'm going to die,' he says. A pause.

'Me too,' she says.

'No, I mean I have a disease. Huntington's. But not just that. I'm making arrangements to go to Switzerland. Zurich. Next year, probably June.' An almost imperceptible glance to the side before she looks back at him.

'Then I won't love you,' she says. She holds his gaze, her eyes taunt him. An emotional impasse. He looks away.

'In Spanish they don't say *te amo*, I love you.' He realises she is talking. 'Well they do but it's general, for everyone. They say *te quiero*. It means I want you. It's different. It comes from that feeling deep in your stomach. It's more urgent, more beautiful.' His throat constricts.

'I have to go.' At the door she hugs him; her lips brush his and his stomach flips. He walks slowly down the stairs. Behind him he hears her key turn in the lock.

*

Phil had heard them come in. It was the music that kept him from sleep. Or maybe the sound of raised voices. He could hear his mother getting louder, more aggressive.

'Go,' she shouted. 'Go on, leave. You're just like all the rest. Too fucking chicken. Too scared to take on a woman like me. You probably couldn't get it up anyway. Go on. Fuck off.' Phil withdrew into his duvet. He knew how this played. She went out, picked someone up in a bar and brought them home. Dimmed lights, mood music, dancing, laughter. It never ended well. From time to time it was a lesser disappointment. He would mumble to an embarrassed stranger on his way to the bathroom. More often it ended like this. In the morning his mother would cry and beat herself up. 'I'm sorry,' she'd say. 'I'm sorry.' Over and over. Phil would sit in awkward silence and study his hands. He knew the unpredictable moods weren't her fault. He knew this. But it was hard to bear just the same.

*

Four in the morning and Phil stands, as instructed, outside 25 Clinton Street on Manhattan's Lower East Side. An old red-brick building is squeezed into the space between a Chinese supermarket and a massage parlour. It's biting cold and he pulls his coat around him, folds his arms across his body and pats his sides. His feet stamp, a rhythm-free beat at odds with the laconic blues music that sidles towards him from the club further down the street. He is about to push the buzzer again when he hears the lock and before he can turn he feels her arms around his waist. His body fizzles – the body that began to let go of its calm in his late twenties, a decade earlier than expected. Now, in his thirties, Phil has forgotten what it is to feel still.

'What's up?' she says into his back. She lessens her grip and moves to face him. Her breath warms his face and he leans to kiss her. The faint but familiar taste of garlic and wine. She steps in closer and tucks her head beneath his chin.

'So your favourite song, huh?' he says across the top of her head. 'This the place?'

'Yep,' she mumbles and steps back. 'Changed a lot since the seventies. No Puerto Rican neighbourhood any more. You should be glad I didn't make you wear the blue raincoat. Come on, let's go inside.'

The room is small, with a faded grey carpet, and smells of soy sauce and ginger. A crimson quilt is thrown over the bed that dominates the space; the colour bleeds into the walls and floor. She removes first his coat and then her own. On tiptoe she throws her arms around his neck. He pulls away slightly, strokes her cheek. She tilts her head. He kisses the place just above her collar bone at the base of her neck. She shivers. He knew she would. She gasps and he looks up, touches his thumb to her lips before kissing her again.

Te quiero. The words fill his mouth. *Te quiero.* I want you. He kisses her harder, more urgently. I want you. I want you. I want you. The words jostle all other thoughts from his head. *Te quiero.* I want you. They take hold, flow through his body. He begins to lose perspective. *Te quiero. Te. Quiero.* I want. He's confused. It's no longer about passion. I want. I want. *Te.* I want. It's not about her. *Quiero.* It's about control. Not of her. Of his body. I want you. *Te quiero.* I want, I want. It's control of what little time he has left. Harder. Rougher. Control. Fear. He can barely breathe. I want, I want. I …

The warm, brackish taste brings him up short, clears his head. His lip bleeds. He's not sure if he bit it himself or if she did it. Not sure if it were in passion or defence. Her hands are on his chest. She looks directly at him. He closes his eyes and the world turns red.

*

The stopover in San Vicente de la Sonsierra in La Rioja is Phil's indulgence, in the same way New York was hers. *Semana Santa,* Good Friday, 11:20 a.m.: they stand with their arms around each other. The procession is due to start in around ten minutes. They had arrived an hour earlier in order to find a spot with a good view. The town follows a road that winds around a hill, topped with a church – box-shaped, painted white, with a simple cross. They chose a place about a third of the way up.

A hush crawls along the crowd. Feet shuffle. The crown of the head of the Virgin breaks the crest of the rise in the road. And then they are there, the *disciplinantes,* right in front of him. Men in white, knee-length tunics. A flap peeled away at the back reveals a triangle of flesh stretching between the shoulder blades and narrowing at the top of the waist. Angry whip welts stand out on the exposed skin. The men walk backwards. Their faces are covered by white hoods with eye holes cut out. A collective gasp.

The hair on the back of Phil's neck stands up. Why do the men walk backwards? So they are constantly reminded of the sins for which they seek penance? To offer a blank, bloodied canvas to be cleansed by the light? It's late April. Only two more months.

'God, they're shackled. Look.' Ellie points to the women walking directly in front of the cart. Dressed in black with thick veils over their faces. Three of them, their feet chained together. Flanked and led by men in black cloaks. Phil looks at his feet. He shivers, sees his mother's body, her lips and fingertips blue, the colour of the flashing lights. A parade of men in green uniforms. The pale pink roses of her cotton nightdress in the moonlight, a barely visible floral tattoo winding around her body. They found her in the woods at the back of the house. Hypothermia, they said, an accident. The cold claws its way up through his feet and comes to rest in the pit of his stomach.

*

In the end stages she lost weight, became confused, struggled to control her body. Dignity seeped out of her life. Phil grew to resent the look of hopeless humiliation on her face.

'She must've wandered out in her confusion in the middle of the night,' they said, after the ambulance had arrived and they had removed her body. He knew otherwise. He knew because they had listened to the radio programme together. The climber on his way to the summit. A woman on the side of the path. Pleading eyes, freezing temperatures. The decision to leave the person where she was.

'She'd be dead within half an hour,' the climber had said. She was. It haunted him, the climber said, the decision to carry on his ascent, but there was nothing to be done.

The temperature was well below freezing the night his mother died yet she was wearing a summer nightdress. It wasn't confusion, it was about taking back control one last time. It wasn't an accident, it was her chosen way to die. Phil knew and admired her for it. That's when he decided.

He was relieved he had managed to travel to Zurich to meet with the doctor while he was still fit enough. A thorough medical examination and final discussion with the psychologist had earned him a provisional green light. Once all his legal papers were handed over and approved, the requested date would be agreed.

*

They return to his flat in Edinburgh in early May. He walks ahead of her up the path through the small front garden; past the bench garbed in rust, with the slackened middle of old age. Outside the door he tries to control the shake of his hands enough to get the key in the lock. The musty smell in the air and the warm breeze at his back tell him spring has arrived ahead of them.

'Sorry I can't carry you over the threshold.' His voice is hesitant. He laughs and feels the colour rise in his cheeks. They aren't married and never will be. Anger burns in his body. 'Why me?' The words force themselves out of his mouth. 'Why me?' He slams his fist against the door. Breathless and unsteady he has no idea of what his next move should be.

The journey has exhausted him and he spends the first few days in bed. Ellie dislikes the tartan bed cover. Two days after their return she appears in the bedroom doorway with a new set of bedclothes to celebrate the time of year. She gives him the packet to open while she strips the bed. The new cover is cream with huge flowers in primary colours, a pattern called summer. He looks at her; she shrugs and throws a pillow at him.

*

Ellie lies with her head on the right side of his chest, just below his collar bone. She has on a faded T-shirt that hangs without certainty on her small frame. It's the one Phil has chosen to wear to Zurich. He wants to smell of her when it happens. Her body is curled up next to him, her legs entwined with his, her toenails the red of a polished fire-engine. He loves this part, where it is difficult to see where one ends and the other begins. Too soon it will be over. He roughly shoves aside the thoughts about the time in the future when she will lay her head on someone else's chest, entangle her limbs with another.

In the corner of the room their bags sit side-by-side. Her battered red suitcase with the piece of tartan tied round the handle. The material is a remnant of the bed cover she had made him shred before she threw it away. She flies out of Zurich the same evening. She hasn't told him where she will go. All he knows is that she intends to leave Switzerland as soon as possible. He presumes she will carry on running from whatever it is that stalks her. Nestled in close, his small rucksack leans against her case. It contains his passport, the final legal documents, his ticket, and a bar of his favourite chocolate. After the drink is given to him they provide chocolate to take away the bitter taste and he wants it to be his choice, not that of some anonymous clinic employee.

'You're going to the country renowned for its chocolate and you want to take some cheap Scottish crap.' She had leant over and tickled him, but he was adamant. It's the last piece of his childhood, a final reminder of his mother.

The bag also contains a CD he wants them to play. The decision on which song to pick had involved hours of discussion and several days of listening to his music collection. In the end he settled on 'Rock 'n' Roll Suicide' by David Bowie, not to be ironic but because it reminded him of when he first left Inverness to move to Edinburgh. He had a ticket to see Bowie at Ingliston.

At the end of the performance Phil was disappointed that the song had been overlooked. In the last gasp, the lights blacked out and a single spot back-lit the singer. He pulled the microphone towards him: 'Time takes a cigarette,' he sang, 'puts it in your mouth ...'

Phil's not sure if it is the sight of the bags or the youthful memory that finally brings the tears. He doesn't know how to stop. She holds him, dry-eyed. He can't see her properly but he can feel her breathing, calm and even. He doesn't understand how she remains so emotionless. She lays her body along the length of him. He inhales the vanilla scent of her shampoo. His nose runs and he sniffs violently. He sees her again in the sun-filled plaza, feral and vibrant; hears the song about the heart.

*

The afternoon sun streams into the pale green room. It soothes the sharper edges cast by clean-lined Scandinavian furniture. The polished hardwood floor sports a brightly striped rug and the bed huddles in the corner against the wall, swathed in a cream duvet with large bright flowers in primary colours. A young man is propped up in the bed, the neck of his faded T-shirt grazed by blonde curls. An older man sits in an adjacent armchair. His lined face is kindly but sombre. He is dressed in navy trousers and a white smock. Next to the bed stands a young woman with dishevelled hair and somnambulant eyes. She is bare-legged and flip-flopped. Her painted toe-nails send flints of fire along the edge of the floor. The young man drinks from a cup with a straw. The woman hands him something. He puts it in his mouth, lies back and closes his eyes. She brushes the edge of her thumb across his lips. Time draws on a cigarette.

Alison Irvine

BROTHER'S RUIN

We scattered Mum yesterday. We took the urn to the high hill and let the wind spread her ashes in flurries of white around us. Then we planted an apple tree; me, Michael and Philip, her bad apples. And my daughter too. Michael made a performance of pushing on the spade, leaning all his weight on the handle and grimacing. He said, 'God give me strength,' like Mum used to say, and my daughter giggled. I told Michael to have some dignity and I shook my head at Chloe. She stopped giggling. Philip just looked down the hill at the city he hated.

We never had a father. My mum said, 'You don't need one. I'm enough.' But when we grew up she said, 'You're your father's fault. You've got his bad genes. Bad apples the lot of you, love you as I do.' I didn't care. I barely listened. I had a picture of my dad that I'd found in the bin and she saw it one day. She shook it at me and said, 'What's this? What's this?' I'll never forget her face. Disbelief and tears and maybe panic.

Michael pressed his foot on the turf around the apple tree's trunk. Chloe helped him, patting the earth with her hands. Her shoes and coat got dirty.
    Philip spoke. 'What are your plans?'
    'Me?'
    'Yes, you, Michael. Now you're back.'
    Michael paused. He looked up at Philip.
    'I want to stay in Mum's house for a bit with Karen and Chloe.'
    'I fucking knew it,' Philip said. He kicked the tree and Michael yelped. Then he grabbed the spade from Michael's hands. He held it as if he'd shove it hard against Michael's face, then he let it fall. Chloe picked it up and that seemed to stop Philip. He took the spade off her, said, 'Come on, kid,' and the two of them walked away, back towards the car. Philip had a stressful job and a wife we'd never met.
    I touched my fingers to the leaves on Mum's tree then Michael and I followed the other two down the path.
    I didn't know what to say. My brother looked healthy. His hair had thinned but his face had filled out and his clothes were clean. We hadn't seen him for five years.
    'He won't apologise,' Michael said. He meant Philip.
    'Have you apologised?' I asked.
    'Not yet.'
    I listened to our shoes clicking on the tarmac and watched Philip down

in the car park helping Chloe into her car seat. Then I said, 'So you've won your battle?'

'God grant me the serenity,' he said. Then, 'I'm sorry for what I did.'

'Apology accepted,' I said, 'but I won't have you two fighting today. If you fight, you're out.'

When we got to Philip's car, Michael sat in the back with Chloe, not a word to Philip. Philip held Mum's urn and waited for me to settle myself into the front seat. Then he passed me the urn and closed the door on me as gently and reverently as if I were Mum herself.

They fought on my wedding day and I blamed them all: Mum, Philip, Michael and Him. I wore an empire line dress to conceal my six and a half months. Michael was fresh from a stint in a live-in place. Philip was getting ready to disappear, though we didn't know that then.

Mum said to me on the morning of my marriage, 'You don't have to marry him.' I was so shocked I laughed, and then she was away around the house locking windows and shutting doors.

She stood behind me as we waited for the taxi on the front steps and poked me between my shoulder blades. 'Karen, don't be a wisp,' she said. 'There'll be times in your life when you'll need to fight, like me.'

I turned to look at her muscular face and thought she'd never stopped fighting.

Then Philip walked me down the aisle to wed Stuart, Chloe's dad, the show-off lad with the terrier and the van and I thought, thank fuck, I'm out of here.

After the wedding we drove to the hall. My Aunty Di and Uncle Derek went ahead to turn on the ovens.

At the door Michael said, 'Coats!'

I didn't trust him. I followed him into the cloakroom and said, 'You keep your hands out of the coat pockets.'

'I don't do that any more, Karen.'

'Good. Don't be tempted. Behave yourself.'

He crossed his heart and smiled and winked.

Stuart couldn't stand him. Stuart had lent him three hundred quid to get him back on his feet and he'd pissed it up the wall with drink or drugs or whatever he'd been into at the time. Philip had stopped lending him money well before then. But my mum always wanted to believe him. Since he'd been back he'd fixed the guttering and put a draught excluder under the front door so she thought he was better. I didn't.

The hall was filled with round tables that I'd decorated the day before, and the guests were sitting down or milling about. A few kids had taken off their shoes and socks and left them scattered on the floor. The DJ was setting up his decks. I checked on the buffet. My Aunty Di had done me proud. The cold stuff was out already and there were spaces on the table for the warmed-up bits.

But then Stuart caught my wrist and said, 'Where's the drink?'

'What drink?'

'The alcohol. There's only orange juice or tea.'

'I've banned it.' I heard my mum's voice from across the hall. She clattered towards Stuart on stubby heels. She wasn't afraid of him.

'What's going on? It's a wedding.' Stuart looked hateful. He turned and raised his arms as if to show my mum all his guests.

'Karen's pregnant and Michael's recovering so we can avoid it for one simple day.'

'They can avoid it! Tell her, Karen.' He squeezed my wrist. 'I don't have to avoid it.'

'We can all avoid it.' My mother seemed alive with defiance. Her eyes shone, her lips glittered.

If I'd spoken she would have ignored me so I picked Stuart's fingers off my wrist and walked away. Philip was already organising a run to the off-licence. I expected he'd make some money out of it.

We got through the food and most of the dancing. Guests sent the kids under the tables to pour gin into their orange juice. My mum beamed. She even said to me, 'This is better than I expected. I shall need to rest for a week when it's over but it's coming off well.'

I didn't care what she thought of my wedding.

'Where's Michael?' she asked.

I looked around. 'He's with the coats.'

'Have a sniff of him for me, Karen. Check he's not drinking. Tell him to come to me if he's tempted.'

A girl was in the cloakroom with Michael, lolling her back against the wall and sticking her pelvis out.

'I knew you'd understand,' Michael said to her. He twirled a cigarette between his fingers, put it between his lips then took it out. 'It's so difficult. My family don't understand me. They think I'm a prick. But I'm not. I've been reading some studies. There's a gene for what I've got.'

'I've always liked bad boys,' the girl said.

'But I'm not a bad boy. It's in my genes. I can't blame everything on that but Philip's got no excuse. There's no gene for violence. There is for addiction.'

'Come here, baby.'

The girl held out her arms, he took a swig of orange juice then reached for her.

I left them and told my mum a girl was taking care of him. My mum smiled. She liked it when girls looked after her boys. It was only me she didn't like getting love off anyone.

'As all is well then,' she said, 'we need a speech.'

'They don't want to, Mum,' I said.

'Who?'

'Philip and Stuart. They're too sober. They said they'll do it later.'

'Don't be so bloody ridiculous. I'll do it myself.'

The DJ said he had a microphone but he couldn't unhook it so my mum would have to come where he stood and speak from behind the decks. I stood near her and waved Stuart over. He put an arm around me, touching his fingers beneath my shoulder straps.

'Ladies and gentlemen, thank you for attending today on my only daughter's wedding day,' my mum said. She tapped the microphone. 'Can you all hear me?'

'No!' somebody shouted.

'Is he joking?' She looked at me fiercely. I nodded my head. We could hear her.

'Well, I only wanted to say that despite appearances, this is no shotgun wedding. Karen actually loves Stuart, God help her, and I hope the two of them are mature enough to give their baby a good start in life. They've no idea how hard it will be, but no one ever does.'

She tilted her head and smiled and a few people said, 'Quite right'.

'I was determined her life would be different to my own,' my mum went on.

My Uncle Derek tapped me on the shoulder and put his mouth to my ear.

'Where's your money box gone, darling?'

I turned around and pointed to the table. 'It should be there.'

'It's gone, sweetheart. Can you think of anyone who might be looking after it for you?'

Of course I could.

My mum was going on. 'I didn't expect her to drop out of life so quickly by having a baby. I did tell her about contraception.' She paused, for the laugh, then continued.

'Stuart, the money box has gone walkabout,' I whispered.

'Your fucking brother,' he whispered back, hard into my ear.

We did the wedding as cheaply as we could. Gift wise, we needed everything – saucepans, towels, sheets, you name it – but we had debts too so I decided to decorate a shoe box in white paper and ask for cards and money. 'They all do that these days,' my mum had said.

'Is it really gone?' I said, starting to get upset.

'I'll make some enquiries, sweetheart, you stay there,' Uncle Derek said. 'I'm afraid your brother Michael's with us today and things tend to go missing when he's around. Shh.' He put his finger to his lips and gestured towards my mum. I watched him walk away and tap Philip on the shoulder.

'No, perhaps she went as far as she could go,' my mum was saying, 'but I did as much as I could, which was more than my mother did for me. She's a good girl. So I would like you to raise your glasses. I'm sorry we've only provided soft drinks but as you know we have our reasons. I would like you to raise your glasses to my daughter Karen and her husband Stuart and their happy future.'

She held her glass out above the decks' flashing lights. Chairs scraped as guests stood up.

'To Karen and Stuart and their happy future,' they said.

Then it kicked off.

'You're a fucking lowlife arsehole!' I heard Philip roar.

Then I heard Michael's scream, and footsteps, and chairs going over.

'Drop the box!' It was Philip's voice again.

I turned to see Michael running with the money box under his arm across the back of the hall and Philip and my Uncle Derek chasing him. Philip got to him and pushed him to the floor. Michael dropped the money box and all the cards and money fell out. His arms flailed at Philip's fists. Then Uncle Derek kicked him in the side and put the boot in his balls too. Michael squealed and he kept saying, 'I'm sorry I'm sorry I'm sorry, I can't help it, what did you expect?'

'It's your sister's fucking wedding day!' Philip said and shook Michael, knocking his head against the ground.

Stuart ran across the floor and gave Michael a kick too. 'That was my money!' he said.

I felt sick. I didn't think those men would stop. The baby gave me one hard kick which nearly toppled me.

'Okay, enough is enough. Everyone.' It was my mother's voice. She was still behind the DJ's decks. 'This party is over.' She waited. Philip held Michael's shoulders. All the guests stood turning their heads from my mum to the men on the floor. 'Enough!' Mum said finally. Philip gave Michael a last shove then sat with his head in his hands.

'I don't know what my son has done. I expect it is abominable, yet again. I told my daughter it would be risky to invite her brother – my own son – to her wedding day even though I wanted him here, of course I did. So I expect he has done something dreadful. But I will not have men fighting here. I will not have you knocking out that boy, on the floor of this hall. This wedding party is over. God give me strength.'

The DJ had a good sense of timing. He pulled a plug and the speakers cut out with a hot pop and the lights stopped flashing. My mum stood behind the decks, grave and thin. Then she lifted her hands and shooed everyone away from their tables and out into the car park.

I didn't move until Stuart said, 'Our cab's here.' Uncle Derek put the money box in my hands and patted my arm.

Two days later her heart gave out. All of a sudden. No warning. She dropped dead.

After the funeral, Philip disappeared. So did Michael. Stuart and I moved into her house because our debts were piling up. She saved us, in a way, dying when she did. I kept her ashes in the urn in the living room for five years. And I began to miss her. Especially when I needed her, when I was elbows and knees and feet trying to keep him away from me, when I didn't know what I'd done or how I could predict or prevent anything.

It took me four years to get rid of Stuart and another year to summon my brothers, despite what state they were in, and scatter Mum.

After the scattering we drove in silence back to mine, Mum's, ours. At the traffic lights, with the tick-tock of the indicator to steady him, Michael apologised to Philip. Philip apologised to Michael for hurting him. And they both said sorry to me for leaving me to cope with everything I'd coped with on my own. 'You're strong,' they said. I realised I was more like my mum than she or I would ever have imagined.

'So, what do you think?' Michael said, as we turned into my road. 'You going to let me stay for a while?'

'For a short while,' I said, and Chloe, who I thought was sleeping, told Michael he could have her room and she would sleep in with me, as she often did anyway.

'I won't let you down,' Michael said.

Philip pulled up outside the house and left the engine running. He took his sunglasses off and put them on the dashboard. I saw our front steps and remembered my wedding day, with my mum at my back.

'What about you? You coming in?' Michael said to Philip.

'No.'

'Oh, go on. Spoilsport.'

'I'll call by soon.'

'Bring that missus of yours so we can get a look at her.'

'No chance.'

They're back, I thought. If I want them. My mum would have had them back instantly, just because they were hers. But Chloe was mine. I had Chloe to think of.

The reverence again as Philip opened my door and helped me out. And my strength as I waved goodbye to Philip and let Michael into the house. For now. For the time being. One day at a time.

Helen Jackson

CITY OF WORDS

GOOD.

Three-metre-high letters, brushed into the January snow in Princes Street Gardens. A snowman holding a broom stood by. Two points for 'G', one for each of the 'O's and two for the 'D': a total of six for Bobs, winning her the game. It was the final tweet from her account; her last word.

Two weeks later, when the snow melted, it revealed a word in the grass below. @DoneEdin tweeted the photo, hashtag #EdinburghWords. It showed the first flowering of snowdrops. BYE was spelt out in delicate white blooms; letters only twenty centimetres high, but clear nonetheless. The bulbs must have been planted in the autumn. Who could have planned that?

*

The game had started the previous summer, with the four of us hanging out at Katie and Przem's flat. Katie tiny, short-haired and intense; Bobs patchouli-scented and imaginative; Przem meticulous, studying us through thick-rimmed glasses; me pleased to be part of the gang. We'd been inseparable since university.

'Do you ever feel someone's trying to get through to you, Fiona?' Bobs asked me, interrupting a daydream.

'Sorry, Bobs. Did I miss something important?'

'I don't mean that. I mean someone, out there, trying to send you a message. You know?'

I didn't know. One of Bobs's fancies, I assumed. Like the belief she could hear the dead, which had obsessed her two summers earlier, or her flirtation with hypnotic regression.

'Someone out where?' I asked. By this time Katie and Przem were listening in. Bobs blushed.

'Oh it's nothing, I guess. Don't listen, Shem, you'll hate this.' Przem smiled politely and waited for her to continue.

'Today on Princes Street I walked past seven buses in a jam,' she said.

'Nothing new there,' said Przem.

'No, but the first letter on each numberplate spelt out Roberta.'

'Freaky!' said Katie.

'But just coincidence,' said Przem.

'And no-one calls you Roberta except your mum,' I pointed out. 'Maybe Lothian Buses got the wrong Roberta?' That earned me a laugh from Katie and Przem.

'A week ago, though,' said Bobs, ignoring us. 'Going up the Mound, that cut grass smell in the air. Someone was doing a bad job of mowing the lawn by New College, cutting stripes into the middle. It looked like the word "ill", with the gardener as the dot on the "i".'

We were less impressed by this than the buses. I shrugged.

'It's like the city was speaking to me,' she said.

'Not much of a message,' I said.

'Tell you what, though,' said Przem, slowly. 'You could play a kind of city Scrabble like that.'

'Whoa, Shem!' said Katie. 'That'd be brilliant. Like, in graffiti and stuff. With points.'

Katie liked games she could win.

'No graffiti,' Przem said, 'nothing permanent. And no found words. Make a temporary word out of things in the city, take a photo, upload it to Twitter.'

'Double or triple word scores for, I dunno, artistic merit and things,' said Katie.

'Artistic merit or cleverness,' said Przem. 'Double for one, triple if you manage both.'

He seemed to have it all worked out. It was like him. His madcap ideas were always practical.

'Who decides?' asked Bobs. 'What makes clever clever or artistic artistic?'

'I decide,' said Przem, drawing a chorus of complaints. He spoke over us: 'I won't play, I'll just be the scorekeeper. We can use my travel Scrabble.'

Przem let go Katie's hand, pulled a black plastic box from the coffee-table drawer and opened it. He handed out three tile racks. The travel sort have a flippable cover so you can put them in your pocket without losing your letters. Przem shook the green drawstring bag and passed it round.

'Seven letters each. No looking. You have to use the letters you draw, but you don't have to connect to anyone else's word.'

I drew O T K I O L P and put them into my rack. The others took their tiles, looking serious.

'You have your mission,' said Przem, pulling the drawstring tight and putting the bag on the table. 'Now, have another drink and I don't want to hear anything more about it until you tweet me a picture. Hashtag #EdinburghWords.'

*

Katie went first, of course.

KatieKatz1977:
@PrzemThinks Early bird **yfrog.com/GubqINw**
#EdinburghWords

A flock of pigeons, feeding on the pavement below Katie and Przem's front room. The birds spelt out WING in wobbly letters.

'How did you get them to do that?' I asked.

'Borrowed carrier pigeons and trained them,' Katie said, deadpan. I must have looked impressed. She punched me in the shoulder and laughed.

'You nana, Fiona! I put birdseed down in the shape of the letters, then nearly gave myself a coronary running up the stairs to take the picture.'

Przem deemed the ornithological link clever enough to award a double word score. Sixteen points to Katie.

I managed less than half that. The Edinburgh Festival was in full swing, so I worked with flyers. I found a noticeboard alternating yellow postcards, showing a marionette *Waiting for Godot*, with red ones advertising a Latvian Flamenco circus troupe. I re-arranged them to form big red letters on yellow: PLOT.

Both the pigeons and the flyers were heavily re-tweeted. The *Guardian* interpreted PLOT as an ironic comment on Beckett so it did the rounds of the literati. It wasn't a surprise when someone gatecrashed the game. Edinburgh in August? Anything goes.

DoneEdin:

@PrzemThinks Hello! **yfrog.com/gaeMEtr**

#EdinburghWords

A CCTV still, showing the airport car park in grainy black-and-white. Row upon row was filled until, in the middle distance, an area was mostly empty. The few cars formed letters: GREET.

'Nifty,' said Katie. 'I dunno how you'd set it up.'

We'd met at the Café Royal and were perched on stools around an under-sized table.

'Must have put traffic cones in the other bays,' said Przem.

'That'd be a lot of cones, Shem,' I said, dubious.

'Double word score for cleverness,' he said.

'They're not in the game!' said Katie. 'They don't have any tiles, so they're cheating.' Przem awarded twelve points to @DoneEdin anyway, tweeting from his phone.

'You're still in the lead,' he said. Katie wasn't mollified.

'Weird coincidence, though,' said Bobs.

'What's that?' Przem asked.

'I was thinking of playing GREET. Look.' She laid her tile rack down. She'd separated the letters into two words GREET AM. Przem took out the letters and shuffled them on the beery tabletop.

'You can still do GREET,' said Katie, a bit too quickly. She'd seen a better word. 'Whoever @DoneEdin is, they're not a proper player.'

'They're pretty clever,' I said. I'd been thinking. 'Greet means cry in Scots. What are the two things you do at an airport?' They didn't catch on. 'You welcome people, and you weep when they leave – you greet and you greet.'

Przem whistled his approval. He'd put Bobs's tiles back; they now read EMERGE T. Katie glared at him.

'Just giving you some competition, Katie-Katz,' he said.

*

Bobs didn't play EMERGE. She had her own agenda.

    LibrarianBobs:

    @PrzemThinks Me, myself and I **yfrog.com/tRMeGae**

    #EdinburghWords

I followed the link. Two laughing tourists, wearing bright waterproofs and rucksacks, next to Greyfriars Bobby. The first had his hands over his head in the 'M' pose from 'YMCA'. His friend was in danger of falling over. Both arms and his left leg were stretched out to the left, right arm over his head, forming the three horizontals of an 'E'. Rain poured down.

Only four points for the letters, but another double word score for the Bobs-Bobby link. I was in last place; Katie was first.

We picked replacement tiles at the pub. Przem carried the bag everywhere that summer. We'd turn at the rattle of plastic squares, knowing he'd walked into the room.

I met him for lunch a week or so later. Katie had cancelled at the last minute; Bobs had a doctor's appointment. I didn't often see Przem on his own, but I was glad. I wanted a word with him. That week, Bobs had played TARGET and @DoneEdin had contributed AYE.

'Is it you?' I asked, as soon as Przem sat down.

'Is what me?'

'@DoneEdin. Cos I think you should stop. It's freaking Bobs out.'

'Of course it's not me. I assumed it was her.' Przem had a point. Bobs had always been fond of stunts.

'She called me last night,' I said. 'She thinks the words are messages intended for her, like the buses and the mower. She's seeing her GP today because they told her she was ill.' Przem just looked at me. It did sound unlikely.

Who am I kidding? Even now, even with Bobs gone, it sounds more than unlikely. It sounds insane. Back then, I blundered on.

'She said she played ME and TARGET to ask if @DoneEdin's greeting was for her,' I said.

'Fiona, that's crazy,' said Przem. 'How would @DoneEdin know what she meant? ME followed by TARGET could mean anything.'

'She thinks AYE was the answer; that they said yes.'

Przem looked thoughtful. 'Aye doesn't only mean yes, does it? It means always, too.'

'She's always the target? Does that make sense?'

'None of it makes sense.'

'Not the point, Shem. The point is, Bobs believes it. Well, I think she does.'

I stopped. I wasn't sure what I thought.

'Look, if it is you, just don't, okay?' I said.

*

Next, Bobs played WHO. Another question? Was she trying to find out who @DoneEdin was? I had no idea. We went for coffee, but she didn't mention the game and I didn't like to bring it up. She'd lost some weight. We talked books and films, ate cake, laughed. She said the doctor was sending her for tests. What for? Another thing I didn't like to ask.

I bumped into Katie and Przem in the supermarket a few days later.

'You haven't made a word this round,' I said to Katie.

'I'm looking for the right canvas,' she said.

'Oh, give over,' said Przem, uncharacteristically impatient. 'You can't hold everyone up while you wait for artistic inspiration.' They walked away towards the freezer aisle, bickering.

*

Katie's next word was DRIVE, written into the dirt on the back of a van. She thought it clever. Przem refused to give double points. Bobs accepted the resulting discussion as playful banter. I wasn't so sure.

The game had exposed a fault line between the couple, one I hadn't known existed. If there was a rift between those two, what did it mean for our foursome?

We chose our tiles and then I carefully changed the subject, but we still left the pub early.

The next day, Bobs took four street maps, made them into letters, origami-style, and hung them from a tree in St Andrew Square. It made a beautiful photo, scoring for artistic merit. Her word: CITY.

There were storms that night. Power cuts hit the New Town. We huddled around Przem's iPhone looking at his Twitter feed.

'No way!' said Katie. 'That can't be real!'

An aerial photo from @DoneEdin showed the New Town in darkness. Except: street lights were lit in the crescent of Drummond Place and running north–south up Dundonald Street and onto Nelson Street.

'C' followed by 'I'.

A 'T' was formed at the intersection between Dundas Street (north–south) and Northumberland Street (east–west). The 'Y' was malformed, thanks to the New Town's grid, but recognisable: a north–south vertical along Vincent Street plus North East Circus Place running out to the right.

Another CITY.

'Wow,' I said. 'That's amazing.'

'It's got to be photoshopped,' said Przem. He and Katie were in agreement, for once. 'And even if it isn't, if it's a real photo, it's a found word so doesn't count. No-one could have caused that.' He awarded zero.

'It's the same word as you, Bobs,' said Katie. 'Maybe someone really is trying to send you a message.'

She was joking, but I saw Bobs shudder.

*

Fake or not, that CITY trumped our efforts. The game meandered on, but we struggled to get up enthusiasm for words fashioned from litter or sticks. @DoneEdin was working with Edinburgh's fabric; we shuffled around in its detritus.

The following week, down at the Barony Bar, an argument kicked off. @DoneEdin had played HUNGER.

'You should have disqualified them for cheating after the last round,' said Katie. 'Whoever they are.'

@DoneEdin was well ahead of her by then. Possibly just to spite her, Przem awarded a double word score.

'Twenty points,' he announced.

'That's not right, Shem,' said Bobs, 'it should be sixteen.' We were surprised to hear her voice. She'd been quiet that evening.

'Four for "H", two for "G", and one each for the others. Ten, doubled, equals twenty,' said Przem.

'The "G" is a blank tile.'

It couldn't have been any blanker than our faces. Bobs pulled her tile rack and a notepad out of her hemp backpack, pushed our drinks out of the way, blotted up a spill with a beer mat.

'Look,' she said, 'it's using my tiles. Remember GREET? Next round, I had G R E T A Y T and they put down AYE. It made BELOW from Y O E L W H blank, using the blank as a B. We both made CITY. I didn't use the blank, so I still have it now.'

Her tile rack contained E L U N H R and a blank tile. She rearranged it: HUN[ ]ER.

'Something's talking to me,' she said. 'Nothing human could have arranged that power cut. It's the city below us. It knew I was ill. It's hungry.' Her voice rose as she spoke, panicky. She'd obviously thought about this, but maybe it didn't seem real until she said it out loud. 'What's it hungry for? Why does it want me?'

I ignored the questions. What could I have said?

'They can't know your tiles,' I tried. 'Can they?'

'Of course they can't,' said Przem, the voice of reason. 'It's coincidence. Stop thinking about it and let me get you another vodka tonic.'

He scored it at sixteen, though, and docked six points from @DoneEdin's total for the blank tile in BELOW.

'She's doing it herself,' he said, when I phoned the next morning. 'There's no-one else it could be.'

That weekend Katie and I met, accidentally, on the Meadows. Autumn had shaded into winter. The fallen leaves were soggy from overnight rain.

'Do you think Bobs is okay?' I asked.

'Who knows, with Bobs,' said Katie.

She had her own concerns. 'I can't figure out what to do, Fiona,' she said, showing me one of her tiles – the 'Z' – and pulling a face. I thought she couldn't make it into a word; thought she was taking the game too seriously. She'd always been competitive.

'Sometimes I just want to do my own thing, y'know?' she said.

*

I only saw Bobs once after that. She came out of the pharmacy carrying one of those little paper bags they put medicine in. What had the doctor's tests found? I was on the other side of Leith Walk. I shouted and waved, but she didn't hear. If I'd known it was my last chance I'd have chased after her. I wish I had.

The game was still running, although we didn't get together to pick tiles. Przem sent mine through the post. Katie got four final points for TOTE, a couple of days later, made out of full shopping bags. Przem didn't tell us for weeks, but she left that day. Packed a suitcase and went, to her family in Fort William. Didn't say a word.

It felt as if everyone was changing, moving on – leaving me behind. I didn't know how to connect with Bobs or Przem. I flipped between anger that they hadn't talked to me, and guilt that I hadn't asked.

Game over, I thought, but @DoneEdin had different ideas.

DoneEdin:

@PrzemThinks World-building **yfrog.com/ErsToIS**

#EdinburghWords

It was scaffolding, half-up on a tenement block in Tollcross, just opposite the Cameo Cinema. Most of the poles greyish metal, some painted blue. The blue ones spelt out STORIES.

Was @DoneEdin hungry for stories? That described Bobs perfectly. Had she found a kindred spirit or was she talking to herself?

Her reply, of course, was GOOD. Did it comfort her, the hope of joining the city, of sharing stories under Edinburgh, after?

*

I found out too late Bobs had been taken into hospital. I'd been round to her flat several times, rang the bell, got no reply. She didn't answer her phone either. Instead of persisting, I retreated into myself. Another thing to regret.

The night after the funeral I discovered my tile rack at the bottom of a rarely used handbag. Alone and maudlin, I pulled it out. All vowels. I realised I could make a one-letter word – an impossibility on a Scrabble board. I collected pebbles and, in the wee small hours, arranged them in one of the shallow-water ponds outside Parliament. The water's cold was knife-sharp, the ripples hypnotic. Traffic noise faded to a distant burr. Arthur's Seat loomed to my right.

My word was I. One point. As low as I could get.

*

I've made friends at work, joined a book group, signed up for evening classes. I see Przem occasionally. We meet for coffee, talk about our jobs and what's on TV. Katie's settled on the West Coast, teaching in a village primary, stays in touch through Facebook. I wonder if she still has Przem's 'Z'?

I found out a nurse from the Royal Infirmary had spelt out GOOD and built the snowman, Bobs's final tweet. Bobs gave him instructions. She couldn't do it herself by then. She needed a stranger to help her.

No-one's admitted to the snowdrops. A last message from the city? I like to think so. They're the image that stays with me, when I think about those months on my walks around Edinburgh; perfect little impossible flowers. A perfect, little, impossible farewell.

Bridget Khursheed

THE CLOVENFORDS VINERIES

All the world purled through glass
and not sure whether this is heaven with
fruit and pools and ferns
or the de'il's place all heat and aisles
sprung with the little spored fronds
that touch and bend

outside the clatter of coal in clarty carts
to keep growth warm from April to dead winter
and the coalman's clunking refracted
and the trainbound grapes packed soft in
Thomson's own mossed crates
bound for London, and the braw shop
in Castle Street; outside
impossible to walk up that hill

put a hand out and it is swallowed
by maidenhair, love apples, Black Alicante swells
next to Muscat of Alexandria and Gros Colman
table grapes eaten with a knife, fork
and a pair of silver scissors, cold lips
plump above the Arabic grate
five miles of hot water pipes
and five boys shovelling anthracite.

Pippa Little

BLACK MIDDENS

Crows flap the cold towards us
coming in low on undertakers' coat-tails.
Snow smells of tin soured by mountain water
and blood's black glaze on a dropped-too-soon's
sodden tangle that never got warm,
picked blue in the ditch to innocent bone
by February's end, forgotten.

Years since we came to church.
Sins and secrets, long-winded as the river
on its stony course, do their disappear, dissolve
in us. Attend their own purpose.

RIDDLE WITH TWO ANSWERS

What is it but
a hall or hame: in winters hackle-laden
with thorny haberdashery,
in high summer, cobweb cupboards'
handsels of love-entangle, heliotropes –

who helms this hotch-potch,
this crinkle-crankle habitation?
Who sews the hem
haphazard, who braids with tendril, hyphen,
who hitches it together, broached and bridled,

homespun handenhold,
the heart's deep holt?
What loops and leads one within another home,
more than its sum, sore through long dissolve of frost,
dreich as an abandoned nest, pin-prick of sorrows:

is nothing but a labour, a common commonplace:
bent, bowed, knocked, cut back, but
still fusing into new, season after season,
maze where small birds sing,
a tower of Babel, a secret helter-skelter,

a breathing loom
through which dark, myriad shuttles dart,
silver strands that for one moment and for perpetuity
pin the evening star inside its cage:
what but this

brilliant, difficult,
open-ended conversation of itself,
how it grew from its own growing,
sorrow-hardy but hopeful yet –
in all its brangling, over-brimming?

The Two Answers: 1. A hedge;
2. A long marriage

Sarah Lowndes

BOOTS

Laura is washing up the last of his dishes when she hears the sound of a key in the door, then Joan sniffling as she hangs up her coat and takes off her shoes.

'Hiya, Laura.'

Joan collapses on the kitchen sofa, resting her feet up on the coffee table.

'God, look at my ankles. When I get up in the morning I look relatively normal, but by the evening … it's like I've been inflated with a bicycle pump.'

Laura laughs. Joan is tiny and looks no different from usual.

'D'you want a cup of tea?'

'God, yes, thanks; I got really cold waiting for the bus. Actually, Laura, I'm glad you're here, there's something I wanted to talk to you about.'

Laura feels her face flush.

'Oh – I'm really sorry that I'm still staying here – I've been looking at loads of flats but they've all been so awful – I'm going to see more tomorrow.'

She fills the kettle and turns it on, bends to hunt beneath the counter for a cup.

'No – it isn't that, it's lovely having you here.'

'Do you want that rooibos tea?'

'Laura, can you sit down for a minute?'

She sits down next to Joan on the sofa. Laura had sewn new yellow chenille covers for it last week on one of the nights Jack was out at the studio. She rubs the fabric against the weave and then flattens down all the wee nubs again.

'I've been trying to catch you for a few days but keep missing you.'

'Yes, I've been trying to keep busy.' *And stay out from under his feet.* The kettle is boiling. Laura watches the plume of steam rise from the kettle and then flatten out beneath the ceiling, a disappearing mushroom cloud.

Joan takes a breath.

'The thing is, I don't want to interfere in something that isn't my business … but when you were away with your friends at the weekend … Rhona stayed the night here.'

Joan's fingers cradle her small bump.

'I was talking to Mary about it and she said that it's been common knowledge for years that Rhona is after Jack.'

Laura thinks of all the postcards Rhona sends him from her numerous holidays, sometimes three postcards, even when she just goes somewhere for the weekend, and all the presents she brings him back from abroad.

What did you hear through the wall, Joan? Stupid things go through her head, like him saying to her at the club one night, all excited,

'Rhona has such cool boots on. I thought they were vintage, but they're not, they're new and *expensive*.'

Once they had had a row about how he would often meet up with Rhona for coffee in little weird cafes, why Laura would never be invited. While they were arguing, he had gone over to the drawer and put on this tribal headscarf that Rhona had brought him back from some safari in Africa and started dancing around the room. When Laura had pulled it off his head, he had shouted,

'What the fuck is the matter with you? I thought it would cheer you up.'

Laura exhales.

'Thanks for telling me. He mentioned it already, I did know – he said it was innocent, it was just too late for her to go home so she stayed over.'

She hears her voice as if from far away.

'He said nothing happened.'

Joan raises her eyes and looks at her.

'To be honest I think Claire had the same problem.'

*

Mel answers on the third ring.

'Sure, I'm in, come over whenever you like.'

Laura looks at her watch. He'll be back from the studio soon. She stuffs enough clothes for a couple of days into a shoulder bag. He hasn't cleared out a drawer for her to use so most of her things are still packed in the big bag in the corner, she'll come back for that later. Later. She crosses over to the futon and sits on the edge. She lies down on his pillow and breathes in the smell of him. Her eyes alight on the bookshelf, on his copy of *Hiding in the Light*. Pressed in its pages, she knows, is the red head of the gerbera daisy she gave him on their first night. She sits up, wipes her eyes and grabs the bag.

*

'You look miles away,' Danny says.

'What? Sorry – I'm just a bit … what were you saying?'

'I was just saying we're going to crack this flat hunt today.'

He smiles. 'Are you finished?'

Laura looks down at her plate; she has only taken one bite out of the sandwich. She flexes her left hand, looking at the silver ring on her engagement finger. He had given it to her the night before she left, engraved inside with the words STRENGTH TO LOVE.

'How're the plans coming for the magazine?'

'Oh – good. I met this guy at a place called Mentor, he's a sort of a business advisor, I'm to meet with him every week.'

She thinks of Jim Glen's hairy knuckles and Masonic ring, his habit of using phrases like, 'the only nigger in the woodpile'.

'Is it one of those ET things?'

'ET?'

'Yeah – Extra Tenner.'

She laughs.

'I guess it is. I'm eligible for some start-up funding, from the Prince's Trust and something called Women into Business. I was thinking of calling the magazine *Portent* – it's from that Richard Hoggart book, *The Uses of Literacy* ... he uses that word to describe working-class youths.'

'Yeah?' Danny is smiling, stirring his tea.

'What? Am I boring you?'

'No – totally the opposite. I think it sounds great.'

Danny leans forward and puts his fingers on her wrist. The noisy chat of the people around them, the smell of steam rising from wet coats recedes. She looks at his hand, his fingers are warm and tanned, his flat nails have a bluish tinge. He says, 'Everything is going to be okay, you know.'

*

The windows in Mel's kitchen are steamed with condensation. She is stirring a big pot of pumpkin soup.

'I couldn't resist when I saw them outside Roots and Fruits. They always have such great displays this time of year.'

Mel ladles her out a bowlful.

'Here: sit, eat. You're skin and bone.'

Laura sits. Mel grinds black pepper over the yellow surface of the soup. It is already congealing. The spoon feels heavy in Laura's hand. The phone rings. Mel answers and then covers the phone with her hand. She mouths to Laura – 'It's Jack'. Laura rises from the table. Joan must have told him where she'd gone. She takes the receiver.

'Laura, are you all right? I'm really sorry about coming back so late from the studio last night.'

'It's got nothing to do with you coming home late.'

'Well – what is it then?'

'Lots of things, but I don't want to talk about it over the phone.'

She looks at Mel, who is making a 'wanker' action.

'Don't you want to stay here tonight?'

'No – I don't. I just need some time away from you. In fact, me and Danny found a flat today so I won't be coming back to yours – I'm staying at Mel's 'til I move in.'

There's a pause and she hears him sigh, then a faint rasp as he rubs his hand across his stubble.

'Oh Laura ... have I been doing your head in?'

'Yes, you have.'

*

He is standing at the door to meet her when she arrives at the landing, something he hasn't bothered to do for ages. Lately he's just been leaving the door ajar for her and doesn't even turn around from his computer to say hello. He tries to move in for a hug but she steps backwards and puts her palms up. In his room, she gathers up her things as fast as she can. Jack follows her around the room.

'Look, stop that for a minute, will you? Let's talk about this, I want to try to sort it out.'

'I don't know if you do – you seem to want to have all these girls hanging around – you can have that, but not me as well. I mean, am I supposed to be *happy* that you slept with Rhona the minute I turned my back?'

'I didn't sleep with her. I mean, I did sleep with her but I didn't have sex with her. I've told you before, it's totally platonic, she's just a mate.'

Laura thinks of times she's shared the same bed with a friend who's a boy. Mostly nothing did happen. She remembers sharing a bed with Danny and one of his skater friends after a house party one night in Dundee. She had slept in between them both, all of them in their underwear and drunk. Nothing had happened, sure. Their bodies were so warm, everything shadowy in the dark, the pins and needles light in someone's attic room. The shifts: the tiny pressures of skin on skin. They had all woken up laughing and hungover, sorry it was already morning.

She looks around the room for other things that are hers. She feels too tired to argue any more. Jack tries to hold her, she pushes him away, he grabs hold of her forearms.

'I don't want to be unhappy. I don't want you to be unhappy. It can work between us, please don't throw this away.'

'I didn't.'

As she is struggling out the door with the big bag he calls her name and she turns around, thinking he is going to tell the truth, maybe they can start again. He is holding out a woman's sweater. It is pale green, cashmere.

'Don't forget your nice jumper, you'll be needing it.'

He is smiling, holding it towards her.

She looks at him for a long beat.

'That isn't mine.'

*

He keeps calling her. Twice, three times a day.

He says, 'You asking for this space has made me think more of you than ever.'

He says, 'I really do love you, you know.'

He says, 'The flat is horrible without you. I don't want to be alone, I want to be with you.'

He says, 'I'm not speaking to Joan, fucking interfering bitch. Sooner she moves out the better.'

*

Laura goes to see Amy in the record shop. She says, 'It's about time for my lunch break, want to grab something to eat?' At The 13th Note, they walk past the big waltzer booths in the windows and two tattooed guys playing the table football to the darkened restaurant at the back. It's a new waitress, she has blue hair and a pierced lip and a thin smile. They both order the veggie burger and Amy waits until she's headed off towards the kitchen before saying, 'So, how are you, missus?'

Laura starts crying.

'That good, huh?'

Amy hands her a tissue from her bag, and lights up a fag. She blows a stream of smoke sideways and then taps her cigarette twice sharply in the brown glass ashtray.

'I hate seeing you like this. You know yourself there was a reason why you decided to finish with him in the first place. He's the one acting like a total arse, not you. I spent my twenties in a really bad relationship. For seven years I just adored my boyfriend and didn't do much else. He's either with you or he's not, please don't get stuck like I did. That's what's making you feel so bad, having a foot in either camp.'

Laura nods, more tears dripping down her face onto the plastic wood-effect tabletop.

*

The night before Laura moves to the new flat Mel is choked with the cold. Laura goes out to hire a video and get some honey and lemons. It's only seven o'clock but already it is pitch black. On a whim, she buys a carton of Jack's favourite juice, and walks on, down towards the lane to where his studio is. She taps on the window but there is no answer. Through the curtain she can see the cornelian crystal she gave him for creative energy, sitting on the windowsill. It occurs to her that he may not have been at the studio all those times that he'd said he was. A middle-aged woman comes through the gate at the back of one of the garages.

'Excuse me, dear – are you looking for someone?'

*

Danny puts the last box down in the hall. He reaches back and pulls off his sweatshirt with one arm, his T-shirt riding up to reveal his stomach. He pulls it back down, wipes his forehead with his arm.

'God, I could murder a beer after that. Tell you what, I'll dive down to the offy and get some. What kind d'you guys like?'

'Oh, I'll drink anything', says Mel, arching an eyebrow.

'Hang on, I'll give you some money ...' Laura says.

'No, it's cool.'

He ducks out the door and they hear him going down the stairs, two at a time. Mel pretends to swoon against the door.

'Mel, stop it!'

'Why? Did you see those muscles … it must be all that skateboarding.'

'Mel!'

'What? Just because you only like self-obsessed a-holes.'

'That's not true.'

'Well, I'm telling you, you could do a lot worse.'

*

Danny passes Laura the tub of yoghurt with the spoon in it.

'This tastes so good.' Laura takes another spoon, passes it back to him. 'Or are we just really stoned?'

'Yeah, that, and high on paint fumes …'

'You know, I think we've done a pretty good job, here.'

'Yeah, me too. I can't believe they wouldn't let us throw out all those stinking carpets and mattresses though, I thought we'd never get them all in that fucking cupboard.'

'Jesus, me neither. Let's not ever open the door again.'

Danny stretches and smiles.

'So – what shall we do now?'

The buzzer sounds.

'You expecting someone?'

'No, you?'

*

Jack cracks his knuckles. 'So, looks like you're settling in all right. Very cosy.'

'It's not the nicest flat, but we're trying to make it nice.'

'So I see.'

Laura looks at him. 'What is it, Jack?'

'I was hoping we could go out for dinner tonight, be good to talk.'

*

He takes her to this microbrewery place called The Canal at Anniesland. It's deserted. He always seems to pick these places in the middle of nowhere.

'I've never been here before, didn't know it existed.'

'No? I thought we had been here.'

He's been here with someone else. Who?

He smiles at her.

'I thought it would be nice and quiet.'

*

He is unbuttoning her jeans, tugging them down off her hips. He's breathing hard.

'No-one's ever felt like you in my arms … I can't stand the thought of you being with anyone else.'

'I don't want to be with anyone else.'

He unbuckles his belt.

'Tell me you need me and you want me.'

Laura hesitates. 'What?'

'Say it, I want to hear you say it.'

*

Afterwards he laughs. 'We'll probably still be sleeping together when we're sixty.' He falls asleep quickly but Laura lies awake. She thinks about the single he slipped in her bag before she left, Dolly Parton singing 'I Will Always Love You'. It wasn't a song she knew, apart from the chorus. Yesterday, when she'd got her record player set back up, she'd played it and realised that it wasn't about enduring love at all. *Who was the 'I' in the song: who was the 'you'? Had he meant she was in his way, or was it the other way around?*

*

In the early morning she climbs over him to get a drink of water and stands for a while at the kitchen window watching a man out on the all-weather pitches marking out the white lines. Ever since she came back from America she's had the feeling that nothing she says or does is really real, that nothing is real. She remembers her last night in LA, sees Trina running up the stairs at Traction Avenue, smiling as she comes through the door. 'Guess what? I've found you somewhere ... my friend has a room to rent in his house in Venice.' But Laura had already booked her ticket home.

*

The next time she wakes it's broad daylight and he is already up and putting on his trousers.

'All right, love, that's me off. I'm going to be pretty busy for the next few days, but I've got a new club night opening on Thursday, at the Belmont Lounge. It would be great if you wanted to come along, tell me what you think.'

*

Mel bangs the kettle down on the worktop.

'I'm not coming with you.'

'Come on, it'll be fun.'

'No, it won't. Here's a wee prediction. You'll go there all dolled up, he will blank you all night, and flirt with anyone else in a skirt. You will get all upset and come home in a right state.'

'He says he really wants things to work out between us.'

Mel puts both palms of her hands on the table and looks at Laura.

'Tell me this: do you really think this so-called relationship is making you happy?'

*

Laura is still lying awake at four in the morning. She's stopped crying now. She thinks it's possible that he might come round after the club to apologise but then again, he might not. She's not even sure if he noticed her leaving. She watches the orange headlights of passing cars sweep across the ceiling. The clock ticks on as she listens and waits. Four thirty. She hears a taxi draw up outside. She tenses, waiting for the buzzer. She hears the slam of the close door and then Danny's familiar step on the stairs. As his key turns in the lock she throws back the covers with a smile. Maybe they can have a joint and a cup of tea together. Then she hears a girl laughing and Danny saying, 'Shhhh, my flatmate's asleep.' Laura lies still. She hears the girl laughing again, saying, 'Hey, where's your loo?' She doesn't recognise the voice. A minute later the toilet flushes and then she hears the door of Danny's room closing.

Pàdraig MacAoidh

AN SGRÌOBHADAIR

Mus do chaidil sinn còmhla a' chiad trup
dh'òl sinn ar slighe a-steach dhan oidhch',
agus leth-rùisgte an dèidh *strip poker* a chluich
thòisich sinn a' sgrìobhadh air ar dromannan,
gob na biro geur air ar cneas. Gu socair
shlìob mi strapainn do bhrà od ghualainn
gus dealbhan borb a dhèanamh air do shlinnean –
hieroglifean 's sifirean 's sgrochladh de rùn,
comharran gus gairsinn a chur ort –
agus mo pheann a' lùbadh sìos dod dhrathais,
ga gluasad às an rathad gus m' ainm-s' a sgrìobhadh –
fon ainm Calvin Klein – air mullach do mhàis.
Cha robh fhios a'm riamh dè sgrìobh thus' air mo chùl
ach bidh do dheòthas gam sgròbadh gu Latha Luain.

THE WRITER

Before we slept together that first time
we drank our way into the night
and – half-naked after playing strip poker –
you had us write upon each other's backs,
the biro's nib sharp on our skins. Gently,
I dropped your bra-strap down your arm
to etch rough pictures on your shoulder-blade,
hieroglyphs, ciphers, scrawls of lust
designed to send a shiver down your spine.
My pen meandered down towards the pants
I pushed out of the way to write my name –
instead of that of Calvin Klein – above your bum.
I never found out what you wrote upon my skin
but will feel your desire scrape *ad infinitum.*

Richie McCaffery

MacATTEER'S

It was the local store at Ballylair,
a bazaar where everything needed
in life and death could be found.
(They did funerals)

They made coffins out the back,
a bead-screen to hide the work
but once I heard them hammer
out of sight.

Hard to tell, given MacAtteer
and his sons did everything,
if they were making a box
or nailing someone in

or the dead chapping a door
somewhere for attention.
Perhaps a faulty product bought
but MacAtteer never did returns.

Linda McCann

SPECIALIST SUBJECT

Monday.

A doctor came to see my dad today, to prove he doesn't have to pay the Poll Tax.

He flipped back the ancient tongue of his Gladstone bag, extracted papers from the mouth, straightened his bow tie and poked his glasses.

'And tell me – eh – George – do you know what day it is today?' He looked at my dad over the top of the half-moon specs.

'It's Friday, of course,' said my dad.

'That's fine. And can you tell me who the Prime Minister is?'

My dad sighed. 'Can you no look these things up?'

'The Prime Minister?' said the doctor.

'Aye,' said my dad. 'Thingmy. The Big Yin. Maggie.'

'Uh … huh. And can you tell me, who's on the throne?'

My dad looked at me. 'Imagine a doakter, no knowing that?'

He looked the doctor in the eye. 'The Queen.'

'Yes I know, but what's her name?'

'Emperor Ming. Thatcher.'

The Parker pen was ticking and scratching in boxes.

'That's fine,' said the doctor. 'Thank you very much.'

'No bother,' said my dad, getting up to show him out. 'Let us know if you don't know anything else!'

I bird-nested my dad's elbow until he sat back down.

The doorbell rang.

My mum brought the doctor back in and I handed him his coat.

'Forgot my raincoat!' he said, waving to my dad.

'God help me, kid,' said my dad. 'You're as bad as me!'

My dad's hat smelled of Brylcreem and diesel, and Brasso from polishing the number on the Corporation badge. Sometimes he'd drop it onto my head when he came home. Even now, I breathe that hat, and sunshine swells behind my eyes, filling the early summer morning when my dad took me with him on his bus, and I sat on any seats I wanted.

My dad always walked bus routes. We took the 11 road. The gnomes in the pampered gardens of Knightswood glowed like the colour plates in my *Grimm's Fairytales*. We chanted the rhyme about the Glasgow Coat of Arms, with the bird that never flew and the bell that never rang. The streets were cross-garlanded in the lost language of birdsong, which blew like green glass from every perch, the smithereens snatched on the wing by the bickering chorus.

My dad was in his apple green summer uniform, and I swung from his arm, quick-skipping in counterpoint, my other hand trailing the wet hedges with no time to look for caterpillars. He told me that soon there would be no bus conductors: a terrible idea. I quietly approved, because I thought it meant you wouldn't have to pay.

As daytime took hold, and the trail of Woodbine doubts was cast behind us, I listened to my dad's tales of the Northwest Frontier, their folds already familiar but their colours unfaded. Tales so tall you couldn't see the top of them, my mum said. The shadows split open like sacks of jewels, as he recalled the heat, the green curry, the time he met Ghandi, the parrot that used to swear at officers.

He even told me 'The Heidless Drummer'. I knew how it started, but my mum would always say, 'Wheecht, you – you'll knoak that wean daft.' My dad was marching behind the bagpipes of the Highland Light Infantry, when swordsmen attacked. The band stopped playing, all except the drummer boy. Laughing hyenas ran off with his head, but he stayed on his horse and carried on playing his drum.

Then we were there. Behind the garage, the dark-treacle slap of diesel fumes, then, on a strip of black gravel pocked in oily puddles the colours of pigeons' wings, stood the Daimlers; a green and orange Chinese dragon of more buses than I thought there were in the world. Underskirts fringed in diamonds, they sparkled like a line of debutantes in wellies. Our bus was in front, in a generous slice of light.

Beneath a doodle of smoke, the conductor was sitting on the warmed platform, his back against the pole. My dad winked at me, and we said good morning in Hindustani.

Wullie said, 'What're yous talkin aboot? I'm fae the Gallagate.' He laughed when I said was that in India.

I followed my dad to the front, and he stepped up into the high seat and banged the door shut. The bus shoogled and blurred, then purred like a cine-camera running under mud. He rested his arm in the open window. 'Mind, if the inspector gets on, you've to kid on you've not got your ticket yet.'

*

I skipped back round to Wullie. In a puff of cigarette smoke, he jumped to his feet and swung round the pole. He stepped on his doubt, skliffed it off the platform, slung himself into his ticket machine and took a bow. 'Right,' he said, his voice echoing like applause. 'All aboard!' The punch on his ticket machine was for punching noses.

I climbed onto the threadbare magic carpet and up the turn of boxy stairs, with my hands and my feet. I'd never been up this early before. My mum wasn't even home from the nightshift. I wondered if she'd cleaned our bus. The high handrails converged in unprinted beams, and the notice at the front had the familiar scratched-out letters: 'To   eat 57 passengers. No s itting.'

Wullie dinged the bell twice and we glided into Great Western Road. I wished the bus had paint-wheels, printing the streets in my dad's hand-writing. We rattled down the middle of Lincoln Avenue, and when the trees stopped, the focus jumped back and I waved up to my empty bedroom eight storeys above. I used to explain to children that Santa didn't need a chimney at my house, because we had a veranda. Obviously, that was why I had a talking Barbie and Stacey, and a Barbie case with all the outfits, and all they got was Tiny Tears.

If Rapunzel lived in my tower, the prince would have to take the lift to the fourth floor before he could climb up her hair. One day when the teacher asked us to talk about the view from our homes, I was embarrassed, almost too modest to admit that my view was the whole city.

People had started to get on. After the flats, the trees thickened again and each time we stopped, the branches clattered a jazz tattoo and burst in through the open windows, clapping and bowing as they departed. Toasted marshmallow shavings of pink and white petals drifted the upper deck. The windows reeled a long close-up of stonework studded in the open closes and closed curtains of soot-crusted sandcastles full of sleeping children.

A Waltzers sensation in a brightening gap, and the buildings were covered in statues, gilded in the sun, red velvet in the shade. As the chatter grew loud, I was squished in at the window, my coat balled on my knee. I crafted a breath-cloud and squeaked my initials on the window, but halfway through they faded like invisible ink, or the paint on the Forth Bridge. When it got too smoky, I moved downstairs.

I could see my dad in his cabin, swapping double toots with other buses as they passed us along the eightsome reel. The bus-shaped shadow skated beside us, folded itself sharply into the kerb, then leapt aside and poured along walls, roller-coasted over shop windows. All the long morning, the sun bounced high like a dancing ball over the words of a song.

Friday.

We each have a place which stands blackened and gothic in our nightmares and on a hill above our town. Its shadow is cast within us and in every pavement crack we sidestepped as children. 'You'll end up in Woodilee.' 'Lennox Castle.' Once I knew what mine was called, the very name could trip my heart. Our secular, privatised Hells are the end of the line on the wrong road, and we go there first as visitors.

Sam and I arrived in a sprinkle of summer rain, the air full of Christmas trees and wet roses. In the turreted shadow of the asylum, the short-stay is a long bungalow in a bright border of manicured pansies. I wanted to get back in the car, but a nurse had seen us coming and opened the doors.

I followed Sam inside. In the corridor, old men drained to the bone were walking like premature ghosts through a foot of invisible water, only enough aware of others to avoid them. At either end of the maze branch were padlocked doors with wire-threaded windows frosted in fingerprints, and every first time, the men retraced their steps to where they went wrong.

The nurse showed us into the dining room. Around blue formica tables, men sat, ticking and chiming like a lot of old clocks in an auction room. My dad gave us a polite nod and we sat down.

He said, 'Well, I must've done it.'

'Done what?' said Sam.

'Oh, it's terrible, son. I killed a man. I've got to pay my dues.'

'You never killed anybody,' said Sam. 'You were a cook in the army. You're no that bad a cook.'

'Oh aye, son, I must've done it, for I'm in here, but I've no recollection. You've got to serve your time, boy.'

'Don't be daft,' said Sam. 'You'll be getting home soon.'

'Oh I don't know about that,' said my dad. 'You think so?'

'Aye, you'll be going home in a few days.'

'Oh that's great news,' said my dad.

'What's that, George?' An English nurse was resting a tray-corner on our table and delivering a plate of Empire biscuits, three mugs and a jug.

'Aye hello, dear,' said my dad. 'How're you the day?'

'Can't complain,' shouted the nurse, smoothing back my dad's hair. 'Georgie Porgie,' she said. 'This your daughter?'

My dad turned and looked at me. 'Well, I cannae mind your name, hen, but you take a hell of a bucket.'

The nurse looked at me, puzzled.

'He thinks I'm my sister,' I said.

'That's lovely, eh, George, having your daughter up to see you? And who's this?'

My dad looked at Sam. 'Well, I don't know.'

'Aye you do,' I said. 'It's Sam.'

'Sam as well, eh?' said the nurse. She moved on to the next table.

I was clutching my handbag like a float. I took out the pound of pick 'n' mix. A squawk of metal chair legs, and men were rising and approaching from all sides like birds to a packed lunch. I uncrumpled the paper bag and held it open.

'Thank you,' they said, in turn, each man taking only one sweet.

'What d'you say?' sang the nurse, pouring us a pleat of tea.

'Thank you,' they chorused.

A small queue began to form, the men on the end of it still chewing.

My dad snatched the bag from me. 'Tellin you – smoke all yer bloody fags.' He hid the sweets under the table, and the men wafted away again. In the slow-puncture ward, each moment is swept clean of the unclaimed bookies' lines of life, each world shrunk to a mug, a mint humbug.

Without warning, my dad lifted his cup by the rim, swung out his arm, and opened his fingers. A tick of tea lashed the air and sank into a new stain in the carpet. The mug bounced to my feet and I put it, still warm, back on the table.

'I waant the pink,' he said.

'We'll bring you the pink tomorrow,' said Sam.

The pink started the day I brought him the Cremola Foam.

My mum said, 'He doesn't like Cremola Foam.'

I made some anyway. He wouldn't touch it.

'Telt you.'

My dad went away, came back with the tupperware from the bathroom and clacked it down.

'I waant that.'

I emptied the 'Best Dad' mug into the pink. It was scabbed in old toothpaste.

He took a sip, said, 'Aaah, Bisto,' and wiped his mouth. 'And by golly it does you good.'

*

When we started to say we should be going, my dad looked at Sam. 'You got the car out there?'

'Yes.'

'Okay. Let's go.' He stood up.

Sam and I cupped an elbow each of this bone china figure who once was my dad. I don't want to see the identifying marks under the loosened sleeves, the blue lady a crone, red roses mouldering on her straw brim.

We edged our way over the dining room as if crossing a prairie in high winds. When we reached the door my dad wriggled free, stretched out his arms, and clung to the doorframe as if about to parachute into an unknown valley. He couldn't let go. Then he took a few steps and stopped again, in the middle of the corridor. The men flowed around us without noticing.

Suddenly, he shouted like a sleepwalker, 'Tommy!'

Sam and I said, 'Shoosht. It's okay.'

'Tommy!' It was louder this time, and minor-key moans rocked the flotsam of men. I'd never heard him say that name. Thomases were always Tam, but Tommy was my dad's brother, killed in the shipyards when he was fifteen.

'Rise and shine!' My dad turned and smiled as if he was dreaming me. He winked, rolled his eyes and shook his head.

The procession had thinned and the exit was blocked by a drift of men, scarecrows for the angel of death. The light's off but somebody's in. The nurse was behind us with the key.

'Say cheerio, boys,' she said.

'Cheerio,' said some of the men, shuffling back from the doors.

'Okay, George? Say bye-bye.'

My dad turned and warned her, 'You're wasting the day, Tommy.'

I hugged him goodbye, and I felt him kiss my cheek for the first time.

Sam took my hand and we waved to everyone.

The nurse hooked her arm through my dad's and patted his poke of sweeties. 'Didn't you do well! Come on, Georgie.'

'Puddin and pie,' said my dad.

Alistair McDonald

DOUBLE EAGLE

'Jean Ellen Alice Neville,' she said firmly, precisely and with a clear diction. There was pride evident in her voice. She paused and her voice lowered, sliding down the scale to contralto. 'That is not, of course, my real name. If I told you that, I should have to kill you. It would be too dangerous for you to know. Dangerous to me and to others; but you must tell no one that that is not my name. Dear me, I ought to have made you promise before revealing a secret.'

'We won't, miss! We won't tell anyone. Solemn promise!' said Agnes.

'So,' Miss Neville spoke. 'So, let us all promise together. Repeat after me: (she licked her right index finger and held it up). Finger wet, finger dry, cut my throat and hope to die.'

Catherine, Agnes and Simon held their fingers up eagerly. Paul looked scornful but Catherine kicked him and he held his finger up too.

'Excellent. That's settled now. You are all bound by the Official Secrets Act, just like me.' She spoke briskly and firmly. 'And now that you know who I am, who are you?'

The children looked from one to the other. The tallest spoke first.

'I'm Catherine.'

'Paul.'

'Agnes.'

'And I'm Simon. I'm the youngest.'

'Yes,' said Miss Neville. 'Fourteen, thirteen, eleven and nine years old. You live on the second floor left with your parents. You moved in three weeks ago. Today is only the second day of the school summer holidays and already you have broken the kitchen window of the ground-floor flat. Congratulations.'

The children looked embarrassed; Agnes stared at her shoes. Miss Neville looked fierce and then she smiled broadly at them. 'Come inside,' she said, gesturing to the open kitchen door.

The children trooped into the large, bright kitchen, which was surprisingly modern, considering how old Miss Neville looked.

'Catherine, open the cupboard under the sink and take out the dustpan and brush, please. Do you think that you could sweep up the broken glass?'

Catherine nodded and did as she was asked.

'Simon, can you open the lid of the bin for her?'

Simon rushed to help.

'Agnes, fetch that tray on the shelf, if you would.'

She pointed to a blue tray in a corner. Agnes, too, was eager to do as she was told, trying to make up for damage done. Only Paul stood still, hands in pockets, looking sullen.

'Paul,' Miss Neville said gently, 'I need your height. Will you get five glasses out of the cabinet behind you?'

Paul said nothing but he nodded and began to get the glasses down from their shelf in the cabinet. Meantime, Miss Neville brought a cake tin out from another cupboard and put it on the kitchen table. She took the tray from Agnes, placed it on the table and nodded once to Paul who was holding five glasses in his hands. Paul put the glasses on the tray. Miss Neville smiled at him then. She opened the cake tin and cut five slices of fruit cake with a large knife. She paused for a moment, looking thoughtful, and then cut a sixth slice of cake. Putting the slices of cake on a plate, she opened the fridge door and brought out a large jug of orange juice. Simon, she saw, had a hopeful expression on his face. Catherine finished sweeping up the pieces of broken glass and put them in the bin.

'Let's sit down, now that things are tidied,' said Miss Neville. 'In here will do. Take a seat, please.'

The children sat down at the nearest places round the kitchen table and the old lady sat down too, at the head of the table, with Catherine and Paul at one side and Simon and Agnes at her other side.

'Orange juice for everyone?' There was a chorus of 'yeses'. She lifted the jug, poured the juice and handed round cake. All five concentrated on the cake and juice without saying anything. Simon finished his piece of cake first. He sat looking seriously at the extra slice. Miss Neville handed it to him without saying anything.

'Thank you!' he said simply and began to demolish it quickly.

'Simon!' Catherine sounded scandalised.

'Well,' he said, 'it was there.'

Miss Neville said mildly, 'I cut an extra slice because I thought that someone might be hungry.'

'Pig!' said Paul.

Simon just shrugged.

Miss Neville gathered up the glasses and put them in the sink. 'Now that we have introduced ourselves, perhaps you would like to tell me why you decided to throw stones at your downstairs neighbour's windows.'

'We didn't. At least, we didn't mean to.'

'It was just one stone and it was an accident.'

'We didn't throw it at the window, just … just … sort of missed.'

The children all spoke at once – except for Paul, who was silent at first, then said, 'It was my fault. I threw the stone.' He glowered at Miss Neville. 'I'll pay for it. Out of my pocket money. At least … at least as soon as I can.'

'No,' Miss Neville said in a pleasant but firm tone. 'That will not be necessary. I pay an extortionate sum in insurance premiums. Time they stumped up something in exchange. All I want to know is why you were throwing stones.'

'We were trying to knock a can off the back of the bench in the garden,' explained Agnes. 'Paul said it was easy.'

Paul looked hate at Agnes.

Miss Neville laughed. 'Come on outside and let's have a look at this.'

She picked up a large tapestry knitting bag, with needles sticking out of the top of it, opened the back door and stepped out into the garden. The children followed her, one by one, Paul last of all. As he went out, he stooped quickly and picked up a white pebble lying on the floor. He gripped it tightly in his right fist, then thrust it into his trouser pocket.

There was a green painted wooden bench on the lawn with a shiny Coke can standing on the back of it.

'That's it!' said Simon. 'The idea was to stand over there' – he pointed – 'and throw a stone to knock it off.'

'Better to stand at this side,' Miss Neville suggested, 'and throw the stone away from the house. That way, if you miss, you'll hit the garden wall. Let me see how you get on. Come on, Paul' – she pointed to the gravel path – 'you first, pick up a stone and have a shot.'

Paul seemed reluctant at first but picked up a pebble and threw it. He missed. Catherine, Agnes and Simon all took a turn and missed wildly.

Miss Neville shook her head. 'Not very good shots, I'm afraid.'

Paul was stung by this. 'I suppose you can do better?'

'Oh yes, much better.' Miss Neville sounded very eager. She laid the knitting bag down carefully at her feet and pulled out a pistol. It was a very large, heavy, black pistol; quite frightening to look at; not at all like TV. Catherine and Agnes gasped; Paul looked quite shocked; Simon's eyes were wide with fascination. Miss Neville grasped the pistol in both hands, levelled it at the can and squeezed the trigger. There was a sharp crack and the can flew off the back of the bench.

'Just an air pistol,' the old lady said, with a hint of regret in her voice. 'It's all they'll let me have these days.'

Simon's eyes shone with admiration.

'Could you do that again?'

'Put the can back on the bench, Simon.'

Miss Neville reloaded as Simon replaced the can. She took aim, there was another crack and the can fell over again. She reloaded once more as Simon scrambled to pick up the can.

'Throw it up in the air this time, Simon.'

Simon threw the can up as high as he could. As it came level with the bench Miss Neville fired again. The pellet hit the can and sent it spinning across the garden. She put the pistol back inside the knitting bag and stood up straight again, smiling. Somehow she seemed very much younger.

'Thank you, children. That was fun.'

'Can I have a shot?' begged Simon.

'You can all have a shot – but not until you can hit the can with the stone. I'll leave you to practise. Perhaps we'll see each other soon.'

Paul nodded, then smiled for the first time since meeting Miss Neville. 'I'm sorry about the window,' he said.

'Don't be,' said Miss Neville. 'I'm not.' And she turned and went back into her flat.

Ellie McDonald

GHAIST LICHT
*'What we seek is some kind of consolation for what we put up
with.'—Haruki Murakami*

Hauf six i the mornin an this auld toun
still couried doun in sleep turns itsel
tae welcome in anither day.
An wi that shift a kitchen licht gaes on,
here an here an there till I hae
aa my universe tae muve through.

The polis, shiftin gear tae tak the hill
think on o bacon rowes washt doun wi tea
syne hame tae sleep.
The druggie lifts his heid, sniffs,
yirks the blanket owre his shouder
an listens tae the dreep, dreep, dreep
o waater skailin fae the rone
an rinnin doun the auld stane waas
whaur purple buddleia blazes.

Fuitsteps on the pavie nou.
Here's Tam McGlinchey girnin tae hissel
about the cauld. Gwaa back tae bed, auld man.
Nae bummers blaa thae days tae cry ye
tae the mill, nae Bowbrig or Rashiewell.
The sun itsel is sweir tae rise. Gwaa back tae bed
whaur you b'lang an whaur the wife
wi paps an hurdies happt in flannelette
spreids hersel across the bed.

This toun aye sent its laddies tae the war.
You name it – we wis there.
Aye, even Hitler feared the Hilltoun Huns.
An efter, through the smoke they brocht us words
tae hing like medals fae our mous – lest we forget
our daaies dee'd fur King an Country.

Conjure if ye will an urban myth.
'the solidarity o the workin class'
syne see a warld o fowk stappt intae a hauf mile

o closies, pends an backlands.
Sweeten it a tickie wi names
like Rosebank, Chapelshade, Bonnethill
an Bonnybank. Taste it like the waater-brash
afore the white slick o history rowes like
a spring tide owre reality.
Fur we wis aye Jock Tamson's puirest bairns,
draan thegither bi the lang threid o poverty
that hants this hill.

Haud about an listen tae the endless scriff o feet
traipsin owre the cassies. Whas voice is that nou
chitterin i the haar? Immigrants an refugees
blaan about i the stour o this warld's turnin,
syne cuist up on this hill toun tae fend fur thirsels
agin a wecht o waes that bou the back mair shairly
nor the stey brae I cry hame.

Fowk heiter on, bi auld lands, auld howffs,
auld kirks. Aathin's smoored in a ghaist licht.
I haud forrit wi the lave tae the unkent day
an a glisk o sun heizin itsel abuin the Tay.

James McGonigal

LIFE SENTENCES

Walking beside me in a dream, not touching,
you asked whether I really understood that this
        was a life sentence.

West wind, wet wind, is bending and polishing
        the holly boughs.

Is it better never or always to forget, he wondered,
and thought of the look of a cliff facing down its
        Atlantic.

Always look in a baby's eyes; always breathe
        in a baby's ear; always smell a baby's skin.

Regarding magpies: look but don't trust.

It is difficult to write two sentences at the same time,
        but not impossible, so long as they do not merge.

The second curse involved feathers.

I was using a dead man's paper and pen to write
        an account of his death in my normal handwriting.

White shirts are haunted by the ghost of sweat.

Years ago he told me what it was like
        flying upside down.

Showering, I still drive the soap down favourite roads
but this morning some of those vistas appear to have
        vanished.

Middle-aged trousers hang in your wardrobe
        like tubas awaiting their promised concerto.

Lambs'-wool is always a comfort when shoving your head
        into the pelt of the day.

Last night a wolf curled up to sleep in the clearing
          at the foot of my bed.

Listen: from the owl's point of view each tree
          is a cash-point.

We walk through sunlit rooms this morning
          to the fridge-hum of expectation.

I stood at the crossroads wondering
          why it reminded me of hair.

Should we bury his ashes or leave them
          for rain or dogs to lick at?

Old newsreels are grainy with brick-dust and blood.

Mistakes in my writing I always attempt
          to scrape clean, with imperfect success.

On the hottest days, our pavement shadows
seem to scrabble for somewhere cool and dark
          with blackened hands.

You need to create some space for yourself,
          the poet in his linen jacket advised me.

The barber shaves each stubbled throat with precious
          care, his customer hopes.

I just don't want to draw a line under those thick necks
          of geese eager to dip into northern waters.

Cloud-prints across a winter sky are remarkable
          for the way they drag one leg.

The old man mistook me for someone else,
shook hands vigorously then apologised, staring
          right into my eyes.

Meandering, maundering, I still claim to be
        searching for the straight and narrow.

The pattern on this carpet has a secret plan
        for the next decade.

A journey's journal – page after page after
        page of *Paradise Mislaid*.

Hills under mist, the curve of them,
        their spectrum of silvers, the shades of them.

Birds were up and about their usual piecework,
        stitching earth to air.

And as winter wore on, the writer continued
        to type out his novel set amidst desert sands.

There are many who fall asleep miles from the one
        they love best – and some who still lie there awake.

In time we come to appreciate the qualities
of darkness: its colour, tone, pitch and so forth,
        its forthrightness.

Please send me your latest disaster by
        return – I enclose a cheque for £17.99.

She was the kind of woman who lived
        much of her life in italics.

We lack evidence about how autumn leaves
        really feel as they fall.

That woman with the unattractive voice has written
        some gorgeous poems, it's true.

We wake and start to walk about its surface,
        getting the earth rolling.

When I showed him the letter that said
I was clear of the cancer, he pointed out
        that the date was wrong.

Someone is watching from inside your head
        and you twist around to see who.

Who was it passed me just now,
        her coat brushing my hand?

By a trick of the light her face half in shadow
        looked something like mine.

Walking on the earth we sometimes remember
        people in the earth.

This clear weather tells us that our daily lives
        proceed mainly through mist.

Where we first heard the joke is often recalled
        better than its punch-line.

That tree raising its hand at the end of the road
        wants to ask the sky a question.

Sitting here we draw up memories from the deep well
        of a teacup.

Our best hours in life are like earthenware pots,
        concealing what they contain.

An envelope is the heart's haversack, of course.

We need to slap a restraining order on those branches
        lashing out at our walls.

Beach sand that gives way, that gives
        away – he thought death was like that.

These nights you sleep lightly enough to hear
        your own nails growing.

His hair, when I met him years later,
looked like an emulsion brush –
      his whitewashed life, no doubt.

At a certain age he decided to accept
      the consequences of every move she made.

Travelling to the poetry reading, he took the wrong train
and wandered off the beaten track of his usual verses,
      the ones we all know.

The girl was wearing hiking boots, but travelling
      in courteous company.

When the time came to adjust the blinds,
sweet daylight filled the bedroom's cup
      to overflowing.

In another life, I will have wanted to engineer time-travel
      in a complex Latin tense.

Sorrowful snow, shovelled aside and frozen again
      like a painful memory.

I dreamt of a grand house where the butler ascended
      the rocky slope of a staircase.

Travelling to our capital city, it is always best
to consider how a cat would act
      in your shoes.

Watching your children holding sons and daughters
of their own, it's time to start another chapter in your
      History of Arms and Legs.

So full of life back then, I was aged 58 before realising
that I would die too – by now of course just a touch
      late in the day.

Lindsay Macgregor

MISS PETRIE

On buttermilk Sundays,
thirled to the stoup
of St Perdita's kirk,

straining stale water
from vases of lilies,
Miss Petrie surrenders

to ramsons and sorrel,
the floor of the forest,
the charcoal, the clinker,

the embers, the rust.
Even buttermilk
curdles when cursed.

Sharon MacGregor

INDEPENDENCE

You said I
was a clarty besom
that ma housekeepin was
enough tae scare the craws
but the mess on your sheets
is mair mingin and clingin
than anythin this dirty woman
could ignore.

Ah've had it with the stains
from your couplin, a pairin
stuck as fast as the grease
on your palms. You've dipped
mair than your finger
in the dark and glossy slick that runs
at ma core.

There's nae stoor sucker big
enough fur tae clean up the mess
of your mockit mind. So
haud yer wheesht, the tainted words
you whisper cannae sullie
this woman's thoughts. Not now
not ever.

It's your health that's failin;
ma weans are grown,
they niver died a winter yet
from feeding aff your germs.
We're cleanin up our act;
boggin is for losers. Aye,
we said you.

Christopher Whyte

LISTENING TO AN IRISH POET READ IN ENGLISH
IN LJUBLJANA
'De kis nemzet titokzatos, magányos nyelvén írni: egy író
*számára nagy lehetőség is.'—Sándor Márai**

When I reached the garden of the writers' residence,
I noticed him at the bar. I recognised him from
the pictures on the covers of his books, but he looked
smaller than I had expected, his unruly
hair forming a half-moon, speckled grey, that hid
his face and his head from sight.

He was the reason I was there.
I found a table, sat down, ordered a beer,
and said a word or two in English to
the woman who was sitting beside me.
At first we heard from a young Catalan poet,
a restless, nervous man, who would raise his arms

above his head at the end of every poem
as if he were a footballer, and had put the ball
into the net with an unusually skilful aim.
Perhaps he wasn't sure about the nature of the sport
in which he was taking part. A Slovenian
translation followed every poem that he read.

Then the Irishman got up, and loudly declaimed
his verses written in the speech of our oppressors:
not the long, complicated poems that made him famous,
but instead poems that were shorter and simpler,
about his family, and how he had grown up.
Though we had been born on opposite sides

of the same cold sea, there was very little
difference between what we experienced
of prejudice and suspicion, on account
of religion and, as people imagined, of race.
But he had made a different choice of language.
I am not sure what I was supposed to feel

---

* *'But writing in the mysterious, isolated language of a small nation also offers huge possibilities.'*

Crìsdean MacIlleBhàin

AG ÈISTEACHD RI BÀRD ÈIREANNACH A' LEUGHADH ANNS A' BHEURLA AN LJUBLJANA

'De kis nemzet titokzatos, magányos nyelvén írni: egy író
számára nagy lehetőség is.'—Sándor Márai[*]

Nuair a ràinig mi gàrradh taigh nan sgrìobhadair,
mhothaich mi dha aig a' bhàr. Bha mi eòlach air
bho na dealbhan-camara anns na leabhraichean
aige, ach bha e coimhead na bu bhige na
bha dùil agam, 's fhalt mì-riaghailteach 'na ghealaich
làin, leth-liath, a rinn a ghnùis 's a cheann a cheiltinn.

B' esan an t-adhbhar a bh' agam a bhith ann. Rinn
mi suidhe aig bòrd air choreigin, dh'òrdaich mi
leann, is thuirt mi facal no dhà anns a' Bheurla
ris a' bhoireannach a bha 'na suidhe rim thaobh.
An toiseach leugh bàrd òg Catalanach, a bha
an-fhoiseil, nearbhach, is a thog a ghàirdeanan

thar a chinn aig ceann gach dàin, mar gur ball-coisich'
a bh' ann, air am bàlla a chur san lìon le cuims'
anabarrach sgileil. Math dh'fhaodte nach robh e
cinnteach ciod e an spòrs san robh e gabhail pàirt.
Lean eadar-theangachadh gu Sloibheinis gach nì
a leugh e. An uair sin dh'èirich an t-Èireannach

is ghabh e gu h-àrd-ghlòrach, àrd-ghuthach na rainn
a sgrìobh e ann an cainnt ar ceannsaichean, cha b' e
na dàintean fada, ioma-fhillt' a rinn allail e,
ach dàintean eile, na bu ghiorra 's sìmplidhe,
mu dheidhinn a theaghlaich is suidheachadh àraich.
Ged a rugadh sinn air taobhan eadar-dhealaicht'

dhen aon mhuir fhuar, cha bu mhòr an diofar eadar
na thachair ris is na thachair riums' de chlaon-bhàidh
agus nàimhdeas, air sgàth a' chreidimh, 's mar a shaoilte,
air sgàth a' chinnidh. Ach bha roghainn eile aig'
a thaobh na cànain. Chan eil fhios cinnteach agam
dè bu chòir dhomh a fhaireachdainn, is mi 'g èisteachd ris.

---

[*] *'Ach tha e 'na chothrom mòr cuideachd a bhith sgrìobhadh sa chànan dhìomhairich,*
aonaranaich aig poball beag.'

as I listened to him: envy, perhaps, since
he had benefited from taking a course
that seemed wise and feasible
– a professorship in the United States,
books and essays written about his work,
a good salary, students' interest and respect,

a widespread audience for his work ... But there,
surrounded by a language that was almost as
small and incomprehensible as my own,
that a hardy people, indifferent to the wider
world's opinion, has nursed and nurtured,
his achievement seemed different. I remembered that

languages are not just there for understanding,
but in order to establish boundaries between
one community and another,
so that one can tell the difference between
what is known and familiar, and what is foreign;
that the ultimate wish and aim of the vapid dream

of general, common, widespread understanding
is to wipe out all foreignness. But people need
difference, strangeness, incomprehensibility!
I pondered all the borders running here and there
in the shadowy garden, and I was not sure
that any less of my Gaelic would make its way

into the understanding of the listeners,
if one were reading before them in this language
rather than in English. Slovenian
had brought a kind of equality to proceedings.
If my language is like the closing of a grave,
shutting over me finally, if every

Eud, math dh'fhaodte, 's uimhir a leas ga chosnadh leis
bhon a rinn e na bha coimhead glic, reusanta
is so-dhèanta – proifeasarachd, mar eisimpleir,
ann an oilthigh Ameireaganach, leabhraichean-
sgrùdaidh is aistidhean air an coisrigeadh dha,
pàigheadh mòr, meas is ùidh nan oileanach, sgaoileadh

farsaing airson obraichean … Ach an siud, 's cànan
gar cuartachadh a bha, cha mhòr, cho beag 's cho do-
thuigsinneach ris an tè agam fhìn, a dh'altraim
is a leasaich poball stòlda, gun ùidh am beachd
an t-saoghail mhòir, bha dreach eil' air na bhuannaich e.
Chuimhnich mi nach eil cànanan ann a-mhàin air

sgàth an tuigsinn, ach cuideachd gus iomallan a
stèidheachadh eadar coimhearsnachd is coimhearsnachd
eile, los gum bi neach ag aithneachadh dè
tha eòlach agus càirdeil dha, 's dè tha coigreach:
gur e rùn deireannach is cuimse aisling bhaoth
an tuigsinn choitcheanna, chumant', ioma-sgaoilte

gach coigreachas a th' ann a mhilleadh 's a chur às.
Ach tha uimhir a dh'fheum aig daoine air, na tha
coigreach, neo-aithnichte, do-thuigsinn! Smaoinich mi
air na h-iomallan uile bha a' ruith an siud
's an seo sa ghàrradh dhubharach, is cha robh mi
cinnteach gum bitheadh na bu lugha dhe mo Ghàidhlig

a' drùidheadh a-steach gu mothachadh an luchd-
èisteachd, nam b' ann sa chànain seo a bha duine
a' leughadh romhp', an àite na Beurla. Oir bha
an t-Sloibheinis air seòrsa de cho-ionannachd
a thoirt don chùis. Mas ann mar dhùnadh uaigh' a bhios
a' chànan seo dùnadh mun cuairt orm mu dheireadh,

word and discourse of mine is destined to vanish,
the sods above the coffin will be green again.
But it could also be that it closes like the
doors of a spaceship, as I disappear from view
on a course whose direction no one living knows.
Does a poet in a great language have a more

powerful craft, or a bolder journey? I didn't
regret that I had not become a Caliban,
that I did not accept the victory of those
who forced us to use their words, with each strange sound;
that my loyalty did not go to the one language,
generally used as it is, but to every human word.

Translated by Niall O'Gallagher

's gach facal is gach searmon a bh' agam a' dol
gan call, bithidh na fòidean os cionn uain' a-rithist.
Ach faodaidh cuideachd gur ann mar dhorsan fànas-
luing a dhùineas i, is mis' a' dol à sealladh
air astar nach bi fhios aig neach beò air aomadh.
Bheil inneal-siubhail nas cumhachdaich', no turas

nas dàine, aig bàrd cànaine mòire? Cha robh
aithreachas orm nach do dh'fhàs mi 'nam Chaliban,
nach robh mi deònachadh ri buaidh na cuid a cho-
èignich sinn gus am faclan fhèin a chleachdadh, leis
gach fuaim àraid – nach deach mo dhìls' don aon chànain,
ge coitcheann i, ach gus gach facal daonn' a th' ann.

Mary McIntosh

TESTAMENT

Despone, convey, mak ower,
by-ordinar wurds
mak short shrift o ware
frae their smaa-boukit lives.

Auld carles,
wha kent naethin
but the tyauve
o wersh grund,
wrocht reid clay
smoored in snaw
intil their banes.

Boolie-backit bodies
bowed aneth
the wecht o the wund
gurlin roond
frae the heid
o Lochnagar.

Sair-riggit fowk
laid doon in this laund,
haud constant as bairn's portion
the glaur that clorts my buits.

Whigmaleeries haud nae wurth
tae the heritor o this estate.

Lorn Macintyre

THE BARD IN THE MACHINE AGE

'I Hear You Calling Me': Father played
McCormack's rendering of the song incessantly
on the radiogram in the tower of our house
in Tobermory, until the stylus began to stick,
and another had to come on the steamer from Oban.
I didn't appreciate the beauty of the Irish tenor,
to understand that my male parent was a romantic,
but I never saw him give flowers to his spouse,
though generous to a fault to his sons. An eccentric,
he kept a Gaelic Bible under his bed, not because
he liked to read a chapter before sleep: it was for
the beauty of the language, not the theology.
He worshipped at the shrine of Celtic lore.
He was a banker, but when he slammed the door
on the massive safe and turned the several locks,
climbing the stairs to our spacious residence
he became a bard, typing out humorous poems
on an old Remington that went clack clack
like a machine gun. When he came to the end
of a line he slammed the carriage back.
Sometimes in the heat of inspiration two keys
would collide in mid-air and stick together.
He clawed them down, and the racket went on and on.
The way the letters punched through the page,
you would think he was creating Braille.
'My head is bursting!' Mother would wail
and go to bed. He wakened her to hear
his latest ode, and then shone the Anglepoise
on the Biblical page, and read Revelation
in what he liked to call 'the language of Eden'.

Shena Mackay

GRASSHOPPER GREEN

Agnes Cameron was one of the many exiles living in a university city on the south coast of England. She was sixty-two years old and in her address book the names of the dead outnumbered the living. Once her hair had been as bright as a red squirrel; now it was more like the grey-tawny pelt of an English squirrel, but it was always beautifully cut. Her small house was at the top of a hilly street and at night she could hear ships hooting in the docks and the putter of fireworks from celebrations on board the cruise liners, while yellow beams like searchlights criss-crossed the sky. During term time the desolate-sounding bellows of students out on the town reached her garden and sometimes she heard the cries of owls and foxes, the night people living their lives.

She had come here with her English husband and after their divorce she stayed on because she had an administrative job at the university. In every household there is one person who controls the weather and Michael had created storms and gloom. She had been a widow with two grown-up daughters when she met him and married him out of loneliness. Her girls and their families gave Agnes her greatest happiness but at the present time they were all living abroad. Some people take to gardening when they get older, others to charity work. Agnes had chosen birds. After both her beloved cats died she had installed a metal pole like a double-headed shepherd's crook from which were suspended feeders of diverse nuts and seeds that attracted an enchanting variety of visitors.

It was Agnes's habit to open the back door last thing at night to let the ghosts of her two cats run inside and up the stairs to bed. One violet autumn evening as soft and moist as if a giant sponge had been squeezed out after a steamy bath, she was standing on her back porch in the moonlight, watching a procession of delicate slugs making its way up the wall of the house. The steps leading to the garden were studded with minute tender-shelled snails. Hearing the rustling noise of some animal under the hedge, she leaned too far forward, triggering the security light which extinguished the mystery of the garden. Highlighted in the yellow glare was the hooded figure of a young man on the balcony of one of the opposite flats. He was looking directly at her.

Agnes couldn't sleep. She had noticed him before several times, assumed he was a student, and felt nothing beyond a slight annoyance that he was always catching her staring through binoculars as if she hadn't anything better to do. Now she had an uneasy feeling that he had been spying her.

She was dreading the morning because she had accepted an invitation to lunchtime drinks from a woman she disliked. She patted the bed where the cats lay. She switched on the radio. Music might prevent the grotesque cavalcade of a lifetime's blunders and regrets from trooping through her head, and divert her from imagining her parents' night-time loneliness and pain in old age. It was always Radio 3, because the World Service could be relied on to plant some atrocity in your head which would be with you for ever. Sometimes at night Agnes wondered if she was actually in a care home and everything else was fantasy. Perhaps she was really lying helpless at the mercy of a sadistic nurse, gazing through the window at the empty bird feeder dangling from a tree, with the television out of reach and blaring out some sports programme. One of her grandsons was in the room. 'I never knew you were into rugby, Granny,' he said and turned up the volume as he left.

*

A chance meeting had brought about the invitation to the drinks party. After being made redundant from the university two years ago, Agnes had the good fortune to get a job at Hazelwood Hardware in the row of high street shops which served the local residents when they didn't take the bus or drive to the malls and precincts of the city. She loved everything about it; the Hazelwood family who owned the shop, the rest of the staff, her green pinafore with the hazelnut logo on the pocket, the stock – from household utensils and mats and cleaning products, nails, screws, light bulbs, spring and autumn bulbs, garden tools, candles, doilies, Christmas fancy goods – it was often remarked that you would always find what you wanted in Hazelwood's. Agnes bought her bird food there in bulk, at a discount, and one of the Hazelwood boys dropped it off in his van. Then last week, out of the blue, Old Mr Hazelwood, now retired, had gathered the staff together to tell them that Hazelwood's was closing down. Everybody, including Agnes, had cried.

A couple of days later Agnes was taking her lunch break, feeling desolate at the prospect of the coming closure, filling the time by drifting in and out of the charity shops. 'Sixty-two years old and still nobody to play with at dinner time,' she thought, remembering how interminable an hour seemed in a school playground. Things improved when her little sister Jeannie started school; at least they had each other at playtime.

She bumped into Vee Saunders, whom she knew from the university, in the Salvation Army shop. Vee was a folklorist whose profession, Agnes thought, lent respectability to a relish for cruelty. She was also a specialist in children's literature and was of the mistaken opinion that all children delight in the gruesome and yukky. Always in a hurry, she would gallop into Agnes's office to use the photocopier, like a superannuated Rapunzel with a flying plait of grey hair which hung to her waist.

Vee was examining a fringed and tasselled brown and mauve patchwork suede tunic.

'Oh hello,' she said. 'I was just looking for something a bit glitzy to wear on Sunday. We're having people for lunchtime drinks.'

Agnes spotted a silver-grey jacket with mother-of-pearl buttons which she herself had donated, and held it up.

'This would suit you. Oh – sorry, it's a ten.'

'No, it's a tad on the dreary side. I think I'll settle for the suede.'

'Isn't it more folklorey than glitzy – borderline woodcutter?' Agnes was tempted to say.

Vee grasped her arm. 'I say, how awful of me! You wouldn't like to join us on Sunday, would you? Do say yes! I haven't seen you for ages, except in Hazelwood's of course, and it would be lovely!'

*

Agnes was up while it was still dark, before the birds were awake, to blitz the house in case anybody offered her a lift home and accepted her invitation to come in. When you live alone vigilance must be your watchword. Nobody thinks anything of scattered newspapers and coffee cups and dented cushions in a family house and the lingering smells of last night's garlic, candles and wine only add to its homeliness, but the singleton's residence must be beyond reproach even if no visitors are expected. A Jehovah's Witness might catch you napping, or Kim and Aggie from the TV show *How Clean is Your House* spring out from your bathroom cabinet in their white lab coats, snapping on their marabou-trimmed Marigolds. At the back of her mind hung a faded sampler whose cross-stitched legend read 'Thou God See-est Me'. She knew from her parents' declining years that there was a slippery slope ending in ketchup and Pepto-Bismol bottles rubbing shoulders on the dining table, corn plasters in the fruit bowl, crepe bandages uncurling into the tub of margarine smirched with crumbs and jam and pills and tubes of unspeakable remedies muddled up with piles of junk mail. She spent hours shredding her identity from her own post. And as you get older there's always the danger of leaving the house with a fleck of toothpaste mocking the brooch on your lapel or a dribble of soup down your blouse from a treacherous spoon, because even your old faithful possessions turn against you.

*

At eight o'clock she ran her bath. Then she saw it. How could it be? How, today of all days, could there be a grasshopper on the bathroom ceiling? It was out of season as well as in an impossible place. It should have departed with the summer, to wherever grasshoppers go but, verdant and sappy, it made its plight hers. Despite last night's mugginess, there was a definite chill in the air this morning, and bad things happen to grasshoppers in the winter. They have to go begging for a grain of corn to the industrious ants, who will turn them away saying, 'You sang all summer long, now you can dance!'

Oh why had she looked up at the ceiling? Why was it always her fate to be the one to notice the injured bird, the trapped butterfly twirling in a spider's web, the ladybird toiling up the window of the bus, climbing and falling, climbing and falling? As a child she had ruined many a family outing by sobbing over some poor dead creature, like a big wet lettuce or a dying duck in a thunderstorm.

If she managed to catch the grasshopper, using an inverted glass and sheet of paper, without breaking off one of its legs, and put it outside a bird might snap it up. If she didn't, it could unfold those tensile legs and spring into her bath and drown. Or frazzle in one of the halogen ceiling lights. Or be discovered at some later date, dead or alive, in her makeup bag. She turned off the lights and opened the window, hoping the grasshopper would have the sense to leap through it, and went to make some toast. Maybe she could use it as an excuse to get out of the party, saying that an unexpected visitor had turned up.

'Oh do bring her along,' Vee would cry. 'The more the merrier! Or is your visitor a he, perchance?'

'I'm not really sure.'

'Intriguing! You are a dark horse, Agnes!'

And then she would pitch up with the grasshopper in her handbag and Vee would start banging on about Aesop and La Fontaine.

*

Agnes always ate her breakfast standing over the sink, with binoculars at hand so that she could watch the birds. She spotted a nuthatch walking backwards on the metal pole of the birdfeeder and raised the binoculars. A flash of sunshine caught the window and the lenses of the binoculars, signalling to the youth she suddenly saw on his balcony. She dropped the binoculars and her toast fell into the washing-up bowl. She hadn't seen him come out for his morning cigarette, wearing his usual hoodie, boxers and flip-flops. Then he turned and appeared to be fixing something to the wall.

The telephone rang. It was her sister Jeannie in Elgin.

'I found a grasshopper in the house this morning,' Agnes told her.

'"Grasshopper Green is a comical chap—",' Jeannie began.

'Not when he's on your bathroom ceiling, he isn't,' Agnes interrupted. 'Listen, pet, can I call you later? I've got to get ready for a lunchtime drinks party.'

'Get you,' said Jeannie. 'I'm impressed.'

When Agnes went back into the bathroom the grasshopper was perched on the rim of the bath. Agnes succeeded in catching it, and put it outside the back door. The garden glittered with spiders' webs.

*

The Saunders home proved to be an Arts-and-Crafts house hung with scarlet Virginia creeper, and self-righteous solar panels ruining the roof.

The front room was already crowded when Agnes arrived. She recognised several people but knew none of them well. The handsome Saunders children were handing round cocktail sausages on silver foil platters, £4.99 a pack in Hazelwood's. Vee had let down her Rapunzel hair and was wearing the suede tunic over ribbed grey leggings and fringed pixie boots. She gave Agnes a quizzical look, as though she was about to comment on her unremarkable dress and thought better of it.

'This is my old colleague Agnes Cameron, Drew,' she said to her husband, a short man with an arched nose which he wrinkled to expose tufts of hair. Agnes knew that he was some kind of scientist. He stared at her.

'I've seen you in Hazelwood's, where I'm working now,' Agnes told him.

'Let me find you a glass of wine,' he said.

The wine went straight to her head and she remembered she had had no breakfast.

Drew's nose hairs glittered humorously at her.

'So, Agnes Cameron, from the land of the deep-fried Mars bar, where do you stand on this Scottish independence lark? Looks a bit inevitable now, don't you think?'

I don't know, she thought irritably. I can remember my granny calling it a piece of nonsense years and years ago.

She heard herself saying, 'When anybody asks me that, for some reason I think of a board game my sister and I used to have, called Touring Britain, or something like that. You had to throw a dice and move little cars about on a yellow map of the British Isles to get home to Ullapool or wherever, and when people talk about devolution I'm always reminded of that game and it's as if a little saw, a jigsaw, is cutting through the border, widening a blue gap, until Scotland floats away like an island. I expect you're sorry you asked.'

'So. Hazelwood's, eh? I always say you can get anything you want there.'

'Actually, Hazelwood Hardware is going into receivership.'

'That's a pity,' he twinkled, as if she hadn't just informed him of the death sentence on a family firm passed down through three generations. 'I was about to invite you to give a paper on fork handles to my students.'

'I was never an academic,' she informed him. 'Incidentally, I've often wondered what exactly goes on in the Life Sciences Building?'

'Ha ha ha,' he answered.

'So you are about to doff the green tabard,' said Vee, who had joined them. 'What will you do now?'

'I've decided to move to Edinburgh, and edit a small philosophy journal with learned contributors, and collect the works of the Scottish Colourists.'

'We'll miss you,' Drew said, refilling his own glass. 'I suppose we could always look you up when we come to the Festival. We'll crash on your floor, as the kids would say.'

'How marvellous, Agnes. The life of the mind is paramount. That's what you must aspire to,' Vee told her. 'By the way, will Hazelwood's be having a closing-down sale?'

Yes, the life of the mind has its attractions, thought Agnes. She had seen them demonstrated by more than one former professor. She could grow a beard and load up a backpack with books from charity shops and ride around on the buses all day reading them, not noticing that nobody ever sat beside her, because her mind would be on higher things.

*

Of course no-one offered her a lift home. She stood at the kitchen window watching the birds darting and swooping onto the feeders. She had absolutely no idea what she would do when Hazelwood's closed down. Blue tit, great tit, coal tit, long-tailed tit, woodpecker, jay. Thank goodness that horrible student wasn't on his balcony. Then she saw what he had been fixing to the wall. A camera.

She stared at it, too shocked for thought, then pulled down the blind and sank into a chair, clutching her head. Ugh! There was something sticky in her hair. Her fingers were all enmeshed in a spider's web clotted with tiny flies. She must have brushed against it when she put the grasshopper out. Vee and Drew had let her stand there at the party in a dreadful cobweb hairnet. Like the heroine of some grim fairy story Vee had dredged up – 'The Tale of Little Cap o' Flies'. No wonder people were looking so oddly at her. She was sure that some of them were sniggering.

What to do, what to do? That terrible camera. It was like a CCTV camera. This must be the student's revenge. He had thought she was spying on him and he was getting his own back. She went icy cold, then burned with shame, as a dreadful certainty possessed her. The boy was taking pictures of her to post on YouTube. The invisible woman exposed to the herd of students who had trampled her on the pavement the other day and galloped on regardless. Old Bat In Dressing Gown Dropping Toast Into Washing-Up Bowl had probably gone viral by now. How many hits would Woman With A Grasshopper Crashing Into A Spider's Web score? Could the camera penetrate her bathroom window? Her grandchildren would witness her global humiliation. She must hide. Flee. But where? It could only be Scotland. Maybe Scotland would welcome her home with outstretched arms, like a kind granny framed in her doorway saying, 'Come away in!'

Agnes went through to the front room to telephone Jeannie. If she hadn't kept the blind down for the rest of the day she might have seen the student come onto the balcony and unhook the trainers he had hung out to air. Close up they looked nothing like a camera. Then, lighting a cigarette, he pulled his phone from his pocket.

Peter Maclaren

AT THE ASHMOLEAN MUSEUM, OXFORD

On papyrus, from 2000 BC
a letter of complaint.
It appears that two beekeepers
have made inadequate returns,
and honeyed words
have not averted
a dismissal.
A scribe writes to his superior
asking for firm action
against the survivor.

Later that morning, ten years after,
my own time and motion study
in the Quaker garden
behind the traffic
as I sit beside a birch tree
planted in your memory.

We visited here
within ten weeks of your death,
learning of the dirt road,
African sky hot to the horizon
the earth scarred
and honeycombed with termites,
receiving you early,
chattering creatures stilled.

Ten weeks, ten years,
four thousand years
let all the time there is
blow its careless breath
through these papery winter leaves
and caress your body
through to the shoots of a new year.

Translated from the German by Donal McLaughlin

THE PRESIDENT'S ORANGES
Translated from Abbas Khider's Die Orangen des Präsidenten
(Nautilus, 2011)

1990

On one of the many never-any-different evenings in custody, Adnan, the capo, spoke briefly to the guards, then returned to us and reported, 'Tomorrow is the twenty-eighth of April. The birthday!' His eyes were shining.

'Allahu Akbar, Allahu Akbar!' Said celebrated. 'I've been waiting months to hear that!' He fell onto his knees, put his forehead to the ground and began to pray. The other older prisoners jumped up, too, as if possessed by a djinn, and took each other's hands as though meeting for the first time. A few hugged and kissed, like young lovers. Bedlam, there was, as they raced round, shouting, like chimpanzees in the jungle. Even the normally reticent Hasan, who for months had been as silent as the walls in their cell, laughed out loud. His voice was brittle from the many months of silence but, coughing and clearing his throat, he announced, 'God has not forgotten us!' And from his tiny brown eyes rolled tears that showed he was overwhelmed.

'What the hell's got into you all? *Whose* birthday is it?' I asked, not understanding why, suddenly, they were all so pleased.

'Haven't a clue,' Ahmad answered, checking out the others with a similarly confused look in his eyes.

'Whose do you think? Not Richard the Lionheart's, that's for sure! Or Salah Al-Din's!' Dahlal scoffed. Having made himself comfortable on the hard cell floor, he was caressing it as gently as a lover's skin. 'It's our leader's birthday!'

'What? Saddam's birthday? Have you taken leave of your senses, or what?' I hissed, disgusted.

'Is there another leader, like? – All the best! All the very best, my friend.' He was congratulating me, as if out of his mind.

'I don't get it. – Have you gone off your heads, all of a sudden? Is it stir-crazy you're going? Has malnutrition wasted the last of your brains finally? Saddam has made our lives hell, you fools! Any more of this, and I'll smash your faces in!'

'Come on, Dahlal, stop winding the boy up. Tell him what's happening!' Adnan said, to appease me.

'On this day, the doors of Heaven open,' Dahlal continued, as if he hadn't heard a word Adnan said. 'And semi-naked angels, draped with gypsy jewellery, will dance through the cells wildly and willingly, surrendering themselves to us like the virgins in Paradise …'

'Your brain cells, more like, will be dancing wildly and willingly, you fool,' Adnan said to Dahlal and their fellow prisoners laughed. He turned, with a conciliatory look, to Ahmed and me. '*I'll* explain it to you, then. Right, April the twenty-eighth really is Saddam's birthday, and the most important day in the life of every political prisoner in Iraq. In the past, there was almost always an amnesty for all political prisoners on this date. So we've been longing for this day for months. It's our one chance to get out of here alive …'

I was lost for words and felt numb. The whole night, I sat, silently, at my place in the cell, staring ahead disbelievingly. Was what he'd said true, maybe? Should I believe it? I wished I could just close my eyes and – without a thought – savour the moment like the others, but though I should have been happy and hopeful, I was tensing up with fear. Every spark of hope that had attacked me in recent months like some rabid animal, I'd suppressed for as long as possible. Hope had seemed ridiculous to me, and distant and also dangerous, and so I'd ignored any thought of it with all my might. Now, though, it was as if it had been flung in my face like a bucket of icy water and I felt how, gradually, however much I resisted, life was beginning to return to me. I began to feel human again, and my heart, having for months, as it were, hibernated, was now beating strongly, pumping warm blood into my veins. I felt like throwing up and my head was thudding.

Later, the others' still-good moods began to infect me. The way they were behaving, you'd have thought we were on a cruise liner, on a few days' holiday. They were starting to get cocky, the still vague prospect of freedom was like a will-o'-the-wisp they were rushing after, blindly. They got careless, forgetting what was at stake: the last of our dignity. That last hint of mental strength, the thing enabling our weakened bodies to function at all. If this was all just a trick, it would be ripped out of us like a vital organ, and Saddam could hang it round his neck – like a necklace of death. In captivity, there was nothing worse than hope: it cancelled out the indifference you'd pulled on like armour, and made you feel the pain again: of all the suffering, all the abuse. Our hope disappointed – that would've been the death blow for each and every one of us; worse, much worse, than being told we'd be spending the rest of our – no doubt – short lives here; we assumed that, anyhow. But I could no longer resist. My feelings, an easy prey now, surrendered to hope, in all their naivety. Had someone told me previously that, one day, I'd feel pleased on Saddam's birthday, I'd probably have said he was mad, or beaten him up.

In days gone by, when I was a child still, pupils didn't have lessons on 28 April, but were allowed to sing and play. The teachers lured us with sweets and toys. And at noon, a huge ceremony was held in the playground, in honour of Saddam. Now, as an adult in jail, I found myself looking forward to this day again and couldn't sleep, the whole night. I dreamt of many things I'd do with my life, once released …

When the guards' barking voices tore me from my sleep, if was as if a beautiful woman had been torn from my arms; our life together, bombed to bits. I'd slept differently, more peacefully, calmly, and hadn't wakened so easily. The mere prospect of an amnesty had changed me. They demanded we stand there in silence. The command was superfluous, actually, as – in our joy and excitement – we'd all lined up obediently, like soldiers at roll call. A few minutes later, police interrogators appeared, together with a man with many stars and decorations on his sleeves and chest. Maybe it was a general from the President's palace? I held my breath. Such an important visitor, in a hole like this, had to be the proof. I stared, longingly, at the general's lips, waiting for him to utter the word that, for us, was synonymous with Paradise, Life, Miracle or Messiah. 'Amnesty,' I repeated, carefully, inwardly. This word was our Ark, the last refuge that would save us from the Flood!

Two more guards entered the narrow corridor and laid two large boxes, carefully, at the general's feet. Maybe the amnesty documents were in there? I speculated. 'Silence! Listen, everyone!' a warden commanded. The general started to speak. 'On this day, the birthday of our President, our holy leader, Saddam Hussein, may God go with him' – everyone present applauded – 'all prisoners, thanks to his infinite goodness, are to receive a gift. The gift is from the President, may God go with him, himself' – again everyone applauded. 'I shall now ceremoniously hand it over and, from the heart, wish you all the very best for the future!'

The general gave the guards and policemen a lofty look, turned on his heel and left. They followed him, as ants would their queen. Only the guards with the two mysterious boxes remained. One carried a box – as carefully as you would a newborn child – over to our cell and ordered us all to sit on the floor. Once we'd done so, he asked, 'How many of you are there?'

'Twenty,' Adnan answered.

The guard opened the box as we all pressed as closely as possible to the bars – each wanting to be the first to see his 'second birth certificate'. For a moment, time seemed to stand still. The lid fell back into place and the world – the entire universe, indeed – shrank to become the small square opening in the box. It was as if the gate to Hell had opened and we'd looked into the flames. It took a moment for me *really* to grasp what I was seeing. In the box lay – in tidy rows – shiny, sturdy, juicy, blood oranges.

*

On the Day of the Oranges, when the realisation dawned on every last one of us, all hell broke loose. We behaved like wild animals. Some were tearing their hair out, screaming, howling, battering their hands off the wall; one curled up on the floor as if he had cramps; our weak hands and arms tried to grab the guards. The latter lashed out at us with truncheons. After a matter of just seconds, our strength was spent: we were, physically, too weak to be able to live out the unbridled hate and immense disappointment within us. I staggered round, then slumped inwardly, like a pile of wet washing.

However much I was forced by my emaciated body to lie there and not move, my spirit was raging. I wanted to torture Saddam, the dirty pig, this son of a gravid river rat, wanted to slowly cut open his skin and, inch by inch, remove it from his body, in order to see with my own eyes his rotten innards and absence of a heart. I'd beat his face to a pulp, break every bone in his demonic body, then throw him in an acid bath and watch as, in great torment, he dissolved slowly and vanished from this planet once and for all. No corpse, no physical trace would remain of him. But not even these cruelties seemed sufficient; I sensed my mind wasn't capable of matching the scale of Saddam's sins with an appropriate punishment. The sins went beyond what I could imagine. You'd probably have to extract from his own sick brain the deadly medicine that, in a just world, he should be given. His supporters weren't safe from my unholy anger either. I'd torture each of these ants, each and every one of these programmed-by-propaganda torture machines. An invisible demon, I'd haunt their homes and rape and impregnate their wives, their mothers, their daughters. For the rest of their lives, the assholes would have to look at my face; would see it in all their future children. I'd put a curse on them, an everlasting curse that would pursue them and their heirs for all eternity!

Imagining such things for a while calmed me a little. On the other hand, I was shocked by myself. I knew only my placid side: was someone who, in the past, might, at most, occasionally have *thought* of giving someone a hiding, someone who – like the bigger boys at school – had attacked me first, and for no reason. But wanting to *kill* someone? Visualising it so clearly, as if it were reality? And feeling a deep satisfaction as you did? That was how far they'd driven me. Mentally, I'd already become what I despised most.

The desire for revenge was controlling not just me. It had beset practically every one of us, like an illness – dormant within us for months – that had now erupted, suddenly and violently. I want nothing to do with it, damn it, I shouted, to bring myself to my senses. In the past, I'd had only my pigeons and a simple life – and been completely happy. But how was I to protect the good angel within, if everyone round me – the policemen, guards and even my fellow prisoners – unleashed demons in me?

Sometimes I got afraid *of* myself, and *for* myself. If one of us died; if I became very hungry; if I couldn't sleep; if the bedbugs showed no respite; or if the guards practised their karate on my face again … Sometimes, rage had a hold of me for a very long time, like in the weeks after that fateful day known as Re-education Day.

Once or twice a month, an officer came to us, who disciplined us in special ways. Once, in the corridor, we'd to crawl on the floor, from the main door to the opposite end of the corridor. The men in uniform climbed onto prisoners' backs and jumped around on them, bawling, 'You're sheep, and we're the wolves!' Crushed to death, almost, the prisoners struggled along the corridor, while the soldiers pretended they were stamping on irritating vermin. 'Come on, you worms – keep going!' Anyone unable to continue, and who stopped, was 're-educated'. Once, it was 25-year-old Mohammed whose weak body could no longer withstand the burden, and who froze on the ground, motionless. At that, he was educated very severely – punched with closed fists, and finally handcuffed, naked, to the main door where he dangled like a slaughtered beast till the next morning. That was in icy-cold January. Several times, the guards threw water over him. His thin, weak body shivered the whole bitterly cold night. The rest of us had tears in our eyes, from rage and helplessness. The feeling of being at their mercy choked all of us. It wasn't just Mohammed hanging there: we were *all* tortured, inwardly, if one of us got to enjoy these methods. The next day, Adnan fetched Mohammed back to the cell. For two days, he shivered and was feverish. On the third, two guards came and, without explanation, took him away. Adnan said, gullibly, 'No doubt he's being taken to the hospital.' We never saw him again, though. He was either transferred to another prison, or died of re-education and was buried somewhere in the Nasiriyah desert.

The education methods varied greatly, were well thought-out, had been perfected. Once, some Kurds had to line up in the corridor and repeat, loudly, one hundred times: 'Down with Kurdistan!' All the while, the guards hit out at them, for fun, or out of boredom, till they were breathless. On another of these Re-education Days, a very handsome young officer appeared outside our cell with six other guards. He was, as I later learned, a Sunni, and called Omer. We all stood up, anxiously, staring at the floor to avoid all eye contact as this often had the same provocative effect on the guards, as on rabid animals. He see-sawed, cheerfully, in his fashionable black shoes; stepped right up to the bars to examine each of us closely. Finally, he stopped before Adnan.

'Are you Adnan?'

'Yes, sir!'

'How are you faring here?'

'Excellently, sir!'

'I want to see all members of the Shiite parties in the corridor immediately. The others, Kurds and Communists, are to stay in their cells. Do you understand me?'

'Yes, sir.'

He then gave us a sharp look. 'Which one is Mahdi?'

'Me,' I said, swallowing with difficulty.

'You stay close to me.'

'Yes, sir!' I stammered, mad with fear, almost.

I stood, trembling, beside him, not knowing what was going on, my heart beating, though, like a woodpecker gone wild.

When the Shiite prisoners had gathered in the corridor, a guard ordered them to sit down. The officer lowered himself to the floor, too, and signalled with his hand to me to sit beside him. A guard handed him a thick green book. He held it up.

'What's this book called?' he asked.

A short silence.

'I want an answer!' he shouted, angrily.

Everyone answered. '*Mafatih Al-Jinaan – The Key of Paradise.*'

I remembered the book immediately. My mother had had it at home too. She'd read in it after almost every prayer. I've seen it in the mosques too. It always lay on the windowsill and was a very well-known almanac of Shiite prayers.

He opened it. 'Today, we'll read Kumayl's Prayer of Supplication. Who knows it?'

He gave Adnan a strict look. 'You perhaps?'

'Yes, sir! I know it.'

'Tell us its genesis, and when it should be read.'

'Yes, sir! It is by Imam Ali. He taught it to his companion and pupil, Kumayl, who passed it on to us. That's why it is known as Kumayl's Invocation. The faithful read it on many occasions, particularly in the night from Thursday to Friday.'

'Then we'll read it now! It's Thursday, after all.'

The officer began to read. The prayer was very long. He was rapt in contemplation as he read, like a deeply religious monk. Often, he repeated sections several times, his voice quivering with passion. Some lines he even read with his eyes almost closed, as if he knew the text by heart.

O Thou who art the light! O Thou who art the most holy!
O Thou who existed before the foremost! And shall exist after the last!
O God! Forgive me those sins that would affront my modesty.
O God! Forgive me those sins that would reverse divine favours.
O God! Forgive me those sins that would affect my supplications.
O God! Forgive me those sins that destroy all hope.
O God! Forgive me those sins that would bring us tribulations.
O God! Forgive every sin I have committed, and error I have made.

When he'd finished, he gave me his hand. 'God bless you!' he said, theatrically. He stood up, looked at everyone and – in an unctuous manner – commanded, 'Brothers, now we shall greet our covert imam who, finally, is covert no more. Imam Al-Mahdi.' He pointed with his hand to me. He then knelt before me, put my left hand on his head, then took my right and kissed it. Finally, he turned to the others and, with a sneer, said, 'Please!'

In a flash, the guards reached for their truncheons and began beating the prisoners. 'Go on! Kiss the hand of Al-Mahdi!' One after the other took my hand, now numb with disgust, and put it on his head, bowed, then kissed my right hand. The guards beat those who hesitated or refused. When they'd all kissed my hand and returned to their cells, crying, bitter tears were welling up in my eyes too. The officer, from whose hideous face every semblance of beauty and youth had vanished, turned to me. 'Your Holiness can now return to his cell,' he said, cynically, and laughed like a horse.

aonghas macneacail

there are days

there are days when i'd like to
close the news bulletins down –
that man gone crazy in texas, who
left a bungalow full of corpses,
and the mouths sitting on an ocean of
coins, promising that you won't be
on the dole one moment longer than
their regulations will permit
for they don't wish that you,
were you poor as a death notice,
should exploit taxes that they
are not willing, at all, to pay –
nor do they really want you
in their big society, no matter how
much golden eloquence weaves among
the benches, in their palace of speeches
– and when the oily sweetnesses of
their capricious voices can be heard
trading bargains in the lobby,
understand that it's not at all for you,
neighbour, but for their bottomless
pockets, and, in order to keep your
attention on possibilities of threats
of devastating attacks by enemies
where we hadn't observed any
enmity, they'll broadcast accounts
of those dictators' deceptions
their bluster read as menace,
so that we will go, in the name of
justice, to murder thousands –
elbows, shoulders and heads
ripped away from bodies – so
much blood, and we wishing
we could feel guilty – were there
time to bear it, and if we could
make some sort of cold count
of the corpses, could there be
easing of conscience, though it was
under orders, and without inclination
that we aimed, sullenly, at heads

aonghas macneacail

tha làithean ann

tha làithean ann nuair a dh'iarrainn
na naidheachdan a dhùnadh sìos –
fear ud às a chiall ann an texas, a
dh'fhàg a bhungalow làn chlosach,
's na beòil tha suidh' air cuan de
chuinn, a' gealltainn nach bi thusa
air an dòl aon diog nas fhaide na
cheadaicheas an cuid òrdachaidh
oir chan iarr iad gum biodh tusa,
biodh tu cho bochd ri sanas bàis,
gabhail brath air cìsean nach eil
iadsan, idir, deònach pàigheadh –
's chan iarr iad gum biodh àite
dhut 'nan comann mòr, ge b' e dè
'n òr-chainnt a tha suainte tro
na beingean, am pàileas nan òraid
is nuair a tha binneasan mèath
an guth teumnaich rin cluinntinn
ann am bathar bhargan anns an
trannsa, tuig nach ann idir dhutsa,
a nàbaidh, ach dham pòcaidean
gun aigeann, agus, gus an cumar
d' fhaiceall air cùram mu bhagairt
ionnsaigh sgriosail bho nàmhaid
far nach do mhothaich sinne do
nàimhdeas, craolaidh iad sgeul
mu mheallaidhean deachdaire
– am bagairt a bhith na bhagradh,
gus an téid sinne, airson ceartas,
a dhèanamh murt air mìltean –
uilinn is gualainn is ceann air an
sgaradh bho cholainn – na bha
siud de dh'fhuil, agus sinne son
a bhith faireachadh ciontach – ach
àm ri ghiùlain, 's nam b' urrainn
dhuinn seòrsa de thomhas fuar
a dhèanamh air na closaich, am
biodh faochadh cogais ri fhaighinn
ged a b' ann fo reachd, 's gun deòin
a thog sinn amas stuirteil air ceann

Kevin MacNeil

HIGHLAND HAIKU AND LOWLAND SENRYU

Highland Haiku

Loneliness. Even the moon
is gone. Sitting here thinking –
another peat on the fire?

a morning so still
the crows' cackles
are sudden harmony

sunlight on the loch
the fence trembling
– her hand on my shoulder

sunk to the bottom of the loch
an oar
six feet from the moon

Lowland Senryu

sorry to startle a sparrow
bathing
in a sundrenched puddle

two boys scream
in the waiting room and hurl
dinosaurs at each other

it's probably
benign, says the doctor,
frowning

in the East End, a kitten
crosses the street
with a swagger

darkness gathering
even the beggar's 'any change?'
seems ominous

Rosa Macpherson

THE BLEED

Agoh wrung the daw's neck. The scavenger managed to bite his arm with its black beak just before its windpipe snapped. Its dead daw eyes fixed on him. Never mind. He tore off its head and buried it in the red earth.

'Can I see it?'

'Lia, we're at the dinner table for fuck's sake!'

'Here, knock this back, Agoh. Leave them to it.'

The Moor poured Agoh another whisky. He sliced himself a piece of salami as the two women left the table and made their way to the veranda.

Mona handed Lia the spotted handkerchief. The marks reminded Lia of strawberries. She remembered strawberries. She took the cloth into her upturned hands; quivered as she held it tentatively near her face. She sniffed. The scent was gone but it didn't matter: the perfume of dried womb blood was never to be forgotten.

Both women smiled. It was true. Mona's bleed had returned. She was the first, perhaps the only. Lia held the handkerchief to her cheek before she gave it back. There was nobody more deserving than Mona.

Mona folded the handkerchief carefully and put it in the pocket of her dress.

'Right, let's continue the celebrations! Drinks for the ladies,' she laughed and banged her glass on the table. Moor shouted to Mona to get her arse over here and pulled her onto his lap. Mona began to shriek.

Lia picked up a napkin and wiped her nose.

Later she got into bed and took a sed from the bedside cabinet.

'Stop snivelling, you're too old anyway.'

Lia cried louder.

'It never happened before so fuck knows why you thought having your bleed back would make any difference. Fuck. It might take years and you're too old already.'

Lia turned her back as Agoh climbed into bed. He did not need this. Not now. Fuck. They were lucky to be alive, any of them. But he knew how she felt. Trust Moor to be the one.

He turned his back on Lia and stared at the dark.

He needed to pee. He half opened his eyes and saw something red across the floor. He couldn't make out what it was and thought for a minute that something bloody had been spilled. Then he noticed where it was coming from; the window blind. It had failed to close properly and red light was coming through the slats. Even when he got up and lifted the blind he had to rub his eyes; his brain could not process what he was seeing. Maybe he'd had

*a haemorrhage. The world was red. All he could see was red, red dust, every-
where. It covered the autos, the road, the garden, everything. Even the grass
was red. Everything was red. Red was drifting through the air, slowly, drifting
and settling where it wanted, turning the world to blood. Then he saw it, the
daw's disembodied head sitting crookedly on its fat shiny body. And it had
something pink and wriggling and dripping in its black beak.*

Agoh woke up sweating. His heart was racing and he put his hand on
his chest, trying to calm it. The fucking dream again. The Lab had said
they'd get flashbacks of the blast but he'd not had one for months, not until
tonight and that fucking handkerchief. The daw was back too. He thought
he'd buried that dream a long time ago.

Lia was snoring softly, her eyes swollen. It had brought everything back
for her too. He nudged her and pushed her over to her own side of the bed.
She whimpered then grew quiet.

He sat up. Even if Mona had started to bleed again, that didn't mean the
Moor had stopped firing blanks, did it? None of them knew what the long-
term effects of the blast were on the guys, did they? Not really, not for sure.
Just because Moor was always acting like he was ready to jump Mona didn't
mean his drive was really back. Everybody was all show. There was no
proof, not for sure.

Acid started to ferment in Agoh's stomach: whisky and salami and fucking
bile. He reached for the gutmed at the side of the bed and drank straight
from the bottle. At least something good had come out of the blast – new
meds. Gutmed was revolting but he was growing accustomed to the taste.
It would help him sleep, a little buzz, hopefully without dreams. There'd be
no more fucking daws trying to peck at his heart. His heart was where it
was meant to be: tucked safely deep inside his chest.

*

'I'm telling you, buddy, he wants to have a beach party tonight – on the
actual fucking beach. One day after the beach clean and he thinks we should
be dancing naked on the chemicals.'

Agoh accepted the joint from Roddy and took a deep drag.

'It's cool for him and Mona, yeah, starting to get it back and, you know,
but I swear he's losing it, man. Thinks he's superman. His head is right up
his arse.'

'Or hers,' Roddy said and fell back laughing. Agoh threw him a cushion
and they both started to guffaw.

'Hey, bring us some peanuts, Lia. I'm getting the munchies,' Agoh shouted,
as Roddy's head started to droop onto his chest.

Agoh watched as Lia struggled to open the pack. Roddy was lying on
the cushion now, his eyes closed. Grinning.

'I can't manage it,' she said throwing him the packet.

'Useless twat,' he said and bit it open with his teeth.

*

'I've got a bottle of Jack Daniel's from before,' Agoh said to Moor. 'I'd been saving it for a special occasion. Was really tempted after the blast. Thought we were all fucked. Was going to have myself one last blast.'

He started to laugh, realising what he'd just said. 'You know what I mean. Anyway, it's yours, man, for tonight. Can I take a stab and guess it's baby-making time of the month? Real reason for the party?'

Moor took the bottle, smiled and nodded towards the couch, indicating that Agoh should sit.

'Heard you've been a bit worried about the celebrations, Ag. Don't you believe we've been cleaned up? Or is it just not worth celebrating?'

Agoh rubbed his eyes.

''Course it's a momentous occasion for you both, Moor, potentially for us all, but why take risks out on a recently virused beach? That was all I meant. Dunno what Roddy was getting at.'

Moor brought an apple out of his rucksack and started to eat. Agoh tried not to stare.

'And, it's Lia, to be honest. She's really really happy about Mona, but, you know, man. Women. It's never ever happened for us and now, well, she's not likely to bleed again, not ever.'

Moor bit into the round red fruit.

'Are apples good for fertility?' Moor asked, wiping his mouth.

'Where the fuck did you get it?'

Moor cupped his hand over his groin.

'You're not the only one who thinks we're momentous. Doors are opening, my man. The Lab's had us over for tests. They say that if Mona's definitely fertile we'll both need all the supplementary support going, so there'll be more of where this came from.'

Moor let out a deep sigh.

'The whole commune wants to know about it. We're celebs, man, Mona and me. The new fucking Adam and Eve.'

*

'And he says he could actually get strawberries? Real strawberries? But how's that possible? There's been no fruit for years, even before the latest blast.'

Lia was brushing Mona's hair.

'Dunno, Lia. Just telling what the Moor told me. Strawberries. Fucking real strawberries. Can't believe it. How bizarre can this get?'

'If anyone deserves this, it's you. You're the first, Mona, perhaps the only. Just think, there could be a baby growing inside you one of these days.'

'Oh, don't I know it. Moor's been high for ages.'

'He's always been full of himself, so what?'

'Well, I don't like it. I think I prefer him stoned.'

'What do you mean?'

'Since the bleed. It's as if. As if he's the one, you know, responsible for it; as if he was the one making it happen. Fuck sake, I just started to bleed, that's all, and it's great and all that, of course it is, but he's sort of fucking me off. The beach party's fine; I love a riot but he's really getting off on this …'

Lia shushed her.

'… and now he's saying that I need to hype up the hankie. Thinks it's going to be a fucking holy relic or something. Thinks it'll bring in cash.'

'Well, if that's what he thinks. Who knows? Maybe he'll turn out to be right, Mona. Let's just wait and see.'

*

strawberries n apples ain't what this old ddddddddaw wants, no sirree, what he wants is to ppppppeck out your little black heart with his little ole beak, peckpeckpeck

'Wake up, Agoh. Are you stoned, man?'

Roddy was in the doorway, singing, using a can of something as if it was a microphone. Agoh looked round, expecting to see the jackdaw but it had gone, vanished. He relit the joint then poured himself a stiff whisky. His eyes scanned each corner of the room. He looked up onto the ceiling, around the back of the couch. It was definitely not there.

Out on the beach the party was starting to happen. He could hear music floating up.

*

Lia looked at her naked body in the mirror. Outwardly, the blast had not caused any physical deformities but it had, until now, stopped fertility in both men and women. It was the slow route to death but, as Agoh said, a much more pragmatic way to conduct war. There had been other casualties; agricultural lands virused, selective famine, they had all become incapable of seeding. She was watching annihilation in the mirror.

She ran her hands over her flat belly; imagined rattlings; dried peas in a pod. She tried, really tried, to remember what desire felt like. A tiny moustache of sweat appeared along her top lip. She stepped closer towards the mirror and stared at it: perfect little beads in a row. She licked it clean with her tongue.

'Fuck sake, cover yourself, will you?'

She could see Agoh in the mirror. He really needed to shave.

She held Mona's handkerchief up to her face and sniffed it. She watched as her own eyes narrowed, flickered.

'What the fuck?' Agoh said and grabbed the handkerchief from her. 'You are so gross. What are you doing with this? How the fuck did you get your hands on this?'

Lia reached out to stroke his face and he pulled back.

'I just took it. Borrowed it. To see it, if it. I just wanted it.'

'Get dressed,' he said and grabbed the handkerchief from her. He threw it on the dressing room table and wiped his hands down the front of his trousers, as if the thing was still wet. He turned to walk out then changed his mind. He carefully lifted the handkerchief and put it in his pocket.

Lia sat on the edge of the bed. She crossed her arms over her breasts and sighed.

*

Roddy and Agoh stood on the veranda watching the party below. Someone had strung lights around the beach hut; the barbeque was smoking and the music was loud.

'S'great, man. This is so great.'

Roddy started to move in time with the music.

'Come on, lighten up,' he said, opening another bottle of beer. 'Things are getting back to normal. Soon it'll be everybody celebrating like the Moor and Mona. It's a sign, man.'

Agoh could see Roddy's lips move but he'd learned to tune him out a long time ago. He'd become very skilled at it, being here and somewhere else at the same time. As usual, Roddy would be talking shit and peace. Well, apart from the nightmares the blast hadn't affected his life any. He'd never felt the need to procreate. So fucking yahoo about a bit of blood. Let the world die out after him, what did he care?

He put his hand in his pocket and touched the handkerchief. He smiled. On the beach the party was growing wilder. Mona and Moor were carried down on beach chairs, waving as the commune cheered. Someone had placed some sort of green leafed crown on the Moor's head and he raised his arms in a mock salute. They were all pished or stoned, laughing and dancing and shrieking.

'Roddy, have you seen the handkerchief yet?'

'Fuck, no, man. Not yet. The Moor's been planning to show it tonight, said the crews might even be here. He's one shrewd dude. You gotta give him that.'

'I can't wait,' Agoh said.

'You'll have to give it back, Agoh. I only borrowed it. Give it back.'

Lia crossed the room towards the veranda, her hand outstretched. She tied her dressing gown tighter when she saw Roddy there.

'What are you tying that for? You think Roddy's interested in seeing anything you've got? Stupid twat.'

'Give me it, Agoh. We need to give it back.'

'Why? It's just a cunt rag. Or you not remember that far back, Lia?'

Agoh laughed and waved the handkerchief in Lia's face. Roddy gasped. 'How the fuck?'

Agoh grabbed Lia's hair and pushed the handkerchief in her face.

'Man. Cool it. You're hurting her.'

'Don't, Roddy. It doesn't matter. He won't hurt me.'

On the beach the music stopped. Somebody called out, 'Let's see it, then. Let us see the blood.' Then a drunken chant began: 'blood blood blood'.

'Hey, don't spoil the party. Let her go. Fuck.'

Agoh pulled at Lia's hair until her knees buckled. He pulled her onto the floor.

'Give it back, Agoh. Please. Why can't you be happy for them?'

'What the fuck is wrong with you, man?'

Roddy tried to pull Agoh away from Lia and Agoh punched him in the mouth.

'Come on, you're stoned. Stop this, man,' Roddy said, wiping the blood from his lip. Agoh started to bang Lia's head on the floor.

'Am I not hurting you, Lia? Doesn't that hurt? Doesn't it? Doesn't it? Stupid fucking bitch. What do you think of me now, bitch?'

He forced the handkerchief deep into Lia's mouth. She started to gag and choke until Roddy pulled Agoh from her. Agoh grabbed a bottle of whisky and took off. Roddy cradled her until Lia could breathe again.

If he could just remember where he'd buried the head then he could be sure it was dead, really dead and it wouldn't be able to mock him like this, fucking him up, fucking him up, looking for his heart to peck out his heart, what did he think, stupid fucking daw, that he'd wear his heart on his sleeve just waiting for it to be pecked out?

Neil McRae

RED RIGGS

Bha mi mìos shìos a deas
Ach air rathad an Eilein a-rithist,
Nuair a shiùbhail mi leth-rathad
Taobh Shasainn dhen a' Chrìche;

Bha e air aithris gun deach cath
A chur uaireigin san sgìre.
Thug mi an aire
Dhan t-soidhne bheag chrìon –

Homildon. Chaidh mi a dh'fhaicinn,
Agus chunnaic mi an cnoc feurach
Far an do thuit fir Alba,
A maithean is a mith-shluagh.

Ged nach robh sanas
No fiosrachadh ri fhaicinn,
Fhuaradh a-mach leam
An sgeul ro aithnichte:

Gun deach iad deas an deagh òrdan,
A thogail creich air an nàmh;
Ach thug cleas nam fear-bogha
Bàrr air braisead is àrdan.

Red Riggs a chaidh èigheachd
A-riamh bhon uair sin
Air an leathad far na dh'èirich
An call a bu mhotha;

Bu chrò-dhearg na h-iomairean
Leis na leagadh san àrach;
'S an tìr bhon do thriall iad
Uair eile na fàsach.

Alba bheadarrach,
Nach iomadh latha dhiubh seo
A bha is a bhitheas
Do mhuinntir mo dhùthcha.

Translation:
Beloved Scotland, is it not many Homildons that your people have known and will know.

Ian Madden

INADVERTENT MUNIFICENCE

'What with the money you'll have from selling that cow, you'll be replacing the rusty bolt on the door of your privy.'

Jessie scowled her annoyance. Not that it was an indelicacy to mention the outside water closet but it was a nerve for that lanky creature to shout across at her. And get off his bicycle in order to do so. Lachlan, whose opinion of himself as a bit of a joker went unshared throughout the island, always had this effect on his neighbour.

'Or have a party, maybe.' He hoisted his leg over that ancient contraption as if it did indeed have a male crossbar.

Holding a doubled-up pinafore bulging with chickenfeed, Jessie continued flinging. She shouted back, 'We'll be having a party; that we will.'

Rusty bolt? She'd give him rusty bolt. She'd show him. She had plans.

Shortly before she sold her cow – and once or twice in the months that followed – Jessie had been to see the minister. That could have only one explanation: there was something she wanted him to read for her. Most people had an opinion as to what she might be up to. On such a remote isle what else was there but the land, the beasts, the roiling sea, the biting winds and other people's business? But not even the speculations of the wiliest islanders were as audacious or as practical as the truth, when finally they managed to piece it together.

Clapping bits of feed from her hands, Jessie once again wondered where the notion had come from. Might it, somehow, have been to do with the last war, the one against the Nazis? Whatever it was, she could envisage as clearly as if he were an old friend the unknown man who had had the idea. In a grey jacket with a row of sharpened pencils in his top pocket; at a desk in an office that might even have a fire to keep him warm in winter. He'd have a map of the islands on the wall. And there'd certainly be a ledger. Thick pages it would have; blue lines across, red lines down; with the sort of edge that looks like it's been splashed with inks of different colours. On its pages the man had – or, heaven bless him, had not – done the adding up. Chances are he'd become drowsy while doing his sums. Was an over-heated room to blame? Like as not he hadn't ever set foot on the island. And, with luck, he never would.

Jessie had stopped herself from calling out after the departing figure on the bicycle to announce that when she gave her party, it wouldn't be the usual – a load of men standing round drinking tea or coffee, talking about their cattle or sheep or the plight of the ferry boat. There'd be music, whisky and something to celebrate. But she wasn't one for rushing into things. A shindig she would have; but only when the grounds for it were firmer under her feet.

Rather than say this Jessie, realising her mouth was open, had called out after Lachlan, 'Your front tyre needs pumping up.'

Some people sang to their cows while doing the milking. Jessie didn't. She placed fetters round their legs – wooden contraptions inherited from her grandfather. So, as she sat, her hands on the udders, Jessie didn't sing; she remembered – or tried not to.

Her intended had been almost entirely bald when he proposed to her. In his early thirties, Sholto was from a tiny village in the Highlands and spoke only English. Jessie had been in her early twenties. On first meeting her daughter's suitor, Jessie's mother, in front of the man who was to become her son-in-law, said in Gaelic, 'A fine man you have here. When you wake on a morning and look at the pillow beside you, you'll not know whether it's his face or his arse you're looking at.'

There were to be only two years of Sholto's head on the pillow. He died early one evening after coming in from the field. It was difficult to say which Jessie resented most – her husband for dying and leaving her with all the work of the croft, or the beasts for needing tending.

Just as a man might dislike his hoe or milk cog – anything that smacked of toil – so Jessie loathed her livestock. She felt burdened by them. One day she took a bucket of water out to the horse. It was lying at the far end of the field. When it didn't come to get a drink, she strode across to the animal.

'Get up! Get up, you brute.'

Eventually swinging her foot at it.

Not even when Lachlan's father told her the beast was dead did she stop trying to kick it back to life.

There were those – Lachlan among them – to whom their headage of cattle was a mark of social standing. They took pride in it. Not so Jessie. She had it in for them. She blamed the cows for the tuberculosis which had, so she believed, carried off her husband.

For a long time it had been Lachlan and his father who had been her nearest neighbours. Now it was just Lachlan. He was in the habit of cycling past two or three times a day. If she was in sight, they'd call out to each other. Sometimes, if he had something to tell her or she indicated – by straightening up – that she might want to hear something, he'd dismount and walk alongside the drystone wall.

While doing the milking Jessie thought with satisfaction about what her neighbour dearly wanted to know. It hadn't been the possibility of a frivolous addition to the lavatory door which had attracted his curiosity. It was the disposal of her third cow, leaving her with just the two. But Lachlan was too intrigued, too mystified to mention it straight out. So he'd come at it from an angle.

The milk pail full, Jessie stood up and gave the tops of her legs a few slow rubs.

Swathed in long dark skirts and shawl, Jessie was nearly always bent double. Either she was tugging at recalcitrant weeds or doing something complicated but less identifiable to the earth at her feet. Even on the rare hot days of summer, her head was covered. So it was – bending or squatting in thick wraps of black – that she kept watch from outside on the men working in her croft.

What the men were up to was a puzzle. Word got round that there were some labourers at Jessie's doing building work. They weren't even from the island. Or any of the surrounding islands. They slept in the byre for the nights they were needed. How she had arranged for workmen to come from the mainland, no one knew.

When she'd had enough of the company of beasts Jessie would sometimes drop in on one or other of her neighbours. This involved a very long walk.

'We thought we'd come by.' Even though she had been a widow these forty-odd years, Jessie never reverted to using the first person when paying a call.

It was during these visits that she had seen other peoples' lavatory doors. Most had bolts. Her own outdoor convenience had never had a lock. There'd never been any need. When her husband was alive she knew where he was; he knew where she was. There was no need for anything as extravagant as a bolt. There was a door; the door had hinges. That had been enough.

Jessie's parents had an unusual history when it came to hospitality. More than seventy years ago – the first time they called as a couple on the McClouds – there had been another guest, the oldest crofter on the island. Jessie's father and mother seated themselves and started reminiscing with their fellow guest, ignoring their hosts completely. As an infant Jessie had been taken on some of these not very social calls. It was always the same; the couple talked to their child or among themselves – never to the people whose guests they were.

As an adult, Jessie paid calls in the manner she'd learned from her parents. She'd accept refreshment but would feel no obligation to pass the time of day. The few neighbours she visited had long since stopped expecting her to speak. There would be a greeting but once Jessie was over the transom that was it.

Jessie and her husband had been hospitable in their way. Once a friend of Sholto's from his village turned up unannounced. They told the man he was welcome to stay with them. In the middle of the evening this visitor was seen by Lachlan's father running away and crying out, 'I'm not staying here among thieves and vagabonds.' From the doorway Jessie threw the poker at him. It barely missed. This was the last time Jessie extended hospitality; until, that is, the day of her proposed party nearly half a century later.

The day after the workmen left, Lachlan was cycling home when he saw and heard something that made him gape in disbelief. To have waved or raised his voice in greeting would have been to let Jessie know that she had been seen. So he turned round and pedalled back the way he'd come – along the cart-track that led away from his home. Down in the dip, Lachlan dismounted. The way he suddenly straddled the cycle, if it hadn't been a woman's he'd have done himself a mischief.

Lachlan's hands twisted the rubber grips of the handlebars. His father (not to mention the minister on Sundays) had always warned against saying things that weren't true. Bursting as he was with the news, he knew he'd never tell anyone.

Kicking at stones in the grass by the track, Lachlan recalled the record player he'd never been allowed to own. The one with the Rexene cover and the gold lettering he'd seen in a shop on the mainland and had embellished on the journey home and for years afterwards. Just the words Solid State were enough to make him twelve years old again. But could an actual machine ever have been as marvellous as the one he had owned in imagination? The sounds blaring from Jessie's doorway moments ago told him the answer might be yes.

He had seen her before he heard the music. She had her back to him. As usual her frame was stiff under the concealing black of a lifetime. But hidden under several thick layers her right leg seemed to be leading a disobedient life of its own. Her pelvis had momentarily escaped the permanent disapproval of pulpit and preacher. Her legs performed repeated buckling motions inside her down-to-the-ground skirts. The black billowed, in and out, in and out.

Not sure whether or not he had seen something shocking, Lachlan lingered out of sight until he judged that Jessie had finished whatever it was she was doing.

Jessie must have caught sight of Lachlan as he emerged from the dip. Between the muddy ruts, her right leg slightly lame, she hurried towards him, avid.

Her lope as much as her face announced that she was the bearer of momentous news. Lachlan's first thought was that something must have happened; something that would need another pair of hands (and maybe a ladder) to fix. Had the rope on the bucket to the well snapped? Was her roof raining in? Or, worst of all, did she know she'd been spotted dancing?

Her call was as indistinct as it was urgent.

More often than not, he'd remain on his bicycle, nod and go past. Sometimes he'd slow down; occasionally he'd stop and stand astride the bike while talking. But now – on his second attempt to get home that afternoon – there was something about Jessie which made Lachlan slide forward off the seat and push his cycle. He wanted the bike between him and his agitated neighbour.

Then he was within earshot. From between pegs of teeth, Jessie was calling out in resounding Gaelic, 'We're shitting indoors!'

In her own time – that is, more than a year after getting shot of that third cow – Jessie let it be known that those neighbours who wished to call would be welcome at her croft on Friday at twilight.

On the appointed evening, Jessie's home took on the atmosphere of a church. That is, a place where people who usually couldn't stand each other were in close proximity. Such was the prevailing curiosity that enmities were very nearly suspended; those who took the furthest pew from each other every Sunday now maintained an equivalent distance while under Jessie's roof. Difficult given the limitations of space – but this was an occasion no one wanted to hear about second-hand. And the possibility that not a word would be uttered made it seem less like they were persisting in age-old animosities as respecting a peculiarity of their host and her long-gone parents.

A few of those present – hardy, grown men – had gathered beforehand and agreed that they'd speak only if spoken to. (No one had partaken of Jessie's hospitality; would she expect her guests to behave as she herself behaved when under someone else's roof?) So no one spoke – to start with. Some availed themselves of the Reestit mutton. Others had the stems of their pipes on which to chew.

As dusk settled, Jessie moved among the menfolk, all still in work clothes. So at ease was she, the shawl covering her head got pushed back an inch or two. Never had she looked so rakish.

There was drink. And from a corner of the room – and filling its every other corner – there was music. On the revolving black disc, steady under that magic needle, an American man was singing a ditty about patting a baby's 'po-po'. Lachlan wasn't sure whether this was the tune Jessie had been dancing to. He couldn't take his eyes off the record as it span round. He was in awe. It hadn't been the cost of the record-player nor the noise it would surely have made – though these were among the reasons he wasn't allowed such an infernal machine; his father had denied him a gramophone for fear he'd set the thing going on a Sunday.

'God favour and keep that man,' said Jessie.

'What man?'

One crofter, mellowed by the fumes rising from his glass, thought she meant Pat Boone.

'We're in his debt, whoever he is,' she said.

What crossed her face next may well have been a smile.

Over the coming months there were to be several similar celebrations – some given by guests at this, the first such party. Every islander had heard a version of the rumour about the recent law which decreed that if you were a crofter with three cows, your situation was deemed liveable; however if you had only two cows this entitled you to financial assistance. Crofters with three or more animals enquired no further. Many bridled at the thought of this new rule. They couldn't believe their ears. Jessie couldn't believe her luck.

She motioned for the men to accompany her. The island's first recipient of what she thought of as 'the cow allowance' led the way to the part of the croft that was the reason for the gathering. Whiskies in hand, her guests followed without a word. The walls on which the builders had been working had yet to be painted. They still smelled of plaster. The door to the new room was untreated wood. Jessie gave it a reverent push and stood aside so nobody need crane their necks. After a suitable pause she edged past them then slowly reached above the gleaming white marvel to the chain dangling from the porcelain cistern and gave the coarse wooden handle a single authoritative tug.

David Manderson

UNION RULES

Kenny jumped up.

There was a big guy standing over him. A student from the HNC class – McDaid, McCaig, something like that. Third row from the back of the classroom, over to the left.

He hadn't heard him come in. Although he wouldn't. The door to the workroom to be left open except for lunchtime. Management policy. Students wandering in and out as they liked.

Lank strands of black hair hanging down the big guy's face, some kind of tattoo up his neck, green and gold like the tail of a dragon. Piercings in his lips, big black stones in long droopy earlobes. A grey beanie hat to top it all off. Chewing slackly, heavy jaw moving.

Stupid bastard standing there waiting to be noticed.

'Aye? Whit is it?'

Kenny bobbing up at him, glasses flashing.

'Ye goat ony pho'o paper? Pho'o paper fur room eight?' Accent as thick and dull as pebble glass, Aberdeenshire or something.

'Photo paper? You mean copy paper? Photo paper's something different.'

Kenny shook himself and jiggled his shoulders. The big lad chewed and thought.

'Eh, aye.'

Kenny laughed, showing sharp white teeth, his thin chest heaving, and ran to get it, a wad of new paper in its shiny slick wrapper in the store off the workroom. He brought it out, a full packet, passed it to the guy. Pushed it at him till the big slow guy reached out and took it.

'Hunners a different papers out there.' Kenny at his desk gesturing at the window, the view over the scheme outside, bouncing on his heels. 'Grades, types, finishes – aw sorts. Satin, smooth, matt. Ye no know that?'

The big guy mumbled something. Ambled off, the square of paper under his arm.

Kenny thumped down on his seat. Stupid arsehole whatever his name was, meant to be doing graphic design and didn't have a scoobie, not a clue, no even any interest. Didn't get what he meant. Didn't care either.

Now, where was he?

He tapped his mouse. The image he'd been working on sprang back onto the screen.

Oh aye.

Mouse clicking, images jumping, his eyes tightening, widening, darting.

This to do and then a union meeting at one p.m. Downstairs in the big main hall, everyone there, place packed to the rafters. Crunch time. Again. Cutbacks, shortfalls, mergers. Another offer on the table. Encouraged to apply. No guarantee you'd get it, of course. Dead in the water if you went for it and didn't, bobbing around in the surf waiting for them to finish you off. Encouraged to apply anyway.

Kenny ground his teeth, tightened his mouth, tapped his mouse again, went on the web and started flicking through files, snipping out the pictures, moving them off. Nighttime city skyline, lines of dancing revellers, a neon-lit alley, skyscrapers, big fiery chemical orange sunburst letters. A flier for a gig he was working on, an outside client, a ton in his pocket if he got it done on time. And then he'd a load of marking tonight, a couple of dozen portfolios to get through. But that was no problem. He could knock out a poster like this in a couple of hours. Nothing to it.

Images jumping, collapsing, flitting over each other, bits slipping off and sliding together, slotting into place like a jigsaw.

Aye, yet another fucking union meeting, yet another announcement and then a couple more hours teaching, a few more transferable skills transferred to a couple of dozen of the bastards, slow as fuck and dopey with the heat, the computers on constantly, nine to five every day, hardly alive they seemed sometimes, staring like drowsy cattle at their screens. While he ran about. Getting them paper, getting them through the software, through the fucking work. Keeping on at them, winding them up, poking and prodding – getting them to *do* something, for fuck's sake! Noses to the grindstone, that was the only way! Get them up to professional standards, industry ready, used to working hard, fast. So they could get the jobs, the poor sods, that wis what they came here for, employability they called it these days. Not that there were any jobs out there but they could always freelance if they were halfway good enough, which they weren't, hardly any of them. They'd know all about it then. He'd done it hims—

The phone on his desk purring.

'Aye? Whit is it?'

'Oh hi – is Vicki McGrath there?'

Polite Scottish voice.

'Naw, not at the moment, she's teachin.'

'Oh, eh, this is Laura McKee. It's just – eh, I've got, well, a bit of a problem.'

'I'll tell her to call ye back.'

'See I'm trying to enroll and I can't – I can't get—'

'I'll tell her to call ye. Right. Bye.'

Mouse clicking, images sliding, flitting.

—done it himself before he'd come into this game. Ran his own business for ten years, loved it, the whole thing. But ten years was long enough. His

old boss Eddie from his first design office, Head of Department in the
college by then, they'd always kept in touch. A few part-time hours going:
Eddie'd given his old apprentice the nod. And then up to full-time – he'd
kept the design work going on the side of course. And then the old guy'd
taken the pension and his old sidekick was a senior lecturer himself now,
practically running the place, this bit of it anyway. Who'd've thought it?
Seven years in the college and the place had grown and grown, more class-
rooms, more computers, more and more students, arses on seats, unbelievable
software, the industry changing, getting faster, going digital, but he could
manage it, he could keep up – good pay, pension, a steady job. And then—

'Eh – sorry—'

It was a girl this time hanging over him. Tits in his face like melons almost,
hanging out over her green army vest. Plus a whiff of something, sweat
masked with deodorant. Those rooms were stewing. Lisa something. Dark
hair, big eyes. Year One. Sat down the front.

'Whit is it?'

'Ehhh – memory stick?' She'd her head to one side, her eyes wavering
over the same way, hand up at her hair, twisting a strand round her finger.

Kenny laughed and jumped up, his thin chest pumping.

'Memory stick? Ye no brought one? Ye're supposed to.'

'I kno-ow. I forgo-ot.' She'd a low, sulky voice. She half smiled and moved
her hips and her eyes over to the other side.

'Looks like ye need a memory stick yerself.'

There was an iron cashbox on the window ledge. Kind of lost property
box where they stuck things the students left behind. Keys, coins,
whatever.

'Awright, here's one. Okay?'

'Tha-anks.' She reached for it.

He snatched it back.

'What's up, ye not get it? Whit's the matter wi ye? Eh? Whit's the matter?'

She kept reaching for it half smiling, he kept laughing and pulling it
back. His thin chest bobbed. His teeth showed sharp. Eventually he let her
take it.

'Away ye go then.'

She smiled up one side of her face and walked off. He stood a moment
watching – the vest and the green army trousers disappearing through the
doorway. Lisa … Rodwell, Dobwell, something like that. Totally useless.
Sat down the front and stared at you, fiddling with her hair. Not a clue, not
a decent piece of work all year. Mind like a sieve.

Where did they dig them up? Christ, they came in here, thought they
knew it all, knew all there was to know about art and design – Kenny turned,
stood jigging slightly, up and down, up and down, staring out the window.
Mile after mile of council house rooftops shining wetly after the rain, the

sun coming out over the low hills, the woods along their tops fresh and green. The cemetery, away down there under this eighth-floor window, dark under its trees, all overgrown paths and cracked headstones. They'd shot a bit of a film there. The big school a few blocks away on the other side, bang in the middle of the scheme, they'd used that too, grim grey walls, wire fence and a concrete compound like a prison.

Aye, where the fuck did they find them, pouring in here year after year, scores of them, school leavers with an A in Higher Art wanting to go on to Art School, thinking they were artists – Christ! Hit them with the real stuff, the stuff the employers said they had to have, and that soon sorted out the wheat from the chaff, the ones that had it from the ones that hadn't. Wait'll ye get out there, son.

He sat at his computer. Stuck his headphones on to cut out the world.

Eyes, images, clicks, shapes.

Lunchtime and the union meeting, it was all a game. Stay with the herd, stay in the middle, one eye on the bloke beside you, the other on the pension. Keep your nose clean, your head down and wait. Just like old Eddie. That was the way it was. The way it always would be.

He clicked his way to the BBC site.

Aww Rangers, Ra-angers, what're you doing? Fucking Division *Three*? And for what? A bit of success? Mind Gazza running through on the ball, flicking it up over his head, over that big guy at the back, big blond Scottish bloke they used to call Braveheart, fucking joke, turning him inside out. They'd hammered Scotland that day all right, showed them up for what they were, a fucking wee parochial team. And the other ones that'd come up, Hateley and Roberts and the big guy at the back, the best of the lot, Butcher – and Christ he was well-named – they knew how to play, those English lads, they'd shown the Scots what fitba was all about. Never stood a chance playin for these wee nothing teams, Brechin and Morton and fucking *St Mirren* for Christ's sake. A joke, the whole thing!

Different class.

They should've split away then, the Gers, gone it alone, got themselves into the big time, the English league, and then there wouldn't've been all this stuff now, this fucking shite, this—

A hand tapping the desk beside him in the corner of his eye. A waft of perfume.

It was Vicki. Asking him something, her mouth moving.

He tore off the headphones.

'Are you going down to the meeting, Kenny? The union thing?'

'Aye – eh, naw. No just now. In a minute.'

They were all coming in after class, Sally and Liz and Vicki and Fiona. And they'd all go down to the meeting together and sit in a group, the Graphic Arts section, third or fourth row from the back, but no him. He'd

sit somewhere else, well away from them. He stuck the headphones back
on. Pulled them off again.

'Aw hey, Vicki, that girl phoned. Laura what's-her-face.'

Vicki rolled her eyes. 'Aye right, I'll call her later.'

He went back to clipping the images, aware of the room around him
filling and emptying, the women gathering up their things, jackets and
purses and sandwich boxes, leaving. Vicki walking backwards pointing
and mouthing lock-the-door before she went out.

No, he wouldn't be sitting in the witches' coven, thanks very much. God
knows what they were up to today, never knew where you were with them.
You had to be careful, watch your back. That time Liz'd put the complaint
in about him. Bullying, she'd called it. Bullying! All he'd done was try to
talk some sense into her.

Not that he'd anything against women, not at all. Not that way inclined.
Christ, he was married himself, two times now. So there you were.

Images flashing, leaping, moving.

Better working at lunchtime somehow, you got a bit of peace, bit of a
rest, head-space, the classrooms empty, all the little buggers down the
canteen, you could get on with things, concentrate, finish what you needed
to do, catch your—

But what was the—?

He glanced at the clock, swore. Grabbed his sandwich, jumped up.

*

Bastards!

Dirty stinking pieces of—

Fucking *union* meeting! Job security? Pension at the end of it?

Settlement? Fucking *settlement*? Fucking Scottish government, bunch
of fucking *wankers* in their stupid wee parliament – never done an honest
day's work in their—

Back upstairs, back upstairs and—

'Uh … soarry—'

'Whit? Whit d'ye want?'

It was the lank-haired, daft-eared, gum-chewing one, leaning over the
banister. Catching him at the wrong time, aye, him and all the others who'd
stared white-faced down the tiers of seats in the lecture theatre at the white-
faced union reps staring back up. So *this* was what it came to? A few fat gits
in Edinburgh makin up their minds about things? Think they knew about
colleges? Think they gave a fuck? Think they cared about the working
classes, the ones that needed the jobs?

Fuckin shock of it – waves of it coming off their words.

'Merger will take place possibly within a year … management stress
there is every likelihood of redundancy.'

Every likelihood? Every *fucking* likelihood? Think he didn't know that, think he hadn't seen it coming? Seen it a mile off.

Aye but *when* or *how bad*, that was whit ye never—

'Whit the fuck is it?'

Kenny on the lower step of the eighth-floor flight looking up at the big guy, trembling from head to foot, his thin chest heaving, showing sharp teeth, the big guy backing off at the look on his face, shuffling his feet, mumbling.

'Fuck d'ye want!' Kenny shouted.

'Paper … fur the – fur the—' The big guy brought his hands up.

Kenny lost it then. Felt the world go black. Could hear a voice shouting, his, a voice far away cutting through everything, the rage inside corkscrewing out his mouth, burning out of him like a storm, and he was laughing inside at the same time too, letting it all out, letting it all go – not really seeing the guy in front of him, just the stupid white shocked-looking face, the thick strands of black hair, the slow-moving lips—

useless *bastard*! useless fucking—

—and then he was striding along the corridor narrow chest heaving, smiling, feeling good, like he was flying, swooping through the air with his—

stupid little treacherous arseholes, fucking *politicians*—

Fucking no surrender ya bastards! Independence? Independence fuck all! Vote *no* ya bastards vote fucking *no* and then out with the flags and the songs, the old red white and blue. *Scotland* ya bastard? – ye can stick it, tear it down, tear it down and scrub it off the map, stupid wee nothin country, fucking destroy it, rip it apart brick by brick, them and their fuckin—

god save the queen ya fucking huns and the—

the *union* ya Scottish *bastards*—

get intae ye ya fucking *cunts*!

Heather Marshall

SUBSTRATA

Remember when we rode down the hill beside the primary school, legs stuck out because the pedals on our fixed-wheel bikes turned too fast for us to keep up? Remember the bite of the rain on our cheeks, red and chapped from being out in that harsh winter? Remember coming in? You do, don't you? We dripped a muddy puddle on the floor, tried to mop it up, the pair of us wiping those hopelessly large sheepskin mittens and woolly scarves across it, trying to make it right and instead smearing mud into the wood and the wool runner. 'Go,' you said, there on your knees, 'before he gets here.' I couldn't. It was my puddle too. Besides, I had nearly an hour until dinnertime. What would I have said if I'd walked in the back door, found my mother standing at the kitchen counter, paper spread open, as usual, reading other people's horoscopes? That I'd made a mess and then run away, abandoned my friend to his father, the front room, the choosing of a belt.

He came in, curly hair like yours bouncing on top of his head, his white to your blond, asked what you'd done. The next part, and the next, I'm sure we'd both rather not remember.

Was this the beginning?

What I remember is being left alone in the room with his father, waiting, straining for a sound of my best friend down the hall. The racket of my own heart swirled; my blood swooshed in my ears. I got hotter and hotter as I stood under the gaze of Craig's father. It seemed ages before I heard the creak of the hall cupboard door, so faint I might have conjured it for respite. Mr Sullivan tipped back on his heels, clasped his hands behind him as the slight clink of the belt buckles bumping reached the front room. His face softened. I thought he might smile, plump out his cheeks and show his teeth, yellowed and dull. He rocked a little, heel to toe in his heavy brown lace-ups, striped tie swinging out and back.

When Craig returned to the room, the belt dangled from his hand, shaking. His father commanded him to unzip his trousers, pull them down, bend; Craig's face turned the colour of the poppies we sold for Remembrance Day. I turned away.

'You are to watch, young lady.'

I watched Mr Sullivan. I pulled every ounce of defiance into my eyes, held his. It took me over a decade to realise that was what he wanted. The belt flashed across my vision, cracked against Craig's skin. I held still, rooted, unflinching. My body jumped within itself as he swung once, twice, again, ten times.

'You will pay attention the next time you enter this house.' He dropped the belt. He smiled. He left. I heard the ice, two cubes, clink into his glass. I heard the slosh of liquid that followed, then another, fizzy sound.

I don't write this – I haven't come all this way to drag Craig through my experience of his pain – I skip instead to what happened next.

I went to the window, rain streaking down, while you pulled up your trousers, slid up the zipper, put back the belt. You came to stand beside me, slid your chapped fingers into mine.

'Sorry.' We said it at the same time.

Remember?

We stood, there at the window, silent, until you whispered that the trick was to pick one broad and thick enough to satisfy him. Too flimsy and he'd go back and get the worst of the lot. You had to gauge him in the moments he marched you to the front room, made you name the infraction.

Did you wonder if you might have selected a flimsier belt? Suffered a little less? Did you take any solace from the feel of our palms pressed together, there at the window? I did.

I had to go. By then I was late for dinner and wishing I had the kind of mother who would come roaring down the hill, bang on the door and ask had they not the common courtesy to send a child home on time.

The whole way home – out Craig's back gate and across the grass to the skinny paved path that led to the green and then to my street – the image of Craig's father rocking on his heels felt as though it was emblazoned inside the centre of my forehead. At the same time, the perfect warm roughness of Craig's hands lingered in my palms. I hardly wanted to lift my knife and fork at the dinner table, knowing the cool stainless steel would rob me.

We switched to walking in the woods after that. Spring would be coming soon. We'd found those hatchlings the year before. For years, I thought I was the one who decided to look for old nests in the bare trees. Now I wonder, had a tendril of the phobia begun to grow by then? Was it nests you wanted or the safest places to build them?

In my recollection, we decided to set out the next day, on foot, into the woods, a pad and a pen and a tape recorder to take down our observations, the size of the nest, materials, the surrounding trees. First we knelt, side by side on the skinny bed in your room. I loved the feel of the two of us huddled in that little bump-out in the attic. What is it – ten feet by ten feet? I think we were both glad none of your siblings was around that day.

We opened the book of birds, read sparrow, robin, thrush, blushed at each of the tits – blue, coal, crested, great, long-tailed, marsh, willow. We read

about ones who migrate, who weather the winter, who look for last year's nest
and the ones who build them freshly every time, abandoning the old.

By the time the buds on the trees began to unravel, we were back on our
bikes, thinking ourselves very grown-up at twelve years old, needing a wider
roaming range. We coasted down Kilmabry Road, heads tilted back to watch
a hawk catch invisible drifts of wind. By summer, we wanted the shore, sixteen
miles, one way, farther than you were allowed. We both knew the risk.

I made us ham salad sandwiches, wrapping the slices of tomato separately
in foil so they wouldn't make the bread soggy. While I stood at the end of
the counter, spreading what I hoped was the perfect amount of butter, my
mother asked Craig what was the date of his birthday. I slid the sandwiches
into my rucksack and pressed my palms on Craig's back to usher him out
the back door; my mother stood with her finger on Virgo, proclaiming
something about the moon's transit in Venus and Craig's brilliance shining
through. I could see her, through the window, still standing there when we
rolled off into the street. How long did it take her to realise we were gone?

On the shore, the waves wandered the sea up around us. Farther out, a lone
puffin, bright beaked, spotted us too late and scurried back to his nest between
the rocks. You sat on your haunches, clutched knees to chest. 'He's too far
south,' you whispered. You said you feared for the little bird, at our latitude,
just below Scotland's waist, N 55°34'33", and building his nest alone.

Later, the *he* struck me. It sounded like an assumption my father would
make. I stopped at the top of the hill on Mannock Road, panting. 'How do
you know it was a he?'

Craig smiled as though I was years younger than he. 'It's always the male
Atlantic puffin who builds the nest.' He pushed off, took four strong pedal
strokes and then coasted down the other side of the hill, his heft putting
easy distance between us.

Was it that year that you found the house martins nesting in a hole under
the eaves near your room? You said they are supposed to nest in cliffs like
puffins. Pushed out of their natural habitats, they make do with holes in
houses, offices, whatever presents itself. Was it then that you told me that
fossils of puffins have been found from thirty-four million years ago? That
they have adapted their wings and feathers to be able to swim underwater?
Or was it three years later, when we boarded the train to Fife, and then the
ferry to the Isle of May to see them, safe with their colony of thousands, in
their farthest south habitat, 56°11'16"? I thought, with the power of public
transport, you would soon be safely away. Now I see the tendril of the phobia
had already begun to coil around you.

You huddled in the belly of the ferry, recited facts about how much difference degrees of latitude might make and what other factors matter.

On the island, you settled us beneath a sheltering crag. We watched the puffins waddle in and out of nests the males had tunnelled into the soft strata beside the rocks.

'They live in there, one male and one female, for life,' you said. The wind lifted your curls in all directions. 'He lines the burrow with grass and leaves for her. And then she lays just the one egg.' You took my hand, entwined your long fingers with mine. 'They take turns holding the egg against their brood patch with their wings.'

I laughed at brood patch, made some comment about a love patch, and tugged at yours, the only facial hair you had then. You laughed, too, explained about the birds losing feathers on their bellies near the end of the egg-laying period, about the supplemental set of vessels that bring the blood supply to the surface of the skin to help keep the offspring warm, about the regrowing of the feathers to keep the adults warm at sea.

'We're lucky to see them here,' you said. 'Normally puffins don't find the proper place to thrive below Caithness, at 58°25'00".'

When did you begin to become stuck at the latitude of your room?

We went again, before my father started my family's westward migration. He moved the three of us to various cities on the east coast of the United States. No matter where we landed, we sat at three sides of our huge, polished table. It seemed to get larger at each new location. My mother read his horoscope when she served his evening meal. When I was young, he used to tell her which parts were correct. By the time of the migration, he'd taken to staring straight ahead, one hand planted on each side of his plate, pressing hard against the gleaming wood, as my mother read.

The first few years, we came back annually, but not at the same time each year. On our last trip, we didn't even sit together on the plane. My mother found three seats on which to stretch herself. My father, one over from me, shut his eyes before we were airborne. Later, I came alone.

I felt the pull back to Scotland – to Craig – as a thing beyond words, so primal I might have passed it to offspring. Craig seemed content to stand at the window of his front room. I came to feel that if I was indeed a bird, migrating back and forth over the open sea, I must be doing it in the wrong seasons and with the bright beak of summer long gone.

Do you remember the next-to-last time? I wrote to you that I had followed a boy to Chicago, become pregnant, then abandoned, that I had booked the airfare back to Glasgow.

You drew a map to the place where I was to go for the termination.

You ran out the front door of your house when I came to collect you in my hire car. You called out the directions to a section of the city we'd never dreamed of visiting; you even knew where to park. I followed you on foot from there.

What were you thinking when I grabbed your arm as we released from the crowd, turned down that narrow alley and felt the press of rain-soaked sandstone on either side of us? Was that safer for you?

We had spilled out of a multi-level car park in the edge of the city centre into a tight throng. Craig's pace quickened immediately. I struggled to keep track of his blond curls, bobbing ahead of me as he manoeuvred too deftly between people, like someone possessed.

'Stop,' I said, pulling him close. My breath was heavy. A wave of nausea began to rise. 'You don't have to be here.' I let go, bent and pressed my palms against my thighs. I spoke mostly to Craig's knees, noticing the bony marks in his jeans, faded places that indicated he had been kneeling or else sitting for a long time on his haunches. 'I can find my own way home,' I said.

You bent, lower than I, looked up into my face. Were you on the brink of tears? 'I want to be here,' you said. You stood. 'It's so hard.' Your clenched fist hung at my eye level.

On the way back to your house, suddenly struck by a compulsion to stand in open air, I clutched your knee. 'Stop. I have to get out.' I ran around to the driver's side and pulled you out. You took three gasping breaths and then bolted to the holly trees at the edge of the woods where we had rested as children.

Standing between the holly and chestnut, you pointed to two nests, one low, near the trunk of the chestnut, the other messy, high, near the edge of a branch. 'Look how different they are, Nellie,' you said. You shimmied away from me, into the branches of the chestnut. I called out to you, saying you could come, escape, migrate with me. 'Did you know that all the chestnuts in America are dead?' you said. Your back was to me, head tilted slightly back.

Do you remember that second trip to Caithness, when you told me that your father had explained how some girls became soiled goods. If just the sex act made someone too stained to claim, what had I just done in Glasgow?

I thought you were disgusted with me.

Craig's father, by then, had begun to shake. The last time I saw him, he was sipping his first gin of the day, neat, looking so true in the cut-glass tumbler. He needed both hands to hold on, there at the shiny table, eyebrows furrowed, knocking it back, then thumping the glass down on the table. A little sloshed over the side. He put one finger in the liquid, making the dots join.

'Mother,' he yelled. 'Mess.'

She started out from the kitchen, wiping her hands on her apron, dark eyes shining.

'I'll get it, Mum,' Craig said.

'Do it right.'

While Craig wiped, his father stood, pushed back the chair, left it out from the table. He caught my eye, smiled his yellow smile, and marched out the back door. I almost exhaled, and then he returned, bending to nestle his head on Craig's mother's shoulder and reaching around her with a bunch of perfect honeysuckle blossoms he must have plucked from the vines that grew wild just outside the high, brick wall that enclosed their back garden.

After that time in the holly and chestnut trees, I drove, alone, from Chicago, west. I don't remember what roads I took, with the few belongings that mattered crammed into my hatchback, to get to the edge of the continent. Your photo, propped on my dash, led me. I stopped at 45°52'54", nearly 10° south of where I began. If my mother read any of this in the horoscopes, she gave no indication.

I came once more after that, at Christmas time. I stood on the front steps and asked you to go to Caithness.

'If you'd said that's what you wanted,' you said. 'I could have planned.'

You put one hand on each of my elbows, pulled me inside, closed the door and then pushed me into the front room. Beside the hearth stood the same silver tree that had been there when we were children. You took my hand, your fingers still long, smoother than I remembered them, and so perfectly warm.

'Nell,' Craig said. He faced me, his curls still thick and a little too long, shrouding his face.

'Craig.' His father's voice, following the thump of the glass, hurtled down the hall.

I couldn't watch whatever it had become.

'Come with me,' I said.

'Craig.' The voice this time accompanied by the rhythm of footsteps.

I slid into Craig's hand a slip of paper bearing my new address. 'Haven't you always wanted to fly?'

When I first left, you wrote page after page. I still have all your letters, tied in a bundle.

Craig's mother contacted me, nearly a decade after that last migratory journey. *Dear Nell,* she typed, in an email. *I hope this is the right Nell. Please reply, even if you want to hear no more, or are unwilling to do as I ask.* She'd racked her brain to think of what had got him out of his room in the past.

Didn't you two have an afternoon in Glasgow? It was the farthest, apparently, Craig had been since the agoraphobic episodes began.

She says Craig has been in there for the month since his father died. He took his place in the receiving line at the funeral. As the crowd moved towards them, Craig walked briskly away. They thought he would come out in a day or a week, as he had before. One of his brothers suspects that he climbs out the window and moves from ledge to ledge down the side of the house. No one has actually seen this.

Did your mother tell you I was coming? Did you get my letter? She isn't sure.

The last season you wrote, a spring, a rainy one for me, some years after my last migration, each of your letters contained only an image of a nest or an egg or a bird. The last featured a bird tumbling from a nest, one wing outstretched. I didn't know how to reply. I'm sorry.

The excuse I gave myself was that my father had tired of my mother reading his future to him. Perhaps she was, too often, wrong. Or right. He remarried and moved to Maine. My mother migrated south. She lives in Florida, at 27°56'N, her skin growing hard and dark. I imagine her a turtle, huddled near the dunes, her lone hatchling having scurried towards the sea in the moonlight, floated away, not returning to lay her own eggs. Mother still reads horoscopes. She calls when there's doom or love on the horizon. I left her clucking to my voice mail, closed the door on her predictions to cross the broad body of land and then the wide sea to return to where I began. I realise, now, how well I have adapted to my new latitude. How long will I be able to sit here outside his door, feeding notes underneath, waiting for a sighting? Am I foolish to imagine that now, at last, I could find the words to lure him from his nest?

Will you come with me now? Will you come to Cannon Beach? Sit with me on the edge of another continent? We can carry our memories there, build a fire on the beach in the evening, toss the pages we'd like to shed on the flames, watch the edges blacken and curl. Come with me and watch our ashes rise, watch the wind pull them away. There is always a breeze. In the morning, we can awaken, there on the beach, just before dawn. You can slip your hand in mine as we walk to Haystack Rock, where the tufted puffins nest. By the time the town rises, they will have returned to their tunnels, safely cradled within the rock itself. We can watch as they scurry in, these tufted puffins, not quite so round as the ones we watched years ago, and with comical yellow tufts on their heads.

When tufted puffins make their nests, when they dig their tunnels into the strata, through the grass and soil and into the soft heart of the rock, the female works just as hard as the male. They are lovely to see.

R. A. Martens

THE BIOVOR AGREEMENT

Dawn at the three-acre Biovor compound, and nature, having lain quiet and sly in the dark, grows raucous with the rising sun. The Fuel Creation Plant hums away inside its sealed enclosure and Sheena, wife of director Doug Grant, opens her eyes at their home in another part of the compound, trying to discern the uncommon sound that woke her. It has stopped. Maybe she dreamt it. She swings her feet out of the bed, not waking her sleeping husband, and reaches for her dressing gown.

Outside the closed curtains of the Grants' bedroom, the source of the sound has crawled, dragging, injured, across the damp grass of their lawn and into a wooded area at the edge, leaving a slick, dark trail. A man in a hazmat suit observes from the centre of the lawn, lifting the head covering to wipe the sweat from his face, his cheeks red with exertion as they huff out misty breath into the cool half-light.

'Yup,' he says. 'You're done. Let's see what happens.'

The door of the Grants' house opens, and he turns his head at the noise. The director's wife is standing there half dressed.

'Mrs Grant.' He touches the side of his head, an unconvincing nod at deference. 'A little early for you to be out, isn't it?'

'Good morning, Brighton.' She pulls the gown tighter around her. 'Something woke me. Early for you, too.'

'Patrol. Security chief's work is never done. You should go back to bed.'

'I have work of my own, thank you.'

They wait, each refusing to cede the territory to the other. Eventually, Brighton says, 'Well, I must be about my business.'

'Yes,' says Sheena. He moves off.

Back in the bedroom, unable to return to bed since it has become an instruction from Brighton, she sits heavily down on it to wake her husband.

'Brighton was outside just now,' she says.

'What time is it?' Doug reaches for the bedside clock.

'Exactly,' says Sheena. '"On patrol", he said.'

'So?'

'In a hazmat suit.'

'So? He's thorough. Come back to bed.' He reaches an arm around her waist, and tries to pull her towards him.

'I can't, I have to see to the staff.' She wriggles herself free, and stands up. 'There's something about that man ...'

Doug sighs and lies back. 'Don't start that again, he's a good guy. We're lucky to have him; people who understand loyalty are thin on the ground, these days.'

'But we don't know anything about him,' she says. She feels her unbuyable heart writhe and twist within her at Doug's easy confidence in the stranger.

Doug rolls his eyes. 'I know the stuff that matters.'

'What if—' She waits for Doug to finish a weary sigh, and presses on. 'What if SpillCorp spun us a line so we'd take him on; relieve them of an embarrassment? What if he took the rap for that "political situation"' (she lifts and kinks her fingers to surround the obfuscating and disturbing phrase) 'because he *caused* it? I've heard things about their operation in Chile—'

Doug tugs the bedcover back towards him, irritated. 'You should know better than to listen to media bullshit. We've had our share of lies printed about Biovor, haven't we?'

That is true. But just because the Biovor stories were lies, it doesn't necessarily mean the SpillCorp ones are. Truth and lies are so tangled together everywhere these days, it's a life's work to sift them – and Sheena already has a life's work to do. SpillCorp's violations or lack thereof will have to be somebody else's business; for Sheena they are no more than a contributing factor to her pressing unease with Brighton. 'Loyalty', she thinks, sniffing in disgust and folding her arms. The man had better be swimming in the bloody stuff, after they paid off the gambling debts that came as part of the Brighton package. If only she could give Doug a reason for the feeling that seeps through her when the man is around, as though cold things were making their way into her skin. Doug needs reasons; feelings are her remit, not his. She will just have to find a way to translate her feelings about Brighton into language Doug can understand.

It is a rare occasion when Sheena wishes her husband were more overtly empathetic. Mostly, it is supremely restful to be with Doug after all those thankless years of fundraising for supercilious charities. 'A roaring bag of egos, same as any other organisation,' he had said when they met at a benefit dinner. 'It's just a competition for who's the most outraged, instead of who's the richest.' She had dissolved in ecstasies of laughter and release. Many of her erstwhile 'colleagues' had their opinions about Doug, even after he funded her Foundation. He'd provided the means to build over a hundred clinics in the first year they were together. He is as compassionate as any of those self-righteous bores, if not more – but quietly so; he does not drown her out. She leaves him in bed, and goes to the kitchen.

Afsana is there, baking already. She looks up, and Sheena congratulates herself inwardly that she no longer flinches, even slightly, at the woman's ruined face. It had been a devastating blow to discover a tiny minority of the women were not robust enough for the decontamination process. Of course, Sheena had insisted they be given work at the compound – people in the outside world could be so cruel to the disfigured, and these women had suffered enough. Their presence here serves to remind Sheena constantly of the decision she made, and requires her to make it anew every day, strengthening her resolve: yes, this is necessary.

'Early, Mrs Grant.'

'Yes, Afsana.' She likes to use their names, pronounced properly. *Afsana*, it is, the stress falling on the first syllable. 'Something woke me, and I decided I may as well make the most of the day.'

'Breakfast? Mr Grant?'

'He's still sleeping. I'll take some cereal.'

Afsana nods, without making eye contact. Sheena hates to use the word, given everything the woman has been through, but Afsana is, undeniably, sullen. Sheena corrects herself. She cannot imagine how she would be, in Afsana's place. One must never judge. But her thoughts trip again to the thousands of women she has delivered unharmed to freedom, and judgement there is hard to avoid. Not one of them ever sought her out before leaving; she has not received a single letter or call in the three years since the plant began work, and it rankles. Doug tells her she was a fool if she ever expected thanks, and of course, that is not why she does what she does. But. But. She has sacrificed so much for women's freedom – living in this compound, on this island, far from her friends and family. A little gratitude would make it easier to bear.

When Doug developed the Biovor Fuel Creation Process, it had finally offered the free world an escape from its servility to oil-producing despots. There was a problem, of course – wasn't there always? Costs required that workers commit to a full year in the sealed plant, and the unions (men who, she itched to tell them, did not know they were born) had haggled over insignificant details of the Plant, and eventually walked away. Doug came home from the final failed negotiation to find Sheena in tears at her computer screen. One of her clinics had been treating a woman for months for the burns inflicted by a jealous husband. She had finally left, only for them to hear today that he had killed her.

'I can't bear it,' Sheena sobbed, as Doug stroked her back. 'If only I could get them *out* of those vile countries; keep them safe.'

Doug, brilliant Doug, saw the solution to both their problems.

She wished she understood the Fuel Creation Process, but it was *so* complex – there was no point in asking; her brain would fog up within two sentences. Science was Doug's remit, not hers.

'Promise me it's safe,' she had said.

'We've done two thousand safety checks on the plant,' he replied. 'No exaggeration. It's way beyond legal requirements, but the unions are asking for more just to throw their weight around. It's *absolutely* safe, I swear.'

She held his head in her hands and tried to read his mind. He twisted away.

'Look, the decontamination process is not nice, okay? But it's safe and it's short. There's no getting around it, I'm afraid.' He smiled. 'And any woman who's given birth will wonder what the fuss is about.' He looked her in the eyes for a long time. 'That's it. That's the only thing.'

'Okay,' said Sheena. 'Let's do it.'

Doug had met with the government the following week. Women treated at the clinics were offered work in the plant, with citizenship on completion of their contract. The Biovor Agreement meant her Foundation could finally offer women the real, concrete, permanent safety of emigration to a civilised country. It was their only way out. She reminds herself of this, again. The sun is up; she will eat her breakfast in the garden.

Brighton has already eaten breakfast. He is sprawled on his sofa in the house next door, his hazmat suit tossed in the steriliser and an online poker game flickering on the screen in front of him. His housekeeper limps in, her drab brown Biovor staff overalls shapeless and uninviting. The baggy trouser leg hanging over her messed-up useless limb twitches and dangles beside her crutch. They are all like this, the ex-plant workers in the compound. They have gimpy legs like hers, or eaten-away arms or horror-movie faces. It's like a zombie apocalypse around here; enough to put you off your food.

'I bring you a drink, Mr Brighton?'

'No,' he says. 'Any calls?'

'No,' she says. She raises her eyes from the floor where she has very quickly learned to keep them when her new boss is around, and the look on his face sends them quickly back, as she rephrases: 'No, sir.'

Brighton has that satisfied feeling of a good breakfast on top of a good workout. It was very interesting, the interlude with the woman he took out of decontam last night. Shame he had to wear the hazmat gear for it – such a barrier to real interaction – but it was stimulating, nevertheless. Brighton is a man who requires intense amounts of stimulation from his work. He has always been very interested in people, how they tick; the fascinating differences and similarities between how they will behave in extreme circumstances. Security is a good career for someone with an enquiring mind such as his, but this latest posting is dry. He wasn't made for patrolling fences, he was made for dealing with conflict, and it annoys him when he has to manufacture it. He thinks of Mrs Butter-Wouldn't-Melt this morning; standing at the door covering herself up as though he was some rapist. She wishes. Those do-gooder types always want it rough, deep down. Time is dragging again already; things will have to be nudged along.

'Get me my radio,' he shouts to his housekeeper, wondering whether she might have the capacity to be a fascinating person.

The handheld radio left on Doug's bedside table emits a piercing crackly burst, hauling him out of sleep. He answers it and listens for a moment, then says, 'Call the hazmat team, right now'; stumbles into his trousers and goes to look for his wife. The cook tells him Sheena is on the patio, and he rushes out to herd her indoors.

'That was Brighton, there's been an absconder from decontam,' he says as she protests his rough, urgent manner. 'There's a chance she came this way.'

'A what?' she asks. 'From decontam?' This has never happened before. 'Did Brighton say how it happened?'

Doug frowns an injunction against any comments Sheena might be about to make on the subject of Brighton, tired of her unsubstantiated dislike. She tries to shake her thoughts into shape over her misgivings, but something refuses to make sense.

'Why would a woman throw it all away when she's so close to getting her citizenship?' Sheena asks.

Doug shrugs. 'No point trying to understand it.' He means, do not question Brighton.

Sheena sees frustration rising in him, and does not want to provoke it with old arguments. She regroups; banishes Brighton from her thoughts for a moment, to see how blame looks when draped on the woman. Here's something: 'If she doesn't care about herself, couldn't she at least care that she could contaminate others?' Yes, that is not inconsiderable.

'Well gee, I guess not.' Doug pulls a face. 'Really, are you still surprised that they only think of themselves? My beautiful wife and her unending faith in humanity.' He kisses her. 'Don't worry, Hazmat are on their way. You'll be out in the garden again in no time.'

If this woman's foolishness results in an innocent worker being contaminated, thinks Sheena, I will find it very simple to take sides. However damaged someone is, they must take responsibility for their actions. Decontam may be unpleasant, but it is *necessary*, to protect the women as much as everyone else. The materials they have been working with, whilst absolutely safe within the controlled environment of the plant, must not be allowed outside.

Doug rubs his face. 'I'm just going to make a call; I need to make sure there's no chance of the press getting hold of this.' He goes to his office.

Biovor has few enough friends in the press already. Despite, or, as Sheena thinks in her more cynical moments, *because of* the contribution she and Doug have made to human rights and democracy. Of course, the journalists all spout their bile, their talk of Foundation clinics as 'recruitment centres,' from within buildings powered entirely by Biovor fuel – but it would be inconvenient to acknowledge this. Just as it would be inconvenient to ask them what their own proposals might be for the emancipation of women from oppressive regimes. These people will not allow that the problems faced are complex, and do not have easy solutions. The fact is, when such core values are at stake, the processes by which they are ensured may not be ideal. This is the way the world is. Compromises have to be made, and high-minded press and academics would rather sit around sniping, *sniping* at the people who trudge through the mire of compromise, than enter it themselves.

There, she has worked herself into a state again. She goes to the kitchen for some chamomile tea, and calls for Afsana, who doesn't answer.

The cook is outside hobbling across the lawn, following the trail of blood and clinging for support to her friend Deka's good arm. She stumbles, rushing towards the end of the trail whilst unable to bear the reaching of it. Eventually, she does. She falls to her knees, hit square in the solar plexus by what she sees. Her mouth twists and collapses, writhes in an effort to form shapes that will let something out. Small squeaks and stillborn croaks are all that will come until Deka puts a hand on her shoulder and releases from her a huge and unearthly howl.

'Hush now,' says Deka, pulling back her friend's hand as it reaches to touch the body of her sister. 'Don't touch, you know you can't touch. Hush,' she says again, wrapping an arm around Afsana's shoulder; holding her away. 'I know, I know.'

What does she know? She knows what it is like to see your loved one's body after decontam. She knows that there is no way to escape from decontam, much as you might wish it; that you can only leave when someone permits it; and that, therefore, someone permitted this. She knows also the pressure of keeping almost all of yourself inside a tight, screaming compartment while what is left whispers, over and over, 'I am still alive, still alive, still alive.' She pushes herself up and holds out her hand.

'We have to go. If they find us here, they'll call the new man.'

Her friend's eyes widen for a moment: they have all heard about the new man, who is a certain kind of man; excited by certain kinds of things. Maybe he will not be here long if he allows his entertainment to spill onto the boss's lawn, but for now he could come at any minute. Deka gently shields Afsana's eyes as she stands, and turns her away, back towards the house.

'Shit,' says Doug at the front door, minutes later. 'You sure?'

The Hazmat guy looks at the floor. 'No, boss, not sure. But there's a definite risk. They were seen outside. We can't be sure they didn't touch the body.'

'Shit,' says Doug again. 'Fine, right, tell Brighton to take them to decontam.'

The Hazmat guy moves off.

'And tell him to do it fucking quietly,' says Doug. 'My wife is going to have my balls when she finds out they're gone – I want to delay that as long as possible, if you don't mind.'

The Hazmat guy nods, and Doug goes to find his wife.

Sheena, however, having exited through the kitchen in search of Afsana, is already outside. Brighton (she guesses from the size of the suit) is holding Afsana's hands behind her back and putting on handcuffs, while a Hazmat guy does the same with Deka, the gardener. There is a thick, opaque tarpaulin over something on the ground beside them. Sheena takes a deep breath, and looks Brighton in the eye, through the Perspex window of his suit. He is angry and happy at the same time; excited and frightening; a monster.

'These are my staff,' she says. 'Let them go. That's an order.'

'Sorry, Mrs Grant, I can't do that. They've been in contact with the contaminated body.'

'Body?' says Sheena, looking at the tarpaulin. 'The absconder died?'

'Most certainly did,' says Brighton, smiling. 'Hardly a shock, is it? They pretty much all do in there, eh? The gimps like these two here are the lucky ones.' He waves a hand at Afsana and her companion, and sniffs. 'At least, they *were*, until they touched the body. Have to go back in now, don't you?' he says, pulling Afsana's face round to his. She is grey with tears, and shaking, held up only by his grip on her arm.

Sheena does not register the women any more: Brighton's words have scooped out her guts and laid them on the ground in front of her.

'Doubt they'll manage a second time, Mrs Grant,' he says, pulling Afsana away and speaking over his shoulder. 'Best find yourself some new staff.'

Doug will tell her it's all lies. And she will want so much to believe him, to hold the monster Brighton responsible for her broken heart. She will perhaps even succeed for a short while. It is not possible, after all, for so many women to disappear without questions being asked. Only, women disappear all the time in other countries – why not here? For a government that is heavily invested, as hers is in the success of Biovor, it would be a small thing to hide the disappearance of a few thousand immigrant women. When she at last gathers the courage to seek and find the evidence that what Brighton said is true, Doug will pretend shock; he will need someone to blame, someone to soak it all up. Brighton's loyalty was a prescient investment; a sturdier thing than her own after all.

All those women who never came to thank her before leaving the compound: why didn't she try to find out about them? Because she didn't want to know – what other reason is there, ever? She was too tired to hear the answer. She sees them now in her mind, leaving in piles of bags, like so much rubbish. All those women she rescued, all those ungrateful women.

David Miller

LOOKING FOR WILLIAM ARCHER
On trying to make life real, again

From where, precisely, does an author create someone – some body: the eyes you'd like to look at, the lips you yearn to taste – when writing a novel?

Philip Roth put it like this, in an interview with *The Paris Review*, and I hope I see what he means:

> I'm also trying to believe in what I've written, to forget that it's writing and to say, 'This has taken place', even if it hasn't. The idea is to perceive your invention as a reality that can be understood as a dream. The idea is to turn flesh and blood into literary characters and literary characters, into flesh and blood.

It is something that has bewildered me for over twenty years, not only working as a literary agent – where *do* these imaginary people come from? – but before that and since then, as an honestly innocent reader ready to be corrupted by words. On one level, I desire to know how a fictional person is born psychologically so I can hold that figure up to the light to see some centre hold – but, if there is a hint of manufactured flaw, the whole thing falls apart and I am disappointed, the book dismantles itself. When it works – well, it is the miracle of fiction: when an author presents someone who you talk about as if they were here, if she or he had actually existed – I think of Emma Bovary, whoever Kurtz is, Jay Gatz, Claudia Hampton, George Smiley, David Lurie – it's when you see that writing can transform the way we all can see the world.

A description of a conversation with Joseph Conrad gives an insight into how a novelist can secularly reverse transubstantiation and make flesh into word.

'Look', said he, 'see that man over there?'

I looked up and saw an oldish man with a short straggly beard, a big nose and a gaunt face, bending over his plate, concentrating on his food.

Conrad said, 'You know, that man – he does so-and-so, and so-and-so', and he began spinning a yarn. Listening, I looked at the man, and was astonished at how true the story rang – I got to believing it.

'I'll go and ask him', said I.

'Don't do that. It probably isn't so, but it might be so.'

The creation of life and character challenges me again, this act of imagining the imaginable, as I've now begun purposefully to chart a second novel. I had no intention of writing more fiction after my first novel was published. I had nothing else necessary to say. That book had come from a strange, dark fusion of grief after the death of my father together with my slight obsession with a woman called Lilian Hallowes, a woman I had never known (she was a secretary who worked with Joseph Conrad from 1904 until his death twenty years later, so I hadn't much of a chance) but a woman with whom I felt profound affinity.

The book I have embarked on – in my head, read around, thought about, begun on scraps of paper – took shape in an equally sudden way. I was clearing books in shelves from a bedroom and hadn't looked at an Ibsen play since I was at school (*An Enemy of the People* for 'A' level) over thirty years ago. I had seen one play – Paul Schofield, Vanessa Redgrave and Eileen Atkins in *John Gabriel Borkmann* in the summer of 1996 – and had been struck by its humanity. I took down the black-spined Penguin Classics and then, a day or so later, started reading a play I knew nothing about: *When We Dead Awake*.

It is Ibsen's last play, a strange dreamy piece about a sculptor and his wife, on a holiday retreat after his return from exile to Norway. The sculptor and his wife peck at each other, but not in a nice way (at one point he says to her, 'I must have someone who can complete me,' suggesting, perhaps, she can't), and then he sees a woman, a figure in black, slowly revealed to have been the inspiration or muse or would-be-fuck behind his greatest, most notable work. There is talk of art, of life, of love, of dying and the whole thing ends with deaths in an avalanche. It is a superb, inspiring mess.

Go: stage that! I thought, as I finished reading, which had me wondering. Where *was* the play first staged? The answer: the Theatre Royal, Haymarket, on 16 December, 1899. Why in London, not Norway? I found out Norway's National Theatre was opened in 1899, five years before that country became a nation. I dug around to find out who translated the play, slowly piecing together that the performance was given (for complicated copyright reasons) by the publisher William Heinemann together with five others, all of them now somehow pivotal to this infant book – most particularly, an actress born in Kentucky, Elisabeth Robins, and the theatre critic, playwright and champion of our own National Theatre – as well as one of Ibsen's first translators – William Archer.

It turned out Archer had been born in Scotland. I found out he had been born in Perth and grew up for a while in Larvik, in Norway, where his family were shepherds and fishermen. I thought of Archer, Perth and Norway, where I had never been, and thought of landscape and Scottishness and the theatre and without really knowing why I began writing, on the night of 15 November 2011. The first paragraph read then like this:

William is sitting in the stalls.

It is taking ages, but he understands why, now.

He hears the director's voice: 'Slowly,' and suddenly – how does memory work? – he is back, outside Perth, and with his father.

He is stood in a stream and his hands are in very cold water. He thinks, now, he might be three. He is standing in the stream as is his father and the water is above their ankles. His shoes are not just wet. His mother will be cross. His feet are now cold, getting colder, as are his hands, and they lie on a gravelly bed of mud and sand and stone and

'Slowly,' his father whispers, his mottled hands, their stubby fingers, are in the water too,

'No, no,' and he says nothing for a while and William stands in the water, finally sees the fishes coming, and his hands are almost white with cold but he waits and his father then says

'Now!'

and William doesn't even think. His palms flick up – two fish leapt in the air: one lands on the bank, the other slithers back into the water.

It is then that William knows he is in love.

There was my William Archer, but he was in a stream, as well as in a theatre. I was obviously happier with him in Perthshire as a child than as a man on the London stage (and rightly so: I soon found out there was no director of *When We Dead Awake,* and Archer wasn't in the stalls but actually on stage) but reading this passage now I see what I knew but did not realise then: William is not just with his father, but here he is my father, who had grown up in Perthshire near Bridge of Earn, had told me stories of 'guddling' with his twin brother (another William – Will, to me – but perhaps also my second son, Billy), and those hands and fingers are seen in my mind, my father's: Jock's. The words he says are mine, as is the view I have for him there, innocently cloudless skies over Perthshire or Larvik. But also I have made him one of my sons, as another voice – his father, a grandfather – is guiding him. Most of all, I am still surprised by that last line. *It is then that William knows he is in love.* It seems like a hurried, unconscious challenge to myself: *You've written a book about death: can you write a book about love?*

I began looking for William Archer. I read more about Ibsen. I took an opportunity to travel to Oslo, and was struck by the light there – I was there in December – how I woke in darkness and almost finished lunch in dusk. I went with a friend to Ibsen's apartment and we slipped off our shoes to stand in a sensitively restored space, where this complicated divided self had spent his last years, the two of us asking the guide questions she'd not really been prepared to answer. I was taken to galleries to look at Norwegian art – not just Munch, but the divine, deep, almost desperate blues of Sohlberg. Oslo is tiny, but Norway is dramatically huge in scope. *When We Dead Awake* takes place in the mountains: I have yet to go there, but I shall. I also visited Stockholm – made a trip to Strindberg's flat, flinching at his narrow bed, the anally tidy, almost schoolboyish desk with pens lined up, the balcony where he greeted crowds before he died – as I attempted to understand recent Scandinavian history, by which I mean since 1860. The similarities between the places where Ibsen and Strindberg each died still fizz in my head.

I spent a fortnight in Edinburgh during the London Olympics, every now and then thinking of William Archer as he might have been had he walked either way from Howe Street to Royal Circus, the muscles in his legs tightening as he stomped towards the ramparts of the Castle, or tottering as he walked down, looking over the blue of the Firth of Forth to the dazzling quilt of yellows and greens that make up a slice of Fife. Or just looking at grey: fifty, sixty, seven hundred shades of grey. Or looking at the railings on Wemyss Place and Abercromby Terrace and thinking of what Scottish society wanted to keep out, what it would let in. I was reminded of something Bruce Chatwin wrote of Robert Louis Stevenson and Edinburgh:

> In the winter the city slumbers all week in blue-faced rectitude, only to explode on Saturday evenings in an orgy of drink and violence and sex. In some quarters the pious must pick their way to church along pavements spattered with vomit and broken bottles.

And every now and again I'd see a man at a bus stop, a moustache, tobacco-stained fingers, a reddened nose, a wart on the hand of a woman holding a shopping trolley – all moments, features, none of which I wrote down but somehow have been stored and will bubble up when I write the book, an attempt at gaining veracity.

*

I took my nieces, mother and Billy for a day out in Dunfermline. You would be hard pressed to find William Archer there but he surprised me in myself, in my theatrical disdain for the land of my father.

Having played thirty-two holes of pirate-themed Crazy Golf, because it understandably started raining, we went indoors to play what seemed like three more hours of ten-pin bowling (none of this helped by the fact that my mother became ruthlessly competitive throughout the day, behaving as if she was in a sudden death play-off in the Women's Open at Carnoustie and not diddling in the drizzle with four under-thirteens in North Queensferry).

Dunfermline has two train stations, one near the Leisure Park near enough to a hospital, which was where we needed to be. A bus drew up.

My (by then pretty pooped) mother said, 'Ooh, this is the bus to the hospital.' I said, calmly, that this wasn't the bus, that we needed a 72C or the 82C. My mother insisted, pointing at the passengers already on board.

I said, 'Mum, every bus in Scotland looks as if it's going to a hospital, because everybody here looks so bloody ill.'

It was the William Archer line. He may never have been capable of saying it, but in my imagination he could be – even better, he would.

*

The most recent passage I have written reads like this:

> He stands up and sees there is blood where shit should be. The paper in his hand is sopping, the liquid splashed to pinkish tears against the dirty white ceramic.
>
> 'It doesn't look good,' he thinks as he sits.
>
> 'Slightly worrying,' said Dr Mason a week after the first incident. 'Happened before?'
>
> 'No,' he said. 'But I am worried. I haven't been, a, the, I've not been – um – solid, for a few months. I've never seen – it's never been just blood before.'
>
> 'So, you've been loose.'
>
> 'Loose is one way of putting it.' He looked at his cuffs licked by dry grime.
>
> 'I assume you eat cabbage,' was what the doctor said next.
>
> 'Oh yes. And I drink milky tea.'
>
> 'Don't we all – don't we all. Do you want a smoke?' Mason asked.

Where did this snippet come from?

Thinking about it, I had a comic doctor in *Today* based on the description of a locum in Jessie Conrad's memoir, so there's a nod towards that, and my grandfather was a GP who worked near a place called Elmer's End (as a child I conspired with myself as to why and how my grandfather might have killed Elmer). His wife, my grandmother, is either mercifully, or mercilessly, still (at the time of writing) with us, aged ninety-six, a lolling head with barely no hair, her lips squashed into a meaningless space by her toothlessness, her voice no longer capable of talk, more a raw, animal squawk; her blackened legs like thick twigs. She is barely living in a communal house in North Berwick. My mother and her sisters go to see her as frequently as they can bear to do so and, the Sunday before we went to Crazy Golf, my second son and I joined her on one of those trips. Billy needed a pee when we got there: I see now that that is where the ceramic bowl comes from, for the bowl was not as clean as it could have been when he used it, streaked with shit and some blood. And probably the cabbage, as the place was pervaded by that smell and the aroma of disinfectant (I've left that out, anachronistic). The cigarette is there as relief, for someone other than me would have lit up. And also this, which I still don't know: is the man on the pan William Archer, or someone else entirely?

Fiction has to be real. It may be about bringing the dead alive again, but it's also about life, about how people respond and communicate to now as well as then. The funniest thing about this book – which isn't written and doesn't yet have a title – is that it took me months to discover that the first performance of *When We Dead Awake* was given on a Saturday morning, by a cast of six, in Norwegian, before an audience of – probably – nobody. Miss Robins had come to England because her first husband had committed suicide by throwing himself into a river weighed down by a suit of medieval armour – none of that Virginia Woolf pebbles-in-the-pocket stuff. It turned out William Heinemann (who spoke the part of the Hotel Manager) had ludicrously large ears and was madly in love with Robins, but she was sleeping with William Archer, who was married.

You couldn't make it up.

So. I am trying to do so again (that word 'so') and – thus perform the Lazarus trick that most fiction is and rightly resists against – trying to make flesh and blood word, and put skin on dry bones and, whilst doing so, I'll be doing something which Henrik Ibsen wrote about in his plays, finding something else that, for a while, makes me look at the world in a different way, makes me question if these word people are real or could have been, makes me understand a culture and a time and a situation, and makes me think about what my book should be about, which is love. All that will help complete me as I undertake this but all I can hope now is that whenever I have finished it, if it is ever published, if anybody ever reads it, what might happen is that that reader may also glimpse what I have imagined, they might see someone I have thought up to be real, they may feel a little like I do as I continue on this way.

Lyn Moir

UNLESS

Ten years, and I've just seen
the horizon headland's not a gentle slope
to beach, but wrinkled cliffs ...

unless a giant hand with spoon
has overnight scooped up red ribs of earth,
shaping the coast again to its desire;

unless my hawk-clear distant vision
has unveiled another layer so what I saw
was just a backdrop now hauled up;

unless this is the clearest afternoon
this decade; unless I've drunk
more than my cellar ever held

in one fell swoop; unless ...

M. J. Nicholls

A DISQUISITION ON INADEQUACY AMONG THE
SALARIED CLASSES

Jed wants to talk to Jim about the deep-seated fears of inadequacy, impotence and humiliation that he faces on a daily basis, but Jim is already talking about the new Kevin Kline movie. Jed won't find a window before Jan, Jim's girlfriend, arrives and asks for a summation of the conversation so far, leading to a repetitive analysis of the merits of Kevin Kline from his amusing stints in *A Fish Called Wanda* and *In & Out* to his absence from our screens in recent times. At which point the moment to discuss Jed's deep-seated fears has passed since Jim can only squeeze in drinks with Jed on Fridays due to film and gig and Jan commitments, and Jed can't see Jim nowadays without Jan, and Jed can't open up to Jan because Jan is a mocker and a talker: the information about Jed's deep-seated fears would pass to Jan's friends with various cutting asides tacked on, leaving Jed forever embarrassed before Jan's intolerant face. So Jed will wearily contribute to the banter once Joe, Jon and Jay arrive, but his attempts to make light-hearted remarks and suppress the throbbing need to express his deep-seated fears to Jim will lead to his gradual phasing out of the group through his unmemorableness and occasional dourness, leaving him without a friend in which to confide his deep-seated fears of inadequacy, impotence and humiliation.

Hello, dear reader! Perhaps you can help solve this narrative problem. There's this rather upset chap who can't see the point of living. Poor fellow has lost his wife and daughter in a car accident, and now he feels nothing but pain, loneliness and despair. What do we tell him?

    a) Snap out of it, old boy! People come and go, that's the circle of life for you. Hakuna Matata!

    b) Seek medical help: psychiatric counselling or antidepressant medication.

    c) Become what the youngsters call a player, have some fabulous sexual intercourse!

    d) Grieve. Oh, he should grieve, feel that pain month after month, year after year. Cry, cry, cry.

You selected:

    a) Don't be ridiculous! No reader would believe such a casual dismissal of two life-long emotional bonds!

    b) And what an exciting narrative that would make, I shouldn't think!

c) So soon after his loss? What is he, a monster?

d) Here's your art. A meticulous dissection of pain so people might better understand their own pain and be more compassionate towards the pain of others. Huzzah!

I sat down to add another fragment to this fragmented narrative, but an email blipped in my inbox. Serious. Responding took me an hour. And yes, I have tried disconnecting the internet, but it's in the air now, it's wireless, it'll always find some way of seeping into the laptop. And so I pottered around for a while being neurotic and anxious, mapping out the ramifications of this (actually semi-) serious happening and exaggerating all the bad things, drawing the line at waterboarding or disembowelment, conceding as usual I am bad at living life when the words end and the numbers begin. Then I had lunch. It's two o'clock now. Then a handyman came around to install new brushes to the washing machine. He's friendly but slightly invasive, quizzing me as to my occupation (writer/dosser), the occupants of my flat (me and one Laura), and the plans I have for the long-time-coming fourth debut novel I completed last week. As I write this, the handyman is still skulking in the kitchen, and as I sit before the screen, twitchy and restless, I realise writing about the endless untameable distractions a writer faces, especially when he can't sit still long enough to keep his nerves in check, will make for a pertinent addition to this toddle around the minutiae of the everyday, the things beyond art no artist is tedious enough to describe. But now I sound like that decadent-little-twerp-in-the-other-room, writing dross like this while honest hard-working men like him are out making a living and fragmented narratives are hardly *work*, are they? And haven't people like Nicholson Baker written about the minutiae of the everyday before … this just goes on and on. It's now three o'clock.

The Tomas Family Plot

John Tomas, 1873–1957. Stockbroker. Repeatedly beat his wife and youngest son Frederick, lavished praise and attention on daughter Louisa.

Mary Tomas, 1880–1920. Knitter. Repeatedly beat the servants, overdosed on opium on her fortieth birthday.

Frederick Tomas, 1910–1995. Industrialist. Mistreated his workers, started slave trade factories in Nigeria.

Louisa Tomas, 1920–1960. Teacher. Sacked for abusing her pupils, beat her daughter, overdosed on heroin on her fortieth birthday.

Daniel Tomas, 1950–2012. Stockbroker. Created one of the largest computer companies in the world. Left no children.
Lilith Tomas, 1952–1968. Slashed her wrists at sixteen.

Crest: 'No use trying to escape us.'

Jan sort of wanted to do something in the catering business but she wasn't quite sure what and Jim kind of wanted to be some kind of artist but he wasn't sure what, a painter maybe, he was reviewing his options. Jan wasn't that sure about meeting Jim for a drink because she wasn't sure if she liked his big hands and Roman nose and if she preferred shorter men, and Jim wasn't sure about tanned girls like Jan who wore lip gloss and dyed their hair, but went along anyway. They sort of got on okay, they liked each other enough, about as much as they liked anyone else, so a second date followed where Jan reluctantly went to bed with Jim, she had to sleep with *someone*, then they became an item, which worked for them while they sort of pieced their adult lives together, never the way they expected, then split up for a while, got back together and so on, increasingly frightened they would never find the perfect partner, drawn back together in the mistaken belief their frequent association had led to a sort of closeness or intimacy through simply being around, available, a recognised face. Then they married. They begrudgingly had a child they sort of loved and they kind of drifted apart, thinking of that day they met and kind of liked each other, without ever knowing why.

Right now: An Essex teenager bites into a ham sandwich. A long-term dieter sneaks a furtive éclair. Two businessmen cut one hundred employees from the payroll. A man sneezes too loudly in a dentist's waiting room. A receptionist called Nina answers the telephone. Scientists pour liquids into beakers. A rabbit dies. Someone listens to The Clash's second album. Forty people sit around doing nothing then get up and put the kettle on. A priest imagines a vagina. A xylophone is played badly by a lazy music student. A man dies. A woman dies. Another rabbit dies. Someone writes a dreadful sentence.

Claire started her own business: E-Claire Online. People could access, for various fees, different parts of her life. For ten pounds a week, the viewer could watch her go to work, get the shopping, and watch the telly. For fifty:

talking to her partner, her parents, her friends. For one hundred: undressing and bathing and lovemaking. *The Truman Show* online, with a woman, and for real! Cameras were rigged all around her flat, on her clothes and head-gear, to gain twenty-four-hour access to Claire. The everyday Claire, the close-friend Claire, the intimate Claire. She made thousands in the first week alone from intimate subscribers, eager to get their fill of Claire, this junior communications and operations assistant at K-Tech & Co., this twenty-eight-year-old with an accounting BA.

For the first three months she could do no wrong. Viewers lapped up her discussions about protocol management within her subdivision or how aubergines made her feel peaky, feeling close to Claire's quirks and com-plaints and passions and routines. At night, people lusted for Claire's imperfect body, her puppy fat and unshaved legs. Oh Claire, Claire, Claire! All around the world, in Japan, Malaysia, Mexico, viewers sat enthralled at her moans about Dan in Acquisitions' general gittishness and wondering whether to go back and do an art degree or how she's too tired for sex tonight or she wonders if she should put red streaks in her hair and how she can't wait for the new Haruki Murakami and whether to go to Juarez or Minsk on holiday this year.

Soon, Claire was a worldwide phenomenon. Hollywood went bankrupt, television became obsolete as a medium (in the same afternoon). This impacted Claire's life in crippling ways. Fans, whose only purpose in life was to stare at this dowdy clerk from Greater London, flocked to her flat in Ruislip to see Claire in the flesh. Now the broadcast consisted merely of people staring at Claire staring at the people staring at her, like a very boring hall of mirrors. She asked for food. Nothing. She asked for freedom. Nothing. Her boyfriend called across the room: 'Shut down the site, love.' She did so, then looked out the window. No one there. She switched on the TV. Channels back in operation. No mention of her. Online, fifty billion people wanted their money back.

—Greetings. I am Narfwald. Here is what I do. I receive demands for council tax or overdue rent arrears. I pulp these forms down into paste, then add milk, flour and sugar to the mix. Once the base is prepared, I add cream to the centre and create cake. When the bailiffs arrive, seeking their unpaid contributions, I offer them a slice before I am arrested.
—Hola. I am Bilxram. Here is what I do. I attend rock concerts, bop along to the music then ask ladies to come home with me please. When we return I offer them a pasta bake and a glass of blackcurrant cordial. Upon their departure, I bury my nose in the seats they occupied, licking the leather until it is sated with saliva, then perch there all night.

—Boo! I am Ginglah. Here is what I do. I apply for paid work in offices. Once I am successful, I work in these offices for fourteen years, speaking with as few people as possible, then kill everyone with a semi-automatic assault rifle, including the night cleaners, who I shoot when dusk comes. I then move on to the next office, repeating the process.

'Kevin Kline, Kevin Kline, on the decline!' all the kids at the LA Pubic School (someone had stolen the L) shouted as he strolled past with his *LA Times* and muglet of coffee. He wiggled his little pinkie, mocking them for being children. They replied with obscene pelvic grinds and further shouts: 'Kevin Kline, Kevin Kline, dirty old swine!' He knew he should've bypassed the school via the K-mart, but hey ho. It was true, though. Kevin Kline was on the decline, not the incline, in career terms. His funniest moments on screen had passed. His finest performances were done. The best he could hope for was a bit-part in some dire romantic comedy he could write in his sleep, voiceover work, or the occasional badly paid TV cameo. Yes: Kevin Kline was *over*. He searched for the pistol he kept under his bed for protection and filled the chamber with bullets. He wrote the following suicide note: 'The end. Thank you, darlings!' then put the gun in his mouth but didn't pull the trigger since the phone rang at that exact moment. 'Kevin – *Sophie's Choice 2: The Revenge*? Whadayasay?' his agent said. Kevin removed the pistol from his mouth so he could reply. 'Can I direct?' he asked. 'No,' snapped his agent. 'Then I pass,' Kevin said. He put the pistol in his mouth again.

Niall O'Gallagher

'NA CLUINNEAM NACH EIL SUBH-LÀIR ...'

Na cluinneam nach eil subh-làir
  agad air fhàgail sa bhùth;
tha mo ghaol-sa gam feitheamh,
  na bris, a fhir-reic', a dùil –

thoiream bagaid dhiubh dhachaigh
  far an gabh sinn, fear seach fear,
ri ithe gach meas' mìlse,
  gu còrdadh rithe gach dearc

(gus am fàg sinn an soitheach
  's e a' coimhead falamh, bàn,
gun ach duille na caithne
  a' rosadh fhathast sa chlàr).

Mar sin, a dhuine fhialaidh,
  is math as fhiach iad a' phrìs –
na can rium nach eil cuibhreann,
  blasad suibh-làir dom ghaol fhìn!

Kim Patrick

from PROVENANCE

I

Wittgenstein is why you are at home during the day. Wittgenstein, language and philosophy. I know you have no-one else to talk to. For two reasons. We have never had a conversation and I am nine. You say you are learning German. You would like to not have to read Wittgenstein in English. I resolve to never read Wittgenstein in English or German. To find language in other containers. To accept that it may have been you who taught me that language is something to talk about.

II

Perhaps, if I read to you. There are only six or seven books here. Hospital books. They are not about hospitals or illness. But they are yellow and infected. You have never read a book. I think of the books I started and didn't finish. Think to make a donation. This is not a collection of books, but a shelf with books. And so I begin. And my voice soothes me. I think if you could, you would take this book from me. You are all piss and panic. But if you let me read to you, you will have my voice, language and come to know a safer fiction. I don't finish books because they do not end as I please. There is nothing more real, nothing less fictitious than what is happening. I carry endings for days. Often longer. Listen, I want to read to you. Let me interrupt you. You will not be still. For some time I have wondered at your imagination. You see everything in relation to the facts of electricity. Sockets and plugs, cords and cables. Lightbulbs, alarms, microwaves, toasters. Nothing grand, just everyday household objects of electricity. In multiples. In their boxes. In their carrier bags. With receipts. Televisions and remote controls, kettles and coffee makers, radios, telephones, microphones and batteries. I do not care for the word 'obsessive'. You have your little fascinations. Nor 'compulsive'. And those other words. Never learn them. 432/8965, 423/5895, 430/1042. These are the goods that got you here.

III

Day is one day of the *New York Times* retyped. You say it doesn't matter which day. You can tell me that day was a Friday. You say that you started from the upper left corner. Eight hundred and thirty-six pages. Seven by ten by two. One thousand, three hundred and seventy-six grams. Forty-nine fluid ounces. Twenty dollars. Day can be read. I know this is not your intention. I ask you about Kurt Schwitters. You hit me over the head. And ask me where my art history is. I have been reading books at seven pounds and ninety-nine pence. I tell you I am trying fiction. Language, you say, can do better than me.

IV

I read. You say. Knowing if you speak loudly enough, you will never need to discuss what I have read. And what you have not. What of language, and its actions? I would say. But you are fearful of dialogue. You speak only of what you know, for sure. You do read. You consume. And tell. You tolerate no illness, but literature – this you catch like a common cold. You ask me why people give you books. And a dead tooth drops on your plate of leftovers. I think of the thirty years between my teeth and yours. And I smile. I will buy you books. Volunteer to feed you pages when it comes time for liquids only. This is not academic. Academics would not have you. This is a principle. Held quiet and close. Swallow.

Colette Paul

DARK NIGHT OF THE SOUL

James pops into the toilet just before six and when he comes out the office is empty, all the lights are off. He can't believe it. He goes to the door and shakes it gently, even though he can see that the grille is pulled down. He laughs a bit, to try and reassure himself. He's beginning to feel a sinking sort of panic. 'Hello?' he shouts, quietly at first. 'Hello, is anyone there?' It's pitch dark apart from the red lights of the alarm. There are nine of them in the office. How could no one have noticed he was missing? He usually walks to the bus stop with a few of them. He tells himself to stay calm. He turns off the alarm and pushes the light switch. The flat fluorescent tubes buzz on, one by one. The office is down a lane overlooking a disused railway line, tucked away from the main road. There's no reason for anyone to pass by.

He sits down at his desk. He needs to work out what to do. He doesn't have his boss's home phone number. He can't call the police or the fire brigade, not for something as daft as this. Once he's accepted that he's stuck here for the night, the prospect is not so bad. There's no one waiting for him at home, and he doesn't have any plans for the evening. His only worry is what his work colleagues will say. They already have him pegged as an eccentric: they'll think this is a great story, him getting locked in for the night. They still laugh about the Christmas party when he choked on a rogue bay-leaf in his soup. Fortunately he'd been clear-minded enough to perform the Heimlich manoeuvre on himself by running to the restaurant staircase, coming down the railing on his stomach, then using the banister post as a fist. 'It could only happen to you, James,' said Robbie, the man he sits beside. 'Whooshing down the banister like that.' He doesn't know how or when it happened, but he seems to have been allocated the role of office clown. He decides he'll hide in the toilet in the morning and emerge when everyone is in the kitchen, making coffee.

It's now quarter to seven. He walks upstairs to the kitchen and makes a cup of black tea. Recently he's been regulating his diet, trying to avoid wheat and dairy on the advice of a Chinese herbalist he's started visiting. He often feels sluggish; he gets bad stomach pains. Sometimes he wakes up in the middle of the night, his heart beating too fast. His doctor can't find anything wrong with him, and he suspects that she thinks he's a hypochondriac. He thinks she's probably right, but it doesn't help alleviate his anxiety. It's got worse since the choking incident. In idle moments he'll find himself wondering how long it would take to discover his body if he choked one night and couldn't save himself. He's in regular contact with his parents, and Mr Brewer, his boss, would probably phone after a day or two. He couldn't count on his neighbours noticing anything. Apart from the man upstairs, he doesn't know what his neighbours look like, and he only knows the man upstairs because he flooded him on Christmas Eve. He's an alcoholic, skinny, stooped, his face caved in with emphysema. At night James hears him coughing through the ceiling.

He drinks his tea, then turns on his computer. He may as well catch up on some work. But tonight his powers of concentration fail him. The quietness distracts him. He imagines the bars and nightclubs and cinemas filling up, people thronging the streets. A group of them from university used to meet up at the Fox and Hound every Friday, but this year their arrangement has finally fallen apart: Andy and Dave have moved to London, and Kev has got a girlfriend. It was James who spotted her first, at the wedding of another university friend. Emma was dancing with one of the children, birling her round, laughing. She was very fair, with an appealing mild, round-chinned face. Her cheeks were pink with exertion, her hair flying around. This image of her in motion, her old cardigan flapping behind her, has stayed, imprinted, in James's mind. He can recall it at will. He was surprised, when he came back from the bar, to see Kev talking to her. Kev usually went for the most attractive women in the room, and Emma was not pretty in the conventional sense. (James likes to think he has unique taste.) She came back to sit at the table and Kev introduced her, but it was noisy and James couldn't join in on their conversation. He spoke to her heavily made-up friend, whose failed attempts to overcome her awkwardness matched his own. She pulled at her sparkly dress, which was too tight, and gulped down drinks while making sarcastic comments about the couple getting married. In an odd way, he felt they recognised each other, and were disheartened by what they saw. He left early and the next time he saw Kev, Emma was his girlfriend.

A few months ago they moved in together, and at the weekend James often goes round for dinner, or to watch a DVD. These evenings – even the thought of these evenings – both sustain and pain him. Emma quizzes him about his love life, half-seriously, in the way that you might tease a younger brother, and says she will set him up. She is only twenty-three, nine years younger than them, but she seems older. She has painted Kev's living room yellow, and bought cushions for the couch, a picture of waterlillies for over the mantelpiece. She sits between them, linking her arms through theirs. There is a note of sheer physical pleasure in all her movements that James finds attractive. He's never felt at home in his body. Sometimes she lies back on the sofa, resting her feet on his knees. She has small white feet, with squarish toenails. One night last month she asked James to massage them, talking in that light, playful way she has to him. James became angry. He wasn't a eunuch, he wasn't a monk. He felt he was being used, although he didn't know to what end, and he didn't know what to do about it. It wasn't to make Kev jealous. He sat in the La-Z-Boy, smiling benignly and strumming his guitar. That night James decided that he'd had enough. He'd rather spend his weekends alone. But at the door Emma said, 'Are you okay? You look fed up,' and she seemed genuinely concerned. He said yes, just tired, you know how it is. She gave him a hug. 'You know you can come over anytime,' she said. 'I feel that me and you are friends now, you know, apart from Kev.' And he said yes, I feel that too.

At thirty-two, he has not had much experience with women. His longest relationship, in fourth year at university, lasted eight months, and ended badly – for him, anyway. 'I'm sorry, James, but now that we've got to know each other, I find you quite boring,' she'd told him one afternoon in the student union. He had not protested. 'I used to think you were mysterious,' she continued, 'but you're just quiet.' Actually for the last few months he'd been in the process of going off her, but he forgot that once she finished with him. He stopped going to his history lectures in order to avoid her. (He'd ended up with a 2:2, scuppering his chances of doing a PhD.) Things had only looked up once he met Camilla. They worked together in Waterstones the year after he'd graduated. She was in the Socialist Workers Party, the Smash the Nazis, and the Palestine Solidarity Campaign. James had never belonged to a club, but he was impressed by her moral confidence. He went leafleting with her a few times, and attended one meeting of the Palestine Solidarity Campaign, where it was decided that volunteers would boycott an Israeli pianist who was playing at the Royal Concert Hall. She hadn't replied to their email asking if she supported their cause.

He watched the films Camilla recommended, and read the books she mentioned. He found her absolutism bracing. His problem, she told him, was that he could see all sides of an argument. He enjoyed being told what he was like, even if it wasn't complimentary. No one had ever paid so much attention to his personality. He even enjoyed being told what to think: all he had to do in her company was breathe. After spending an hour with his parents at his birthday she said, 'Your mother's depressed and you're father refuses to acknowledge it. He's very controlling.' Until that point he'd thought, if he'd thought about them at all, that they were happy.

In fact his parents' separation had coincided with the end of his relationship with Camilla. After the summer she'd started teachers' training, and he saw her less. She began to cancel their dates, and when they did meet up, she seemed withdrawn. James didn't broach the matter: he was afraid. Finally, over the phone, she'd told him she couldn't make him happy. James said she did make him happy. She begged him not to make this any harder than it already was, and said she hoped they could stay friends. The next week, in the spirit of friendship, he bought her an expensive biography of Karl Marx for her birthday. He went to her house to deliver it, but she was out and he had to leave it with her flatmate. When he didn't hear from her, he began to worry that the flatmate had forgotten to pass the book on, or even stolen it. Why else would Camilla not have contacted him? He tried to call, but she didn't pick up the phone. One night after the Fox and Hound he stood under her lit

window shouting, 'I'm not drunk, I just want to talk to you,' until her flatmate
said he was obviously unbalanced, she'd call the police if he didn't go away.

There's been no one since. Recently, under Emma's persuasion, he signed
up for a free three-month trial with *Guardian* Soul Mates. Even before it
got to the meeting-up stage, he had two automated rejections and one
strange message reading: *Sorry to learn about your disability. I probably
won't choose to have a relationship with you. But I feel sorry for you and will
pray for you.* None of the three dates he's been on has come to anything.
The first woman ('Literary, lively & a few pounds overweight!') emailed
him the next day to say she thought he was a nice person, but that she hadn't
felt any chemistry. The second woman ('Shy but picky. Hates litterbugs &
liars') talked bleakly about her ex-boyfriend all night. None of their photos
matched the reality by a long shot. James had picked an unflattering snap
of himself, feeling that there was nothing to be gained in gilding the lily;
nevertheless, he'd registered date number two's disappointment as he
approached her. 'I usually go for tall men,' she'd told him. 'You looked tall
in your picture.' (She'd looked a glamour-puss in *hers*.) The third date, last
weekend, was the worst yet. She had emailed him on Friday to say that her
dentures were being repaired, would he mind if she came without them?
His heart sank. No, he wrote back, he didn't mind. They arranged to meet
in Beanscene at seven o'clock. He sat near the door, fighting the temptation
to look up every time it opened. She hadn't turned up by eight, when he
ordered another coffee, or at quarter to nine, when he decided to go home.
Later that night, just before he went to bed, he got a text message: *Sorry, I
fell asleep on the train. Just got home. Sorry x. Sorry x. Sorry.* For some reason,
he's been unable to laugh about the incident. Even just thinking about it
fills him with a nameless horror, a hopelessness that cuts across his soul.

It's eleven o'clock now, quiet apart from the soft swoosh of traffic passing
by in the distance. He walks round the office, trying to keep warm. It'll be
Christmas in two weeks, and then there'll be the ordeal of Christmas Day,
of trying to arrange things so that he sees both of his parents and neither
feels left out. His mother is less of a problem because she's got her new
husband, Philip. James tries to find fault with him, out of loyalty to his father
who hasn't got over their separation. He was forty-five when he married
James's mother, reconciled to being alone. Now, at seventy-seven, he is back
to square one – or so it seems to him. Nothing can console him. He has
become loquacious in his grief – to his family, to strangers, to his church
buddies. He is not ashamed to admit he still loves James's mother, will always
love her, would have her back in a flash. Often his eyes well up before he
has time to wipe them. People feel sorry for him – James feels sorry for him,
and guilty too. The idea of his father's loneliness nags away at him. But he
also realises that, in some perverse way, his father is enjoying himself. He

has taken to victimhood like a duck to water. Even his walk seems calculated to suggest a poor soul, a poignant figure barely holding himself together. James has many thoughts that he tries to censor from himself, and this is one of them. He feels it exposes some fundamental personality flaw in his father; something shameful, weak, unmanly.

He makes himself another cup of tea, and eats a few digestives from the communal biscuit tin. He feels even hungrier afterwards and has a look in the fridge. There's a few microwave meals, but they have the owner's name printed on them in warning capital letters. After the Strawberry Müllerlight fiasco, he wouldn't risk it. He's just about to turn off the light, when he hears a scream. At first he thinks it's a woman. He rushes over to the window and lifts the blind, his heart thumping. But it's a fox, a big one, stalking up and down by the rubbish bins. He watches it move in and out of the darkness. The screams are spaced out, as if waiting for a response. He's only ever caught quick glimpses of foxes, never anything like this. It's eerie. He begins to feel as if the cries are getting under his skin, entering his bones. He watches for a long time but no other foxes appear.

Afterwards he feels unsettled. He goes downstairs and walks around the empty office, up and down, up and down. The quietness is that frozen, charged kind that feels like the aftermath of something. His sense of unreality is so strong that for a moment he imagines himself dead. He thinks about what he would regret, if the next few hours were all that remained of his life. And it's then, feeling a loneliness too absolute to bear, that it comes to him: he must tell Emma how he feels. He picks up his mobile phone and stares at the screen. As if on cue, it begins to ring.

'Frank?' a woman says. 'Frank, is that you?'

His head is so full of Emma that he feels momentarily disorientated. 'You've got the wrong number,' he says.

'This isn't Frank?' the woman says. 'Who is this?' There are people talking in the background, and music. Before he can answer, she says, 'Please, Frank, I just want to talk.' Her voice is slurred and he realises she's very drunk. 'I know you're there,' she says.

He tells her again that she has the wrong number, that there's no one called Frank here.

'Who are you?' she says.

'I'm James,' he says.

'Please, James,' she says. 'I need to talk to him.'

'I'm sorry,' he says, 'he's not here.' The woman has begun to cry. She says something else but he can't make it out. Everything is muffled. He presses the phone hard against his ear.

'Maybe you should try him in the morning,' he says, not knowing how to end the call. She is still crying. 'I need to go,' he says finally. 'I can't really hear you anyway. I'm sorry.' But before he can hang up, the line goes dead.

Afterwards he thinks, for the first time in twenty years, of Frank Ross, a boy he was at school with, who was bullied mercilessly. He was two years above James so they weren't friends; they lived next door to each other. He used to see the McDonald brothers following him home: *I love your trainers, Frank. Frank, I love your anorak. Did your mum get them for you, Frank? Frank, why won't you talk to us? Aren't we good enough for you, Frank?* He wonders what's become of him. He thinks about other people he used to know and wonders where they are now. He remembers his best friend in school, Ben, and how they used to call each other on the phone for hours. What did they find to talk about? There was a girl Ben had a crush on whose favourite term of abuse was *ignoramus*. Her father was an ignoramus; the boys in her class were total ignoramuses. One Saturday him and Ben and her and her friend took the bus down to Ayr for the day. It was the middle of July, a hot, cloudless afternoon. They raced along the beach, high on the few cans of cider they'd shared. Later on, when Ben and his girl had disappeared, he had his first kiss with her friend. Afterwards they'd sat on the beach wall, big, noisy gulls swooping above them, and James had wanted to put his arm around her. 'Do you see those girls over there?' she'd said. 'They're laughing at me because I'm fat.' And even though he thought she was lovely, he said nothing, because he was shy. She'd got MS, this girl – James remembers someone telling him when he was home from uni. By that point Ben had finished his plumber's apprenticeship, and his girlfriend was pregnant. Their friendship just sort of petered out. James's life went down one path, and Ben's went down another.

He should try to get some sleep. He worries when he doesn't get enough sleep. Such a strange night. His chest is tight, his mind whirring. He turns off the lights, and the darkness surges into him. He puts his head on his desk. His heart is roaring. What if he's having a heart attack? There's a tingling sensation in his arm. He tenses his weight against the darkness.

He wakes up twice. The first time, at three o'clock, he's disorientated. His neck is stiff. He's so cold. A rectangle of flat, white moonlight lies over the carpet. A feeling of utter dereliction takes hold of him. This night will never end. He thinks to himself, *After the night comes the morning. After the night comes the morning.* He remembers it from church.

At five thirty, he wakes again. It's still black outside, but the world is slowly coming into focus. In an hour, an hour and a half, grey light will edge the rooftops. The streets will begin to fill, feet pounding over the wet pavements. He pictures it as he waits for the dawn, as he waits for today to be here.

Nalini Paul

CAPTURE

A flutter in the heart
stirs ashes awake;
wings scrape the walls of soot.
Debris falls into the hearth,
nothing but dirt.

In a vacuum, time takes flight,
a universe of unspoken words:
bird, trapped, chimney ...

The hourglass aperture was too small
for life of that sky-spanning magnitude.

RETURN

As if wings could swim in air
locked wide open
head tucked in
        eyes shut –
a snapshot of flight.

A tremble inside the box
then out again to safe hands
        garden breeze
        water to baptise sooty eyes

before the world awakens
and off it flies.

Alison Prince

SLATE

This flake of slate is heavy in the hand,
blotched with fool's gold like medals won
in the battled centuries of being rammed
tight by the slow forces of tectonic shift.
It comes undone
easily now, its layers as thin
and black as carbon paper, yet
shoals of it slither underfoot, rock-hard,
blocks of it form the harbour wall
and low-crouched houses, keep the wind
out of the pub where talk goes on
far beyond all rules of licensing.
Cliffs of it still rise
out of the quarries where the sea roared in
to end an industry.
Its royal names live on. Queenies
and duchesses still roof the paying world
and this princeling
grants its small, intense weight
to a common palm.

Margaret Ries

HALF-LIGHT

There was something about the light that pulled her back the second time, after a year spent circling the world. Sure, the history, breaking out of its forty-plus-year cocoon, was interesting, even thrilling, but it was the light that hooked her. A sun that never seemed to set, a night sky a shade of royal blue she'd only seen in paintings and thought was imagined, an atmosphere of play as long and deep and luxurious as the light licking the sidewalks, outdoor cafés full to bursting. Warm, but not hot, not so hot that everything – and everybody – went into meltdown.

She met Til on one of these forays out, when the day totters on the fulcrum of night, finally tipping back into day again. She'd sat, feet up on the chair opposite, a Pils at her elbow, a book in her lap. The sun was coming up. Three a.m. and the sun was coming up. Wild, she thought, shaking her head.

One of the two men at the next table got up and crossed the street. She watched as he went into a Turkish café, ordered a coffee, and sat down at one of the tables. The Turkish men stared at him for a moment, but eventually dealt him a hand of cards. He waved at his friend through the café window and then settled, frowning, into the game.

'*Wahnsinn*,' his friend said, laughing so hard he spilled some beer on his shirt.

'Pardon?'

He wiped the froth off his shirt, picked up his beer, and came over to her table. In all her evenings of café-going and people-watching, this had never happened before. The frivolity of the summer spilling over in her direction.

His English was flawless. Her German came in erratic fits.

'Would you look at that?' he said, pointing at his friend.

The friend made a dramatic show of throwing his cards on the table and storming out of the café. By the time he reached the table, his shoulders were shaking with laughter.

'Never play cards with Turks,' he said. 'You'll lose every time. But I got the last laugh. See how far they get without this.' He slapped a card on the table. The ace of spades. Til slid it across the table to her.

The three of them ordered another round and then another. They abandoned the last to sweat in the sun as they headed off to another café for breakfast. Joachim, the friend, peeled off en route, leaving them alone.

They were alone that day and the next, when they took the S-Bahn out to the Wannsee to wrest a patch of sand in front of the lake from the multitudes. On the third day, it rained and they spent the day playing cards in the apartment Til had squatted in the East. She only used her extra ace when she really needed to. He forgave her every time.

As she was packing up her things to go, he reached out and touched her hand.

'Don't you want to stay? I mean, really stay?'

She thought about her rented cupboard in the widow's house in Steglitz. Not only had she suspected the woman of rifling through her stuff, but Steglitz itself was a problem. Once, when she'd gone to a new club in an abandoned building in the East, it had taken her an hour and a half to get home with the night bus. A place for pensioners, not someone who'd just turned twenty-four.

She looked at the square of gold in Til's otherwise green left eye. When the sun shone, the square soaked up its light and seemed to glow. She wouldn't mind waking up to that every morning. And Til had two rooms.

She set her backpack down on the floor.

*

The summer continued, each day a brighter pearl than the last. Til warned her that he wasn't usually like this, that it wouldn't always be like this, but she didn't believe him. Til had a lot of friends and they went out every night. His friends opened their circle easily to her and were patient with her college German, which improved with each beer she drank. She and Til stayed out late and slept late, spooning each other under his light summer duvet. Once they got up, they headed to one of the cafés that had opened in the East for breakfast, served until six p.m. Afterwards Til read the paper and she people-watched – or woman-watched – for fashion ideas. Black stretch was in. Her khaki shorts and Lacoste T-shirt were not. Sometimes they hung out there all afternoon, coffee turning to beer, one friend pulling up a chair, then another, until the circle was complete and the evening in full swing.

*

Til handed her a cup of coffee. 'What are you going to do today?' he asked.

'Do?'

'Joachim and I want to get together and talk about getting our study group going again. A bunch of us want to do a *Schein* this semester.'

The coffee was hot, with two scoops of sugar and lots of milk, just the way she liked it.

'I don't know. I guess I'll have to think about it.'

*

Til was in the second year of his law studies. The question became more pressing after the semester started. He wanted to do his second certificate, in criminal law, and when he wasn't in class, he was either studying or meeting Joachim and a few other students at the *Staatsbibliothek* to review the material. She suddenly had a lot of time.

It was a relief, in a way. She'd been worrying, vaguely, about the state of her liver. Her money was running out. And she had to do something about living in the country illegally.

*

She tried to call the *Ausländeramt* to find out when they were open. The phone rang and rang. Not even a recorded message. She figured out where it was on the map, which U-Bahn to take.

'I think you better try and get there early,' Til said.

Eleven a.m. seemed early enough. When she got to the turn-of-the-century building in Schöneberg, she saw that the times were seven-thirty a.m. to twelve p.m. Monday through Friday. She looked at her watch. Five past. She shouldn't have stopped for a *Milchkaffee*. She pushed on the door anyway. It was open. The foyer was empty. A weak sliver of sun from the back window made the brown linoleum look greasy. The walls were full of pieces of paper, stuck up at haphazard angles with yellowing tape. Official notices printed on flimsy, recycled paper, as though the message-givers didn't believe in the durability of their message. Or didn't care.

She followed one of the arrows painted on the wall up the stairs and into a hall. It was dark, windowless, the doors clamped shut on either side. She stopped in front of room number 125, where another recycled missive stated 'R-T' in microscopic print. She knocked on the door and stuck her head around the edge. The two desks, covered with files, were vacant. She could hear voices in the interior office.

'Hello?' she called out as she walked towards them.

A group of middle-aged women sat around a low table, smoking, drinking coffee, eating cake, chattering like chickens.

'Hello? I was just wondering …'

The women stopped mid-cluck and turned to glare at her. One woman stubbed out her cigarette, pushed back her chair, and grabbed her by the arm, fingers pressing to the bone. She escorted her out of the office, down the hall, down the stairs and out the front door onto the steps.

'I don't know who you think you are, but don't you ever do that again. This is a government office. You'll have to come back during our opening hours, just like everybody else,' the woman said.

The lock turned and she stood for a moment, watching the colour slowly return to the five white spots on her upper arm.

She didn't go back after that, deciding instead to concentrate on finding a job. Maybe her future employer could sort it out. She poured through the classifieds each Sunday, highlighting anything that sounded like something she could do. Sales, secretarial, reception, bookkeeping, word processing, data entry. Then she got up early on Monday morning, dragged the phone into the bedroom, closed the door, and made her calls.

'I read your ad in the paper?'

'The job has already been filled.'

She didn't understand how all the jobs in the paper could be gone by nine o'clock in the morning, but maybe they were to anyone with imperfect German and a foreign accent. She had a nibble at a secretarial job when she told them that she could type a hundred words a minute without a mistake, but they lost interest when they heard she didn't have a secretarial degree.

'But I have a degree from Princeton. You know, Princeton, as in Ivy League, as in one of the best schools in America?'

'I'm sorry, but we are only looking for qualified secretaries. I don't imagine you can take shorthand either, can you?'

She set her sights lower, and lower, and eventually got some work cleaning house a couple times a week. She didn't need a work permit and it was all paid under the table. One job was in her old stomping grounds of Steglitz and another was in Dahlem, a rich corner in the south-west of the city. Particularly there, she saw the other cleaning women, climbing the steps to the villas in the morning, heard them talking in their foreign tongues as they met friends, other maids, after work, their hands swollen red tomatoes at the end of their sleeves. Turks, Poles, Ukrainians. No Americans.

They were morning jobs and since she didn't earn that much, she started walking home afterwards to save on U-Bahn tickets. Eventually she started putting on her coat and heading out on the days she didn't have to work. The apartment only had two rooms. Although they had never discussed it, it was clear that the living room, which also contained the TV and the stereo, belonged to Til during the day and most of the evening after dinner. She had the bedroom, the kitchen, and a toilet in the stairwell, if she wanted it. She preferred going out to staying in bed all day.

*

It had surprised her how quickly the summer made its exit. From one day to the next. The chairs and tables disappeared from the sidewalks, the people into long-neglected lives, the sun behind an armoury of steel clouds. The city turned grey, relentlessly grey. Particularly in the East, where there weren't many trees to mitigate the concrete.

She'd never lived so far north and was amazed that it was possible to get up at eight a.m. and still beat the sun. And that by three-thirty, the prison gates started to swing shut again, leaving only a few hours of half-light for one to exercise in the yard. Half-light, half-life. The sentence one had to serve for the beauty of the summer.

She found herself getting up earlier and earlier, slipping out from under the heavy warmth of Til's arm, the down comforter, into the frosty chill of the night/morning. Til liked to save on heating costs, and she could see her breath as she laced up her Doc Martens, fumbled with the buttons of her coat.

Once she even met him when he was going to bed and she was getting up, as though they were changing shifts on the bed. He grabbed her arm just as she was about to open the door. He pulled her to him, wrapped her in his arms.

'It's four in the morning. Don't you want to come back to bed?'

'I told Frau Löhmann that I'd get there early. She's having a big party tonight.'

'Won't she be a little surprised if you turn up at five?'

She slid out from between his arms. 'I wanted to walk. It's so peaceful when nobody else is around.'

'To Dahlem? You must be crazy. That's what they have U-Bahns for. Come on,' he said, unbuttoning her coat. 'It's back to bed with you.'

When she got up again, it was still dark. She was pleased as she thought about easing herself into it. The church bell a couple blocks away struck six.

She put her clothes on in the reverse order she'd taken them off at four a.m., her coat last. She checked the pockets, finding a twenty and her keys. She found Til's wallet in the pocket of his jeans and extracted a blue 100 and his credit card, for good measure. It reminded her of the crazy Greek woman she'd once known, who had advised her to always have a hundred-dollar bill sewn into the tongue of her shoe. 'You never know when you might need to get away.' Twenty years of marriage and she was still sewing.

She had every intention of going to Frau Löhmann's, but once she hit the fresh morning, she couldn't face it. Climbing the steps in unison with the other hired help, ringing the doorbell, having the old woman open the door. Squawking 'Na, wie geht's?' as she took her coat and led her into the dining room for a cup of coffee before they began, together, to polish the silver they'd just done last week, for the dinner parties she never gave. They never got around to any other part of the house, some of which she'd glimpsed on her trips to the dining room, covered in white starched sheets.

Instead she headed for Treptower Park. Somewhere she had always wanted to go, but never gotten to. As she was walking along a street that shadowed the S-Bahn tracks near Ostkreuz, she came upon a huge mountain of garbage blocking the sidewalk. She stepped off the kerb. She'd never seen anything like it before. Washing machines, stoves, refrigerators, sinks, bathtubs – all GDR vintage. Someone had even driven a Trabant into it, abandoning it, hood up, motor gone, half on the sidewalk, half in the street. She wondered what they'd bought instead. What goods, what system.

It took her a while to find the monument in the middle of the park. The entrance was inconspicuous, a plaque, a parking lot, a break in the trees, none of which prepared her for how immense it was. A statue of Mother Russia, head bowed, kneeling before two gigantic triangles of red granite – Russian flags at half-mast – further up the walk. Then, a large square lined with blocks of white marble, marking the graves of the thousands of soldiers who had died trying to take the city. And at the end, on a hill and a pedestal to increase his height, a mammoth Russian soldier, a child in one hand, a sword crushing the Swastika at his feet in the other.

She walked up the steps. A couple of people had laid wreaths, in Russian, at the base of the pedestal. She sat down and surveyed the ensemble. It was strangely beautiful, in its simplicity and symmetry and its overweening grandeur. Peaceful. Empty. She got up and walked around the pedestal. There was absolutely no one else on the square, no one else in the entire city paying homage but her. She ran down the hill, arms out for balance, one toe leaving a long skid mark in the wet grass.

On her way out of the park, she spotted a café set back from the tree-lined boulevard. It sagged in the middle. There was Astroturf on the terrace; inside it smelled like mildew. An old woman was behind the counter, chatting with an even older man, whose butt lapped over the edge of his stool. Each had a beer. She smiled to herself when she saw the faded picture of Honecker above the cash register, wondering if they knew about the Wall. She ordered a small beer and went to sit down at a table to wait for it.

*

'Why don't you have a seat with us, *junge Frau*?' The man slapped the stool next to him, grinning. Most of his front teeth were black. She smiled back and sat down.

'Where're you from?'

'Me? I'm from the States.'

'Oh, I would have guessed Sweden from your accent. Or one of those other Scandinavian countries.'

The woman crossed her arms under the shelf of her bosom. 'And what would you know about that? You've never been out of Treptow in your whole life. No, I take that back. Didn't you go visit your son in Prenzlauer Berg last year? Or was it the year before?'

She smiled into her beer. It was exactly what she had walked this morning. Prenzlauer Berg to Treptow. And now back again. About an hour and a half on foot, fifteen minutes with the S-Bahn.

'Why're you here?'

'I wanted to see the Soviet *Denkmal*,' she said. She noticed there was a yellow stain the shape of Texas on the front of his khakis. It worried her, to think he was being so friendly and didn't know he'd pissed in his pants.

'No, I mean *here* here,' he said, sweeping his arm out wide, as though to include the entire city. The gesture almost brought him off his stool.

'I don't know exactly. It just seemed like a good idea.'

He guffawed. 'I can think of plenty of other, better ideas.'

She drained her beer. 'Yeah, you're probably right.'

*

After she'd walked a couple of miles, she realised that she had to go to the bathroom. Desperately. It occurred to her that she could just go in the street. Pull down her jeans, squat. She had seen so many men do it – some crept into the privacy of a corner, others simply let loose, their penis in full view, against a lamp-post or a parked car – that it almost seemed normal. But she kept thinking about the man in the café. About the yellow Star of Texas on the front of his pants. Would she end up with Texas on the front of her jeans? Or maybe she was already there.

She concentrated and took small steps. When she reached Ostkreuz, she got on the S-Bahn, sitting with her legs crossed. Finally she was at her apartment building, with only two and a half flights of stairs between her and the bathroom. After she made her pit stop at the toilet on the landing, she went up the last few steps to their apartment. She let herself in.

Til came out into the hall. 'Frau Löhmann called. She wanted to know why you didn't show up. I thought you said she had some big party tonight.'

'I quit,' she said, hanging up her coat. She went into the kitchen. 'I'm going to make a cup of coffee. Do you want one?'

'What are you going to do now? It was hard enough for you to find that job.' He leaned against the counter in the kitchen, arms crossed.

'I don't know. I'll think of something.'

'Oh yeah, before I forget. Your mother called. She wanted to know when you're coming home. I told her never.' He laughed.

Soon, she thought, patting the credit card in her pocket. Very soon.

Kay Ritchie

OPUS

At last we pass through an opened door.
Blue. Inside too as cool as
this distant misty Sierra Nevada.

Hats hang in the hall.
Not three cornered.
Just panamas.

Flagstones matted in rush.
All hush as sweet light oozes through
Alpujarra curtains ripe as Seville oranges.

I am haunted by ghosts.
Your cotton-filtered cigarettes dance
will-o'-the-wisp into and out of each room

while Miles sits spell-bound sketching
Spain in some dark enchanted corner. Me
in a blue wicker chair where you and

Federico drew up mysteries and magics
puppets and politics   around
your round table.

When we take our leave I believe you have bewitched me.
I will go home and listen on a loop to 'El Amor Brujo'
then paint my doors and windows bluer than blue.

Angela Robb

GREYHOUND

The dog was Jake's idea. He comes in one day with this photograph and says, 'Do you like her? She's yours.'

I looked at the picture without actually seeing it, if you know what I mean. I couldn't think what to say. So I said, 'I forgot to pick up my prescription.'

Jake pushed the photo into my hands. 'Her name's Bonnie,' he said. 'She's a retired greyhound.'

I'd never wanted a dog. Dogs stare at you, and you know they're thinking something, but God only knows what it is. The dog in this picture was a blonde colour, hefty as a toothpick. It stared out of the photo with these big, wet, sad eyes.

'She's nice,' I said. That was good enough for Jake – he was that desperate to see me happy. 'They say a dog's the best therapy,' he said.

I might have smiled. Next thing I knew he was away, back to the bus station. He was doing the night drives back and forth to Glasgow.

I looked at the photo again. I couldn't cope with a dog. I put the photo on the table next to the couch. My pill bottle was lying there, empty. The chemist shop would still be open. I'd had my shoes on all day, but I hadn't gone out. I'd done other things, spent an hour washing up the breakfast dishes. There was still time to go to the chemist. But I wouldn't go out now.

I put my feet up on the coffee table to study my shoes. They were so comfy, those shoes, flat black ones with laces. The leather was soft and wrinkled, I'd had them that long. I bought them for working at the travel agent's. Well, I must have sold hundreds of holidays in those shoes. I even wore them when me and Jake went to Cyprus for our tenth wedding anniversary. And at Mum's funeral, of course. After that I wouldn't clean them again, wouldn't wipe off the dirt from the cemetery.

I watched some sketch show on TV then went to bed.

In the morning I felt ready for anything. I went to the chemist, then the supermarket. Everything was fair game: cheese, chocolate bars, soda water, glacé cherries. Mixed herbs, digestive biscuits, air freshener. Six cans of baked beans. By the time I got home I was ready for some of those baked beans.

At five o'clock Jake came in from work. I asked if he'd had a good shift. He said aye, and for once sounded like he meant it. Right away he started on about the dog. It had been at the refuge centre for a month, he said. It was still young, as well; greyhounds get retired early. This one's racing name was Shooting Star. She certainly was a beauty, he said. The refuge centre was run by a charity called Homes for Hounds.

'They said we can collect her tomorrow,' he told me. He said, 'I think we should both go along.'

'It's all right,' I said. 'Just you go yourself.'

'No, Tess, you should go too. It's all about bonding with her.'

This was too much. I said, 'You know I've never wanted a dog.' It was a hurtful thing to say and it hurt me saying it, but that just made the words more irresistible. I listened to them like it was someone else talking.

He never said anything then. I knew what he was doing: he was *coping*. I wanted to tell him I was sorry, but I couldn't, of course. Anyway, I wasn't sure if I was sorry. I never *had* wanted a dog.

Later on we looked for something for the tea. But none of the things I'd bought at the supermarket would make a meal. We put cheese on digestive biscuits and ate them with soda water. Afterwards Jake went back to the supermarket. I lay on the bed and pressed my face into the pillow.

The next day was Saturday. We got in the car first thing and headed for the refuge centre. On the way there we stopped off at the pet superstore. Jake got a trolley and we wandered up and down the aisles, thinking up all the things we'd need.

I'd never seen so many dog toys. Squeaky hamburgers, furry bones in six colours, teddy bears with bow ties. And beds: faux sheepskin, corduroy, jazzy patterned fabric. As if the dog can tell the difference.

I said, 'It's ridiculous, all this stuff.' But Jake was too busy studying all the different types of foods. I looked in the trolley. I hadn't a clue what he'd been picking up.

We got to the till with an orange plastic basket, a blanket, a brown collar and lead, two bowls, eight tins of food, a pack of chew bones and a rubber hedgehog. The girl told us the total, and I nearly hit the floor. But Jake never batted an eyelid.

The back seat of the car was a bit too small for all our carrier bags. We shifted them around until they fitted just perfectly. The pair of us got in the front, then Jake said, 'Where's the dog going to sit?' So we moved all the bags into the boot.

Jake put the key in the ignition and hesitated. 'Should we have bought mixer?' he said. 'What is mixer?'

'I don't know,' I said. 'We don't need any.'

We drove on to the refuge centre. In the reception, a woman in a Homes for Hounds sweatshirt was sitting behind a desk. 'Mr Delaney?' she said.

'Aye,' said Jake. 'This is my wife, Tess.'

'Nice to meet you,' she said. 'If you'd like to take a seat, I'll go and fetch Bonnie.'

We sat down. Neither of us spoke. I felt uneasy, hearing all the dogs barking. I didn't know what to do with a dog, and neither did Jake.

The woman came back with this lanky streak of a dog trotting along beside her. Right away Jake was on his feet, fussing over it, and I just sat there, thinking, Oh no.

'Would you like to give her a clap, Mrs Delaney?'

I ran my hand along the dog's back. It was like petting a toast rack.

Jake kept talking about *bonding*, for days afterwards. The first night we had her we shut her in the kitchen with her basket. She wouldn't stop barking this whiny, pitiful bark. I'd never heard that sound in my house. I put the pillow over my head to stop myself throwing a fit, but it only seemed to get louder. Eventually Jake brought her into the bedroom. She lay down at my side of the bed and fell asleep, just like that. I listened to her breathing, slow and deep, and wished it was mine.

It was the same every night. The kitchen was history. Jake said she'd had a bad experience and needed to be with us, needed to be loved. That's just fantastic, I told him – two mental cases under one roof. Every morning I woke up hoping she'd have disappeared in the night. But then I'd roll over and there she'd be, watching me with those huge brown eyes, begging me to love her. It was pathetic, no, worse than that – it was oppressive. Here was this dog – this selfish animal – denying me my basic right to think of nothing but ... well, myself. So I'd get up, let her into the garden. Get dressed, have breakfast. Feed her. Every day was the same routine. Like that déjà vu, or whatever they call it.

Round the park, come rain or shine. Jake said the exercise would do me good, and the fresh air. He never mentioned the mud. Finally I had to clean my shoes.

Thing is, Jake loved the dog. So when he asked, most days, how the two of us were getting along, I'd say, Fine. And at least half the time I did that for his sake. But then there were all those other days, when I'd give him the same answer but only because if I'd said anything else I'd have started crying and forgotten to stop. On those days I wanted him to know the truth. I'd like to say it was sympathy I was after, rather than that I wanted him to share the agony. I'd like to say that.

Anyway, whichever kind of day it was, I could tell he didn't believe me. He tried to look like he did, and he'd say, Oh, you see, I knew the pair of you would hit it off. But you could see it in his eyes. Jake's not really any better at expressing himself than I am. We're a couple of fakers. But he was trying so hard all the time, for me, and there's nothing fake about that.

So, this was me every afternoon: I'd be kneeling on the living-room carpet with a biscuit in my hand, saying, 'Bonnie, come on.' She always came right away, licking her lips and trembling. If I asked for a paw I never got one. I thought all dogs knew about giving paws. Anyway, she'd take the biscuit, gentle as you like, and that was that.

This one day the postman's bicycle skidded on oil, and he came off it just in front of our house. I went outside. He'd broken his arm. Someone called for an ambulance.

Later on I sat on the floor as usual with Bonnie's biscuit. I swept a hand across the carpet, and a whole trail of crumbs sprang up. I did it again. Bouncing crumbs, everywhere. I couldn't remember when I last hoovered. Bonnie came over and took her biscuit. Big crumbs were dropping out of her mouth and landing on my carpet.

I lay on the floor with my eyes shut. I could feel big jagged crumbs pressing into my cheeks. Bonnie licked me and whimpered. I sat up, patting her head to get rid of her. I couldn't look at her sad face.

Jake came in from work. We had a cup of tea in the living room. He sat in his usual chair, still wearing his uniform. A light blue shirt with short sleeves, and black trousers and tie.

I remembered when Jake used to love that job. He'd always say, They're not buses, they're *coaches*. He loved providing a service for people. He never said much about it any more. But we wouldn't talk about that. Instead I started thinking about my own uniform from the travel agent's. A striped blouse and navy skirt. At that moment I felt ready to wear it again.

I said, 'What'll we do when I go back to work?' Jake just stared at me. 'About the dog, I mean.'

He kept looking into his mug, swirling the tea around the bottom of it. 'If you go back,' he said, 'maybe it'll just be part-time though, eh?'

If. 'Aye,' I said. 'To begin with.' I let that hang for a minute. Jake was doing something with his head. He might have been nodding. 'It'll be fine,' he said. 'Cross that bridge when we come to it.'

I kept looking at him. His fascination with the dregs in that mug was really annoying me now. He didn't believe I had a hope of getting out of this house and going back to work. I wanted to shout at him, tell him he was wrong; I could hear myself ranting in my head. But the rant had no words, no sense, because Jake was dead right.

He stood up. It was a lovely day, he was saying, I should be outside enjoying it. I sat in the back garden, trying to make the sunlight play on my shoes, but the leather was too scuffed and grubby. Bonnie lay flat out on the grass. I could hear the hoover going in the living room.

The tea that night was a bit burnt. I counted the lumps in my cheese sauce. The telly in the kitchen was turned up loud. Jake was watching it intently, some kind of quiz show with celebrities.

I told him, 'The postman crashed his bike today.' He never heard me.

The next day the weather broke. Bonnie refused to go out. The two of us stood at the front door like idiots, until I said, 'For God's sake, Bonnie. Forget it, then.' So we sat in the living room and watched the rain from there instead. It really was the most boring rain I'd ever seen.

I thought about lunch. There was a can of baked beans left. 'Beans on toast, Bonnie,' I said. It sounded even better out loud.

Jake always says you feel a lot better when you've got something to focus on. Well, right now that something was baked beans. I searched through the cupboard like there was ten grand stashed somewhere among the soup. Except at that moment I'd have thrown the cash aside to get to the beans.

I found the tin. Bonnie watched me emptying the beans into a saucepan. She cocked her head to one side. 'Yum yum, Bonnie,' I said.

The heat was on high to speed things up. I smelled the warm, sweet tomato sauce, bubbling like crazy. I could taste it already.

Bonnie stared at me as I ate. 'It won't work,' I told her. But I put my last forkful into her bowl, because you do get a lot of beans in those tins. I grudged it nonetheless.

The man on the radio was talking about his dead relatives. I listened while I did the washing up. The presenter – that older one, can't remember his name – chipped in with this story about his grandfather, who used to steam the stamps off his mail and recycle them. The two of them were laughing. You can't dwell on loss, the other man was saying, you have to remember the good times.

I switched off the radio. That's when I heard a noise: a wet, chugging sound, like something being *chewed*. I went through to the living room to find Bonnie with one of my old black leather shoes clamped between her jaws. Next thing I'm running towards her, tugging at the shoe, yelling, '*Bad dog!*' I smacked her across the snout and she let go with a yelp. She slunk behind the couch.

My hands were shaking as I turned the shoe over. It was ripped on the top – only very slightly, mind, but she might as well have torn it to shreds. I sat down, still holding my shoe. I didn't know who to hate most – the dog for doing the damage, or me for letting it happen.

The rest of that day she stayed away from me. I gave my shoes a clean, for what it was worth, and sat in the living room. I wanted the hours to drag. But before I knew it Jake was home and reading me like a book.

'What's the matter?'

'Nothing's the matter.'

'Oh come on, Tess, you've no' even put the telly on.' I could tell he'd had a bad day; no doubt some wee ned had tried to bring a fish supper on the bus. I felt like he was saying, Stop wallowing.

'I'm all right. Just leave it.'

'You know, it hurts that you won't let me help you.'

Help me. My mind would have been in better nick, and hell knows my shoes would have been, if he hadn't gone and *helped* me. 'The dog chewed my shoes,' I said. 'She put a hole in one of them.'

Jake just shrugged. 'Is that all? You were needing new ones anyway.'

I shook my head. I told him, 'I'm keeping those ones. We've only the one salary coming in.'

'Don't be daft! Shoes aren't exactly a luxury, are they?'

'I'm no' getting rid of them.'

'Why not?'

'Because I like those shoes!'

'Tess – they're ruined!'

'Aye, and who ruined them? It's the damn dog I need rid of!'

'Oh, for God's sake, stop being so melodramatic.'

'*Melodramatic?*' I was burning up. 'You have no idea what this feels like.'

Right then, I'd wanted to reach out to him but instead I'd pushed him away. He didn't look angry any more – just sad.

'You're right,' he said. 'I don't.'

We sat there like a couple of strangers who feel like they've met in a previous life. I couldn't explain it to him, my obsession about the shoes, because I knew it was stupid. That's what my rational mind told me, but the thing is, my rational mind never did get a big say.

Neither of us spoke a word at teatime. I kept my head down, eating tiny mouthfuls as quickly as I could. I went to the sink for a glass of water so he wouldn't know I was crying. But of course he knew. He was close to tears himself.

Later on Jake took the dog out for a walk that lasted two hours. I went into our bedroom and took my uniform from the travel agent's out of the wardrobe. I folded it up and put it in a bin bag. After that I went into the bathroom and locked the door. I picked up the razor. I pressed its tip into my wrist until a fat drop of blood oozed out.

I'd decided who I hated most.

The blood dripped into the sink. It dribbled towards the plughole, turning pink and watery. I turned the tap on full and rubbed the soap across my wrist. 'Stupid fool,' I said.

All night I listened to the rain tapping on the window. My brain turned it into a rhythm then added a crazy tune, and an image of us dancing to it, me and Jake, and for some reason – God knows why – Bonnie was dancing with us. Then just before dawn it dried up.

By the time I woke Jake had already left for work. Bonnie sat by the front door while I got ready. I put the lead on and took her out.

We never met a soul all the way to the park. Pavement, puddles, houses, sky – all were as grey as each other. I looked down to check that I was still in colour. I could see my shoes, swinging in and out of sight. The one with the hole was letting in.

We got to the park as the rain began to spit. I let Bonnie off the lead and walked round our usual circuit. I threw her ball and she caught it. I threw it again, harder than I meant to, and she couldn't find it. She bounced around, wagging her tail and barking.

'All right,' I said. 'Calm down.'

I looked for the ball. We were down near the bottom end of the park, where the grass is longer. I felt my way through with both hands. The mud was deeper here, wetter and stickier. Already my trousers were soaked and my hands were filthy. I hadn't a clue where the ball had landed.

Bonnie kept running round my ankles, yapping her head off.

'Stop it,' I told her. 'I'm looking, all right? We'll get you another ball, for God's sake.'

I gave up and looked around for the least muddy way out. There wasn't one. I started back the way I'd come. At least I thought it was the way I'd come, but maybe it wasn't, because I'd hardly taken five steps before I felt the ground swallowing up my feet. I fell forward. My hands were splayed in the muck and disappearing into it. I turned myself around and saw my shoes lying a few feet away, one step apart.

So I started to cry. What else was I going to do? I was crying about nothing, which is the same as crying about everything. Maybe I thought the mud would suck us down, me and my shoes; maybe I hoped it would.

Then I looked round, because Bonnie's nose had brushed against my ear. One of the shoes was in her mouth. She put it down, and I saw that she'd already salvaged the other one. She sat and watched me. I looked at her sad face. It was covered in grot, and so was I, sitting in my socks in the mud and the rain. And then I couldn't help it. I laughed.

'Good girl,' I said. I patted her head and she licked me as I struggled back into my shoes.

I must've looked like I was doing some kind of jig, hopping from one tuft of grass to the next with Bonnie egging me on. I knew Jake would enjoy this story when I told it to him later.

Lydia Robb

ON THE BANKS O THE TAY

The horizon heists its hem up
on a raw o reid clouds.
Fae my sait on the upturnt coble,
a view o river, mountain, sea.
There's the soun o chuckies,
sooked smooth
bi the incomin tide.
Wunblawn wee boats
daunce a wattery jig.
Ae blue yacht, triangled in white sail,
weengs it doon the Fife coast.

Cynthia Rogerson

AFTER

Something strange happens seconds after the boy's car crashes on the A9. A sudden change in the atmosphere of the material world. In a nearby village the light flattens, so anything unbeautiful becomes almost sinister, and the things that are pretty, seem slightly surreal. A breeze arises, a chillier breeze than even this winter day warrants. It eddies in cul-de-sacs and creates small whirlpools of icy dust that sting the eyes of cats and runny-nosed toddlers in their pushchairs.

A middle-aged woman shopping in the Spar, who has never met the boy and now never will, suddenly sighs and slumps inside. She drops a bottle of salad cream into her basket, though it is overpriced and not her favourite brand. She simply lacks the heart to do anything else.

Outside the shop, a recently retired man (whose brother's son once had a one-night stand with the woman above) shivers and zips up his jacket. He suddenly thinks of people who are dead. His old work mate, Jam Jimmy, who always ate ham and jam pieces. His niece with bifocals, who used to sing Hey Nannie Noo Noo.

Across the road at Marty Dunn's garage, a small sticky-faced girl bursts into tears and is inconsolable for ten minutes, though her young mother (who was taught maths by the man above) holds her close. The child hiccups and can't say why she's crying, only sobs as if her heart is broken.

Time passes. The mother of the boy who died in the car accident wanders away from her old life and falls carelessly into another one. From the outside, she seems to be doing okay. She isn't, but she looks like she is. Which is probably true of a lot of people. And the appearance of *okay* must be better than no *okay* anywhere in the equation, right? But this isn't her story – that would take a novel, and there is only this short story. Barely enough room for snippets of the salad cream lady, the pensioner and the little girl who wept and wept when the chill breeze of the boy's demise blew through her. Their lives, well, they aren't going so well. Sudden mysterious depressions can lead to acts of desperation and fatalism.

Tod, the man who suddenly thought of dead people, visits the cemetery and runs into Edna, tending her husband's grave in her housewifely fashion. Fussing with the square of pink gravel, flicking dead leaves away, polishing the stone. Normally he's terrified of women, but when she invites him home for a cup of tea, he says yes. He follows her Lada and notices one of her brake lights isn't working. He's good at fixing things like that.

Bethany, the little girl who cried and cried, who lives across the road from salad cream lady and one street away from Tod, she's now four months closer to losing all her teeth due to the sweets her mother bought to soothe her. Depression can be contagious, like flu, and her mother buys a bottle of port today. Weeps with self-pity after her daughter goes to bed. She keeps thinking: What's wrong with me? Something is wrong with me.

And Linda, the forty-seven-year-old salad cream lady. Since that day when apathy deluged her in the condiments aisle, what's-his-face has dumped her without actually saying so, simply leaving her to draw that conclusion in cold, clammy graduated levels of silence. She'd been so certain he was the one, she feels dislocated. The latest in a very long line of quasi-true loves – no wonder she forgets his name sometimes! She's stopped answering her phone and is having trouble getting out of bed. Feels nothing, and would pay good money to even feel sad. Then, in a brief moment of courage, induced chemically at 1:30 a.m., she logs on to www.match.com.

Nobody knows that years ago Linda was in love with a man who used to climb into her bed every Tuesday and Thursday, never any other day for some reason she never discovered. Tod has skin cancer, has managed to keep this secret from all his family, even his sister Mildred who's sharp as a tack. Bethany's mum wonders if she fancies her best friend, but it's too weird to be gay where she lives. Plus, this friend would probably run a mile if she knew. This so distracts her that she regularly burns the fish fingers.

They're neighbours.

They cross each other's paths most days, and often nod in a friendly way. Sometimes they comment on the wetness of the rain, or the suddenness of the sun. Once Tod offered the information he'd just come back from hospital, but that resulted in such a rush of concern from Linda, he'd avoided her for days after because he suddenly knew he didn't want to be seen as a sick person. She still gives him a warm smile and he returns it, but it's only the weather they touch on now.

More time passes. Maybe two weeks. Things start to improve somewhat. In her midnight house, Linda sits at her computer, drinking red wine and writing to four men she has never met. ROMEO69, MisterBig, PerthStudinsky, and uneedme. Extraordinary. As if the walls of her house have melted, and her life is peopled by men who think she's hot. Well, not entirely their fault. She calls herself msup4it, and has chopped ten years off her age. Writing her profile made her think she should take up novel writing. She imagines these men also alone, their computer screens the only light in their house, their windows the only glow in their streets. And where is the harm in any of this? At least these lonely hours will have passed with the pretence of intimacy. And who is to say what is pretence and what is real? At any rate, the smile she is smiling right now is genuine.

Tod is also awake, but in bed thinking about the widow Edna. Tod has never married. Doesn't really mind, it's just one thing he's missed. He's lived all these years and never hurt anyone on purpose. He's proud of this fact. Tomorrow he's taking Edna out to dinner. How old does Tod feel right now? Aside from the itching from the surgery stitches, about nineteen years old.

And then there's Bethany. She's asleep, thumb planted in mouth. Earlier this evening, she'd willed herself into invisibility (a new skill), took her mum's new necklace and also some Smarties. They're under her pillow right now, and she's dreaming about eating sweets on a polka dot beach, and the necklace makes her pretty as her mum. Prettier!

Her mother is awake, smoking and looking out her bedroom window at nothing. The Nytol works for an hour or two, but never the whole night. Since Bethany's birth, her sleeping patterns have been shot. They live in the council estate snuggled into the heart of the village. A house with small rooms, but they don't need much space. She's not tired in the least, but it'll be an early start, so puts out her cigarette, gets back into bed so at least her body will be rested. Tells herself stories. Imagines entire conversations, seductions, even arguments and making-up scenes. Then she replays the great time she had with her best friend yesterday, the laughs they had over lunch, laughing about ... well, their lives and what fuck-ups they'd been in school. She rolls over again, and thinks: I don't know what I'd do without her to talk to. And then a fish lorry from Wick heads noisily down the dark A9, en route to France. It's loud enough to intrude into her thoughts, but also soothing enough to trick her into sleep.

Time keeps passing. It goes lickety split some days, almost out of breath, and other days oozes like golden syrup in a cold kitchen. Linda, Tod, Bethany and her mother are still going in a direction that began the minute the boy's death jolted them. The adults have contrived explanations to justify their actions. They were tired, anxious about chemotherapy appointments, hung-over, pre-menstrual, menopausal, coming down with the flu, angry at their boss or the neighbour's dog, suffering from toothache. Of course, these things contributed as well; it's all a bit blurry. They don't know where their moods come from. It doesn't occur to them the air might be a soup of emotional exhalations, that moods might be inhaled and exhaled. They live in the same place and know each other's names; they have never been inside each other's houses. They are connected. Not connected. Connected.

Linda sits at her computer and searches for love on Valentine's Day. Sounds sad? But there are millions of people doing the same thing. Another glass of Rioja, and she googles Friends Reunited. Keys in the owner of the lips that'd kissed her own so memorably, years and years ago. Nothing. She tries Yahoo people search, BT telephone directory. She writes to various mutual acquaintances she's never written to before, thinly disguising her wine-soaked stalker mood. She says *I still love you* to him in her head, and it feels true. But then one glass too many, and it begins to seem unhealthy, this need to be in love. When she wakes in the morning, her first act is to switch on her computer and pray that she won't be horrified by what she's sent.

Tod and Edna are in bed sipping a post-coital cup of tea. She looks a decade younger now, soft and pink, and Tod looks older, in a stronger, more masculine way. The act itself has made him feel sexy – he hadn't expected this! So even now, as his sweat dries and his heart slows, he feels the stirrings of arousal again. He gently takes Edna's nearly empty cup of tea and places it on the bedside table, closes his eyes and plants a kiss on her tea-warm lips. She returns it, soft mouth opening, body lowering, arms opening to him again. And from the inside, behind their closed eyes, there is nothing about this act that differs from the lovemaking of a couple in their twenties. Astonishingly, not a thing. They yearn for more, while sated. It feels like they've stumbled on the secret of eternal life. If only they can remember how to find this place again and for ever. Not let it fade.

And Bethany and her mother – their life is improving. Or appears to be. Bethany stopped being demanding recently, and instead of worrying about her daughter's quietness, she simply enjoys the calm. Even has a few nights of solid sleep. Looks fresher, and people comment. Starts locking her front door, though. Either someone's thieving, or she's losing her marbles. Too many favourite things going missing. Her pal thinks they should have a fortnight in Majorca together. Leave Bethany with someone and just go. Her pal is child-less and husband-less, though she's had a boyfriend for ever. An accountant. Bit boring. No wonder she wants to have a girly holiday in Majorca.

Bethany has a new friend. The boy next door, who never wanted to play with her before, now drags his mother next door and demands to be left with Bethany. Neither mother goes to the mother–toddler group, and the children are lonely for other children without knowing it. They don't really play together, they don't know how, but they're happier near each other. Bethany hardly looks at him and never offers to share her toys, but she edges near him. Is unhappily aware if he edges away.

Another chunk of time slides away. Whoosht!

One afternoon, Tod, Linda, Bethany and her mother all use the A9. They drive by the place where the boy died and notice nothing, but Bethany suddenly wails. She's dropped her doll, but these tears are sadder than that. It's been so long since she cried like this, her mother touches the brakes and the car behind her does the same, and the car behind that one nearly hits it. But she doesn't notice. She's soothing her daughter.

'Hey, hey. Stopping soon. Don't cry, baby.'

Later that day, Bethany and her mother argue about a pair of earrings. They weren't that expensive, but she's just found them inside her daughter's dollhouse, where she certainly did not put them. Bethany will neither confess, nor lie. She is crying, but silently, mouth closed. Her mother never really clocked kids before getting pregnant, so she doesn't understand how unusual this is. How disturbing her daughter's descent into biddable silence should seem. In any case, she's too absorbed by her Majorca holiday plans to notice much.

Bethany wishes her new pal from next door was here, making those car noises. Her mum in a shouty mood is not much fun. Suddenly, her mother runs out of shouting steam, leaves the room and opens a bottle. Doesn't notice the click of the back door opening and closing. Bethany's sturdy three-year-old legs take her down the path by the scary bushes, onto the pavement with the dog poo, and up the gravel path of the house next door. Her pal's house. But she cannot reach the doorbell, and no one comes to the door when she slaps her little hands on the door and shouts: 'Open up! It's me!' Then the door opens, but it's not the mother, it's a man.

'What have we here?' he says.

At the same time that Linda answers her phone.

'Is that you, Linda?'

'Aye. And who are you?' The pounding of her heart is visible even under her nightgown and robe. It's leaping like a demented and wanton salmon up the falls of her loneliness. It's three in the afternoon, and she's not even dressed yet. Her house is a tip and smells of sour milk.

'I got your email,' he says. 'That was a shock, I can tell you.'

Her hand squeezes and squeezes the phone. A ridiculous smile spreading.

While down the road, Edna finds Tod's oncology appointment letter and he tells her his first lie. Tells her it's a routine appointment. Just a check-up.

This has the double effect of making him feel he's shutting her out – a sad, lonely feeling – and also it reminds him that his days are more precisely numbered than hers. That he will be found out sooner or later, and she will know of this first small lie.

To distract her, he says: 'Hey, there's a sale on at the garden centre. Fancy going down, having a look, Edna? Let's.'

They get stuck behind a tractor, then another tractor, and Tod forgot to pee before he left the house. Fatal, the combination of forgetfulness and an old prostate.

'Don't you love this time of year?' chirps Edna. 'I don't even mind all the tractors. Look at those fields, look how neat the plough lines are, like stripes. Hard to believe in a few days, there'll be a sheen of green on them. Every single year, it amazes me. Ah, my Crunchy Nut Cornflake, do you not think it's amazing?' She's taken to calling him pet names, usually food-oriented. He likes this, but can never quite do it himself.

'Yes, I love it too. I don't mind the tractors either,' lies Tod, clenching his prostate.

Another month passes. Linda finally throws out the salad cream, unopened. She's now in contact with Kiss-man who shaped her life first by his presence, and later, even more powerfully, by his absence. In fact, he's in her bed right now. There he is, stretched out and snoring. Linda is next to him, wide awake. She's looking at him, but not with the rapture one might expect. She's spent too many years imagining him. His kisses are not remotely as intoxicating as she remembers. But there's not dislike on her face. There's interest. He's an unknown quantity that she's summoned into her life. She misses the familiarity of solitude momentarily, but doesn't beckon it back. She's back on the roller coaster! Her muse, the source of years of infatuation, has come home to roost. It's like she's living in a bittersweet romcom.

Tod, who discovered romantic love with the same naive pride Columbus discovered America – he's telling Edna that he's dying. He whispers this right now to her in her dark bedroom. Edna says nothing, merely burrows her head into his shoulder. And they make love again, but this time as if they'll never have the chance again. The very last time. And a few hours later, they make love again as if for the very last time. Then Tod needs to talk. Says he worries he is literally leaking time. Fights an urge to simply plug it up, seal it over. And also, he feels like he's fighting something else, but not the cancer, something more like a … a … an ebb tide. Yes, exactly that kind of powerful freezing pull away from land. Half the time, he's not even sure he's heading to shore, not further out to sea. Too busy trying to keep his face out of the water.

'Listen, Edna, that ebb tide, well, it's pretty obvious it's going to win, but how can that be? It can't really win, can it?'

Edna listens, he can feel her listen in the dark. She finds one of his hands, and whispers:

'Hey, darling Spaghetti Hoop. Of course it's going to win. Shush now. Sleep time.'

Bethany is in trouble. So is her mother. Her pal has cancelled their Majorca holiday. Her accountant boyfriend proposed, and they'll need to save for their wedding. Bethany's mother is so upset, she sulks for a week. Her pal apologises, but in an impatient way, and a cold silence falls between them. Days pass. Bethany's mother understands that her heart is broken, but this is something she cannot tell anyone. Especially, she cannot tell her pal. It wouldn't make sense to anyone. It seems strange even to herself. It sounds too gay, to miss a mere friend this much.

'So happy for you,' she finally tells her, when she runs into her at the Spar. 'Really, really pleased for you. You'll be great together.'

Bethany has begun to bite her nails, and she doesn't want to play with the boy next door any more. Or anyone, come to that. She becomes even more invisible, if possible. She puts herself to bed, after saying goodnight several times to her mother, who is lying on the sofa, staring at nothing. Bethany wishes her mum was not sad, and her mother wishes she was not a mother. They are both exhausted.

Two years pass. It's a Saturday morning. Linda is cooking a fried breakfast for her new lover, because that's what he likes, and making him happy makes her happy. Personally, she prefers porridge. She met this man in the pub a few months ago. Kiss-man disappeared ages ago, probably back to his marriage, having once and for all punctured her fantasy. Now she looks back and thinks she was a little crazy. Linda has a good feeling about this new one. He sometimes forgets to visit when he says he will, and for Christmas he gave her nothing and she gave him something she'd spent days fretting about, but no one's perfect. He's the one. She just knows it. Any other story would be unbearable.

While Linda flips the eggs and butters toast with determined cheerfulness, a few streets away Tod is dying. He dies in bed with his wife Edna holding him. The last words he hears are:

'Go easy, Big Mac With Extra Fries. I'm here.'

His last words are: 'Thank you, wife.'

Or are they: Thank you, life? Edna stays in bed with him, has a strangely refreshing nap. She's an old hand at death, is not afraid. In her dream, Tod is healthy and laughing that laugh of his. She dreams that her heart is cracking open like a big fat egg, and something sweet (like the cream in a Cadbury's Creme Egg) is seeping out uncontrollably. She feels almost incontinent with the sweetest melancholy. Still in this dream, she holds Tod close, close, as if to keep him warm, or from harm.

Bethany is not safe. At lunch time, her mum is not waiting at the school gate, and she walks home herself. She walks quickly, in the wake of another child, walking hand in hand with his own mum. She knows them vaguely, and it seems the wisest thing to do, given she's not allowed to walk home alone yet. Her front door is locked, and she goes round to the back door, a bit scared because of the shadows and proximity of his house. She goes in her kitchen door, and calls:

'Mum!' A little angrily, because her mum has forgotten a very important mum thing.

Then, 'Mum?'

She sees the shoes first, and her mum's jean-clad legs, and the rope which has been tied to the upstairs railing. But the shoes are still on the chair, and the chair has not been kicked away.

'I'm here, Bethie,' she says, climbing off the chair and lifting the rope from around her neck as if she's removing a scarf she's decided really isn't her colour after all. Crumples up a piece of paper lying on the table and says again:

'Here I am, Bethie. Want a muffin?'

Bethany's neck tingles, as if it's been her neck, and she feels the blood rush back into her heart, as if it's been her heart that was so cold it could not go on.

'Okay,' she says after a second, as if everything is okay.

And just after she turns towards the kitchen, a chillier breeze than the day warrants sweeps around her house, down her street, and into various houses. Some people experience a sudden mood plunge, a slight tension. A fragility of spirit. The clouds above Bethany's estate look bruised for a minute, a heavy purplish hue, and the air feels humid. Two residents reach for aspirin, one suddenly snaps at their spouse. Look at them – so close if one of them screamed, they would all hear. But no one is going to scream today. No one is connected, and everyone is connected.

Right now, Tod is a small cloud of disembodied electrons – he still has substance, but so very slight and not visible, not recognisably himself at all, aside from the self he was when he amounted to two cells in his mother's womb. Fastest rewind in the world. Like everyone who has died. Like the boy who died on the A9 that winter's day, adding his panic to the communal soup. Edna is fighting a sudden sluggishness despite her long morning lie-in next to her deceased husband, and attributes it to grief. Linda is convincing herself that he didn't mean to hurt her feelings with that affectionate comment about his ex-girlfriend; makes her third cup of coffee and considers joining the gym. Bethany's mother is making herself chat to her daughter, while washing dishes, but an endless suppressed yawn makes it difficult for her to speak normally. And Bethany, all she yearns for right this minute is some clear cold air to breathe, air that is not sodden with sadness. And maybe a bowl of Coco Pops with cold milk.

Dilys Rose

YOUNG

It had been a miserable summer, weeks of damp gloom, the grass in the back green too sodden to cut, the shrubs and hardy perennials in the border rotting at the roots, but Mel couldn't care less about the weather or the state of the communal plot. Mid-afternoon, after another all-nighter in clubland, getting up to who knows what reckless, unhealthy and illegal activities, her daughter Bonnie was out for the count beneath a rancid downie, amidst the mingled stinks of booze, weed, takeaway food and adolescent hormones.

Electrical wires from phone charger, hair straighteners, blow-dryer and laptop trailed and tangled through a midden of dirty laundry. Squalor was one thing; a fire hazard was another. The hair straighteners had already scorched the carpet and the dressing table: nothing Mel said about safety in the home or the tragic life of burn victims had any more effect than spit on a conflagration. Nothing Mel said about anything had any effect. Her daughter didn't want to hear her mother, see her mother, speak to her, share the same air. Mel was reduced to skulking around, an outcast in her own home.

Scott, Mel's husband, was off in rural France. His emails told of breathtaking bike rides to sleepy villages, of unbroken sunshine by day and dramatic thunderstorms by night, of jaunts to Paris; of the art galleries, the boulevards, the *confit de canard*, the *coq au vin*, the *vin*. It was a working break of sorts and Mel would have been glad for him had Bonnie's simmering resentment not doubled on his departure. Had her mother pissed off as well, she could have had the run of the place and hosted any number of house parties.

Days went by with barely a word passing between mother and daughter. There was never the right time for meaningful conversation, for any kind of conversation at all. If it wasn't friends, it was *Friends*, or *Desperate Housewives*, or *Big Brother*. Bonnie had to go out, to do something on computer, to phone a friend, dry her hair. Often the computer, phone, TV and hairdryer were all going at the same time, as if her aim were to max out her carbon footprint.

When the rain finally let up, Mel dragged the lawnmower from the dank, filthy shed. The grass was long and lush, bristling with dandelions and hard to mow but it was good to feel the sun on her face and focus on a simple goal. She was about to charge into the last swishing, uncut patch when a fat bird bobbed out from the weed-infested border and shuttled briskly across the newly cut, sweet-smelling grass. It was a gull chick, with downy speckled feathers. A very large gull chick.

Mel completed the mowing, returned the Flymo to its home amongst broken chairs, bicycle wheels, skis – whose were the skis? – and other assorted crap which nobody ever saw fit to take to the dump. Then she stuffed the compost bin with grass cuttings. She didn't like the compost bin much. It was alive with the festering and decomposing. It had a heat and internal busyness which was unsettling. Just imagine falling into all that feverishly composting life.

The chick blinked, turned its back on her and crooed softly; its pillowy bulk quivered. It showed no sign of fear or any intention of shifting from the spot. Had it been injured, damaged a wing? She was bending to check its condition when a fierce screeching erupted overhead. Before she had time to locate the source of the racket, a pair of adult gulls whooshed past her ears so close that their wings skimmed her cheeks. Screeching all the while, the gulls rose up again, twisted in midair and launched a second synchronised assault. Shielding her face, Mel backed off from the chick and irritably took refuge indoors. It was the first fine day in weeks, for God's sakes, and she couldn't even enjoy being out of doors.

Gulls had only recently begun to nest in the city centre but they'd quickly made their mark, splattering walls and laundry pegged on clotheslines, fouling up house windows and car windscreens with viscous, corrosive slugs of yellow-green guano. They bawled to each other from chimney tops and swanked on the pavements with the insolent, proprietorial glare of occupying troops. They basked on sun-warmed bonnets of parked cars and harassed indigenous pigeons over anything edible.

The chick had plumped itself down on a sunny patch of grass and closed its smug little eyes. Mel kept the cat indoors though couldn't put any such restraints on her daughter who surfaced late afternoon, slumped in front of *Friends* re-runs with the volume cranked up so high that canned laughter spilled into every corner of the flat. After gulping down an overflowing bowl of cereal, Bonnie spent the next couple of hours between the bathroom mirror and her bedroom mirror. At dusk, without a civil or uncivil word, she traipsed out into the night – too much cleavage, too much leg, too much make-up – leaving a trail of damp towels, discarded clothes and blistering contempt.

Mel shed a few tears. They came easily these days. Her reservoir had filled to the limit and brimmed over at the least provocation. Though she was under orders not to enter Bonnie's room, she ventured in, glancing around anxiously, as if she expected something nasty to be lying in wait for her, a trap of some kind. But no, just the mess. She switched off all electrical appliances, removed pizza boxes and beer cans and made surreptitious inroads into the mountain of laundry.

As the washing machine sloshed into action, she attempted to get to grips with some paperwork – she'd promised Scott she'd attend to her tax returns and some new forms from the Child Benefit Agency – but soon gave in to maternal brooding. The sky turned fuschia, purple, indigo. The chick was still on the grass, making pointless little forays this way and that. It couldn't fly; it didn't even seem to know it had wings.

Mel didn't like gulls but a chick was a chick and when night fell wouldn't it be picked off by some nocturnal predator? Surely a fox would rip it to bits, or one of the burly neighbourhood cats. Her own cat's furry nose was pressed to the window, its hind quarters keenly aquiver.

Just before dawn, in the midst of another bad dream, Mel woke to a loud hum, a sharp, electronic ping, the clack of stilettos, the slap of unlaced trainers and snorts of drunken laughter. She grumped through to the kitchen where Bonnie and Joe, the friend who didn't seem to have a home to go to, were piling a dinner plate with slabs of cheese on toast.

How many times have I asked you not to use the microwave at this time of night?

Sorry, the friend mouthed, hamming contrition.

It's not night, Bonnie sniggered. It's already morning!

Yeah. And I have to get up for work in a couple of hours.

Sorry, Joe mouthed again, as the pair staggered out of the kitchen, leaving crumbs, smears of butter and strings of melted cheese on the counter.

Joe was a cheerful, polite lad and it was some comfort that, given Bonnie's age, looks and the outfits she favoured, somebody was there to watch her back when she was out on the town. But in the house, his presence was like one of those invisible electric fences between mother and daughter interaction. Mel knew that if she ventured too close, she would be repulsed and punished.

The next day, the chick was still on the grass, looking none the worse for spending the night al fresco. It was making a racket. As its shrill, insistent squeals soared to the pitch of a dentist's drill, a sleek adult gull swung out over the rooftops of the tenements, dipped through the pearly dawn, hung, wing beating, above its overgrown darling, and began to deposit squirming morsels into the gaping gullet. It was an awkward exchange, all thrusts and gulps, jabs and grabs, but there was no doubt that the gull was doing her maternal duty.

Ears pricked, tail stiff and bushy as a bottle-brush, the cat once more whined to be let out.

No. You're staying here. With me.

While Scott was away, Mel had done a lot of talking to the cat but why not? The cat didn't mind, even if he was visibly sulking about not being let out, pawing the floor, raking his claws across the lino and emitting a low, threatening growl. The cat would get over it. His memory was short and he didn't hold grudges, whereas Bonnie had built up a whole barricade of grudges, stretching back into early childhood like a hard-packed wall of sandbags. Why did Mel persist in attempting to communicate when she had to check herself before she opened her mouth? Don't mention that, or that, or that; mind your tone of voice; don't sigh, frown.

If they could have maintained a cordial silence, skirted the edges of each other's lives like strangers in a boarding house, nodding as they passed each other in the hall, keeping themselves to themselves, clearing up behind them as they went, this *phase*, as Scott insisted was all it was, might pass and mother and daughter would emerge unscathed. But was it a phase and how long would it, could it last?

Of course a seventeen-year-old wanted to be off living her own life. Mel and Scott had no desire to hold Bonnie back. They were doing everything they could to help her leave home in the hope that, by helping her go, she'd return in her own good time, of her own volition, as a sorted, adult version of the sweet, self-contained child she'd once been.

Bonnie had signed up for some voluntary work on the other side of the world. Mel and Scott were happy to help out though overseas volunteering certainly didn't come cheap. But since they'd paid her plane fare they'd heard no more about her plans. Couldn't she at least have let them know her departure date, what progress she was making with inoculations, visas? Shouldn't she be cutting back on partying all night and sleeping all day; shouldn't she be sorting out what she needed to do, to take? Was she having second thoughts; would she change her mind at the last minute and kiss goodbye to the one opportunity on her horizon? Her parents, it seemed, would be the last to know.

At work, Mel spent her day attempting to advise young people about their plans for the future; young people who were more than willing to discuss their hopes and dreams. Not to mention their problems. One lass, a little pixie-faced blonde whose round blue eyes repeatedly pooled with tears, spent two hours chronicling her parents' messy divorce, her involvement with an older man, her struggle to focus on her studies. Mel had listened, offered tea, sympathy and tissues. She'd been patient, positive and kind but why was it that she knew so much about her students and so little about her own daughter?

She could hear the blaring TV from the street. Bonnie and Joe, still in fluffy pyjamas, were nestled on the sofa.

Hi, said Mel. Hungry?

I'll get food if I want it, said Bonnie.

Hi! said Joe, extra nicely.

Sometimes Mel appreciated Joe's exaggerated sympathy; sometimes, like today, it felt like mockery.

If I'm going to be cooking I may as well make food for you—

I said I'd get food if I want it, said Bonnie.

One of my students has been near where you're going. She was saying—

Tell me later. I'm watching TV.

You're always watching TV. There's more to life than *Friends*.

It's not *Friends*. You just want to find something to complain about.

I just wanted to tell you—

I don't want to hear what your student said.

Fine, said Mel. Fine. Could you turn the volume down? It will disturb the neighbours.

The neighbours make plenty of noise. You just want to find something to complain about.

Just turn it down, will you? Now!

Mel slammed the door on the screaming sitcom and marched off to the kitchen. This wasn't how she'd meant things to go. On the walk home from work she'd told herself over and over and almost certainly out loud, to stay calm, composed; to avoid any confrontation. She'd failed. Again.

The chick was sunning itself on a brick, its fluffy body puffing over the edges, a look of satisfaction on its well-fed face. As it was a fine evening and conversation with her daughter was now out of the question, Mel thought she'd make a start on weeding the border. She had only taken a couple of steps onto the grass when the twin alarms wailed overhead, the parent gulls swung out over the rooftops and plunged, criss-crossing inches from her face in a blur of beating wings. Bloody birds. Did they ever go off duty?

After a week of the chick commandeering the green, starring the grass with sloppy constellations of shit, of its ever-vigilant parents on double offensive and no improvement whatsoever on her own domestic front, Mel phoned Environmental Health, who said it wasn't their responsibility to remove a chick from the drying green. Under certain circumstances it might be their job to remove a nest, for instance in the early stages of nest building, or if, say, it was blocking a gutter or drainpipe. But as the chick was on the ground, it was – Ha ha! – out of their hands.

She phoned the RSPB who said their remit was the welfare of gulls in the wild but she might try phoning the RSPCA. The RSPCA said that if the gull was injured, they could arrange for somebody to fetch it and nurse it back to health but otherwise, it wasn't their responsibility. And gull chicks wandering about the place, building up their strength to fly was a normal seasonal occurrence and happening all over the country.

While the feathery-voiced woman elaborated on the developmental process of gulls, Bonnie appeared in the kitchen, scowling, arms folded. Dressed now, and heavily made-up. Tarty. No two ways about it.

I need to use the phone, she said.

Just a minute.

Mel couldn't quite believe what she'd been told about the family life of gulls. All those chicks tipped out of rooftop or clifftop nests! One minute they'd be sitting snug in warm abodes made of twigs or moss or plastic – the RSPCA woman hadn't specified what gulls used for nest building – the next, plummet and thud. And what about impediments on the way down; sharp rocks, spiked railings, broken glass? Until then, Mel had imagined that birds knew instinctively what to do when the time came: perch on a branch, take off, flap madly and – hey presto – find their wings and soar.

You're doing this on purpose, said Bonnie.

You'll have to wait. I'm speaking to somebody.

I need the phone now!

Tipping a chick out of the family nest was nature's way of saying it was time to move on but what if the chick wasn't ready to leave? How did the parent birds know when the right time had come?

At that moment Mel didn't want an explanation; she wanted a problem solved.

The parents were the issue, Mel explained, their tactics of intimidation. But the RSPCA woman didn't have any suggestions about how to tackle overly protective parents. She did say that food should not be left out and that it could be several weeks before the chick worked out what to do with its wings.

I need to use the phone! Bonnie snarled. You've been talking for ages!

Do you have to be so rude?

Do you have to be so annoying?

Here, said Mel. Couldn't you have used your mobile?

I don't have any credit! Her daughter snatched the phone and clattered off to the front of the house.

Just remember who pays the bills, Mel said to the empty kitchen.

As a change from talking to the cat, Mel passed on her findings about gulls to the neighbours who, now that the sun was shining and the grass was cut, had begun to spend more time on the back green. A retired man, plump and fluffy as the chick, who made it his business to deadhead roses and assist the Virginia creeper to extend over the fence, admitted to feeding the chick. He'd used his golf umbrella as protection but the parent gulls had torn holes in it; he was happy enough to give up feeding the chick. A single woman whose downturned mouth betrayed her disappointment with life, made the point that bread attracts rats and foxes and God knows there were enough of them as it was. The bug-eyed parents of a baby girl bemoaned not being able to hang out their washing. A mother of twin boys complained that the lads hadn't been able to play out of doors and were driving her up the wall. A childless couple, who were in the process of trying to sell their flat, commented on the deplorable state of the border though Mel had never seen either of them pull a single weed.

Mel envied the retired man. His children were married; settled, as he put it, often. She envied the baby's parents their newborn, sleep-deprived joy; she envied the twins' mother for knowing where her offspring slept at night; she envied the childless couple their devotion to foreign holidays; she envied the single woman for having nothing more to worry about than rats and foxes.

Suggestions were offered as to how to get rid of the chick.

Chase it, give it a scare.

Wring its neck.

Now, now. This is a chick we're talking about.

And there are parents present.

Chuck it over the hedge onto next door's green.

Now you're talking.

On either side, the common plots had long ago reverted to wilderness; nobody ever attempted to hang out washing, read, sunbathe, garden, play, light barbeques. The mention of barbeques sparked an irritable flare of comments on the ruinous effect of sizzling sausages on clean laundry.

The consensus was to relocate the chick but, as the retired man pointed out, the removal operation would require at least two people: one to nudge the chick onto a spade and lob it over the high hedge, another to fend off its avenging parents. There was the safety aspect to consider. Not to mention the prospect of making complete fools of themselves. As was often the case when it came to communal responsibilities, the parley wound up on a positive note but nothing was done.

Later that evening, Bonnie and Joe went out again, this time quickly and quietly, offering no information about where they were going or when they might return. Before going to bed, Mel checked her email. Another message from Scott told at some length of another bicycle ride along a riverside path, followed by details of yet another meal. Did he really think she wanted to know what he ate? Since he'd been away she had barely cooked. As Bonnie refused to eat anything she prepared, it was hardly worth making more than a sandwich for herself.

Scott wanted to know whether things had improved at home. As they hadn't, she postponed replying, removed the most dangerous debris from Bonnie's room, once again switched off the electrical appliances and went to bed. The chick had stationed itself directly beneath the bedroom window. It was squealing querulously. Had its parents forgotten to feed it or abandoned their vigilance? The cat padded heavily across Mel's bed.

When she checked Bonnie's room the next morning, the bed was empty. No message on the phone. Mobile number unobtainable. No clue as to where she might be. Should she try calling some of the numbers of Bonnie's friends, numbers she'd gathered surreptitiously, in case of emergencies? Was she over-reacting? Her daughter was legally an adult. Just. It was time she learned to step back, wasn't it?

She sent off a long, tense email to Scott, knowing he couldn't do anything to help but needing to tell somebody, somewhere. He'd be sympathetic, she could count on that, but sympathy wouldn't solve anything. And sympathy for what – being useless, redundant? It wasn't as if, like the gull chick's parents, she'd had to fend off predators. She'd been denied that role.

Scott emailed back instantly, expressing concern and volunteering to contact Bonnie, give her a talking-to, set things straight about what she should appreciate, be grateful for, not take for granted and so on. No, Mel replied, he should do no such thing. Had he forgotten that any kind of reprimand would only make things worse?

That morning she worked at home, in case Bonnie showed up. Wasn't it today that she had to go for her inoculations? She'd already missed an appointment at the clinic and one at the consulate, related to her visa. At least if Mel was at home and somebody needed to get in touch, if something had happened, she'd be there. For all the good she could do, though, she might as well be on the other side of the world.

The chick was padding about on the grass, giving a little hop and awkwardly, one at a time, unfurling its wings.

That's it! she called out. Keep going. Try again. Flap them. Flap, flap! That's what wings are for! She was shouting, through a closed window, at a bird. But there was nobody to hear or look askance.

Unfortunately it didn't turn out to be a eureka moment. The chick gave its wings a brief airing, a half-hearted flap then folded them away. The mother gull dropped by to shove more sustenance into its big baby.

Bonnie dropped by later in the day. She was grey-faced, lank-haired, tight-lipped. Mel tried to explain how she'd been worried, how all she needed was a text, a message on the answering machine, a note, something to indicate that she was still alive. Bonnie mumbled something which might have been Sorry, or Sod off. She took a shower, changed clothes, made herself a sandwich which, for once, she ate in the kitchen. The silence between them, it seemed to Mel, was more wary than hostile. She was about to risk some small talk about the gull chick and the neighbours when Joe arrived at the door and off, once more, the pair of them went.

Days passed. The chick became a bit less fluffy but no more energetic. For hours it sat plumply on the grass, eyes half closed, soaking up the sun, digesting its last meal and waiting for the next, its curved beak giving the impression of a sly smile. Spoiled brat, Mel thought.

Of course the chick did eventually learn to fly. Mel didn't witness its take-off. One day it just wasn't there. She checked all round the border in case it was lurking amongst the tall weeds; there was no sign of it. And no more air attacks. The border was a tangle of neglect but here and there shrubs which had withstood the weather were blooming. Mel began to yank up the ground alder and couch grass, to free a lavender bush from its choke collar of weeds. She heard birds overhead, calling softly to each other, as if they were having a genteel, avian conversation about the lovely weather. High above their temporary nursery, the gull family – sleek white parents and a fluffy grey chick – drifted in a lazy, contented loop then, gliding on a thermal between the chimneytops, swung out of sight.

Stewart Sanderson

TO THE YDE GIRL

My father the physicist tested Lindow man
not to see if he'd been murdered, but to date
how recently. And in the end two thousand years
of decaying carbon-14 convinced the police
to close the case. Another authority
invoked, then the book shut fast and Lindow man
consigned to a museum case behind plate glass
where no druid with a grudge could get to him.
Safe from eating air and ritual knife and rope.
He lies there still. No leads are followed up.

And so it is with you, the girl from Yde who
rose from the peat a bruckle, brittle thing
of tar and knuckle. Maidenhair like moss
kissed black by fire.

Though you, in my imagination, step
to the water's edge, white teeth and straw-fair plaits,
pink fingernails unstained by centuries
of desiccation. A single blow and now you slip
below the surface of the shallow pool
which will contain you. Do your unbound wrists
make this beatific? As perhaps it was
when they unwrapped your atoms. One ellipse
of C-14, revealing when they hit.

Shelley Day Sclater

A BRIEF BIOGRAPHY

A man in a pale green smock cut you from the body of your mother with a slicing knife. He was flailing as much as you were. He put his shiny instruments into the boiler to wash all trace of you away. He rinsed his hands. He looked across the pale green room in the pale green light; he looked at your mother whose hair was damp, whose eyes were closed. Someone came and stitched up the gaping bloody hole in your mother's belly where they had pulled you out. You started screaming. It was the first sound you ever heard, and you didn't know what it was.

Your father wore a suit, a tweed suit, of a pale greenish colour, made in Ireland, after the moss that coats the damp peat by the sides of the sheep tracks. The weave was rough against your smooth face. Your father had money in his pocket; you heard it rattle. He looked down at you with eyes the colour of the walls. Your eyes, squinting, tiny, did not yet focus. You had no idea who he was, that man with the rough green skin and the walls for eyes.

Now that you had come, your father was thinking of Norway. He was thinking of Golå, of the red wooden *hytte* in the wild green *kve* where the globe-flowers and the harebells and the cloudberries tossed their girly heads in the fine warm grass. It was August. All down the side of the mountain, all the way down to the Golåvann, the fir trees stirred, the scent of resin drifting on the air like birdsong. Across the lake, in the distance, snow-capped mountains rose blue in the haze. Your father will take you to there when the time comes.

You are a child in a portrait painted by an itinerant Spanish artist. You hang opposite your brother on the cold wall of the morning room where no-one ever goes. Your mother is in the blue-painted kitchen, making ginger granthams. She beats butter and sugar in the Mason's bowl until her arm is tired. She looks out into the Hampshire afternoon and thinks of Blackloch, of the small white-painted house reflected in the water where otters dive. She smells bluebells and daffodils, wild garlic in the woods; she worries about the encroachment of rhododendrons and caravans. There's a little boat tied up at the jetty, bobbing gently in the water, in the wispy shadows of the trees.

They send you away to school because that is what they do and they do it. They spend a long time choosing, a good one that will make you into a fine young man. They dream for you: a lawyer, perhaps, or a churchman, like your godfather in Bridge of Allan, or an army officer, like your mother's brother whose name you should be honoured to bear; the uncle you never knew no longer needs a name. The school makes you tired and angry, but that's how things are. The matron is kind and her skirts are warm and in the summer you lie on the playing field and watch the cricket and you eat the biscuits your mother sent wrapped up in foil.

Oh look, here come the horses, your father's passion. In the holidays you ride up onto the hill in the early mornings. You hear the metallic squawk of the pheasant as it flaps in the corn stubble, too heavy to lift off without an effort. Your father takes snuff and issues commands and sometimes he makes you laugh. In the winter, you ride to hounds and they smear fox blood on your face. Your mother puts her hand on your head, but says nothing. You eat your ice cream alone in the dining room. Above the door, in the hallway, the fox's head hangs, its teeth bared.

With your father you walk for days in the Jotenheimen, looking out towards a vast expanse of sky; you're up beyond the tree line, way beyond the fir trees and the bilberries and the tight dry heather and the twisted stubbled birch. The air is light and this is the only place on earth you can breathe with any ease. In the wide green valley far below sheep tear rhythmically at the close-cropped turf, the muffled clank and echo of their neck bells the only sound. Poetry comes to you easily but you tell no-one. Your father makes bloody plans for catching trout; you will help him put the nets out at Little Jetningen, you will help him pull them in, you will help slash the slithering fish open and scrape the crimson guts into the chipped enamel pail that stands outside and attracts flies. Your mother never comes to Norway and you do not miss her.

Alternate years, you go to Galloway. You row the little boat out on the Blackloch, your arms are growing strong. Your mother, sitting in the bow, points out a heron standing like a sentry among the rocks. Gulls wheel and screech overhead and the water is getting choppy. Your oars dip rhythmically as you bend and pull, bend and pull, glancing over your shoulder to line up the jetty. You help your mother out of the boat, and you notice how cold her hands are, how papery the skin. You are young and strong and she is old. She smiles, gathers up her skirt and begins the short climb up the hill. The dachshunds run and leap, yapping on the grassy bank, worrying shadows, as you tie the boat up.

Your mother takes you to Lochnaw, to the crumbling grey castle where she was born. The cold stone kitchen smells of ancestors and thick brown tea is poured into chipped china cups. You eat shortbread and fruitcake and the sound of the wind is hollow in the chimney. This is where your middle name came from.

One time, you walk alone along the cliffs, all the way from Dunskey to Killintringen. You stand for a long time looking at the House of Knock, a big white house that sits on the edge and looks out across the Irish Sea. Your mother, as a child, in skirts and a clean white pinafore, thick stockings and little black boots, is by herself down there on the shore, collecting shells and putting them into the pocket of her pinafore that is already bulging. She does not yet know that her mother will die, that her brothers will die, that she will marry your father, that her own ashes will rest for ever in this place. For now, she is a child, just a child, engrossed in collecting shells. You walk back up the muddy track towards the road. The wind blows from the west, a sticky salty feel to it. Behind you, the waves crash on the rocks and froth and foam in all the little crevices before pulling back to gather up strength again. You walk back under a bruised cloudy sky as the sun is setting.

Kirsteen Scott

AND THE WIND SANG

in the month of Carpe Diem
sand grains in the hourglass

in the month of Signet
dot the line

in the month of the Coracle
abandon the ark

in the month of Depression
name it thief

in the month of Psalms
bare the head

in the month of the Warrior Spirit
unlock the self

in the month of Ardifuar
bless the broken boat

in the month of Pontefract
build a bridge

in the month of Gravity
icebergs calve

in the month of Magenta
sip from fallen plums

in the month of the Otter
leave your mark

and in the month they call Purslane
let cats curl by the fire.

Maria Sinclair

PILGRIM

Dae ye remember that guy wae his beard
doon tae his baws, him that used tae kick aboot
St Enoch Square, haudin bags of newspapers,
toes burstin through frayed shoes,
the skin aw hard and broon right doon
tae his bare sole so that his shoes were kinda pointless,
and I don't think he ever took them aff,
because they didny look like the kinda shoes
ye could put on, it was more like they'd been
moulded there, deliberately, like an auld witch's curse,
and he hud tae keep wearin them till they fell apart,
or some fairy godmother turned his rags tae prince's clobber,
and he never asked for money, even though
if anybody wis gony ask ye fur two bob
it wid be him, and I don't know whit age he wis,
though his hair wis black and his teeth wur black
and his smell wis black and his white shirt
wis black and his shoes wur black,
and he never spoke tae anybody, so I don't know
whit happened or when wis the last time,
but one day he just wisny there, no even his
shoes, though I think I saw him
on a bus once, and I smiled and he looked
at me and smiled back, well it wis more a sort
of a nod, but I could just be makin that up
and anyway it doesny matter, does it?

Raymond Soltysek

LIZARD ISLE

Miriam sits by the river's edge under the shade of a chestnut tree. She is supposed to be sketching the little stone bridge across the river. It is picturesque, three-arched, grey and possibly ancient; but, to be honest, Miriam isn't much of an artist. She once had ambitions, not to be a professional, of course – far too precarious a life – but at least to indulge herself in some way. Teach, perhaps; those who can, Donald would say. Instead, she watches two young boys laughing and playing in their yellow inflatable dinghy on the opposite bank. They are skinny, pale, all sinew and gangle, and they leap off the rocks into the boat, capsizing it and tumbling each other into the water. Behind her, young, handsome, blue-eyed Artur waters the lawn.

This is her widowed, widened life, now. She has embraced the goal of self-improvement: last summer, she'd walked in Catalonia, very well organised it was, with their bags always waiting for them in lovely hotels and a car on hand for those who found the heat too much (she'd only used it the once); over the winter, a cookery course in Florence with a strangely passionate Italian chef. She had made many friends, though she never visited any of them afterwards, and they never visited her. Her daughter has asked her, 'Met any nice men on these trips, Mum?' but no, she says, the thought has never entered her head.

Pink geraniums bloom in a trough in the centre of the wall separating the garden from the river, sunning themselves stiffly in the lack of breeze. One twitches slightly, and a little green flash pops out onto the wall. A lizard, tiny, horny-skinned, pasty-shaped, basks nervously for a moment or two. Then it tips over the edge, walks vertically down the wall in stop-frame motion on its little sucker feet and skittles off into the undergrowth, its tiny arms and legs flailing.

She settles back, running a finger under the chin strap of her sunhat: she finds the heat so uncomfortable at those points where cloth exerts pressure on her skin. Papery, dry skin. Old. Her head rests against the back of the chair, comfortably designed for long periods of artistic sitting; she feels that slipping sensation, of the laughter and the birdsong and the hiss of the hose receding somewhere, gilding the back of her head, and she is happy to let herself drift.

Donald would have considered this an extravagance with time that he would never have countenanced. He planned bus trips to castles and military tattoos. Abroad, moments were filled with activities – 'There are some ruins at the top of this hill'; 'Come on, dear, the guidebook says there's an interesting craft shop down this alley' – and he saw it all through a lens.

At first, it was his Kodak Brownie, but he'd developed a passion thereafter. Leicas and a Hasselblad (Hassel*bad*?; she can never remember) and then on to Super 8mm. Just before he died, he'd bought the latest digital camcorder: it was still in its box, cellophane wrapped.

She remembered Venice especially, prodding her into position for the perfect shot of St Mark's or the Ca d'Oro, all the while an enormous VHS camera on his shoulder like a rocket launcher. When they went home, he played the video on the TV and didn't remember a third of the places they watched. 'But we have it here whenever we want,' he said.

She dozes for a while, and is woken gently by the sound of a voice far away. She opens her eyes stickily: Artur is beside her.

'Mrs Davies. Are you all right?'

'Why of course, dear.' Her lips feel thick. 'I'm fine.'

'You were speaking in your sleep.'

'Oh my. I hope I wasn't saying anything too scandalous.'

He smiles. 'No, not at all. You are much too much of a lady.' He lifts her handbag and her drawing tools. 'I think you should sit in the shadow a little.'

The sun has moved, and she is now in its full mid-afternoon glare. She feels the flush on her cheekbones, the tightness across the skin of her shoulders, and when she levers herself from her chair, her legs give way beneath her.

'Oh my,' she says. 'I'm getting old.'

'Not at all, Mrs Davies.' He offers her his arm. 'We must all be very careful of the heat here.'

He helps her under the shade of an adjacent tree: she notes guiltily that she hasn't completed enough of her sketch for the change in perspective to make any difference whatsoever.

'You are perhaps a little dehydrated,' he says. 'I will ask Anna to bring you a cold drink from the hotel.'

'Thank you, dear. Thank you so much.'

Artur is, she realises as she watches him make his way up the garden, the first naked man she's seen in forty years, Donald always having been a pyjama man. The thought pleases her. Of course, when the art instructor, Julieanne (wonderful colourist, lovely landscapes), had announced that the model usually hired for the Life Drawing session was indisposed, and that one of the hotel staff had volunteered to pose, all the men fervently hoped it would be Anna, a beauty with a long back and low-slung hips they could not avoid watching and who made perfect pizzas and cocktails while flashing dark Italian looks. One of the Germans, a florid man in khaki shorts, had privately professed abject love for her after she had placed a hand on the small of his back as she served dinner.

And the men seem to covet the attention Anna pays to The Sirens. Five of them, all indeterminate ages, they live in a serene and perpetual whirl of things to do. One or two paint, one writes poetry, another apparently composes music – or did they all do these things, but just at different times? – and they gather regularly during the day to share their thoughts on the veranda or in the guests' lounge, unable to contain themselves, eager to tell of the rare bird one has spotted, or the fabulous squid they saw on the fishermen's boats at the quayside after bicycling five kilometres to the coast. Last week, two – in their sixties, for heaven's sake – had jumped off a mountain with parachutes on their backs.

'And how long are you here for, if you don't mind me asking?' Miriam was passing through the lounge one day, overhearing their latest adventures. 'It's just you seem to know so much about the place.'

'That's because we live here now, my dear,' one had replied, and she introduced them all, a coterie of Harriets and Margarets. 'One by one, we all visited here and decided to stay. Didn't we, ladies?'

Yes, they all beamed back, and one patted an empty seat. 'Why don't you join us, Miriam?' She had, and spent the best half-hour of her holiday in an atmosphere of confident relaxation while Anna beamed and served them olives and her famous margaritas. 'Would never have happened but for Anna,' one of them remarked confidentially. 'She took us all under her wing.'

So there was a ripple of surprise – perhaps even consternation – when it was Artur who entered the studio wearing a short bathrobe, and another of undisguised envy when he slipped it off to reveal himself.

There was a complete unselfconsciousness in his poses and no hint of arrogance about the definition of his muscles and the flatness of his stomach. Of course, none of the men could find it in themselves to concentrate on his genitals, but Miriam enjoyed looking at them, the dark folds of skin, the wrinkles, the coarseness of the hair. She couldn't tell how large it was compared to other men – perhaps about the same as Donald in his younger days – but she was certainly struck by its prettiness. She'd devoted a corner of her sheet to an individual study, then hurriedly used the others for less attentive sketches of less controversial parts of his anatomy.

'You've captured his knee very well, Miriam,' Julieanne said. 'There is a real power, a real force in your rendering of the tendons there.' Then she'd tapped Artur's penis. 'This is the best, though.'

The sun reflects sharp shards of silver off the river, and she shades her eyes with her hand as if saluting something in the distance. Her head begins to throb with a tension just above her eyes, and she wishes she'd brought sunglasses too. She stretches her legs out and adjusts her wrap to cover them, settles down, eases into the chair and is still.

Six feet along the wall, another livid green lizard pokes its head out of the geraniums. With explosive little movements, it scrambles onto the top of the wall. She holds her breath so as not to disturb it. In a couple of spasmodic skips, it turns this way and that, then holds one of its front feet in the air and presents a profile as motionless as a photograph. She hasn't moved, but it senses her there, testing the air with its tongue.

Its eye rolls. It stares at her, performing for her. 'Watch this,' it twitches at her. Its jaws open wide, its mouth like pale pink wet dough. A sliver of saliva, thick and reptilian, stretches between top and bottom lip, then soundlessly snaps.

Miriam gapes, fascinated, repulsed. Its jaws widen, widen, until she fears she'll hear the crack of tiny bones dislocating. With a jerk, though, they flip back, over its front feet and scaly neck. There is a gulping motion and, slowly, it begins to devour itself from the inside out.

She gags and retches between her feet. Foamy bile dumps itself on the grass. Her hands knead her eyes and she cannot look up, cannot watch any more.

But she must.

The insides of the lizard's lips close cheekily over the tip of its tail. It quivers and pulsates wetly, then dries quickly in the heat and turns to pale grey, sitting there indistinguishable from the other little rocks perched along the top of the wall.

From behind her shoulder, Anna swings into view, dropping a tarnished silver tray with a clever arrangement of legs before her. 'Drinks and dolmades, Mrs Davies?' she says, bending over the tray to serve her.

Miriam feels the blood drain from her head, sweep down her body. 'I'm sorry ... oh ... I feel really faint ...' She tries to lean forward and almost topples from her chair. Anna kneels quickly beside her and takes her hand.

'Mrs Davies? Are you unwell? Can I get you something? I have brought water: have some.' Anna helps the glass of carbonated water to Miriam's lips: it fizzles painfully in her throat.

'I must have had too much sun. I saw things.'

'What did you see?'

'Oh, nothing. Just stupid heat stroke, I suppose.'

The girl raises an eyebrow, scolding her. 'What did you see, Mrs Davies?'

She gulps more water, then points at the wall. 'Over there. That rock on the wall. A minute ago it was a lizard. I saw it change. Or I thought I did.' She passes a hand over her forehead. 'You must think I'm a mad old bat. Off my trolley.'

Anna's face doesn't flinch. 'But you did see it,' she says.

'Oh come now, dear. You don't have to agree with everything I say.'

She is still holding her hand. 'But you did. I did not say that the lizard changed, just that you saw it. That makes it real. Do you know the name of this island, Mrs Davies? In English?'

Miriam shakes her head.

'The Island of Lizards. There is a legend about a place called the Lizard Islands. They were magical. Strange things took place all the time. Women who were cast out of society found refuge there: they went to the Lizard Islands.'

'They came here?'

'No. They were a legend. But who knows, perhaps this island was the source of the legend.' She lets go of Miriam's hand and crosses to the wall. She picks up the stone and offers it to Miriam, who takes it nervously and tentatively weighs it in her hand, sees that it glistens faintly pink in the sunlight. 'Perhaps someone once came here long ago and saw a lizard change into a rock.'

Miriam feels tears in her eyes. 'I'm very tired,' she says. Anna makes her eat some bread – 'The dolmades will be too rich' – and drink more water. 'I will get Artur to help you back to the hotel for a rest.'

What on earth is wrong with me? she wonders. She turns the stone over in her lap. It is, only, a stone. She is right: she is turning into a mad old bat.

Artur comes running, apologising for leaving her asleep so long in the sun. He has a cold, damp towel in his hand, and he places it across her brow, 'for a moment before I return you to your apartment,' he says.

He places his left arm around her waist, barely touching but there should she need it, and helps her back up the garden and all the way to her room. Anna has already drawn the muslin drapes, turned down Miriam's bed, and adjusted the air conditioning.

Artur leaves decorously as Anna helps Miriam into her nightdress, prising the rock from her fingers and placing it on the dressing table. She pours more water, helps Miriam ease herself onto the bed and puts a cushion beneath her feet. She sits on the bed and takes Miriam's hand.

'I will come back later, to check that you are well,' Anna says. 'I am concerned about you.'

Miriam pats the girl's knee. 'Och, there's no need. I'll be fine. Besides, isn't tonight your night off?'

She smiles. 'It was. I was going out for dinner. But I can have it here.'

With a delighted little shock, Miriam realises that Anna and Artur are lovers. 'Artur is a lovely young man.'

'Mrs Davies! You are a very perceptive and a very naughty woman. He is sweet, but young and he is returning to university in Paris after the summer. We are close for the moment.'

A wash of sadness comes over Miriam at this girl's self-assuredness, her self-possession. That is what is so much better about the world, nowadays.

'You are thinking of something.'

'Perhaps I was. I'm not sure.' She sighs. 'Well, no, I am sure. I was thinking of a time I went out for dinner with my husband. It's not important.'

'I would like to hear. It was romantic, yes?'

'Oh no! Not at all!' Why not, Miriam thinks, it was so long ago. 'Have you ever heard of the Titanic Test?' she says. Anna shakes her head. 'Of course you haven't. Silly of me.

'We were out for dinner with some colleagues of my husband. Lots of boring business, you know. There was a couple, Frank and Fiona, I think they were called. They divorced shortly afterwards, so things were bad. Fiona got rather drunk and gave us all the Titanic Test. If you were on a lifeboat and there was only room for one person, would you choose your partner? All very uncomfortable. "Of course," Frank said. She told him he was a liar, that he'd pick his children from his first marriage. He had to think, then said he'd get them all on but she said that wasn't part of the game, it was hypothetical, he had to choose.

'And then she went even farther. Frank and his children are on the lifeboat and Fiona and his ex-wife come swimming towards them: who would he choose? He went quiet, and she went on and on, "Come on, Frank, who would you choose? Who would you choose?" He said he'd jump in to make room for Fiona, but she said that just shows he'd pick his ex-wife first, so he shouldn't pretend to be a hero. Well, nobody knew where to look.'

'What happened?'

'I suppose Donald thought he'd better say something. Well, he said, he wouldn't choose me because, let's face it, I'm far too fat and would capsize the damned thing. Everybody laughed. Except Fiona.'

'This should not upset you. Your husband was perhaps drunk: I'm sure he didn't mean it.'

'No, it's not that that upsets me. It's me. I laughed too.'

Anna purses her lips – she is so beautiful – then leans towards Miriam and gently kisses her cheek. 'Feel better, Miriam,' she whispers, almost hisses, in her ear, and as she draws her head away, Miriam notices for the first time that the pupils of her dark, ancient eyes are not quite round. 'You are tired. Sleep.'

And Miriam does feel an exhaustion that makes her ache as if her old flesh is falling off her bones, and her eyelids flutter and she slips into unconsciousness to the sight of the girl, smiling at her in a way she recognises from her childhood.

She sleeps all night and wakes feeling clean and scented in sheets that are cool and crisp and white. Someone has been into the room – the window is open, her clothes tidied away – and they have bathed her and brushed her hair and smoothed away her soreness, it seems. She feels different, wonderful even, as if she has been changed at some genetic level.

She gets out of bed and peers through the muslin curtains – it is going to be a fabulous day with so much to do – then looks in the dressing-table mirror at herself looking back: nothing new, but she says 'Good morning, Miriam' at her reflection as if she were saying hello to another person.

Her finger runs along the edge of the dressing table and flips up the plastic lid of her pot of facial moisturiser, letting it fall back with a little clunk. She turns over bits and pieces on the surface – her purse, keys, a necklace Donald gave her she now admits she never liked – and finds herself reaching out for something which isn't there.

The pink stone. It is gone, and written in the dust are the tiny, trident-shaped scratches of lizard feet, heading purposefully towards the open window.

Tom Sommerville

AN EDINBURGH GOD

About an Edinburgh god there are a few certainties:
he would live in a good street in the New Town,
so he could keep an eye on things
and have a wee place down the coast
or up in Perthshire, for the weekends.
He would send his son to the Academy
and would claim that, after all,
it was just the local school.
He would be seen in Glass & Thompson's coffee shop
with Alexander McCall Smith, but not too often.
He would call Gullane Gillane and
he would be a Liberal Democrat so as
not to offend anybody.
He would not be too familiar with the neighbours
so as to retain a bit of the mystery of the old gods
but, more importantly, not to be thought common.
He would have *The Scotsman* delivered each morning,
for the look of the thing,
but would not read it, knowing in advance
there would be nothing in it.
He would talk proper and have no truck with
the Scots language, which he would call bad English,
except in a poem.
He would be seen in Waitrose but never in Tesco.
He would be invited to join the board
of the National Trust for Scotland and become
a non-executive director of the Royal Bank.
He would hate the bacchanalian goings-on
of the young on Fridays and Saturdays
but would do nothing to change them,
because he would not like to interfere,
and, besides, gods aren't what they used to be.
He would leave his curtains open at night
so passers-by could see the good furniture
and his picture collection.

But questions remain:
would he still shop in Jenners
now that it's been taken over?
What would he think of the trams?
Would he long for thunderbolts?
Would he forgive Glaswegians?

Kathrine Sowerby

SONIA DELAUNAY

Last night, I dreamt about Sonia Delaunay.
Her paintings, deep pink and orange, and what a name –
blunt edges tumbling round my mouth in the minutes
before I'm fully awake and I want to stay in the dream,
in the room with high ceilings, busy with the mess of
    activity and ideas.
A girl with long hair folding over her shoulders,
cross-legged with a drawing board on her knees.
My boyfriend who has left me for a more urgent,
    angular girlfriend
working amongst piles of papers and models and photographs.
I look for curtains or sheets to enclose my space but
    the ceiling is so high,
I have so much to catch up on.
Small marks, grey and tight, what I need is colour,
    whole washes of it.
Brushstrokes of orange and sickle-shaped pink, Sonia Delaunay –
bold and bright transparency. I want to paint
like Sonia Delaunay.

Jim Stewart

NEST

They'd troubled their way into
a traffic cone too heavy for the cat
to topple, its hole
too high; and built inside,

driven by their genes, a cup's
thrift of moss and feather, and of web.
The eye would catch
a flicker, in and out

of the red-and-white geometry,
comings and goings
with pinched grubs
for the craws under that rubber.

One day the commerce ceased.
An old story, of fields
toxic with spray, each gathered meal
deadlier than the last,

made clear
they'd come no more. The cone
lifted, showed five young
with blown-bubblegum crops

that stopped the traffic,
poisoned where they lived
and rendered mulch,
never to fly.

Theirs was the common cup;
but its base uncommonly wide
spread the breadth of the cone,
large dinnerplate sized.

The lane once entered,
the signed route kept,
birds had arrived
in their town of children

and couldn't help building out,
to what limits exist,
a space made fast
for their homecomings.

The cat flung off
for simpler kills.
The nest's odd architecture
and unseeing idea

settled in a room of the house
where, working blind,
shadows filled
its fixed bowl.

Richard W. Strachan

INCHKEITH

From the station he crosses the roundabout and heads through the estate. On the other side of the estate he climbs the hill.

We call these streets, and we call these houses. We call these cars, we call this a hospital. But that's not what they *are*. Those are just the names we have given them.

His sister Rachel is waiting for him by the entrance, flanked by smokers and watching absently the skittish progress of two crows across the car park. She doesn't see him until he's almost there in front of her. When she glances up there isn't so much the look of recognition on her face as the same bland understanding as when you see your own reflection in a mirror.

There's nothing to say.

She leads him through the corridors to the palliative care unit at the back. Their mother is lying down, asleep.

Not unconscious, Rachel says. Just sleeping. Although they tell me it won't be long …

I know. I mean, just looking at her, I know.

They sit down on opposite sides of the bed, and after an hour their mother wakes up. He's ashamed and confused at how difficult he finds it to talk to her. He has an almost superstitious fear of her, of her illness. But it's not fear; he directs his eyes to every corner of the room as he tries to isolate the feeling. It's self-consciousness, or embarrassment, as if he is being watched or is under some form of assessment. The last time she was here she was in a communal ward; now it's a single room. No more chemotherapy, no further tussles with the ion stream and the accelerator machines.

Rachel leans over and kisses her on the cheek. He can see the shape of her upper jaw. The sheets bulge around her stomach; she is swollen with her disease. He leans and kisses her on the cheek too, and, as he falls into a tentative hug, unwilling to hold her as tightly as he wants to, he feels the need to lay his hand on top of her head, as if she is a child and the relationship between them has been inverted. She pats her hair back into place. There is nothing of her.

She isn't lucid. They speak on parallel tracks, passing occasionally to catch light of the other's train of conversation, but for the most part he talks about himself, his work, the article he's trying to write, his life, the journey down. He gives her all his current information, it's what she always wanted to hear. She answers in words that don't connect. She seems to understand, but she can't make herself understood. He thinks that all three of them must share the sense that they are talking around the real subject, and that this subject has enormous power only by virtue of its sitting nameless between them.

Rachel talks about what she has been doing lately as well, about her boyfriend and her job and some minor difficulties back at the house (a problem with the fuse box, an unreliable signal on the wi-fi they installed and which their mother has rarely if ever used).

We'll get it sorted though, Rachel says, don't worry.

He thinks, She'll never see the inside of that house again.

He takes his mother's hand and she squeezes back. She understands that. They all sit for a while and hold her hands, her fingers swollen and spatulate, until she falls asleep. A nurse comes in to check on her. The room is stifling, and he is sweating heavily under his clothes. He opens the French windows and walks out onto a patio, a neat lawn of buttercups and daisies beyond it. There is a garden bench and a low wooden table at the side. On the table there is a saucer with three grey cigarette butts swimming in an inch of rain water.

He starts crying, and walks further up the lawn so no one will see him.

Back at the house, he writes an abstract for his article, a short reiteration of the facts to keep them clear in his head.

In 1493 James IV proposed that two infants be placed on the island of Inchkeith, in the Firth of Forth, isolated and free from interference, to determine what language they would speak when they grew up. To look after them, a wet nurse was found who was both deaf and mute, and would be unable to communicate with them by speech. It was assumed that at the conclusion of this experiment, the children would speak the 'original' language of God, the language of the Garden of Eden. There is no record of what happened to them.

He gives up his pen and sits back in his chair. The whole thing is speculative. He is wasting his time. There is no more documentary evidence for the subject than a brief passage in an early-sixteenth-century survey of Edinburgh. Where do we go from here? In the end, the island became an asylum for syphilitics and plague victims. Evidently the king lost interest in his whimsical and sinister experiment. Flodden was twenty years ahead of him. He would die to an English arrow, utterly unable to explain what was happening to him in the moment of his killing.

Picture this scene. Mist hangs heavy on the water. A boat issues from the harbour at Leith, a fishing boat with a small crew, all of whom have been forbidden to speak. The boat's mast-lamp is swallowed in the haze. The island looms ahead, and the caged flame of a warning beacon directs the boat to a stone jetty. The fishermen tie up and unload their cargo – a few crates of food and water, firewood, supplies to keep the rudimentary buildings in good order. A woman emerges from the mist. Behind her, holding hands, are two young children. Silently, enveloped in their mutual silence as in a cool, connecting web, the woman and the children gather up the supplies and take them back to their shelter. The fishermen say nothing. The island's only inhabitants say nothing. The fishermen untie and sail back into the mist.

Pictures would be all you had. Trapped in a perpetual present, for the woman and the children there would be no way to describe it.

Rachel comes in from the garden, knees stained with mud. She is holding a pair of pruning shears and a trowel. She places them in a basket by the back door.

Something else to think about, she says. It's going to pieces out there. What do you know about gardening?

Less than nothing.

Pity.

He has spent the afternoon going through bills and bank statements, title deeds, savings accounts. Everything seems to be in order. He doesn't know what he's doing. He wants to say to his sister that all of this is beyond him, but doing so would be to admit that she is the more successful adult. She has a mortgage, she has a well-paying professional job with a regular salary. It's not a competition, but he feels, like the dark backing to the mirror of this whole experience, the subdued disappointment of their mother in the room.

Rachel washes her hands at the kitchen sink.

Shall we get someone in? she says. Look in the phone book, hire a gardener?

I don't know. What time are you going back up?

In a few minutes. I thought I could stay for an hour or two, then you could take the next shift.

Shift?

So at least one of us is there. It'd be nice for her if she wakes up to see one of us sitting with her.

The strangest thing ... He is most upset when his mind is empty, when he is washing the dishes or blankly standing in the bathroom having a piss. It's when the mind has nothing else to fix on, he thinks. A draining away, a kind of extended present tense, the mind poised only in this moment. It can't range over what has been, or what will be. Just what is. We are lost in this moment, for ever. In this moment my mother is dying.

While Rachel is out he tries to work more on his article. The whole process makes him feel numb with frustration. No paper will take it; no journal or magazine will be interested. And yet the subject compels him, and he cannot let go of it.

From his kitchen window back home he can see Inchkeith; its heavy hull of black stone and dull grass low in the water, its dormant lighthouse, the crags and hollows of its coastline inhabited now by nothing more than gulls and seabirds. To live in a world of such silence that gestures are almost deafening; rudimentary signs, indicating your meaning by way of hand movements, expressions, symbols ... When you have no means of speaking, no language with which you can communicate, how do you make yourself understood? But maybe I'm looking at it the wrong way round. If I have a proposition in my head that I want to communicate, I translate it into writing or speech. But for them, raised like this, perhaps the form and the proposition are one and the same thing, or the relationship between them not quite as abstract? They think and communicate at the same time, in the same gesture. So, the gestures aren't separate, they're the visible contours of their thought ...

He pictures them on that island, the children growing without ever hearing a spoken word, without ever seeing a written sign. It stands to reason that the woman, the wet-nurse, would not have been able to read and write. Where in the medieval city, in a barely literate society, would they have found a deaf and mute woman, living on church charity, who could read and write? (He writes, *This opens subsidiary questions – how did the authorities explain the plan to her? How did they make her understand what was expected of her if she couldn't hear and couldn't read? The uncomfortable suspicion arises that they may not have found their wet-nurse by chance. Perhaps she wasn't deaf or mute to start with, and after explaining what was expected of her they cut out her tongue ...*)

As they grew, the children would have relied on symbols. Think of our early ancestors, before language had even begun to develop. So, the best analogue then is ... cave paintings, or carved symbols. Stone, ivory, bone ... Say, one day, the children felt ill or wanted to be on their own. They placed outside their huts a spiral design carved into a block of wood, or a sequence of shells strung up above their door. Cairns decorated with bladderwrack and mermaid's purses, dotted around the island. Assemblages of stone and rope. Living inside a skein of silence, they left significant arrangements of driftwood where each could see it.

You can't write about this. He looks at the page. You are using an abstraction to talk about an abstraction.

When you don't need to speak, he writes, *when language has been removed from your discourse, whether written or spoken, then you live by the purity of your gestures.*

He crumples up the sheet.

When Rachel returns he is still sitting at the kitchen table, his notes spread out around him. He doesn't look up, aware of her only as a vague bustle beside the sink, by the cupboards and drawers. Eventually she places a glass of whisky by his elbow.

You read my mind, he says.

Special offer over the road. I thought ... why not? So, she says as they sip their drinks, how's it going?

Christ, where to start? He looks at his notes. It's going nowhere. I have all these ideas, these speculations, concepts, some pretty vague data, some rough idea of the period, a few photographs of how it is now – you know how difficult it is to get onto that island? I can see the thing from my house, but I can't find anyone to take me there. I'll end up buying a bloody kayak and doing it myself.

That's not what I meant, Rachel says. How's it going?

Not well. You?

Not well.

How is she?

Not good.

They finish their whisky in silence.

Are you going to head up the road then? Rachel asks him. A couple of hours?

I don't know. Was she awake when you were there? I don't really ... it's not that I don't want to, but if she's not there to see us, if she doesn't know we're there, then I don't ...

It's not just for her, Rachel says. It's for you as well.

Tomorrow, he says, avoiding her eye. I'll head in tomorrow morning.

It was so fast. It gave no quarter once it announced itself. There you were, getting the diagnosis, and a few months later you had mere days to live. Trapped inside this cage. How about that? he thinks. A rebellion, of the thing you rely on most. She had retreated inside herself, he could see that clearly on the first day he arrived. It wasn't so much falling asleep, or falling unconscious, but a way of seeking refuge. The irony of this struck him as unnecessarily cruel, on top of everything else. The body was the thing that was killing her, but it was the thing into which she could slip away as well, to take shelter from the storm. Maybe it wasn't cruel then; it was a form of kindness. It's not killing her, it's helping her on her way. There's no one definition of what it's there for. But if that's the case, then what's the point? Why?

He can't stop thinking about it. He tries to sleep, lying in his boyhood bedroom, surrounded by the boxes of books and clothes that, lacking the space, he can't store anywhere else. He gropes in the darkness for something resembling a point, but he knows that there isn't one.

People cleverer than me have struggled for an answer, he thinks. You die, young or old, and you get a lifetime's worth, no matter what.

He drops off in the early hours and sleeps in late. Rachel has already gone by the time he gets up. He leaves his notes on the kitchen table and sits in the back garden drinking coffee. Early summer sun has placed a cube of white light in the narrow courtyard, so he sits on the bench under the hornbeam in the corner. Soon all of this will be mine ... But what would I do with it? Let her have it. He pictures her surprise at the offer.

They're eating dinner later that evening. He sees for the first time that the skin under Rachel's eyes is dark, that there are lines against the side of her mouth. She picks at her food; Chinese, from the takeaway along the road. He has drunk most of a bottle of wine and she has barely touched her first glass.

I'll go in after this, he says. I meant to earlier, I know, but ... with work ...

That's a good idea, she says. I think you need to.

It's raining. He can't drive, and even if he could he wouldn't be able to with the wine inside him. He doesn't want to impose on Rachel. He takes an umbrella from the rack by the front door and walks to the hospital, half an hour up the road. There are no set visiting hours in palliative care; he can come and go as he pleases. The nurses buzz him in and smile as he stalks to her room, leaving wet prints on their polished floor.

She doesn't know he's there. She's unconscious, not asleep. There is a box tucked under her pillow, hooked up to the tubes that deliver her pain medication. It clicks and whines every few minutes. He takes a chair from the corner of the room.

Her breathing is terrible. She stops for about five seconds at a time, then the breath builds up in a sequence of groans, expending itself in a long, liquid rattle. She's lying straight on the bed, but one hand has been positioned under her chin to stop her head from tipping forward.

He starts crying at once, before he's even sitting in the chair. He takes her other hand and sees that everything has been cleared away from her table, the wheeled table at the side that swings across the bed – all her magazines and cards, the half-drunk bottles of juice and water. So it's soon, he thinks, it's going to be very soon. And it's terrible. He is turned inside out by this weeping, to see her lying there with no knowledge that he is sitting beside her, sitting with her for these last few hours before she dies, it is unbearable this feeling inside him, breaking out in this fit of weeping, of sorrow and self-pity at the strange and awful thing that has happened to her and that is happening to him, he is marooned on this feeling, he can't get off. He has no concept of the world inside her. What do you dream about? Make it something consolatory, please, God. A stretched-out moment as she dies, a prolonged, an infinite, moment of peace. Make her present, for ever, in a single moment that never ends, and make it a good moment, of peace and happiness. That would be enough. If there's nothing else, that's enough.

After a while he is calm again. He sits for an hour, two hours. A nurse enters and reassures him that his mother feels no pain. She sits opposite him for a few minutes, a large and kind and patient woman.

Is she likely, he asks, but can't complete the sentence. He finds his composure. Is she likely to last the night, or …?

I don't see why not, the nurse tells him. It's impossible to say for sure, and I know this looks bad – indicating the laboured breath, the groans, the rattling in her throat and chest – but there is no reason to think that she will not last another day, another two or three days.

It's just, if it was going to be tonight … But if it's tomorrow, I think I'll head back now. I'll come in again in the morning. It's getting very late.

We'll call, of course, the nurse says, if anything changes.

The rain has slackened to a turbid haze that smothers the roof of his umbrella. He walks home, and the midnight pavements are striped with thick, black slugs that have emerged from the drains and the bushes at the side of the road. He takes care not to stand on them. They have emerged as if to feed on the water that surrounds them.

As he walks back he thinks about his article, his failed article, and he thinks about the island. A woman and two children, placed there by a capricious king. If it's innate, this need to speak, then they would have developed something so they could communicate with each other, surely. More than just gestures, or cave paintings and patterns in the earth. Something free of writing, at only one level of abstraction. That's it, he thinks, you have to get down as close as you can between the thing itself and the means of describing it, to bridge that impossible distance. They would have done that, because they would have had to in those circumstances. They would have come up with something. They would swim, alone, in the medium of their collaborated language, and there would be no misunderstanding between them. It was a gift that had been given to them. The woman was there to oversee that gift. I'll write about that. Tomorrow, that's what I'll do, that's the approach I need.

A taxi passes in a lonely swish of sound, its wheels hissing through the water. He crosses the road, comes down the hill from the hospital, walks past a nursing home and a primary school into the backstreets of the estate. On the other side of the estate he crosses by the roundabout and he can see the house ahead. The door is open. Framed in light is his sister, waiting. There is nothing to say.

Shane Strachan

THE STRULDBRUGS

I

Well, he's nae lang for this earth onywaiy, that's for sure, the passengers on the bus from Peterhead to Aberdeen heard Alma Robertson yell down the phone to her daughter. Alma was four years younger than her brother Davie, who would be unaware that it was his seventy-eighth birthday as he awoke that day in an auld folks' home just outside the city. Oh, I better awa. That's ma stop just noo ... ah right, ching ching. She waddled up to the front of the bus, her cream anorak scuffing between her thick arms and bosom.

The driver let her off just past the WELCOME TO ABERDEEN sign. She took her time walking down the pothole-ridden country road towards the Mundurno Nursing Home.

Over the recent summer months, the home had glowed warmly with the golden wheat of the surrounding fields reflected in its windows. Now the fields had been harvested flat, and the rooms inside the home had been lit to fight off the gloom of the morning's dreich skies. In this cold light, the building looked more run down than ever with the moss and dirt spread like shadows across its harling.

Och, it's nae so fine the day, Alma said to the receptionist when she got inside. But I'll maybe still tak him for a walkie. I suppose it's best just to get him oot as lang as the rain bides aff.

Yeah, the receptionist said, not looking up from her computer. Alma took off one of her cream leather gloves and signed the visitors' login sheet. The receptionist buzzed her through the glass door.

In the beige corridor there was a strong smell of broth and the air felt over-warm; Alma saw that the radiators had been turned up high to stave off the oncoming of winter. She took off her anorak before she stepped into the lift and pushed the button for the second floor. As it moved upwards, she dichted at her sweaty brow with a hanky in the mirror. The curls of her red-dyed perm had become lank in the heat.

Out of the lift, she made her way through the corridor, glimpsing into the rooms with doors ajar. Most had a nurse inside, helping the residents up out of bed, except for one auld mannie who lay alone and looked up at his door expectantly. Oddly, the door of the communal room further along was shut, but Alma rushed inside anyway.

I'm sorry, madam, can I help you? asked a young black woman as she made the bed in the otherwise unoccupied and unlit room. Her fuzzy black hair seemed to float in what little light came in through the window behind her.

Eee me, I think I've went on to the wrang fleer. Far's the communal room at again?

Downstair, she pointed a manicured fingernail at the floor.

Och! I'm ah rayvelt the day, so I am, Alma said, a hand on her forehead.

The woman grinned, You'll be joinin us soon.

Dinna say that, Alma tried to laugh as she rushed out of the room.

Back in the lift, she pushed the first-floor button and stood pechin. When the doors reopened, she took her time walking to where the communal room would surely be.

It was a relief to see Davie sitting in his wheelchair by the window at the back of the room. He looked up at Alma as she neared him and then looked away again, as though upset with her, but she knew better. His legs seemed even worse than a few weeks back: they had been slowly twisting around each other like vines since the start of the year.

Hiya, fit like are ye the day noo? she asked as she sat down beside him. It's Alma here to see ye on yer birthday. I winna pull yer hair this time though! she giggled. It'll ah be oot wie seventy-eicht tugs.

He continued to look away with his white-blue eyes, slivvers dripping from one corner of his mouth.

Hud on a mintie and I'll dicht that awa … That's better noo, in't it? We gan to gang oot for a walkie the day then? The sun'll maybe come oot and ye'r sair needin to see it.

II

Out on the cycle path that cut through the fields, Alma pushed Davie towards the beach. He was wrapped in his birthday present: a cotton blanket she'd knitted. It was much larger than the ones she usually did for the newborns of Peterhead.

A burnie trickled behind thick grass along the side of the path: there had been plenty of rain through the night. She could smell it in the air as well; that sweet scent drying wheat gave off. It drifted over to them from the stacks of hay bales in the fields.

Can ye smell that, Davie? Do ye mind on that smell fae fan we were just bairns and Ma and Da still ained thon hoose oot by Philorth?

He bid still and said nothing. Rage and guilt flushed through her when he did this. It made her think she should never have taken him here. It was only because of the one bad fall that she'd thought it best, but removing him from his own house was a mistake: ever since he'd retired from the family business of undertaking, he'd just sat around inside – night and day for years – until its rooms were all he knew. Removing him from that house was like removing his brain.

She could have got a nurse – she could have taken turns with the rest of the family to look after him, but who else would have bothered to help nowadays? And who could have known that taking him to Mundurno would make things worse?

The only thing that had got a response out of him the last few visits was when she sang. During one of her Sunday visits, a minister had been in playing guitar and singing hymns until some of the residents were roused into singing along with him. Davie had been one of the first to join in. What a friend we have in Jesus. Bind us together, Lord. Abide with me, fast falls the eventide …

As she pushed onwards, she thought back to her and Davie's younger days when they'd help their da out with the funeral services. They'd stood in the back pews, leading the singing when the rest of the kirk didn't know the tune. Now that the breeze had calmed, she sang quietly,

> The year is swiftly waning,
> the summer days are past,
> and life, brief life, is speeding,
> the end is nearing fast.

The wheelchair rattled over a rough patch of ground. She stopped singing and leaned over to check on Davie. He stared onwards, his head tilted to one side as though fed up. It was then she decided to turn back. A small weight of sadness hung inside her when she did this: in not going any further, she felt like he was missing out on something, but back they went.

As they made their way towards the home – now just a fleck in the distance – she began to sing again. She was louder this time and drowned out the babble from the burnie.

> As I gid doon to Turra Mairket
> Turra Mairket for to fee,
> I fell in wie a fairmer cheil,
> fae the Barnyard o Delgaty.

Davie had begun to hum along with the last line. She sang cheerily as he rasped along with her,

> Linten adie toorin adie
> Linten adie toorin ay,
> Linten, lourin, lourin, lourin,
> Linten, lourin lourin lee.

He promised me the ae best pair
I ever set my een upon,
and fan I gid hame to the Barnyards
there was nithing there but skin and bone.

A gust of wind blew at them. Though Alma sang on, Davie stopped. She looked up at the thick cloud overhead; it showed no sign of breaking. She pushed him onwards in silence.

As they neared the home, she heard a familiar noise coming from her brother: a small whine like air escaping from a balloon. She couldn't thole it. It was as though he was calling for help from somewhere deep inside. The worst was when somebody else was about and all she could say was, Noo come on, Davie, that's enough o that noises now. Ye'r affrontin Ma so ye are.

Come on noo, stop that, she said the day.

He got louder.

Stop huddin a maneer! She slipped off one of her gloves and slapped the back of his head with it until the noise stopped. Fit sang will we sing noo, eh? she peched. Her hands shook as she put the glove back on and took out her inhaler. Fit sang will we sing noo?

III

Back in the warm communal room, most of the residents were sat round a large TV at one end. At the other, a visiting hairdresser combed the limp white hair of one of the wifies. Alma pushed Davie past them and went up to the untouched bookcase by the window. She sat herself down on a chair next to Davie's and watched as the plump, middle-aged woman scooshed water over the trembling head in front of her before trimming away the ends of the fine hair. Once cut, she blow-dried the remaining strands on a low setting, gently teasing them up from the skull with her fingers. Alma fell into a trance like those around her as she watched. The auld wifie suddenly came to life.

A dinna like it, Mam! she skirled. Fit a sotter! Mam, tell her to fix it!

Alma caught the hairdresser's eye in the mirror as her client squirmed in the chair. The hairdresser winked and shook her head, near laughing.

Oh, somebody's nae pleased. I hope you dinna hud a cairry-on like that fan I'm nae here, Alma said at the top of her voice. Davie looked on, his eyelids starting to droop. Ee, look fa this is comin in the door. Ye mind on Ruby noo, Davie? I didna ken she wis in here wie ye, she nudged at his arm and giggled.

Dressed in a tea-stained nightie, Ruby was helped down onto a seat beside the TV. Although her hair had started to grow in white, the skin on her face still had its dark-tanned complexion. Along with her deep wrinkles, it reminded Alma of mud that had dried and cracked. Nobody would be able to tell that Ruby was younger than Alma.

The nurse went over to the hairdresser and Alma got up and waddled over to Ruby.

Yoo-hoo, Ruby! I've nae seen you in a filie, she said, standing over her. Ruby looked up slowly, as though half asleep. She mumbled something incomprehensible. Aye, I ken. That's right noo, Alma said as she sat down next to her. Has Iris been in to see ye?

More mumbling.

Aye, uh-huh. And do ye see ma breether Davie owre there? Do ye mind on him fae the caravans oot at Turra?

Ruby shrugged the shoulder nearest Alma and turned away to look at the TV. They sat in silence and watched the weather forecast: rain in the afternoon.

When the adverts came on, Ruby seemed to awake from something and turned back to Alma. She placed a thin hand on Alma's shoulder, and, in the same slur she used to talk with in the caravans late on a Saturday night with whisky-laced breath, she said,

Noo, Alma, let Ma tell ye summin … she paused and looked around the room … This place is just full o auld cunts.

Alma sat speechless. Ruby just stared through her. Alma stood up and marched back over to Davie, her face burning. She swiftly pushed him out of the room.

A female nurse lifted Davie into his bed and his eyes rolled with tiredness. Before the nurse left, Alma complained to her that the window must have been left open at some point. Could she not feel it was as cold as the sea?

Once they were alone, she got in beside him; something she hadn't done since they'd shared a bed as bairns in the cottage out by Philorth. Back then, Davie would read her stories and sing ballads in the dying firelight until she fell asleep.

As Davie drifted off, she stared up at the white wall above them. She wondered if he ever managed to sit up and look out at the fields in the mornings, or if he was just stuck staring at the ceiling until somebody came to his room.

She'd been humming a tune to herself as she had these thoughts. The words came to her and she sang in a whisper,

> Days and moments quickly flying;
> blend the living with the dead.
> Soon our bodies will be lying
> each within its narrow bed.

She stopped: she couldn't mind any more. Instead of striving to find the words, she lay still and listened, searched for her brother's faint breaths among the blasts of wind outside.

Em Strang

WAITING TO WATER THE PONIES

It must be summer. The man is naked
on the path, early fog wrapping
his long grey shape, his quiet skin
in its loose, grainy light.

His hands are full – a bag of apples,
an orange bucket with *Fire* written on it –
and he's saying something, lips moving,
sound carrying across the invisible field
to the ponies with uncut manes
and tails thick with mud and rain.

Their summer blood brings them
one by one out of nothing
to the blank man and his bright bucket
in the small corridor between them and us.
They take it in turns to drink
the fire-water and eat the soft red apples
the man has saved.

Valerie Thornton

HOARD

I smell Dad's hands
rising from the blades
as I start to shred
his statements.
I see his Parker nib
turned over for a finer line
of permanent blue-black
Quink which codes each
rise and fall of pounds
and shillings and pence.
I hold my breath
and turn the sheets
to face away, to hide
the slicing of his hand.
My guiding thumbs
with nails as squint
as his, feed scrap
to eager scrap.

SECRET

Of course, my mother didn't
read my five-year diary,
the one from my troubled teens.
It was red and zipped all round.
Its flimsy gold latch
clicked shut like my satchel.

She could have found the key
to me: she could have saved
me from a man twice my age
yet still under thirty, entrusted
in loco parentis.
I can tell now she didn't

read me by her shaking hand
as, for the first time,
she holds my father's
wallet. 'I feel like I'm
intruding,' she says,
and I keep mum.

David Underdown

ARRAN PILOTS IN SPRING

These fellows are old before their time.
Plodders, they sit in silent rows
and wait for weeks to pass,
the earnest dullards of the class.

And in the end they get there,
each in a different way
summoning the energy and nouse
to sprout the necessary shoots.

Come the days' light lengthening
I will find dibber, line and marker sticks
and bury each in its own hole
to find its future.

THE PSYCHOLOGY OF PATHS

The selection of paths

Think first whether you really need one
or if, rather than rely on others,
you might make your own.
Be suspicious of any too broad or even-surfaced
or any leading straight to somewhere popular.
Way-marks are easily missed, signposts reversible,
yet a circular path is fit only for amateurs.
Always choose a path by its cover:
moss is a good sign
or the spoor of rare animals.

The terminology of paths

A tunnel is not a path; a rainbow is not a path;
a corridor is not a path, even in your mind;
lanes are not paths save those with grassy centres.
Flight-paths designed by pigeons or prescribed
for jumbos need specialist skills.
A staccato path results in stepping-stones.
The path of the wind can lead to dunes
requiring major detours.
Rights of way are a reason for scepticism;
paths for the blind may be invisible;
a secret path leads to the spot marked X.

Pathology, the logic of paths

The topography of paths is more than the sum of their parts,
so ponder the motives of those who have preceded you
and be mindful of the interests of those who may follow;
for the logic of paths is a mystery only understood
by those who do not need them.
Remember, each path comes with a purpose
even if it has been long forgotten.
Your rights are leasehold,
your responsibilities surprisingly onerous
so there is no point in arguing the toss about directions.
Registration of paths is a heresy widely misunderstood,
a change to the way of a path contrary to its nature,
to make it straight the height of human folly.
Consider also the unfinished path through the minefield,
or the way to the unmarked grave.

The names of paths

South Vennel, The Cut,
Down-by-the-shore, Badgerbank,
Top Field, The Broomway,
Via Dolorosa, Narachan,
Up-by-Maggie's, Hadrian's Wall,
The Langdyke.

The seductiveness of unmarked paths

A random path is a contradiction
only resolved by discerning its secrets.
In taking the oasis for granted you may forget
that camels often have preferences
which are not the same as yours.
Why, for instance, would you need a path across a frozen lake?
The path taken through Birnam Wood
frequently feels unlike the time before.
A river will find its own path,
a current adapt unerringly to circumstances.
Even a sheep may know its own way.

The mapmaker's urge to destroy signposts

See cairns? Ye dinnae need them.
Signs ur pure rubbish,
way-marks only fit
fir daupet coofs wha couldnae pish themselves.
Gin ye huv a map
jist huv the gumption tae ken yur whauraboots
and gin ye dinna
jist bide at hame in bed.

An amazing way through the labyrinth

The pathway to enlightenment
is a new one on me
needing perseverance and fortitude,
demanding precise answers.
Are we nearly there?
Ask yourself, why are random numbers slippery?
What is the colour of an unsaid prayer?
When is god pretending?
Are we nearly there?

Nacho Viñuela

THE EDGE OF THE TIDES

I

We found the man – for my mother would later tell me it was a man, the first and last one I ever saw – washed up on the beach, entangled in ribbons of seaweed. Mother asked me to stay behind while she put down the basket and started walking with cautious steps towards the uncertain mound of flesh. I opened my eyes as wide as I could and the light of the sun blinded me, dampening the roar of the waves. A quiet sea is a bad omen. Mother was poking the body with a stick. I called her but she didn't look back. A bladder of fear spilled black bile inside me. She crouched over the body. I couldn't help wondering if that mass of skin and meat wrapped in seaweed was something we could eat. My belly rumbled while the thought of whatever it was being alive – and attacking and killing Mother – filled me with dread. I would have rather stayed hungry than alone. Mother always threatened to abandon me whenever I did bad things, warning me that being alone was far, far worse than being dead.

She turned around and summoned me with a toss of her head and then a brisk arm movement. I was never quick enough. I ran to her, readying myself to tear up flesh and bone with my hands and teeth, but she put a hand against my chest.

'It's a man,' she said. 'He's not dead. Help me.'

I stood stunned, my arms limp like broken tree branches.

'Can't you hear me?'

She was only so hard with me, she had told me many times, because it's so difficult to survive being alone. I never knew what she meant by being alone when we were always together. But looking at the man, I understood. We were not the only ones. I felt a pang of pain. Why had she never told me?

I tried not to look at the man but, as we lifted him, I caught a glimpse of the viscous pelt that covered his chest and legs. His skin was burnt. I felt an urge to touch the places where it was red and scarred. Whatever a man was, it was heavy and smelly. Our feet sank in the sand under his weight. The man smelled of rotten fish and drowned bonfires. His smell made me gag and filled me with an exhilarating fear, as if I was looking down from a cliff.

We dropped the man on Mother's bed. His feet and hands stuck out over the edges of the mattress. His head was twisted at an odd angle. Mother propped it on the pillow. The man's swollen lids were closed and his nose was shiny and red. Mother took a knife and snapped the weeds and rags that sank deep into his flesh. Whenever the knife pierced the skin, she winced as if she had cut herself and dabbed the blood with the hem of her skirt. I bit hard on my lips. The man was naked. His body was unlike my mother's but also very different from mine. It was broader and covered in fur. Its swollen, hard flesh seemed about to burst the skin on his shoulders, thighs and chest. And at its centre, nestled in a tangle of hair, there was the dark, bulbous creature I couldn't stop staring at. A metallic taste oozed into my mouth.

'What are you doing standing there?' asked my mother, smoothing her skirt, now garlanded with red stains like plucked rose petals. 'And what's that blood on your lips? Go put some water to boil!'

I ran outside for the water pail and placed it on the stove. But the fire had gone out, so I had to collect dried grass and kindling. I felt a restlessness in my crotch. I wanted to kick Mother's ankles and pull her hair. Instead, I went into the forest and pissed and tried to piss again, because the slug between my legs kept pulsing. I rubbed it, tugged at it and pinched it until it shook and its tendrils shivered up my spine, bursting in my head like a flash of lightning. Mother had told me I carried a venomous creature between my legs and warned me against its hunger. 'It will want you to do bad things,' she said. 'If you give in to it, it will poison your blood and you will waste away.' Now my knees felt wobbly and I got scared. I went back into the hut. Mother came and slapped me across the face and then tied her scarf around my eyes. It smelled of rancid milk and sweat, the smell of her.

'The man can't stand the weight of the blanket on him. His skin is too raw,' she said. 'Even the weight of your eyes on him makes him ache.'

'What about your eyes?' I spoke back, a new note of anger deepening my voice.

'I can trust myself to close them,' she said, pushing me onto a chair.

Even with my eyes covered I could feel the man's presence. His breath and his smell filled the room with something nameless, dense and dark like molasses. Now that I could not see him, the man breathed inside my head, making me giddy. I heard the rustle of Mother's clothes as she moved about and the dripping of water as she wrung out the rag she must have been using to clean him, surely with her eyes open. The man moaned softly and I drove a fist into my crotch trying in vain to quell my creature's hunger.

II

That night I could not sleep. Mother and I were sharing my bed. Her body was too warm and knobbly and she kicked me in her sleep. I could hear the man's laboured breathing, like an echo of the tide coming in. I got up, lit a candle and walked up to him. His chest moved up and down with each breath. The black pelt that covered it glistened like wet grass. A stream of hair trailed down his stomach, thinning towards the thick overgrowth

where the eel laid. I leaned and sniffed him. The coarse hairs tickled my
nose and my lips. I inhaled the smell of fungi and lichen, breathed it in
down to my belly. I felt I wanted something badly, but I did not know what
it was. Something to do with the holes in my body and the creature between
my legs. I listened for Mother's snoring and I touched the man's furry,
wrinkly pouch with the tip of my fingers. He squirmed and the eel rose on
its tail, upright like a tree trunk strangled by swollen vines. My crotch itched
like a scab. I rubbed it against the mattress. The flame above my hand
flickered greedily. Melted wax trickled down the candle, scalding me. I
tilted it and hot wax dripped and congealed on the man's belly. He flinched
and the eel dangled its purple head and spouted a thick poison. Before I
knew what I was doing, I dipped the tip of my finger in it and took it to my
mouth. Certain that I would die I scrambled into bed and cradled in the
nook of Mother's body, sucking up the man's poison from my finger. Sleep
fell on me, sweet and sudden like death.

III

When I woke up, Mother put the scarf around my head. I was hungry but
not weak. The man's creature, I thought, could not be as poisonous as mine.

'Open your mouth.'

Mother fed me with a spoon, scooping the spilling gruel from the corners
of my mouth. 'My poor baby,' she muttered.

'Mother, why am I not like you or the man?' I asked, finding courage in
my blindness.

'What do you mean?'

'My body. Why is it the way it is?'

'You are just a kid. You'll grow up; you are already changing.'

'Will I become man or mother?'

'Don't talk nonsense,' she snapped, thrusting the spoon against my teeth.

After breakfast Mother went out. I was still feeling hungry so I went to
the man. I did not take off the scarf. I used my hands instead of my eyes.
The man flinched when I touched his thigh. My poor baby, I whispered,
while I stroked his creature to hardness. I ran a finger down from the fleshy
pouch and I found the hole between his buttocks. I slid a finger inside him.
The warm, soft muscles contracted around it, like the mouth of a fish closing
on a hook. I slid a second finger in. The man's creature hardened as if it
was trying to break out of its skin. I tightened my grip and the poison
spurted out and whipped my hand. I licked it, savouring its bitter, raspy
taste. Suddenly, it occurred to me that the man must be hungry. I went into
the pantry and felt the insides of the bowls and pans. My hand closed on
a mound of ripe, juicy berries. They would be good for him; I had picked
them myself. With my free hand I felt for the man's head. His hair was
coarse and tangled, it caught my fingers. I felt an ear and a brow, a nose

and a lip. I hooked my thumb behind his teeth. His mouth was warm and
wet. He snorted and tried to pull away. I filled his mouth with berries
and pushed them down his throat. He gurgled and choked. No, I said,
pulling his hair, don't do that, just swallow. He coughed, splattering bits of
berries on my face. I pinched his nose until I heard him swallow. Then, I
stroked his hair until he fell asleep.

IV

I stayed outside for most of the day. When I took off the scarf, the sand and
the leaves on the trees seemed brighter than they had ever been. I brought
water from the well. I watered the plants and gathered wood in the forest.
I mended the nets, all the time whistling the only song I knew. A song with
no words that Mother taught me. I wanted to ask Mother if we were going
to keep the man, but I was afraid. She never let me keep any of the animals
we trapped, no matter how much I begged. She just said no and snapped
their necks.

'You are such a good kid,' Mother said when I went into the hut with the
scarf already tied around my head.

She ruffled my hair and led me to the table. She put a knife and a fork
in my hands. We ate boiled rice with fish. Food seemed to taste better with
my eyes closed. We ate without talking, aware of the man lying on the bed.
The silence was full of him. I went to bed early. When Mother joined me
she was very warm and her breath smelled of mushrooms and wet flour.
I feared she had been feeding on the man. I did not want her to know
what I had learned about him. She put her arm, heavy like a log, across my
chest. I did not move although I could hardly breathe.

V

I felt tired and miserable the next day. I walked restlessly around the hut,
bumping into corners and chairs. My body ached and my joints felt brittle.
My throat was tight and my eyes burned. As soon as Mother went outside,
I went to the man. I sat on the mattress and stroked his hair, but he did
nothing. I pulled the hair on his chest and bit his right nipple. It hardened
between my teeth. He moaned weakly and tried to push me away. I sank
my teeth on his hand and it fled like a fish. The man was too weak to shout
out or to move away. I felt light-headed and my shitting-hole squeezed up
like a jellyfish. I felt hungry there. I took his hand and squeezed it between
my legs. But I heard Mother calling me outside and I had to leave.

Mother waved at me from the edge of the sea. We were going out fishing.
I jumped on the boat. Mother's face was glowing and her eyes twinkled.
She smiled at me.

'You are so beautiful,' she said, running her fingers on my cheek.

'What does beautiful mean?' I asked.

'Beautiful are the things you never get tired of looking at. The things that, no matter how long you stare at them, always seem new and always make you happy.'

We threw the nets into the water and waited. Mother closed her eyes and lifted her face towards the sun. I did the same. The cave behind my eyes was lit up with a warm glow like a bonfire. There, I found the words for the only song I knew and I sang it in my head. Beautiful like trees and rabbits. Beautiful like the backs of dolphins and whales. Beautiful like the stars and the sickle moon. Beautiful like the sun on a shell. Beautiful like the man and me. I opened my eyes and I caught Mother looking at me through a small slit between her eyelids. I feared that I had been singing out loud without noticing. I couldn't know if I had. I blushed. A dark cloud wiped the glow from Mother's eyes.

'You really are changing,' she said. 'I can see you are keeping things to yourself. You don't tell me everything like you used to. It makes me sad.'

I felt I might start crying if she kept talking. I hoisted the nets up. A splattering of fish fell on the deck and flapped frantically, like wingless, featherless birds. Their mouths and gills gasped for water. I watched them dying, as if for the first time. I could hear the cries inside their heads. Suddenly I was afraid. I caught one by the tail and banged its head on the board until it stopped wriggling. And then another. And another.

Mother watched me in silence, her mouth twisted.

'Don't maul them,' she said, 'they are for the man.'

VI

Mother kept a close watch on the man and me. At night she locked her legs around me. For days I could not get near him without her being there. I would wander through the house aimlessly until she shouted: 'Get out. Go fishing, fetch wood. Get out of my way!' She tended the man for hours and sat on the bed talking to him, feeding him small pieces of dried fish. She said, 'You are going to get better; you are doing very well.' She also said other things to him that I couldn't understand.

Those days I could not stop touching myself. A sudden laziness would take hold of me and I would go and lie at the far end of the beach. I pinched my nipples and squeezed my slug and slid my fingers inside me. But it was not enough. I was hungry for the man's flinching skin, his sweet pain. I bit my fingers until they bled. The beautiful things were beautiful no more. They turned their backs on me. I felt trapped inside myself and so alone that I began to wish I were dead.

Mother announced one morning that she was going to the forest to gather medicinal plants. She said the man was getting better and he would live. I asked if he would stay with us then and she said yes. She said everything would be easier with him around. She said he would help us and that I

would learn a lot from him, things she couldn't teach me. She was smiling.
I lifted her off the ground, surprised at her lightness and my strength. We
laughed. Before leaving, she said we'd be a happy family. I was too excited
to ask what that word meant.

The man was lying on his back with his eyes open. He was looking at
me. I felt clumsy walking towards him. The scarf was wrapped around my
wrist. The man's eyes were unfathomable, like those of a fish. I stroked the
man's sleeping eel, but he gave a jolt and his creature would not harden. I
pulled on it but it stayed limp. I feared that Mother had killed it. The man
stared at me with the eyes of a trapped animal and puckered his lips as if
he was about to speak. He threw one hand awkwardly towards me. Did he
want me to go away? I hesitated. I put the scarf over his eyes and fastened
it at the back of his head. I took my clothes off and crawled on top of him.
He wriggled so I pushed his shoulders down with my knees until he gave
in. The hair on his chest brushed my thighs. I bit and sucked on his neck
and his lips. Every time, he writhed and flinched, striking sparks in my
head like on a flint. Trying to get away, he pushed himself against me. His
strength was mine. I felt intoxicated, poisoned with a desire I couldn't resist.
I was tied to the man by bonds of need. I felt his eel swelling between my
legs. I rubbed my arse against it. The man's hand slapped my face. I smacked
him back and took his hand and pressed it between my legs. My slug
throbbed at the touch of his rough skin. He grabbed my face with his other
hand. He seemed strong enough to crush my skull like an egg. I wondered
if he would. I pressed against his crotch and his eel slid inside me, a knife
with a blade of pleasure and sharp edge of pain. I closed my eyes so that I
could be in the same place as him. I moved with him and against him,
riding on silent waves that were the colour of blood. We were coming fast
to a foggy edge, a precipice of light beckoning us. I was ready to fall and
die, ready to take all the light and all the darkness. But I was yanked away
by the hair, dragged out of a vertiginous dream. I felt a slap across my
mouth.

'What are you doing to him?'

My lips burned and throbbed. I looked at Mother but she seemed too
far away. I blinked. She grabbed me by the ears and asked again:

'What are you doing?'

I could feel hot tears running down my cheeks. But she did not get an
answer. Mother slapped me again.

'You have ruined everything,' she said. 'You are evil.'

She kicked me and punched me. 'Evil, evil, evil!' She was crying too.

'I don't want your pain any more. It hurts,' I said, clutching at her wrist
and pushing her away. 'I only want the man's pain.'

'You don't know what you're saying. You're killing me with your evil
words. You've ruined everything.'

Her tongue was very red in the paleness of her face. She had a knife in her hand. I saw it darting across the room, shining like a herring. I couldn't move. A dull pain inside marked the place where the man had entered me. I wanted to keep that pain, to hang on to it. Mother did what I thought could never happen. With one thrust of her hand she slit the man's throat. Foamy blood gushed forth, pushing the flaps of the wound open. The man jerked and sat up and the blood stopped and then came pouring out again. I was watching him dying. Fish fell over me. Their cold fins scratched me as they flapped sliding down my skin. The man gurgled and gasped. He was drowning in his own blood. He fell on his back and shuddered and then he grew still. He was dead, whatever that meant.

Mother spoke with her back to me, the knife still in her hand. Her voice was hoarse.

'It was the only thing to do. One day you'll understand. Everything will be like it was before, like it's always been.'

She spoke but I was not listening. I was running down the beach without looking back. I was pushing the boat, jumping into it. I was inside a dream. Mother's cries were like the screeching calls of hungry birds. 'Come back, come back,' she wailed. She hurried into the water but I was rowing fast, out into the glittering sea. With every stroke I moved further away and she grew smaller until she was swallowed by the sea. There was only water around me. I was alone.

Bechaela Walker

O JESUS O JESUS O JESUS O FUCK

When I wake, the woman is gone. She has sneaked out to avoid me to avoid having to talk to me. I feel sick with paranoia it is not just the hangover. Everyone hates me and that is why I am alone in this bed. It is not just the woman who has deserted me: I have been deserted in turn by men and women friends and enemies my mother my father everyone. I would abandon myself if I could but I can't. I toy with the idea of suicide I imagine sitting on my windowsill, as though to get a better view of a march, and then just tipping myself over the edge and then splat on the pavement. I am not at home I am in another room a large room. O jesus o fuck get to work but that is tomorrow. A fan turns on its axle in the centre of the ceiling it is lined with strips of wood painted white. I pull the single sheet up over my shoulders and notice the other beds 1 2 3 4 5 of them all pushed up against the wall like mine. There is a tightly packed backpack on the bed opposite, a pair of hiking boots next to the bedside table. The other beds show no sign of having been occupied. I didn't notice the beds last night she didn't either. We did it all on top of the covers and I cringe I wonder if I was noisy I hate the sound of my own moans. I moan like porn stars moan to show my pleasure to try and please my lovers but it makes no sense at all. I quiver, the fan is not needed I am a bad lover with bad noises and how did I find her anyway? There is a penalty in this country for that sort of thing it is banned so there are no places so to speak.

I'm back there again at the club, the bar of the hotel. There are honest to god photos of Empire on the wall: white ladies reclining on wicker loungers on immaculate lawns, white families posed for photos on wide wide terraces, black servants smiling by their sides. There is a plastercast statuette of a slave in a turban by the bottom of the stairs smiling welcome sir madame nothing has changed in here. The carpet is too thick for a bar: tartan reds greens heavy, sopping up the syrupy drool of their cocktail glasses the malty spit of their pints. For years. This is the only place to drink legally. For miles. How did I get here ask yourself that princess. I have come alone but to meet other people who are called my friends I have only known them for about 2 months. Come over here you they say and I go to the toilet first. I'm too paranoid to look in the mirror if I'm caught looking at myself that is what really terrifies me. So I brush my hair in the cubicle yes I've remembered a brush and I apply lipstick it's red I've never experimented with other shades. I drink some of my rum gin and coke premixed in a plastic bottle that I carry in my handbag. I decide to talk to John.

I will be brazen and attractive but the carpet disrupts my attempt at gliding into the room, the thick pile keeps twisting short my step. I remember a story about a public private hospital initiative. On the first day they couldn't get wheelchairs across the threshold because of the enormous integrated fuzzy doormat. I try to think of something sexy alluring fun to say but I start on something to do with the politics of education. I mean, it's just a way of getting all those kids ready for what's ready for them anyway I say and John turns to his mate and says see what I mean. He's just 18, shaved head for the part in this TV series they're filming out here they've just finished filming. He's cruel to me and I imagine this might make him an exciting lover him torturing me in a nice way I am sexually pathetic. It's a formal bar, he says, and I curtsy and he says you should have worn the blue dress as though he's my fucking husband or something and we're in the 1950s but I almost turn back and change I am gutted and I catch myself in the mirror it makes him stronger to me. You look like you're about to cry, he says, cheer up do you want a drink or something, she's better when she's had a drink.

I plan my escape. I'm in the tourist wing of Audrey's house Sally must have chucked me out of our room, or I didn't even try to go in feeling it was wrong to fuck in a room with my friend there and such a light sleeper even the roosters wake her in the morning. Vikki Vikki (she says) I think it's time to get up, we'll be late for church. You go to church I'm just not coming it's ridiculous. But all the locals notice and my pupils submit an anonymous story about me:

Miss Gray
Miss Gray is an alcoholic she is very bad. We see her bottles in the dump it is rum and some gin. She also smokes and it is very grievous to health as well it is too smelling horrible. She is not a Christian. We should write to her mother and father in England and let them know that there daughter is a prostitute.

It's in Esther's hand, I should have beat her but I don't do that the other teachers say I'm too lax and they would respect me if I beat them but I say no it's not decent and so I have them doing chores sometimes not this time. I go into the class. Children I say where am I from? They chorus Ingirland and I say no it is not it is Scotland I am Scottish I am from Scotland. Scot land, I write it on the black wall in chalk. Now copy that down I say and next time get it right.

There is water all the way from my bed to the door that leads to the shower room I notice my hair is wet I have already showered but no memory of the act and it is then, o beautiful realisation, that we did it in the bathroom not in front of the sleepers and after came back to the bed. She curled up behind me and pushed her body up against mine there was no space between us that is how I went to sleep. I am not a bad person it is just the danger of it and that is why she has gone and also the only black person in the hostel and I blink I am a nazi in this all white place white walls white nets white sheets white folk and Audrey appears. So you're awake she says and I nod and she says now get up and get out and don't you dare bring one of those damn whores back here ever again you hear me girl you could have had me shut down you silly silly girl she could have looted the whole lot you don't know these people. She wasn't she wasn't I say. And I tell her the story:

I meet her in the lobby of the Holiday Inn so see she isn't a prostitute she is well dressed a conservative I say and she tells me she's been stood up her boyfriend told her to come to Mutare to the Holiday Inn he hasn't shown up she has no money to stay anywhere no money to get back and I don't have any US dollars either so I could at least give her a bed. I don't tell her other things like:

She almost drags me to the toilet she is calling me Miss please Miss Miss Miss like the children at school. I say don't call me Miss I remember that o christ o jesus. I say just call me Vikki and she says Vikki you need to help me. Her skin is shining the light strip lighting her lips she has on purple lipstick a weave it is coming loose a modern bob she says I need to get it fixed he said she says and I say fuck him. You musn't swear she says I give her some rum gin she really knocks it back and she says cmon cmon.

Audrey says, you have an early start tomorrow. Let's forget about all this. And I remember dancing in the bar at the hotel. Cmon cmon dance! Dance! I am demanding this fun out of everyone, the tyranny the tyranny of fun, cmon have it have it and John is saying to them all, you know how I said she was better with a drink, I'm not so sure. I am pulling him close whispering in his ear, let's fuck, cmon cmon and he is up against me, hard hard, and he's pushing up against me and then he just says, you know you could be beautiful if you took more care of yourself and he says I'm off and I'm left there just saying cmon cmon yeah fuck it cmon so what everyone is looking. And stop feeling so sorry for yourself, Audrey says, it's your turn to do the shopping you'll miss the shops dry your hair you can use my hairdryer o dear what a girl you'll have to hitch the bus is gone.

The man drops me at the turnoff. When I start walking I find I have no concept of how long the road is how long I've been walking how long there is still to go. The cold takes my hangover leaves me jangling I worry I worry

I push for the memories they won't come a blackout the truth I am unlikable unlovable. Sally is usually with me we walk home in the light. Alone, I struggle to work out the shapes that come out of the dark at home there are streetlights or where there are no streetlights the afterglow of the city in the distance but here there is no city no afterglow only darkness Tsonzo ahead Watsomba behind. Mutare in the distance. The moon is hidden maybe a mountain I strain to make out the studio backdrop panorama, the hilarious the obvious the clichéd start of the Bvumba range. But where its silhouette should be is a different shape it is something real: a cloud a cloud a cloud it is just a cloud. The shopping is heavy I went when I was hungry I shouldn't have bought fresh milk we don't have a fridge chocolate we have no money rum gin all those luxuries. I try to still the clinking all the other sounds have stopped it is just me the whole plain has held its breath it could be bottles of juice it could be anything how dare you presume but it is booze of course it is and why not. The path has lost all sense of familiarity it is a different path did I miss the village. My bags slow me I loop one over my wrist so I have a hand free to smoke I can smoke in the dark there is no one to see me. I stink yellow my fingers all nicotine no self-control it's no wonder.

I think of the woman where is she what is she doing. I imagine I meet her again I imagine we elope. I ask her name and she says you forget it so easily it's Hazel I'm so glad you found me. We get the bus to Harare we are in love people stare because they can tell or my whiteness but we are careful not to touch we both whisper about our future I'll teach o god I'll just get on with it be thankful she'll start college she wants to be a secretary. We take a small flat in Mbare. The first week the usual some good months to follow and then fights fights. We last for 2 years she meets a man at work he is everything I cannot be he is so much better so much he is strong. I trip and land face down in the dirt just a trip wire no children no giggling they must have left it gone home.

When I get in I'm all dusty red dishevelled fallen. I dump the milk chocolate fags booze butter and the cheese the cheese Sally says how can you ruin our night talking about white privilege and then bring in a bagful of that rubbish she says you've wasted the last of our money it was for the next month. I say use your daddy's credit card I know you have it you told me so use it and don't you dare I wave my finger at her. I hate her healthy athleticism tea totalling maybe a glass of wine if it's nice on occasion and her prim outfits they are outfits and the way she gees me up in the morning to church to church and not even believing in god that's the worst of it. I cut a large chunk of cheese a swig of rum ah and she leaves the room. I know how to make her go. Everyone goes. I don't even like them anyway am bored halfway through conversations a chore to go out meet up catch up. I am a teacher o christ o jesus I will never be a teacher I will never I will give it all up back home. What will I do what can I do there is nothing nothing that I can do inside of it all.

The next morning I make it to work clean myself up keep down a good breakfast I grovel sorry sorry Sally get me bread and some cheese thanks thanks you're a star. The children are scrutinising me can smell it the gin rum, can see my fingers know I am a bad teacher I don't care. Rather a bad than a good but what will I do how will I pay for anything dress feed I will end up what in the gutter. It is Dickens again today set text set unit set class set school. I leaf through the pages I loafe and invite my soul I decide I will not teach Dickens any more no way.

I imagine telling the children I refuse to do Dickens his work is offensive Scrooge the reformed do-gooding capitalist with a heart of with a soul deep down under it all, the plot is unbelievable worse it is simply false. I will tell them there is such a thing as truth it is not all just relative I am frightened terrified of the future of being alone fight fight things always change but for the better I don't know I wish. I see myself walking away from everything men and women friends and enemies my mother father everyone. I am lying in my bed and the woman is curled against my back and the woman is grabbing my arm I imagine eloping with her. Audrey is telling me to go to go Sally has already gone I will meet her later she will forgive me she has gone with John what a state he says what a fucking state. The children are writing a letter to my mum, my dad and I take it from them I post it myself later that afternoon on my way to the supermarket.

I look up the children are staring at me why is your dress dirty Miss. I read from the last page: *He became as good a friend, as good a master, and as good a man, as the good old city knew, or any other good old city, town, or borough, in the good old world.* Discuss, I say. Frankly I imagine fascism. I hate those rich white black capitalists we are not capitalists we live within capitalism and so we work buy goods things a packet of cheese a bottle of gin rum. A capitalist has fucking capital. We work we work and we buy we buy and what do we have.

Fiona Ritchie Walker

WEARING THE BLOUSE

You walk in the kitchen and she's off.

That's my best blouse you've been dancing in,
stinks of smoke,
you're sweating like a pig,

armpits stained white,
borrow my roll-on why don't you,
everything else seems open season.

And you stand there
with the taste of his mouth on your lips,
his name a fat marble
rolling around on your tongue,

this name of the man
who's met your mother on Tuesdays,
lain heavy on her in the back of his car
before her trip to Vonnie's to have her hair done,
before walking to the fish shop, the bakers,
then heading home with her backcombed hair
making her half a head higher,
shoulders pulled back in this blouse
the one that you are wearing
so that tonight he thought –

spinning you round, kissing hard
on the wrong day, on the wrong mouth,
sending the memory of his tongue chasing hers
back home with you on the bus,
making you think about your dad, bent over
in the floodlit factory, all hours.

You feel the name, hard
on your tongue, rubbing against your teeth,
watch your mother's hand rise up.
Try to decide
whether to spit or swallow.

Roger White

THE WOMAN IN A FUR COAT

Istanbul. Late morning on a cold weekday in February. The bitter wind blows all the way from Central Asia, across the wide space of Taksim Square, and funnels down Tarlabaşı Boulevard carrying flurries of snow with it. The vendors of roast chestnuts and *börek* pastries who have taken up their stations huddle behind their carts. A few citizens hurry towards their destinations. The etched glass in the mahogany doors of the opera house reveals the lights of the foyer within. The doorman grasps a polished brass handle from the inside and pulls the door nearest to the box office open. A few flakes of snow are blown into the building. A puff of warm air escapes. A woman sweeps in, a small pug with a squashed nose and weepy eyes scurrying at her heels.

The woman wears a black fur coat, the snowflakes on it already turning to drops of moisture glistening in the light of the chandelier overhead. She carries with her something of the lost European cities of the old Ottoman Empire – Odessa, Sofia, Bucharest – a cosmopolitan but faded self-confidence.

A poster next to the box office announces the theatre's current production – *Saraydan Kiz Kaçirma*. The name of the composer and the portrait of a girl wearing a diaphanous red costume on a sofa in a vaulted palace, her hand fluttering upwards in a show of modesty, make clear, if clarity were needed, that this is Mozart's *Die Entführung aus dem Serail*, set in a Turkish harem.

The woman heads straight for the box office window, tapping her shoe on the floor while she waits for a previous customer to be dealt with. She has removed her hat and reveals her dark hair to be tightly permed. She is middle-aged, wears make-up and has rather too much powder on her cheeks. Her right hand clutches a brown leather handbag, her left grips the pug's lead.

The previous customer completes his business and she advances to the metal grille that divides her and the clerk behind it.

She leans towards the grille and begins speaking.

Her speech is rapid, urgent, muted, as if she is taking up a story in midflow whose previous chapters the clerk has already heard from her. Perhaps he has.

It is clear that she has an issue of some sort with the establishment. She produces a bundle of papers from her handbag. It is not immediately apparent what they are – used or unused tickets; a letter from the theatre declining to refund her for money spent but seats untaken; correspondence relating to some earlier complaint or complaints; perhaps all of these. She concludes by drumming her red fingernails on the brass-topped ledge of the box office, culminating in a single rap of her knuckles as she places the papers down. She pushes them firmly underneath the grille towards the clerk.

Enveloped in the warmth of his office the clerk is in his shirtsleeves. He sports a Zapata moustache and wears spectacles which he removes occasionally, placing one of their arms in his mouth and sucking thoughtfully. In an innovation for the opera house and as required by the management, he wears a badge confirming that his name is Muammer, which any Turk would tell you has a number of meanings including fortunate and lucky.

Muammer takes the woman's papers in his hands, shuffles them to make them neat – and slides them gently back to her underneath the grille. He addresses her as 'madam' in a pleasant light tenor voice and explains that an answer to her alleged complaint lies outside his area of competence and she needs to communicate in writing through the postal system with the management of the house: he waves his arm vaguely in the direction of the office behind him.

The woman leans back in towards the grille. She responds at first to the return of her papers with a pleading, poignant lilt, almost seductive in its tone, allowing an ironic smile to hover for a moment on her face, her teeth slightly bared. Her voice becomes firmer and slower, increasing in volume. If the required destination of a complaint is the office behind Muammer, why can he not merely pass her papers through to whoever sits within?

Muammer remains impassive, the gaze of his eyes meeting hers calmly. He reminds her again that his function is to sell tickets. He repeats his reference to communication with management.

Frustrated by this rejection she takes a step back and attempts a more forceful statement of her complaint, spelling out for him in words of one syllable, both what the situation is that he is failing to grasp and the remedy she requires. For the first time she supplements her words with a raised hand, wagging her finger at Muammer as at a naughty child.

Further potential purchasers of tickets have been admitted to the foyer by the doorman and a small queue is building up behind the woman, the struggle on their faces apparent between a desire to complete their own business as quickly as possible and a feeling that this just might be a show worth watching.

She pauses for breath, gathering her strength for an attack on what she imagines correctly to be Muammer's wilful and feigned ignorance. She is not going to allow this mere functionary to pull the wool over her eyes.

Just as she begins to speak the telephone sitting next to him in the box office rings. Even she could forgive him the accident of fate that causes it to sound out, but when he answers it a look of ill temper passes over her face. Not just answers it but embarks on a lengthy conversation with someone at the other end of the line who is seeking information about some complicated combination of full and concessionary ticket prices and their availability for a forthcoming production.

While he listens and then speaks, she raps the knuckles of her right hand rapidly and with increasing volume on the ledge at her side of the metal grille. It is a threatening rumble, ending with the sort of *whumph* that in an orchestra involves the whole percussion section all banging, hammering and striking at the same time whatever piece of wood, metal or stretched animal skin is to hand.

Muammer replaces the receiver, having at least outwardly ignored the crescendo that formed the backdrop to his telephone call.

He points out that the number of would-be ticket purchasers has grown, that customers are waiting for their turn and he has already told her he cannot help. He does not mention that there is now an ancillary force of extras in the foyer observing the drama – a cleaning woman complete with cloth and a tin of lavender-scented wood polish, the doorman in his uniform, some sort of under-manager lurking on the far side of the foyer hoping not to be seen, and a wide-eyed boy blown in by the cold wind from the café next door carrying a tray of small black coffees and glasses of tea for the back-stage staff.

The woman turns round to view the small audience and smells the bitter-sweet aroma of coffee. She is suddenly deaf to any noise from the foyer and the street outside and a picture comes into her mind. She is sitting on the old sofa in the dark interior of her fourth-floor apartment, the maid busy in the kitchen, one of the long-playing records from her boxed set of *Die Entführung aus dem Serail* on the gramophone. It is the beginning of the third act and the last track on that side of the record. Belmonte has just reached the climax of his great aria about the power of love, *Ich baue ganz auf deine Stärke*. The orchestra's dying notes have faded away and the record continues to rotate on the turntable, the noise of the needle amplified by the loudspeakers – *ssh-ssh-ssh-ssh*.

She sees the faces of the other people in the foyer. Emboldened by their seeming neutrality, even tacit approval – as if she needs it – she turns back to the box office, fortified to face Muammer.

He is tapping the edge of a block of unsold tickets on his side of the ledge – *toc-toc-toc* – and glances up as if he has just noticed her.

Raising her voice, she issues a stream of what might be commands to a platoon of illiterate and particularly stupid village boys, new recruits being drilled on the parade ground at some provincial infantry training depot. On the wall behind the clerk she sees the photo obligatory in every public building of Mustafa Kemal Atatürk, the soldier and statesman who single-handedly raised Turkey up eighty years ago from the mire of a degenerate and decayed sultanate to a secular European state. She suggests that the clerk somehow represents the sloth of the country before Ataturk's revolution. And in tones that might have come from the mouth of the great general himself, she spells out a series of orders to the clerk instructing him precisely what to do, concluding with a passing reference to his badge and the fact that if she has to write to the management about his insolence she will certainly be mentioning his name. She articulates it slowly and deliberately, 'Mu-a-mm-er.'

Humiliated by the scorn in her words and tone, mindful of his status as a married man and father, and stirred by memories of his own military service many years ago, her insults seem to give Muammer courage and he rises from his seat to his full standing height. With the advantage of the raised floor in the box office and using the horizontal bar under his chair to lift and support his heels off the ground he towers a full twenty centimetres above her.

He has had enough. This is not some management nonsense about good or bad customer service, this is an assault on his personal integrity. Now it is his turn to let her know precisely where he stands on the matter.

All the years of frustration explaining the availability and price of seats on the plan of the theatre engraved in the ledge between him and customer, of taking people's cash in inconveniently large denominations and giving them change in notes and coins that they won't reject as too many, too small or too dirty, of answering long-winded phone queries from people who then do not even buy a ticket, and, yes, of being patronised, all of it, spills out and he addresses her as if she were the personification of every awkward customer over all those years, which of course to him she is if she could but recognise it.

Who the hell does she think she is? He has worked in this building for seventeen years, the last twelve of them in the box office. He always strives to do his best, for the honour of the opera house and the modern nation that Turkey has become, as well as for himself: he pauses here and clutches his right hand to his heart. He is a true son of Istanbul, and what would she – nouveau riche bourgeoise that she most certainly is – know about that? The question is a challenging one but he leaves no pause to allow for an answer.

She attempts to join in, brief *sotto voce* protests at first seeking to find the gaps in his monologue where she can be heard, but then more assertively, and his solo becomes transformed into an angry duet that passes outwards across the foyer and rises upwards to the ceiling.

The door of the auditorium opens. Two or three musicians in open-necked shirts and slacks taking a break from rehearsals peer out to see what the noise is, and find a small crowd assembled behind the two principals, as if the siege and conquest of Constantinople by Sultan Mehmet II were being played out to a conclusion in the very entrance to the theatre.

Towards the climax of the involuntary duet, the roles of Muammer and the woman become reversed. Her soaring voice is now dominant and it is he who has to identify when she is going to pause for breath so that he can interject. As he attempts in one of those brief moments to respond to an especially outrageous claim by her of incompetence on his part, she slams her handbag down on the box office ledge, not once but three times, in a gesture that the uninformed might interpret as triumphant but that both she and Muammer know is in fact an admission of defeat.

In a final compensating upsurge of apocalyptic indignation more appropriate to Wagner than Mozart, she backs away from the box office window, pug's lead and handbag now both grasped in her left hand while she raises her right arm to point accusingly at Muammer. She looks him directly in the eye as her voice dies away and she utters a final malediction.

In the silence that follows, her gaze moves swiftly over the onlookers in the foyer. They stand, intimidated, unwilling or unable to return her challenging stare. Callas-like, she plunges towards the front door and the street outside, indifferent to what any of them might think. The doorman manages just in time to open the door as she storms out, the pug dragged unceremoniously behind as he seeks in vain to keep up with his mistress. There is a sense of collective exhaustion in the building.

In that instant, Muammer has a curious vision, that the woman has walked straight out of the theatre on to the Bosphorus bridge, where she is struggling to cross the strait on foot against a fierce headwind. Buffeted by a sudden strong gust, her fur coat is caught by the wind. It inflates like a discarded plastic bag and she is carried off into the distant sky, her arms flailing, a look of terror on her face. To his surprise he feels rather sad at this unexpected image. He sighs and invites the next customer to come forward.

Outside the theatre, the woman pauses under the canopy that shelters the entrance from the extremes of the Istanbul weather, before venturing in her black fur coat into the snow and wind. For a moment it is not clear whether the damp on her powdered cheek is a snowflake or a tear.

Inside, no one notices that the pug has urinated on the frayed carpet in front of the box office. The small damp patch remains there, gradually merging with the scuffed threads until in due time the carpet is replaced.

Hamish Whyte

A LETTER TO MY LONG-LOST UNCLE

Why write now, when you're long gone?
Rummaging in the archive box the other day
I came across a photograph of you
in your ANZAC uniform, about 1915,
a sheepish grin memento.
My mother says you were an engineer
building Australia's roads,
some still called 'Berry' roads.

I imagine you, tenement boy spooling into the outback,
or were you more comfortable with city grids?
My grandfather's brother, you're my great-uncle Sam,
eldest of nine, went off down under.
I have a picture and a story and that's enough,
in a world that bleats family family,
that asks who do I think I am,
where Google knows nearly everything.

Mary Wight

ANOTHER DAY

I wake choking,
daylight pushing against the curtain folds,
jasmine thickening the air,
a blue glass bottle on the floor.

Wound tight in the sheet
you draw in breath as if it's running out
while I lie like a pen in its box,
dreams leaking,
and it is my own fingers
filling my mouth.

THE FIRST SWALLOWS

come arcing through the afternoon—

three black-fletched arrows tipped with gold

hit pitch-perfect notes, inviting us, *sing them.*

Ginna Wilkerson

FORMALLY DEAD

The crunch of bones
is only a drumstick
nicked from the bin
by a naughty kitten –
bones that can
splinter inside
and kill a cat.

And the splinters
of fear
in my own gut,
the sadness
in my veins
riding the blood.
Often, I would trade it
for formaldehyde,
fluid of formality
in dead things.

Formal, like the sleek-shining
bodies in the fish shop
window – freshly dead
with the sea in their veins
and smooth, watery eyes.
I feel embarrassed seeing
them laid out,
eyes wide open –
for all to see.

When they come to see
me formally dead,
dressed for travelling –
Julia, I know you will
close the box.

Colin Will

SELENE

As the bulge of the world's
Moon-tugged waters
travels under the night sky,
whales surf the tides,
turning vertical motion
into migration.

The Moon moves away
an inch and a half every year.
Once it was close, a monstrous ball
of black rock, crazed with magma,
above a similar Earth, with five-hour days
and uncountable eclipses.
I wasn't there – none of us was –
but it must have been something.
Count the inch and a halfs
in 200,000 miles,
and figure how long ago.

Squid, salps, plankton
and their followers
go up and down the water column
in daily cycles, catching food,
being food, as the world turns
about the Sun, the Moon turns
about the Earth. Springs and neaps
follow full and half; apogee
and perigee add their influences.
And we look up, seeing the same face
we've known since childhood,
the white Highlands, the basalt seas.

Christie Williamson

VENTURE

Slippin safe harbour
laek a Bloody Mary
doon da trott
o a eftirnön aff
truth wid wade
fae da mooths
o babes if dey hedna
scuppered dir skiffs
pittin thrift afore
raisin dir een
ta fin da mirk
clearin i da lift.

Accoardin tae da charts
wi'll hae nae clear wattir
til wir sortit da brucks
o dis mettir o time an spaes
slalomin laek salmon at's sookit
da cowld steel o straet on
an towt better o hit.

Sae lang as da haund
bides on da tiller
da tail micht wag
da dug yit. Better
ta brakk apö da reef
as fester an crack
i da grave
o riskin nawtheen
an gainin dat sam.

Rachel Woolf

OF AQUA COLOURED GLASS

Of aqua coloured glass; a limpid hue but of another latitude. Here
the waters veer from leaden grey to Loden green, at the wind's whim.

Aqua; daubed round doorways and windows on Grecian archipelagos
and reflected in the sea from Crete to Thessaloniki

but not to the haunts of the pink-footed geese
of Aberlady Bay.

*

Found on a North Berwick beach, or at a slow meander's reach, a stopper
pristine but for one small chip, churned unraggéd in the tidal stream.

The object speaks of its utility. I fancy it hails from a one time
apothecary, where it sealed a flaskful of a patent remedy.

It kept company for long enough with a hoard of frosted pieces
for a never-realised chandelier of sand salvage and twisted wire

and spent time too with broken bits of blue-and-white; a crackle glaze
of saucers and cruet sets, scattering shards of patterned transfer ware

here and there along the tide line, garnered by me for an unmade mosaic
in a seaside garden, now gone to seed; reaped prior to parenthood perhaps

when thoughts might turn to idle plans for wire-wound artefacts
and extracted from a rattling shoebox, in a sifting of stuff, stuffed in the shed.

*

On a singular occasion, a nocturnal friend and I synchronised time zones,
her morning to my afternoon. Beneath a widdershins sun

we went westerly, walking the wide expanses of Yellowcraigs;
the Forth, several tones and some few shades from aqua,

yet I picked up a hint of it, among the strewn shells and seaweed,
and held it, juggling hope with probable disappointment.

I suggested a turnaround and a cuppa. Before the kettle was filled,
I had fiddled. It fitted. Yay and Yippee!

The tapered stem of the stopper slipped into the sea-glass ring
I had pocketed at Fidra, so snugly, it seemed to kiss the smooth lip

of the first half inch of bottle neck where, perchance, long since,
linctus was slipped into less willing mouths, thrice daily, after meals.

*

I dream about the fortune that united them, two one-off finds
from beach wanderings, separated by years.

Had they come from the hold of a scuppered ship, I would have spotted
other signs of antique pharmacy, in my decades of pottering this shore.

I breathe those yesterday walks, inhaling ozone with my mother, gone;
building sand boats for crews of venturing girls, grown.

Now and then I paddle the Aegean at Skyros, hand in hand
at the water's rim. The stopper from the sea unstops memory.

It's not as if I've located a rare plant after an eon of searching or achieved
the deciphering of a Reformation map to unearth a cache of monastery gold.

That's exactly it. The serendipity, the sheer randomness,
makes treasure trove of aqua coloured glass.

*

Of aqua coloured glass; a limpid hue but of another latitude. Here
the waters veer from leaden grey to Loden green, at the wind's whim.

Catherine Wylie

SPEECH THERAPY

Aye, A've taen up the ukelele.
Ye ken when A heard
the diagnosis
A went oot and boucht
an acoustic guitar –
a real beaut it wis.
But after the operation
A couldnae get my arm o'er
so A oft an boucht ma uke.
It's jist perfect.
A play aw things –
twenties, country, rock.
It's brilliant, so it is.

It's sure helped me –
wi ma speech an a.
Did ye notice?
The words sound better.
A strum and hae a sing.
They folk up the stair
bang on the ceiling
an shout,
Shut-the-fuck-up-doon-there.
But A pay nae attention.
A jist carry oan
sittin up in ma bed
strummin an singin.

Singin an strummin
an gien it laldie.

Eleanor Yule

MUSEUM OF CHILDHOOD

Bernie was always the first one there and the last to leave. His arrival and departure took place in darkness, in the gloomy half-light that washed through the unpopulated exhibition spaces. His long-established routine was always the same. Without hesitation he chose the correct key from the heavy metal bunch, gripped it tightly in his right hand, and inserted it into the large lock. It used to take him ages, not to find the key, but to slide it into the lock, but now, after many years of practice, he made it look effortless. But it wasn't.

He knew he was lucky to have a job, let alone to hold on to it for fifty years. He never imagined himself working with children, he thought he might frighten them, but he found that if he kept a distance, or sat in the gallery corners, they hardly knew he was there.

These days there wasn't a moment that went by when he didn't feel grateful to be here. He was contented, if he was honest. He hadn't always felt like that. As a young apprentice, almost a child himself when he started, he was frustrated and impatient. He was taught to be methodical, to 'start at the bottom and work upwards' or something would get missed. Some tiny object would fail to be illuminated or activated, a seemingly small and insignificant oversight, often the sole reason for a child's visit, could leave a wee one disappointed or tearful.

Bernie was surprised at how much the younger children noticed. They saw things adults missed. They constantly reminded him to observe the small details of life, like the foxes that slipped along back courts of the museum or the coloured light that fell on the floor of the doll's house carpet through its miniature stained-glass windows. He'd realised, over the years, they'd kept him young, the kids that ebbed and flowed through the gallery spaces. Everyone said he didn't look his age. He was fit and lean with a good head of thick grey hair. His dark eyes sparkled with a youthfulness that was hard to explain, even to himself.

In the fifty years he'd done the job, it never failed to surprise him what objects the children were drawn to. It was never the obvious things like cars and dolls. Adults, it seemed to him, were entirely predictable.

Bernie had four floors to prepare for the public over two awkwardly conjoined buildings. One uneven and ancient, the other modern and concrete. Through the years his fellow attendants expressed their views that the building was lopsided, almost ugly, 'a dog's dinner' his new boss told him, but Bernie thought it had a charm of its own. A quiet, individual logic, that over time he'd grown to respect. Even love.

Each floor had its own distinct character. The welcome display on the ground floor was the only part of the museum he instinctively disliked, but since he had never been asked for an opinion, he never gave one. The children never stayed long. He believed, like them, that it was a hotchpotch of contrived oddities aimed at impressing their parents. An over-painted horse with bulbous eyes salvaged from a carousel dominated a display full of monotonous waxwork nippers in red tin cars and under suspended model biplanes. An impossibly agile girl with flying pigtails hovered eternally above her squatting brother in a wide-legged leapfrog, a smile fixed on her rosy-cheeked face.

A pompously framed photograph of the balding 'collector' overlooked all this. Overweight, oval glasses, a thin moustache and small slim hands. He was long gone by the time Bernie started the job. The older staff that had encountered 'the collector' during stuffy council receptions told Bernie that he was 'a bachelor' who hated children. Bernie reasoned that was why the toys were locked away in deep display cases or preserved behind heavy plate-glass windows. It was all kept perfect, never handled or touched. Never played with by any child.

Bernie looked at the collector's unreadable pudgy face one last time. He'd finally worked him out after years of puzzling. The breakthrough came when Bernie remembered a boy he disliked at the children's home where he spent his early years. His name was Denis and he hated sharing things, sweets, toys, even a joke. He wanted to keep it all for himself. So he was never included in any of the other boys' games. He was the loneliest child Bernie knew. Even lonelier than he was.

Next to be lit up was the sizeable antique doll collection, the museum's key attraction. Deep display cases crammed full of pale porcelain faces and dusty frills. Bernie no longer got unsettled by the rows of glassy eyes twinkling in gloom, watching him as he flicked on the banks of light switches.

The second floor was in the old building and was reached by climbing twenty-five narrow stone steps. The keys attached to Bernie's black work trousers jingled out a distinct rhythm, one that he would never hear, as he made his way up the spiral staircase.

The nursery rhymes were first to go on and echoed around the gallery and down stairwells of the old building. Bernie was always careful to double-check that the sound disc was actually turning. The non-stop singing got to some of the other attendants, young children's voices, playing over and over on a never-ending loop. After a while most of them couldn't stand it, some had left because of it, but Bernie was immune, in fact he was envious, he'd give anything to hear the sound of a child laughing.

Then there were the large-scale train sets, next to them were what Bernie nicknamed the 'penny dreadfuls'. The kids clustered around miniature wooden theatre sets, which showed scenes 'of horror and dread', that burst into mechanical life once a five-pence piece was inserted into the slot. The kids could then bear witness to a bloodless decapitation of a paying customer by a butcher with a blunt axe or a ghostly appearance behind an unsuspecting gent reading his morning paper in a gothic library. The adults always complained at regular intervals about the 'penny dreadfuls' but from what Bernie could see the children positively adored them.

Collecting was the next floor up. Bernie loved the stamps. If he looked hard enough there was always a new detail. An antique dragon in a border he'd missed, a mountain in the distance, a scroll in someone's hand. He'd discovered countries he'd never heard of, imagined what it was like to smell their foreign money, feel the heat of a tropical sun on his face and stroll languidly along the idyllic coastlines etched into the surface of the stamps. It was the closest he'd ever gotten to a foreign holiday. Cards, comic books, even cameras on this floor, all in excellent condition. All untouched.

The top floor was more formal. Here were life-sized scenes, a Victorian schoolroom, with a permanent date chalked in copperplate onto a black-board. Another scene showed a party, in some distant idyllic past. Picnics. Party hats. Bunting. Skipping ropes. Hoops. Rackets. A wax boy in dusty cricket whites. The perfect childhood.

Bernie thought he could still see her, sometimes, out of the corner of his eye. Bunched up tight in the gloom. She'd been there a while but he hadn't heard her of course. She might have called out to him for all he knew. The first thing he felt was her tiny hand touching the small of his back. It made him jump. He was tense until he turned around and saw how slight she was and how uncared for.

Bernie didn't need to look at his watch any more. He knew he had twenty minutes left, just time for breakfast before the others arrived and half an hour before they opened up to the public.

He ignored the lift and took the stairs as he always had. Even if he had to climb them fifty times a day he would never use the lift. It was a matter of self-discipline. It was self-discipline had kept him in the job. His foster mother had told him that self-discipline was the secret to a happy life. He never let anything slip. Apart from that one time. He could still feel the imprint of her tiny hand on the small of his back. It almost brought tears to his eyes today.

The staff room was in the basement. A windowless square with a small table and two chairs. Bernie opened his Tupperware box to reveal chopped bananas and bran flakes. He pulled out the carton of milk he'd purchase next to the bus stop and poured it over. He loved this time of day. He would think of nothing. Just stare at the wall.

It was the week before Christmas that he'd discovered her. It had snowed during the night and was freezing cold when he arrived in the gallery that morning. The heating had only just fired up when he found her. He'd pulled her out of the shadows. She was shivering, had probably been there all night. He could just about read her lips but she said very little except that she didn't want to go home. He wasn't sure what to do. He knew he'd have to tell someone but he got the feeling that the child needed time on her own first. He recognised something in her eyes. A caged look that he empathised with almost acutely.

She had white skin and deep blue eyes, black hair and a small smudged rosebud mouth. She looked about seven or eight but Bernie guessed she was small for her age and probably older. She had the tired eyes of an adult.

Even the Christmas tree in the staff room held no magic for her. Bernie felt her profound sadness. He opened up his spartan breakfast and offered her some food. She didn't want that either. She'd brought her own meagre feast. Hastily packed broken biscuits and half a chocolate bar swallowed down with a can of Irn Bru. When she finished he made her a cup of tea, which she drank, with four large teaspoons of sugar that she heaped into the cup herself.

After that she perked up a bit. It was already time for the others to start arriving. She begged him, pleaded with him to be allowed to stay in the museum just for one day. She wouldn't be any trouble. He could show her around. She'd always wanted to come but her mum never had the time. They lived on the edge of the city. She had walked all the way there in the snow. He could see her cheap fabric boots were soaked through.

He reasoned with her. What about her mother, she would be going spare with worry? The girl told him she wouldn't notice. Her mum, she said, worked at night and slept all day. Then she looked at him, deep into his eyes, bold as brass, and asked what was wrong with him. She said one side of his body was like a boy's, the other like a man's. She touched his right arm, which was small and shrivelled and curled in towards him like a lame paw. His left leg was the same, twisted and stunted and not much longer than her own. She asked if it hurt and if it was sore for him to walk. She wanted to touch his hearing aids. He didn't know why he still wore them, they made little difference now. He pulled them off his ears and showed her how to make them whistle and for the first time in his life he broke his own rules and he let her stay.

When he was sitting there, alone in the staff room, sometimes he could swear the building spoke to him. Not in words but in gut feelings. He'd chat through his day, ask for things, get help when he felt down. He'd never mentioned it to the others, they would think he was even odder than he was already. He even confided in the bare walls when he saw someone he'd 'liked'. It hadn't happened often. Never with the staff, he made sure of that. It was always someone he'd encountered briefly. Always married with kids or out of his league. They may only have asked for directions to the toilets. It was always, to his bemusement, men that he 'liked'.

He looked up at the clock. It was time. He closed the lid of his Tupperware box. People criticised him for coming in so early. He wasn't paid for it. Made them look bad. He could have breakfast at home. He didn't see the point, it was time wasted. He preferred it here. This was his home. Not the clinical spaces of the sheltered housing he occupied.

He felt a sharp pain in his heart, a reminder that this would be the last time he would sit here. They told him he was welcome to come back anytime, sit here anytime he wanted, but why would he do that? He no longer had a function.

He'd told the child to wait in the ladies' loos, wash her hands and face and come out when the museum got busy. It wouldn't take long. The Christmas crowds were large and he knew he could show her around without anyone noticing.

He showed her the stamps first, but she wasn't interested, even when he told her they were his favourite. The doll's house left her cold. She even turned her head away from the tiny grocer's shop and the intricate baskets of fruit and the miniature loaves of bread being pulled from the oven. Always a winner with the wee ones. She didn't seem interested in the details and made straight for the 'penny dreadfuls'. He handed her a small fist of coins. She was mesmerised by the butcher swinging the axe, the horror on the gent's face as the ghost popped out. It was the first time he saw her laugh.

His last day at work passed quickly, mainly because he wanted to hold on to it. Everyone was very nice. Envious that he would now become a man of leisure, free to do whatever he liked. He knew they were secretly preparing something. He could lip-read from a good distance.

A recent round of redundancies meant most of the staff he knew well had already left. He really was the last of the old guard. His retirement presentation was a brief affair, at the end of the day. They had clubbed together to get him a new sweater, a deep russet brown that reminded him of the old Victorian postcards up in Collections, and presented him with a small wooden plaque with his name and dates of service etched into a silver panel at the side. In the speeches they alluded tactfully to his disabilities and the courage it took for him to do the job. His long period of service. Somehow it left him feeling emptier than he was already.

They offered him some champagne, which he couldn't drink, but accepted with good grace and pretended to sip while nibbling dry cake that someone had picked up from Marks and Spencer's on their way into work. Then it was over.

As he handed in his pass at reception he remembered that he had bought her a star for the top of her Christmas tree from their gift shop and a bag of Jedburgh snails. He told her to wait for him in the toilets while he locked up and he would escort her home. When he was finished he wasn't surprised to find the toilet empty. The Christmas star abandoned on the floor by the washbasin next to an empty sweet wrapper.

It took him a while to find her. She was in the last place he expected. Her face was pressed up against the thick, cold plate glass of the display case in the dolls' gallery. She was staring at a life-sized china baby doll lying in a smart pram, naked but for a neatly secured cloth nappy and a lace bonnet. The doll was lying on her back smiling with her feet in the air.

She asked if she could pick it up, she wanted to nurse it, to give it a hug. Bernie explained that the cases could never be opened. The dolls couldn't be touched. That was the rule. Only a curator with special gloves on was allowed inside. Her shoulders dropped. She accepted it too quickly, as if she already knew what he would say. When she turned towards him he could see she'd been crying.

They let him lock up the building one last time. And so he switched it all off. Closed it down. Plunged the floors into darkness. Stopped the children singing. Cut the butcher off mid swing. Saluted the collector on his way down to the staff room. He said goodbye to his old friend. He picked up his Tupperware box from the staff room table, set the alarm and locked the main door. If he didn't linger he'd be just in time for the bus.

It took him some time to find the key for the doll's cabinet but she waited patiently. He'd never used it before. The lock was stiff but finally the door opened. He let her enter the case, pick up the baby doll, and watched her through the thick glass as she smelt the top of its head and ran her fingers along the baby's porcelain belly and tickled its perfect pink toes.

BIOGRAPHIES

Gregor Addison lives in Scotstoun, Glasgow, where he teaches English. He has published poetry and prose in *New Writing Scotland, Chapman, Gairm, Gath, Cabhsair/Causeway,* the *Edinburgh Review,* and written the novel *Pure Wool.* Some of his more recent poetry is to be included in Carcanet's *Oxford Poets Anthology* 2013.

Jean Atkin works as a writer and educator, and lives in Shropshire. She is a past winner of the Torbay Prize, the Ravenglass Poetry Prize, the Ways With Words Prize at Dartington Hall and others. Her first collection, *Not Lost Since Last Time,* was published by Oversteps Books in spring 2013.

Dorothy Baird lives in Edinburgh where she works as a Human Givens psychotherapist and runs creative writing groups for adults and teenagers. Her poetry has been widely published in magazines and her first collection, *Leaving the Nest,* was published by Two Ravens Press. She is currently working on her next collection. **www.dorothybaird.com**

Helen Boden is a Yorkshire-born, Edinburgh-based writer, teacher and editor. She sometimes blogs at **helenbodenliteraryarts.wordpress.com**

Jane Bonnyman teaches English in Glasgow and writes poetry in her spare time. Her poems have been published in *New Writing Scotland, Poetry Scotland* and *Northwords Now,* and she has recently been awarded first place in the poetry category of the National Gallery of Scotland's Get Writing! Competition.

John Burnside's latest books are *Black Cat Bone,* which won both the Forward and the T. S. Eliot Prizes for Poetry, and a collection of short fiction, entitled *Something Like Happy.* He works at St Andrews University, and lives, for the moment, in rural Fife with his wife and two sons.

Margaret Callaghan completed an MLitt in Creative Writing at the University of Glasgow. She is working on a novel called *The Last Big Weekend of the Summer.* This year she was shortlisted for a New Writer's Award.

Kate Campbell works in Edinburgh and spends time between homes in the Lammermuir Hills, Scottish Borders and Midlothian. She loves to be out in the hills with a camera. Kate has performed at the St Magnus Festival with the Orkney Writers' Course and was published in *New Writing Scotland* 29.

Jim Carruth's first collection, *Bovine Pastoral*, came out in 2004. Since then he has published a further five collections and an illustrated fable. His most recent collection, *Rider at the Crossing*, published by happenstance press, came out in 2012. He is the chair of St Mungo's Mirrorball – the Glasgow network of poets.

Defne Çizakça was born in Cyprus, grew up in Turkey, lived in Malaysia, Germany, Holland, Belgium, Morocco and is currently in love with Scotland. She is a creative writing PhD student at the University of Glasgow where she is working on a novel about nineteenth-century Istanbul, tentatively titled *Deep-sea Istanbulites*.

A. C. Clarke's latest collections are *A Natural Curiosity* (New Voices Press), shortlisted for the 2012 Callum Macdonald Award, and *Fr Meslier's Confession* (Oversteps Books). She is a member of Scottish PEN and has won several prizes, most recently the 2012 Second Light Long Poem competition.

Stewart Conn lives in Edinburgh and was from 2002 to 2005 the city's inaugural Makar. His most recent poetry publications have been a Mariscat pamphlet *Estuary*, and *The Breakfast Room*, published by Bloodaxe Books from whom *The Touch of Time: New and Selected Poems* is due early in 2014.

Ian Crockatt is a poet and translator. His most recent publications are *Pure Contradiction – selected poems of Rainer Maria Rilke* (Arc Publishing, 2012); *Skald – Viking poems* (Koo Press, 2009); and *Blizzards of the Inner Eye* (Peterloo Poets, 2003). He is currently translating Old Norse court poetry at Aberdeen University.

Caitlynn Cummings is the Managing Editor of the Canadian literary magazine *filling Station*, the Coordinator of the Calgary Distinguished Writers Program, and a graduate of the University of Edinburgh's MSc in Creative Writing. Her writing can be found in *Drey*, *This Magazine*, *Alberta Views*, *dead (g)end(er)*, *Cordite Poetry Review*, *ditch*, and *NōD*. Follow her on Twitter **@Tartaned_Maple**.

Jenni Daiches lives in South Queensferry, writes on literary and historical subjects as Jenni Calder. Published poetry includes *Mediterranean* (1995), *Smoke* (2005), and contributions to many Scottish magazines. Fiction includes *Letters from the Great Wall* (2006) and *Forgive* (forthcoming). Recent non-fiction: *Lost in the Backwoods: Scots in the North American Wilderness* (2013).

Katy Ewing lives in rural south-west Scotland and is just finishing a Liberal Arts MA at the University of Glasgow (Dumfries). She has had poetry and prose published in *From Glasgow to Saturn*, prose in *Earthlines* magazine and poetry in *Southlight, Octavius, Far Off Places* and *Gutter* 8.

Born in Russia, **Elizaveta Feklistova** moved to Glasgow at the age of six and promptly fell in love with the place and the language. Though she left Scotland for Germany two years later, she's been writing in English ever since. She is now nineteen, and studying English Literature at Glasgow University.

Gerrie Fellows is the author of four collections of poetry. *Window for a Small Blue Child*, a sequence of poems about IVF, was shortlisted for the Sundial Scottish Poetry Book of the Year. Earlier collections include *The Duntroon Toponymy* and *The Powerlines*.

Olivia Ferguson was born in Lanark, and brought up in Biggar. She studied Literature and Linguistics at McGill University in Montréal. Her work has appeared in McGill's *Steps Magazine* and *The Veg Literary Magazine*. She now lives in Victoria, BC. She is writing a novel called *The Swim*.

Seonaid Francis currently lives in the Western Isles with her husband and three children. She has previously had work published in *New Writing Scotland* and *Valve Journal* and takes much of her inspiration from the landscape of the Hebrides and the complexities of life there.

Graham Fulton's poetry collections include *Humouring the Iron Bar Man* (Polygon); *This* (Rebel Inc); *Open Plan* (Smokestack Books); *Full Scottish Breakfast* (Red Squirrel Press); and *Upside Down Heart* (Controlled Explosion Press). New full-length collections are due to be published by Roncadora Press, Smokestack, Red Squirrel Press and Salmon Poetry.

Harry Giles grew up in Orkney and is currently based in Edinburgh, where he helps run the spoken word events series Inky Fingers. His debut pamphlet *Visa Wedding* was published by Stewed Rhubarb in November 2012. Credits, videos, and texts about poems and performances can be found at **www.harrygiles.org**.

Rody Gorman: born Dublin 1960. Lives on the Isle of Skye. Editor of the annual anthology *An Guth*.

Alison Grant is a student on the MLitt in Writing Practice and Study course at Dundee University. Her writing has appeared in magazines and anthologies, including Red Squirrel's *Split Screen* and *A Wilder Vein* published by Two Ravens Press.

Katharine Grant grew up on the edge of the Lancashire moors. She now lives in Glasgow. *Sedition*, her first novel for adults, will be published in 2014 by Virago in the UK and Henry Holt in the USA.

Jen Hadfield is currently working on her third poetry book, *Byssus*, due out in 2014. She lives in Shetland. In her sometimes-chaotic creative life, walking, foraging for wild food and material for her visual art are as important as her language-centred practice.

Sylvia Hays was born and educated in the USA. She left Virginia with her young daughter some forty years ago for Oxford, then Edinburgh. Orkney has been her home for more than twenty years, where she pursues her profession as an artist. Increasingly, writing competes with painting for her attention.

Audrey Henderson was a finalist in the *Indiana Review* 1/2 K Award and *River Styx* International Poetry Contest. A contributor to BBC Radio Scotland and graduate of Edinburgh University, she currently has work in *Magma* 54, *Gutter* 8 and *Tar River Poetry*.

After graduating from the University of Stirling's MLitt in Creative Writing, **Angela Hughes** was shortlisted for a Scottish Book Trust's New Writers Scotland Award – 2012 was a great year! She has been a press officer and an English teacher abroad. She now writes and enjoys a simple life in Scotland.

Alison Irvine's novel, *This Road is Red* (Luath Press), was shortlisted for the 2011 Saltire First Book of the Year award. She has recently been awarded a Glasgow Life Commonwealth Games residency for which she is writing a book of creative non-fiction. Her short fiction has been widely published.

Helen Jackson likes making stuff up and eating cake. She's lucky enough to live in Edinburgh, her favourite city. Her stories have been published in the anthologies *Rocket Science* and *ImagiNation: Stories of Scotland's Future*, and in various magazines. Visit **www.helen-jackson.com** for more information.

Born in Baghdad, **Abbas Khider** fled from Iraq in 1996 after two years in jail for 'political reasons'. Resident in Germany since 2000, he has published three novels in German. The first, *Der falsche Inder,* will appear in English in 2013 (*The Village Indian*, Seagull Books, trans. Donal McLaughlin). **www.abbaskhider.com**

Bridget Khursheed is a poet and writer based in the Scottish Borders; she also edits **poetandgeek.com**; her work has been published extensively in magazines and anthologies; birdwatching and A68 obsessive – often at the same time.

Pippa Little is from St Andrews and lives in Northumberland. She has won the Norman MacCaig Centenary Poetry Prize, the James McCash Prize, a New Writing North Award and an Eric Gregory Award. Her first full collection, *Overwintering*, was published by Oxford Poets/Carcanet in 2012.

Sarah Lowndes is a writer and curator and a lecturer at Glasgow School of Art. She is the editor of *The Burning Sand*, and her previous publications include *Studio 58* (2012), *Dieter Roth: Diaries* (2012), *Robert Rauschenberg: Botanical Vaudeville* (2011) and *Social Sculpture* (2010). 'Boots' is an excerpt from her first novel, *You and a Hundred Others*.

Pàdraig MacAoidh is a poet, academic and broadcast journalist. He is the author of *From Another Island* (2010) and *Sorley MacLean* (2010). He lives in Edinburgh.

Richie McCaffery is a Carnegie scholar at the University of Glasgow, researching the Scottish poets of World War Two towards a PhD in Scottish Literature. He has published one pamphlet collection, *Spinning Plates*, from HappenStance Press and has another pamphlet, a collaboration with the artist Hannah Rye, forthcoming.

Linda McCann has published poetry and prose. She has been a Hawthorden Fellow, a recipient of a Scottish Arts Council Writer's Award, and has been Writer in Residence for the Universities of Glasgow and Strathclyde. She has honours degrees in English and Law.

Alistair McDonald, born in Edinburgh, lives in Argyll with his family. He has had poetry and cartoons published, in English and in Scots. He is trying to complete *Double Eagle* and is working on a cartoon strip. While at school, he once dated a granddaughter of Naomi Mitchison.

Biographical notes answer no relevant questions. Only the poem is important. **Ellie McDonald.**

James McGonigal lives in Glasgow. Recent publications include *Beyond the Last Dragon: A Life of Edwin Morgan* (Sandstone Press, 2012) and *Cloud Pibroch* (Mariscat Press, 2010), which won the Michael Marks Poetry Pamphlet Award. He is currently working on a Selected Letters of Edwin Morgan for Carcanet Press.

Lindsay Macgregor lives near Cupar and is studying towards an MLitt in Writing Practice and Study at the University of Dundee. She co-edits poetry reviews for *Dundee University Review of the Arts* and is co-founder of Platform, a monthly music and poetry evening held at Ladybank Station.

Sharon MacGregor lives in Glasgow with her partner and four children. A student of creative writing with the Open University, she writes both short stories and poetry. She has also been published in *Still Me*, an anthology produced with fellow students. The poem included here was the first ever submitted.

Crìsdean MacIlleBhàin/Christopher Whyte's fifth collection, *An Daolag Shìonach*, containing new poems 2002–2007 and uncollected poems 1987–1999, will appear in September, in Gaelic only. A book of Tsvetaeva translations, *Moscow in the Plague Year*, covering the period from November 1918 to May 1920, is due out from Archipelago Books of New York in April 2014. He currently divides his time between Budapest, Venice and Glasgow.

Mary McIntosh, retired teacher, lives in Kirriemuir. Writes mainly in Scots. Published in *New Writing Scotland*, *Lallans* and *Riverrun*, also various anthologies including *A Tongue in Yer Heid*. Ketillonia has published *The Gless Hoose*, a pamphlet of her short stories. Now writes short plays for a local street theatre group.

Lorn Macintyre, poet, novelist and short story writer, was born in Taynuilt, Argyll, and spent formative years on the Isle of Mull, both places being the inspiration for his poetry and prose. He is interested in particular in the relationship between writing and the writer's beliefs and personal development. His website is at **www.lornmacintyre.co.uk**

Shena Mackay was born in Edinburgh. She has written two novellas, eight novels and five collections of stories. Her latest book, *The Atmospheric Railway: New and Selected Stories*, was published by Vintage in 2010.

Peter Maclaren lives in Glasgow where he taught English for thirty-four years (Sundays are now completely different). Time now to garden, to travel, and to watch Clyde trying to avoid the title of worst team in Scotland. Occasional poems published previously in *NWS*.

Donal McLaughlin is both an author and a translator. His translations of novels by Monica Cantieni, Abbas Khider, and Urs Widmer (all Seagull) and Pedro Lenz (Freight) are forthcoming, as is his own new book *beheading the virgin mary & other stories* (Dalkey Archive 2014). **www.donalmclaughlin.wordpress.com**

A much travelled, award-winning poet, in Scotland's three languages, and a songwriter who's had the privilege of working with some of Scotland's best composers, **Aonghas MacNeacail** is delighted to have lived through such a glorious period for Scottish literature.

Kevin MacNeil is a poet (*Love & Zen in the Outer Hebrides*), novelist (*The Stornoway Way, A Method Actor's Guide to Jekyll & Hyde*, the forthcoming *Good Grief, Death*), editor (*These Islands, We Sing*), lyricist (*Kevin MacNeil & William Campbell are Visible From Space*) and lecturer (universities of Uppsala, Edinburgh, Kingston). From Lewis, lives in London. Visit **KevinMacNeil.com** or follow Kevin on Twitter **@Kevin_MacNeil**

Rosa Macpherson's work appears in *New Writing Scotland, Edinburgh Review, The Devil & The Giro, Collins Short Stories* and others. Recipient of an SAC Writer's Bursary, she co-wrote *How To Giftwrap a Chicken*, a Polish/Scots stage play performed at the Edinburgh Fringe. Rosa studied Creative Writing at Napier University.

Neil McRae was born in Galashiels in 1959. He started learning Gaelic fifteen years ago out of interest, and this led to an unquenchable love of the language which, if anything, has grown stronger over the years. He now lives in Skye and works as a locum vet.

Ian Madden's short fiction has been broadcast on BBC Radio 4 and has appeared in the *Edinburgh Review, Wasafiri* and several anthologies including the Bridport Prize.

David Manderson published his first novel, *Lost Bodies*, in 2011, and a collection of short stories, *Best Man*, in 2012. In the past he has run creative writing magazines and film festivals. He now teaches creative writing and screenwriting in a university. He lives in Glasgow with his family.

Originally from Kilmarnock, **Heather Marshall** is currently based in the foothills of South Carolina, where she lives with her children, a pair of

Labrador-cross dogs, a set of bagpipes and a Royal Enfield motorbike. Her works are published in *Northwords Now, Prime Number* and *Six Minute Magazine*. You can find out more about her at **heathergmarshall.wordpress.com**

R. A. Martens' stories have been given various homes. Most recently, *Sobek Refutes the Plover Theory* spent a night at Radio 4. The traitor is currently working on her first novel, called *The Strong and Practised Arms of Mr Friendly* until someone demands otherwise.

David Miller was born in 1966 in Edinburgh, and educated in Canterbury and Cambridge. He has worked in London as a literary agent since 1990, working with Nicola Barker, John Burnside, Stephen Grosz, Victoria Hislop, Kate Summerscale, amongst others. His first novel, *Today*, was published by Neri Pozza and Atlantic.

Lyn Moir has published four collections, two with Arrowhead Press and two with Calder Wood Press. She lives in St Andrews. She is working on a fifth collection.

M. J. Nicholls lives in Glasgow and writes comedic fiction.

Niall O'Gallagher's first book of poems, *Beatha Ùr*, was published by Clàr in the spring. He lives in Glasgow.

Kim Patrick was born in Glasgow. Her poetry has been published by the National Galleries of Scotland, shortlisted for the Bridport Prize, and her short libretto, *Fatal Plurality*, was performed at Wigmore Hall, London. Since being awarded a writing residency at Brownsbank Cottage, Kim has been working on a collection of prose poems titled *Provenance*.

Colette Paul has published one book of short stories, *Whoever You Choose to Love* (Phoenix/Weidenfeld & Nicolson), and is finishing a second collection. Her work has appeared on Radio 4, and in various literary magazines and anthologies.

Nalini Paul's first poetry pamphlet, *Skirlags* (Red Squirrel Press), was shortlisted for the Callum Macdonald Award in 2010. Widely published, she was George Mackay Brown Writing Fellow in Orkney (2009–2010) and worked as scriptwriter for Ankur Productions' *Jukebox*. Her recent musical comedy, *Hens and Cakes*, was well received. She teaches Creative Writing in Edinburgh and Glasgow. **www.whwn.co.uk**

Alison Prince has written biographies of Kenneth Grahame and Hans Christian Andersen, and among other prizes won the Guardian Children's Fiction Award and holds an honorary Doctorate of Letters for services to children's literature. She has published two poetry books and has won the Literary Review Grand Poetry Prize twice.

'Half-light' is the second story **Margaret Ries** has had accepted for publication. The first, 'For Sale', appeared in *Green Hills Literary Lantern XX*. She has completed one novel, *Shadow Jumping*, set in Seattle and Berlin, and has almost finished the second, *The Block of Joy*. She moved to Scotland in 2006.

Kay Ritchie grew up in Glasgow and Edinburgh. She lived in London, Spain and Portugal and worked as a freelance photographer, teacher of English and radio producer. Settled back in Glasgow, she has been published in *Tracks in the Sand, Shorelines* and *The Glad Rag* and performs at various events.

Angela Robb is from Stirlingshire, and has a varied educational background including a BSc in Zoology from the University of Glasgow and an MA in Screenwriting from Edinburgh Napier University. She now works in scientific journals publishing and writes a variety of stories and film scripts in her spare time.

Lydia Robb's poetry and prose has been widely published in Scots and English. She is also involved in various playwriting projects. Her poetry collection, *Last Tango with Magritte*, was published by Chapman Publishing, Edinburgh.

Cynthia Rogerson has published four novels and a collection of stories. Her work has been translated into five languages, produced as book of the week on *Woman's Hour*, won the V. S. Pritchett Prize, been shortlisted for Scottish Novel of the Year 2011, as well as broadcast on BBC radio and included in various anthologies and literary magazines. She is programme director of Moniack Mhor, an Arvon writers' centre.

Dilys Rose has published ten books of fiction and poetry. She is programme director for the MSc in Creative Writing by Online Learning at the University of Edinburgh. A new novel, *Pelmanism*, is due out in spring 2014.

Stewart Sanderson is a first-year PhD candidate in Scottish Literature at Glasgow University. His poems have appeared in various UK and Irish magazines, including *Gutter, Magma, Irish Pages, Cyphers, Poetry Wales* and *Poetry Review*. He co-organises the Verse Hearse reading series and edits *Scottish Poetry in Translation*: **owersettins.wordpress.com**

Shelley Day Sclater is a Geordie lass who lives in Edinburgh. She's been a lawyer, an academic psychologist and a research professor. Since 2007 she's earned a crust by freelancing and now writes fiction. Her debut novel, *The Confession of Stella Moon*, is represented by Jenny Brown Associates.

Kirsteen Scott now lives in Edinburgh but if you ask where she is from, she will say Argyll. She is a member of Words on Canvas, a writing group started in the National Gallery; she likes the taste of words and ideas that flirt with her eye and her ear.

Maria Sinclair is a graduate of the MLitt in Creative Writing at Glasgow University. She has been published in various magazines and anthologies, most recently *Gutter*. She is currently on the Clydebuilt Poetry Programme.

Raymond Soltysek is a Saltire-nominated prose writer, BAFTA-winning screenwriter and a Robert Louis Stevenson Award and Scottish Arts Council bursary winner. Working in teacher education, his materials and courses support creative writing in schools nationally. He is writing an academic textbook on behaviour management and lives at **www.soltysek.com**

Tom Sommerville has spent more than fifty years teaching literature in secondary and higher education. He was an intermittent writer of poetry and stories until he joined a poetry writing class at Edinburgh University which considerably increased his output. He has a particular fondness for sonnets.

Kathrine Sowerby is a poet based in Glasgow with a background in fine art. In 2012, she was a runner up in the Edwin Morgan Poetry Competition and commended in the Wigtown Poetry Competition. Kathrine is a recipient of a 2012/13 New Writers Award from the Scottish Book Trust.

Jim Stewart was born in Dundee in 1952. He teaches writing practice at the University of Dundee. His libretto for Graham Robb's opera *Flora and the Prince* premiered at Carnegie Hall, New York in October 2012. He is poet in residence at Tentsmuir National Nature Reserve, Fife.

Richard W. Strachan has been published in *Gutter*, *The View From Here*, *Litro*, *Spilling Ink Review*, and the *Scottish Review of Books*. In 2012 he was given a New Writer's Award by the Scottish Book Trust, and he has recently completed his first novel. He lives in Edinburgh.

Shane Strachan is currently working on a short story collection focused on life in the Northeast of Scotland as part of a PhD in Creative Writing at the University of Aberdeen. He has previously been published in *Northwords Now*, *Exegesis*, *Metazen* and *Causeway/Cabhsair*, the latter of which he now edits.

Em Strang is a poet in her final year of a PhD in Creative Writing (Ecopoetry) at Glasgow University. She has published work in various anthologies and journals including *Dark Mountain, Causeway, Earthlines*, and the *Glasgow Herald*. She is currently working on a book of poems and illustrations with folk artist Rima Staines. She lives in south-west Scotland.

Valerie Thornton is a writer and creative-writing tutor. She's held two Royal Literary Fund Fellowships at Glasgow University. Her latest textbooks are *The Writer's Craft* and *The Young Writer's Craft*. She has two collections of poems (Mariscat Press) and is proud to have been awarded an Honorary Fellowship of ASLS.

David Underdown was born in England but lives on the Isle of Arran where he is joint organiser of the McLellan Poetry Competition. His poems have appeared in a number of anthologies and journals and a selection can be read at **www.davidunderdown.com**. His first full collection, *Time Lines*, was published by Cinnamon in July 2011.

Nacho Viñuela was born in León, Spain. His flash fiction and short stories have appeared in a variety of anthologies and magazines. 'The Edge of the Tides' is his first story to be published in English. Nacho lives in Fife with his partner, four hens and a cat called Judas.

Bechaela Walker (b. 1979) is a writer based in Glasgow. This is her first published work.

Fiona Ritchie Walker is from Montrose, now living in Blaydon, near Newcastle-upon-Tyne. She made her Radio 4 *Poetry Please* debut in 2012, reading 'Mrs Thorpe's Arithmetic', which is one of the poems in her latest collection, *The Second Week of the Soap*, published by Red Squirrel Press. **www.fionaritchiewalker.com**

Roger White. Possibly the oldest new kid on the writing block. It's festered inside for years and is now breaking out, aided by the Open University and time-released by departure from toiling at the coalface of public service in Aberdeen.

Hamish Whyte has edited many anthologies of Scottish literature. He runs Mariscat Press, publishing poetry. His own latest collection is *The Unswung*

Axe (Shoestring Press). *Pussy Baudrons*, an anthology of Scottish cat poems, is forthcoming this year. He lives in Edinburgh and is a member of Shore Poets there.

Mary Wight is originally from Melrose, and for now lives very contentedly in Edinburgh. Her poems have been published in various literary magazines and she is working on a first collection and also, perhaps foolishly, a first novel.

Ginna Wilkerson anticipates completing a PhD in Creative Writing in spring of 2013 at the University of Aberdeen. She has several journal publications, and her full collection *Odd Remains* is due out this summer. She divides her time between Scotland and Tampa, Florida.

Colin Will is a poet, publisher, gardener and naturalist with a scientific background. Born in Edinburgh in 1942, he now lives in Dunbar. He has had six poetry collections published, the newest being *The Propriety of Weeding*, Red Squirrel Press, 2012.

Christie Williamson likes to write poems. Someday he hopes to gather a whole bunch of them together for people to read.

Rachel Woolf writes in Scots and English. Her poems have appeared in *New Writing Scotland* 28 and 29 and anthologies and journals in Scotland, Ireland, England and the USA. She has been placed in poetry contests, including the annual, ekphrastic 'Inspired? Get Writing!' competition in 2009, 2011 and 2013.

Catherine Wylie has lived in the Stirling area and taught English for a number of years. Her work has been published in *New Writing Scotland*, *Poetry Scotland* and *The Eildon Tree*.

Eleanor Yule is an award-winning writer, director and screenwriting lecturer. Her work includes a recent BBC profile on Finnish writer and artist, Tove Jansson, a BAFTA-nominated 'Bookmark' on novelist Muriel Spark, and *Blinded*, her feature film debut, starring Anders W. Berthelsen, Peter Mullan and Johdi May.